ORPHAN'S TEST

ORPHAN'S TEST

The Core Empire Book I

Richard Coxson

San Diego

This book is dedicated to the unsung heroes
who put their lives on the line, not knowing if
they will come home at the end of the day.

"You will never do anything in this world without courage. It is the greatest quality of the mind next to honor."—Aristotle

"Some people live an entire lifetime and wonder if they have ever made a difference in the world, but the Marines don't have that problem."—Ronald Reagan

"The Creed is not—cannot—just be words. To serve the people, the emperor must embody it."—Cyrus, Emperor of the Core Empire

1

War Games

Naval Quarters #1, Beacon
0935 Local & BBMT 27 April 3463

HUGH CASCADE CREPT THROUGH THE WILD, stalking his prey, his black hair melding into the shadows. Carefully lifting his head, gray eyes barely above the underbrush, he looked all around. There! A magpie perched on a limb, still unaware of him. Sliding carefully back to the ground, he continued his approach. Nearing a tree thick enough to hide behind, he stood, prepared to rush his target. Whipping around the trunk, his eyes rounded with disappointment as the bird flew off!

From the house, he heard his father call, "Hugh! Get in here. I thought I told you not to go far."

"I'm not far!" he yelled back. Besides, he had important things to do out here. When the bird had distracted him, he had just been finishing up a fleet of leaf boats to sail on the stream running through the woods. They would have been done, too, if Danao and Pacho had been here to help, but their families suddenly flew off-planet for some reason they hadn't explained. So, he needed to do it all by himself. After that, he wanted to try to climb that old oak again. The last time his brothers were home from the navy, they had teased him because he couldn't make it up onto the lowest limb yet, especially Drawton, who had entered the academy last summer. Dad had laughingly agreed about him being too small at eight. But he wasn't! He'd prove to them he was big enough and old enough.

"Hugh!" Dad called again. Not exactly a yell (Dad didn't really yell), but when he wanted something, he used a tone that let you know not to ignore him.

"Coming," he answered. Regretfully, he looked over his fleet. Hopefully, the squirrels wouldn't ruin everything before he returned. Hitching up his pants, he headed for the house at a run. He loved to race across the perfectly trimmed lawn. Hitting the back door, he caught sight of his face in the glass. A rather tall boy with a smudged face and grass stains on his clothes smiled back at him. Maybe Dad would go fishing with him, instead of to that stupid ceremony at the palace! That must be it! His gray eyes danced with delight at the thought.

Dad waited at the door in his pristine naval whites with Command Master Chief Petty Officer Ginty Drab, his aide, standing behind him. Dad almost always wore his whites, which meant he rarely had fun or played with Hugh. "Want to go sail boats in the stream, Dad?" Hugh suggested hopefully. "Danao and Packo are gone, and so are Rob and Llew." It never hurt to ask. Occasionally, Dad would come out and do things with him. Not very often, but sometimes.

Imperial Warlord Trevor Cascade smiled at his youngest son, who shared his gray eyes and black hair, "Admiral Davies' grandsons have gone to live on Periastron, but the other two will be back in a week or so. I wish I could launch your fleet with you, but I can't today." He paused to take in his son. "You look like you were in combat. Did you win?"

"Naw," Hugh answered truthfully. "Stupid bird flew away before I could catch it."

Trevor laughed. "Just as well, you probably wouldn't like it if you caught it. What kind of bird?"

"Magpie," Hugh answered.

Ginty chuckled. "You're right, sir, he wouldn't have liked it. Those claws can be pretty nasty, especially on an eight-year-old."

Hugh glared at Ginty. He had no business interfering with stuff between Dad and him.

Trevor laughed. "Watch your back, Ginty. Hugh isn't amused."

"Aye, sir. As the warlord says, I am definitely on the young warrior's target list."

Both of them laughed at him while Hugh clenched his jaw

angrily. He knew Ginty meant to be nice; he just didn't like being treated like a kid. Dad's laugh tailed off, a serious expression coming over him. Uh-oh! Now for the bad news.

"Hugh, I have to be at the Hall of Judgment later this week. I don't have a choice."

Hugh tried to keep his face impassive, as he'd seen his dad do often enough when he received bad news, but he couldn't. A frown dragged the edges of his mouth down. "Ah, Dad. We're goin' fishin'!"

"I know, Hugh, but I can't avoid this. It's important to the emperor and, truthfully, to me, too. Sector Lord Quadros is being judged, and Emperor Cyrus needs my support." Hugh felt mutinous. He never got what he wanted. Trevor knelt down in front of him, gripping Hugh's arms. "That's what duty requires sometimes." Hugh could feel hot tears coming. Dad had *promised*. Why did duty always get in the way? Why couldn't he just be his dad? Trevor hugged him, surprising Hugh completely. Dad hardly ever did that, either. Hugs were always Mom's job. Hugh struggled to fight back the tears that always came when he thought of her. She hadn't wanted to leave—hadn't wanted to die—but the doctors couldn't do anything . . .

Hugh's father continued to speak, and Hugh pushed away his sadness to listen to him. "But I've decided to let you go fishing off-planet anyway. Doña Carlota will take you to Deft."

To Ginty he added, with a sigh, "Trout and some unbelievable local varieties we'll miss out on."

Hugh knew Doña Carlota liked him, but he wanted to be with Dad. Hugh clutched at his father, "But I want *you* to go with me. You promised!"

"I know," Trevor whispered into his boy's hair, "I know. We'll go another time. If things go well, I may even get to meet you on Deft."

Hugh bet that wouldn't happen, but he could hope. Besides, he could tell Dad wanted to be with him; he never lied, to him or anyone else. Ever. But it seemed like Dad never had time anymore, always too busy because of his stupid job, so he would pretend to make Dad feel better about missing the fishing. "Okay, Dad."

Trevor let him go before standing. "Now, don't you have a fleet to launch, mister?"

"Aye, sir!" Hugh promptly responded, doing his best to stand at attention.

"Then you better be about it before the enemy destroys it on the ground!"

"Aye, sir!" Hugh yelled happily before banging out the back door.

Deft

1805 Local/1005 BBMT 1 May 3463

FOUR DAYS AND MORE THAN TWO hundred light-years later, Hugh sat on a canvas camp stool and stared into the fire, tired but comfortable, even with the thin wind soughing through the trees. Wrapped in a huge blanket, with the remains of the trout he had caught hours earlier on a plate beside him, he felt warm and drowsy. Though only a fair cook, Sergeant Jake Daniels had done well with the fish. Some of the other Marines were much better cooks, but it had been Daniels' turn. Across the fire, Doña Carlota Gonzalvez y Rodriguez del Castillo leaned back in her camp chair. The firelight gave an interesting tinge to her russet hair. Hugh thought she must need the fancy chair, given her advanced age. She must be almost fifty! Hugh wished he could have brought some of his friends, but they were all gone, off having fun with their families.

Most of the day he had played scout in the woods, trying to sneak up on the Marines, or made-up armies of bark and twigs that fought each other. Attacking himself had not been as much fun as if he had had someone else to play with, but he had managed. He always won, of course, but it hadn't seemed like a challenge. Even so, he had enjoyed himself. Now, he just wanted to cozy down into his blanket and sleep.

Mitchell, one of Doña Carlota's servants, suddenly approached her. "Ma'am? Emergency message from Beacon."

As Doña Carlota took the computer pad, Hugh looked over, mildly interested. Doña Carlota had insisted she didn't want any messages that weren't life-and-death, but she opened this one. Hugh watched Doña Carlota's face drain of color as she read the message.

"What?" Hugh piped up, sensing something wrong.

"Quadros has attacked Beacon. He's killed the emperor."

Fear spiked in his heart. "What about my dad? Is he okay?"

Doña Carlota shook her head as she looked at Hugh with infinite pain. "I don't know, but he must have been there when the kinetics hit the palace. A shuttle intercepted Quadros on his way to the Imperial Palace for judgment, while a cruiser from Prime Fleet—not even one of Quadros' Twelfth Fleet ships that were in-system—hit the palace and Imperial Fleet Headquarters. Your father, the emperor, most of the sector lords," her voice dropped to a whisper, "my family, were in the palace."

Hugh didn't understand. "But my dad?" he yelled, his voice echoing in the trees.

Sergeant Daniels grabbed him up, holding him tight. "We don't know, Hugh. We just don't know."

Beacon Highridge Training Center
1110 Local/1010 BBMT 1 May 3463

CRAWLING THROUGH THE TALL GRASS, Sergeant Major Sean Ward felt fully alive, something he definitely didn't when sitting at his desk in the palace as the empire's senior noncommissioned officer. At five foot eleven, toned from regular workouts and bronzed from days in the field, he felt completely fit. Or as much as someone could at forty-three after crawling around in the weeds for twenty-five years. The sun had turned his very short hair a light brown, instead of the darker color it became after too much office time.

Wearing fully activated, nanite-impregnated, chameleon skin uniforms, which effectively hid each soldier and his equipment, none of his team or the other Fleet Elite Marines approaching the objective could be seen or found with most sensors. Their sharply honed abilities to remain unseen made them nearly unbeatable. Nanocamo used microprocessors and cameras that worked to almost instantaneously match the suit to its background, as well as absorb sensor signals as if they had not been intercepted. It almost seemed like cheating.

Preparing to stand to take out the guard in front of him, his archeon com buzzed. Angrily, he tapped a *What is it?* signal. Someone better have a good explanation, or they were about to be made very unhappy for interrupting the exercise.

The com whispered in his ear, something no one but a very alert sentry would notice, much less hear, "Code red one, Sergeant Major. It just came in from the palace com center. No follow-up."

Ward's blood froze. An attack on the emperor, probably at the palace. Lord Bartleby Quadros of Twelfth Sector had been credibly accused of treason, and Emperor Cyrus had planned to impose High Justice upon him today. Rarely in the Core Empire's thousand-year history had such a highly placed person been found guilty of treason and sentenced to High Justice. While many in the empire considered it barbaric to execute someone, the charge of treason required it. And to ensure the full impact of the sentence, a number of high-ranking members of court, as well as the civilian government, had been invited to witness the historic event. On some level, he thought it gave the emperor more confidence in carrying out the sentence to be surrounded by those who supported it. Loyalty to the empire above all else!

Ward and his wife Ann Marie thought their son Rod should understand the importance of justice and judgment applying to everyone in the empire, and while Ward couldn't be there, his wife and his only son had gone.

Their other children had died years ago, one from a rare childhood cancer, another while pulling a foolish stunt with his friends. Only Rod had survived, and Rod and Ann Marie were guests of his boss, Imperial Warlord Trevor Cascade, in the Hall of Judgment today. Were they okay? He thrust that thought away. Duty first. He steeled himself to ask, "What word from other command centers?"

"Nothing, Sergeant Major. All com is down with the capital and fleet. Jamming."

"Sound recall. Get the shuttles here five minutes ago. Contingency Omega One until we know more." *Omega One: head for the capital and protect the emperor unless the emperor is dead. In that case, an exposed heir or Tier One imperial official such as the warlord or protector of the succession took priority.*

He needed access to a secure screen to decide what to do next. If the emperor had escaped to safety, a notification code would have been sent. No code, no emperor, but maybe the jamming prevented that. He shook his head, rejecting that hopeful theory. Hopeless, really. With the emperor dead, the warlord had probably died, too, but he could determine that from the priority screen. Which meant he would soon know about Ann Marie and Rod, too. "When are the shuttles going to be here?" Ward growled softly into his com.

"Eight minutes, Top. The colonel wants to know what you're planning to do."

"Tell him that, under my rank as an imperial officer, I am taking command of the battalion. If you feel brave," Ward said with a ghostly chuckle in his voice, "remind him that as part of the imperial chain of command, my rank of major is two grades higher than regular forces. Otherwise, I'll explain it if it comes up. If General Musgrave requests assistance in protecting the emperor, we'll go there. If we can't establish com with the palace, we're headed for the most endangered heir or Tier One official. This may very well be a coup attempt, so all heirs are presumed to be in danger. Tell the drop ship commander to open his sealed orders on my authority. Then report back to me soonest. I should know where we are going by then."

"Aye, Top. I mean, sir."

Speaking into the com, he ordered, "All Viper units, this is Sergeant Major Ward, now acting as Imperial Guard Major Ward. Everyone go live and hot now. This is no drill. I say again, this is not a drill." Ward didn't feel any adrenalin, just an icy cold dread growing, squeezing his heart. *Ann Marie!*

He had never before invoked his Imperial Guard rank, knowing it should only be used in the most dire circumstances. By doing this, everyone now knew just how bad things were. The Marines fell under fleet command. But the Imperial Guard served the warlord and emperor directly, in order to protect the succession. While he maintained his position as the highest-ranking noncommissioned officer in the Marines, he also held the rank of major in the Imperial Guard, giving him authority over almost everyone else in the Core military.

The com squawked in his ear again, *"Ward, this is Garand. We just got an announcement from Sector Lord Quadros. He claims Emperor Cyrus is dead, and he is now emperor. Reports from Faith, or at least from what's left of the capital city, say it's total chaos there. The palace is completely gone. It looks like the emperor didn't get out."*

Ward felt ill, as the last spark of hope for his wife and child died. Only a kinetic weapon strike could do that kind of damage. If one of those hit without the shield up, there wouldn't be any survivors. Clamping down on his grief, he forced himself to concentrate on his duty. Duty to the empire and to his dead friends in the palace. He keyed the mic. "Open your secure connection to Guardian. Tell me who needs us here on Beacon."

The colonel answered quickly, *"All the surviving heirs on Beacon show green. Apparently, their personal security teams are handling any threats coming their way."*

Ward nodded. "Okay. We'll be going farther away. Any first-tier targets listed nearby?"

Garand paused, then said, *"Doña Carlota Gonzalvez y Rodriguez del Castillo, the Protector of the Succession, is the nearest surviving Tier One official. She is with the warlord's youngest son, Hugh, on Deft. He's also an heir."*

"Then that's where we're going, Colonel."

The Core Empire

Planetary Settlement

Like the rest of the galaxy, the planets of the core were settled in several general ways:

- Cultural or religious communities, most often insufficiently capitalized to maintain interstellar civilization, as well as lacking in a large enough population to succeed;
- Penal colonies that lacked the capability to sustain a high level of civilization following the withdrawal of support due to the attitudes and behavior of the inhabitants;
- Commercial endeavors, i.e., mining, agricultural, and industrial planets;
- Daughter colonies of successful commercial systems; and
- Military bases.

None of these, by themselves, would have been able to maintain civilization in the face of the pirate fleets that arose following the destruction of the League of Humanity without the efforts of two unique individuals who lived and died over a thousand years ago: Constantine, or Jack, Jackson (2416 to 2494 AD) and his wife Evie Weltz (2422 to 2515 AD). Very different in temperament and skills, they formed a unique pairing that changed what could have been an interstellar dark age into a twilight struggle to retain civilization.

2

Fool's Quest

Above Beacon
System Centrum GY, Prime Sector
1120 BBMT 1 May 3463

ALTHOUGH HE COULDN'T SEE THE shuttle pilot's face, anonymous under his flight helmet, Sean Ward could feel his tension, his fear, and that of his crew. The Fleet collier *Gratitude*, which had dropped them out here, had blown up behind them as they'd sped away. Ward's own nerves competed with his gut-wrenching sense of loss.

The stream of shuttles headed for the nearest moon as a stop-gap until they could board a cruiser or other ship for the run to Deft. The command pilot had apparently decided that heading back into the maelstrom of destruction closer to Beacon fell in the category of a *bad idea*, and Ward unquestioningly agreed. Through the clear cockpit screen, the view in space rarely showed anything of value; things were just too distant. Not now. The action could easily be seen all around them, too near for comfort. His eyes were riveted on the blaze of lasers, missile explosions, shields flaring, and the horrible glory of ships dying. The awfulness of the destruction almost overwhelmed him.

In his ear, he heard the chatter of the shuttles streaming in four diamonds behind him.

"Viper Three, close up. You're straying out of the flight path."

"Roger, One."

"Viper One-Four, Viper One-Four! Hold tight on my three o'clock. You are getting too near that cruiser."

A shaky voice answered, *"Roger, One-Three. Almost had an unexpected meeting with a missile, which left me little choice, over."*

Humor tinged the answer, *"Congrats on avoiding it. Now get back in formation or you're likely to run into something you can't avoid."*

"Roger that."

Ward quickly moved the focus of the battle hologram around, searching for a ride to Deft, even if he had to go alone. The shuttle's flight veered slightly away from the little moon of Flame as it changed targets, but the rest of the trip proved to be just as exciting as it had begun. And tragic.

"Viper Ten, pull it in."

"I'm trying, Eight. The anti-missiles are just too heavy in your path to stay close."

"Pull it in! You're straying too close to that supernova. You're in her laser self-defense zone."

Clearly panicked, the pilot's voice begged, *"Which way do I go to get out of the target zone?"*

Ward stared at the battle hologram in horror as Ten veered straight toward the supernova *Meteor Strike*. A flash and Viper Ten disappeared, along with its crew of five and the forty Marines of 3d Platoon, Company C, 847th Marine Space Assault Battalion. Which left only 637 Marines to protect their assigned heir, an eight-year-old he knew well, Hugh Cascade, the boy Rod had replaced at the Hall of Justice. What a grim sense of humor fate had.

Ward found a possible way to get to Trevor Cascade's boy and Doña Carlota. On the edge of the fight, beyond the little moon called Flame, lay a cruiser squadron with its associated destroyers, frigates, and corvettes shooting at Twelfth Fleet ships belonging to Quadros that came too close or were trying to escape. "Pilot, take us toward Cruiser Squadron 1-11."

The pilot's head swiveled back toward him. "Are you nuts, Sergeant Major?"

Ward just smiled thinly back at the anonymous face. "Probably. Take us there and connect me with the commodore commanding."

His steely tone indicated his lack of amusement. The pilot's head snapped forward, and the shuttles headed toward the cruiser *Quetzal.* Ward didn't particularly want to rely on a cruiser christened for a planet named after a flashy bird, but he had no real choice.

The com came live, *"This is Commodore Pak Hye-won."*

Ward thought she looked more like her Korean last name than Indian first name, an irrelevant observation at the moment. "Commodore, this is Major Sean Ward of the Imperial Guard. Please authenticate my transmission." The commodore went off-screen to be replaced by a swirling kaleidoscope. Ward spoke his name carefully, followed by the code phrase, "The Guardian never dies."

The swirling colors were replaced by the commodore who looked impressed. "You are authorized to make any use of my command that you need."

"Take the shuttles behind me on board, dump your supply shuttles, and take us to Deft. Do not communicate with anyone else, maintain com silence."

Pak didn't look pleased. "I don't think so, even with your clearance. I don't want to take your men on board or dump my shuttles. I'm signed for the shuttles, and your men could take over my ships. Twelfth Fleet started this, but, other than that, I don't know who to trust and I am not taking a chance. Besides Quadros' fleet, Prime Fleet ships are attacking us, too."

Ward stared at her, his voice cold and hard, "This is essential for the protection of the succession. Check the red, sealed codes in your safe and you will find I am on the list of people you must absolutely obey."

"How do you know about those?" Pak seemed to be more belligerent than before. "Those are need-to-know."

"I do because I am head of the proctors. Now check them and get us aboard. We have an heir to protect, and after today there will likely be a lot fewer, which makes that kid even more important. I understand the protector of the succession is with him, too, so stop being the problem and start helping with the solution."

Ward ordered the link cut and his shuttles to divide among the ships, two per cruiser, and the other seven to a destroyer apiece. Then he waited, half expecting to be blown out of the sky as they neared their ships. Surprising him as much as anyone, they attached without losing another shuttle. As he watched the hologram, the remainder of Task Group 1-3 formed around the nova *Emperor Jamal* and pulled out of the fight. Early on, *Emperor Jamal* and its task group of Prime Fleet ships had suddenly joined the Twelfth Fleet rebels, almost tipping the balance of the fight in their favor. Since then, the ships of Prime Fleet had savagely focused their fire on *Emperor Jamal* and its task group, almost to the exclusion of Twelfth Fleet ships still within range. Ward had cheered silently as ship after ship had died, but now they were running. *Good riddance!* As they left, the rest of Twelfth Fleet cut and ran, too. Standing, he headed for the rear hatch as it locked onto *Quetzal*.

Cruiser *Quetzal*, Limits of Deft System
1340 BBMT 4 May 3463

SEVENTY-TWO HOURS AFTER LEAVING Beacon, Ward stood on the bridge watching the holoscreen as Cruiser Squadron 1-11 slowed to enter the Gantry System. After taking in the new data on the display, he turned toward Commodore Pak. Blood drained from Pak's face. Ahead of them, Task Force 1-3, led by the nova *Emperor Jamal* and surrounded by its swarms of ships, blocked the path to Deft.

"How?" The question hung in the air. It didn't matter who asked the question, but the answer certainly mattered. Who had tipped off the rebels as to where they were going?

Ward automatically glanced at the comm panel, but no one there appeared guilty, only scared or stunned. As his eyes moved away, he noticed the intel officer, who normally sat on the next board, slip out of the hatch. Ward had brought a planning team with him to coordinate with Pak, but they were first and foremost Marines. Growling from the side of his mouth, he ordered, "Bring that man back, Gunny. In one piece, if possible."

Without even an *aye, aye*, three Marines dashed across the bridge, causing a minor hurricane, knocking two ratings and an officer down as they sprinted after the fleeing traitor. Pak said nothing as the three sailors on the deck were helped up and dusted off, one woman holding her arm at an odd angle. Ward had seen enough injuries to figure she'd be wearing a cast in an hour. If they survived that long.

Pak looked at him without expression. Ward knew why. Pak had four cruisers with a total of forty missile bays and eight destroyers with another forty-eight bays plus the eighty on the frigates and corvettes. Normally, one hundred sixty-plus missile bays could handle just about anything, including pirate fleets. But they were facing a task group. It appeared to be short a cruiser and three destroyers, but that still left forty bays on the nova alone, thirty on their three cruisers, and seventy-eight on the thirteen destroyers, not counting the numerous frigates and corvettes swarming around. Almost four hundred missile bays to one hundred sixty-eight. Not good odds. Ward waited.

An incoming priority call chimed. The com officer turned to Pak. "Call from Commander, Task Group 1-3, ma'am."

Pak nodded, half turning to head for the privacy of her flag bridge before stopping herself. "Put him up."

Ward kept his eyebrows from rising. Normally commander-to-commander calls were private, especially when they were between enemies. Pak must want everyone to know what they were up against. The florid, smiling face of Commander Jeffrey Gladstone appeared on the main screen. He wore the uniform of a rear admiral.

Ward had never cared for the man despite his undisputed brilliance; now he truly hated him. Gladstone's smile flickered, likely because he realized he had an audience, but it instantly returned.

Pak knew him, too. "What can I do for you, Jeffrey? Where is Admiral Isulu?" she demanded.

Gladstone's eyes narrowed behind his smug smile. "He is no longer with us. If you want to join him, simply refuse to become part of my command and the Restitution Movement. My people are in the process of taking over your ship and squadron even as we speak."

At that moment, a disheveled lieutenant commander staggered onto the bridge. Behind him, the intel lieutenant landed in an unceremonious heap. The gunny Ward had sent after him stepped in looking nearly parade ground fresh. The other two were equally crisp. Ward simply nodded. There wouldn't be a mutiny on the *Quetzal.* He began speaking into his mic to his battalion, "All Viper units, stand by for redeployment within the squadron due to attempted mutiny. Await further orders." Luckily, his men were already armed, ready for planetary insertion, so this should be a short fight. If one even broke out, which he doubted because, from the look of things, this mutiny seemed to be top-down only. The Marines were only posted aboard the cruisers and destroyers, but that should be enough. Ward doubted a conspiracy like this could have been kept secret if it included officers on every ship. Ward's eyes narrowed as one more thought hit him: Gladstone had been one of the officers responsible for counter-intel, so reports about potential rebels or mutineers had likely been channeled through him and his people. Obviously, a problem.

Regardless, Gladstone didn't seem so smug now, more like a wounded tiger. "You stopped some of my people, but you won't get them all. Your ships will be mine within minutes. Even if they aren't, we outgun you better than two to one. Surrender, and I will spare your lives."

Pak drew herself up to her full five feet five, one hundred twenty pounds. "I serve the empire and the Creed. I will fulfill my mission and do my duty. You murdered your way to that command, now see if you can keep it."

Pak made a cut sign before Gladstone could answer. "Contact Admiral Davies through the planetary archeonA, not the archeonA on the nova. Tell him what's going on here. Then order our squadron to clear for battle." To Ward, she added quietly, "We will get you down, but I don't expect any of my ships will survive." Although Ward generally agreed with her assessment, he disagreed with one thing: he didn't think the battalion would even reach the drop zone.

Viper 1, Deft System
2055 BBMT 4 May 3463

A SHIVER RAN THROUGH THE deck plates of the combat shuttle. Ward felt it but forced himself to ignore the very real danger that at any moment the cruiser carrying his shuttle would explode into an expanding ball of gas, destroying them and ending his mission. *That wouldn't be so bad*, a traitorous voice within whispered, *I could join Ann Marie and Rod if that happened*. The com announced, *"Two minutes to separation."*

He smiled drily. *Two suicide runs on a single mission, a new personal best!* Grimly he settled back, waiting for the gravity change that indicated shuttle separation. He made a private bet with himself that less than half the battalion would make it to the ground. Flying through all that firepower ahead would require all the luck a person used in a lifetime. Before the countdown clock reached zero, the shuttle suddenly detached and sped off at max speed. A moment later, on the hologram above the battle board, he watched as *Quetzal* disappeared in a magnificent and dreadful ball of gas and flame. Most of the other shuttles also detached in the nick of time. Three didn't make it. Another 120 dead Marines. Five hundred seven Marines left, if they all reached the ground.

Appendix D: Imperial Ship Types

Core Navy Combat Shuttle—Identified by the name of the mother ship with the letter A then number, if part of a ship complement, or by squadron designator when assigned to a planet, space station, or other orbital body.

- 140 meters long, snub delta wings, nonretractable. 6 meters tall, 20 meters wide
- Belly and dorsal laser/solid shotgun mount
- 2 anti-missile pods
- Carries 40 fully equipped troops as well as a cabin crew of four plus crew chief; Gunners may be provided by unit receiving lift or squadron support teams
- Limited graviton drive for interplanetary flight. Reaction drive available for atmospheric operations. No extended life support capability. Strong sensor suite. Highly maneuverable
- Max speed 1 light-month per hour for 24 hours before exhausting fuel
- Air lock at rear of deck as well as a drop panel in main deck floor for non-landing insertions; For air insertions, troops are equipped with grav drop belts
- Communications: archeonC only
- Crew: Pilot
- Copilot
- Electronic countermeasures and threat identification, combined with
- Commo
- Crew Chief/engineering
- 2 gunners (unless provided by unit shuttle is transporting)
- During ground operations, can be tied in with other shuttles to create ground combat multiphasic shield

3

Wolves at the Door

Camp Cascade, Thorison Highlands
Deft, Gantry System, Prime Sector, Core
0510 Local 5 May/2110 4 May 3463

FIRE RAGED ON THE MOUNTAINS across the lake, its flaring flames turning the night to day. Hugh Cascade huddled in the shadows inside a deep crack in a huge, old pine. He had always loved playing at army: hiding, skulking, hunting, ambushing, before jumping out and killing all the bad guys. Now things had changed. Kinetic missiles without warheads or built-in guidance–so dumb everyone in the military referred to them as "rocks"— screamed out of the sky before crashing into the planet. Their impacts made his ears ring. The ground rolled and a hot wind blew him over with every impact, even those miles away, over the horizon. He didn't like to play war anymore.

An hour ago, as he had looked through a telescope at the stars, the first rock had fallen. He had followed it down with the scope until it had landed on Yellowbird, a small town where they had shopped for supplies. He hadn't been able to get the image of houses burning or people running into the night out of his mind. The fire had started there and had been chasing them through the mountains ever since.

It scared him that Doña Carlota, Sergeant Daniels, and the others were tense all the time. At least one man, generally two, always watched him now. Worse, as he listened to the Marines, he slowly began to understand those rocks shooting down from the sky were aimed at him, trying to kill him, *personally.*

So now, he hid in the strong, old tree. Suddenly, his ears

perked up as he heard Sergeant Daniels calling to someone out in the dark. He even sounded happy for the first time in days. "Sergeant Major! Took you long enough."

The voice sounded familiar, though he couldn't think of the name that went with it. "Just wanted you to enjoy the rest of your fishing trip before putting you back to work, Daniels. And, for the record, I'm using my Imperial Guard rank of major, which means I'm in charge."

"So, what do I call you? Major?"

The answer came with a slight chuckle, "Whatever you feel brave enough to call me."

Sergeant Major Ward! He exploded out of the tree, dashing up to a tall figure in chameleon skin. He worked with Dad. Now his father would come, and everything would be okay! Sliding to a stop three feet in front of him, Hugh stood tall like Dad had taught him, looked the sergeant major in the eye, then boldly said, "Come to kick the bad guys in the butt, Sergeant Major?"

Ward got down on one knee, putting a hand on Hugh's shoulder, and looked him in the eyes. His hard face broke into a sad smile. "Well, we have a tough fight coming up. With some luck, we'll make it 'til the navy gets here. Can I count on you to do exactly what Sergeant Daniels tells you to do?"

Inside, Hugh felt his courage wavering. *Why weren't things going to be okay right now? The Marines had landed!*

Automatically, he answered, "Aye, aye, Sergeant Major." Then a question burning to be asked popped out. "Where's Dad?" With the sergeant major here, Dad couldn't be far behind. Dad would fix everything.

Ward's face softened, pain deep in his eyes. "He can't make it. We'll talk about it later . . . if we get through this."

If we get through this? Terror threatened to overwhelm him, but he stood up straighter. He suddenly knew Dad wouldn't be coming. If he were on the way, surely Sergeant Major Ward would have told him. Tears began welling up in his eyes. He turned away. He couldn't cry in front of these men; it would shame him and Dad. Dad always said that if you acted brave you would *be* brave, and that's what he'd do.

Ward gently turned Hugh back toward him. "Your dad would be proud of the way you've handled yourself so far. Now, I need you to be brave just a bit longer while we figure a way to fight off the bad guys until help arrives." Ward reached up and wiped a tear from Hugh's cheek.

Hugh wiped his nose with the back of his hand, straightened his shoulders and said, "Okay. Let's do it."

Daniels shook his head. "Sounds just like the warlord, doesn't he?"

Ward gave him a sharp look. "He may need to do more than just sound like him before this is all over." Hugh had no idea what that meant but did understand one thing: war had stopped being a game.

Hugh watched Doña Carlota and Sergeant Daniels relax as the sergeant major took over. *Maybe things will be okay after all,* he hoped.

He thought wrong. As he watched, things became much worse. At first, his excitement grew as around him a base camp took shape, just like he'd seen happen lots of times when Dad took him on inspections. In the field near him, four shuttles nosed in together, Marines working between them. Within minutes, power couplings were quickly run between the shuttles that gave Viper One's generator sufficient power to project a kilometer and a half-wide, semi-spherical, multiphasic shield. Just as the hazy purple shield filled the sky, a rock came screaming in directly for them. Hugh fell to the ground, covering his ears, sure they would die. Above him, the shield bonged when the rock hit, but nothing more. No wind, no heat. All around him, Marines went about their duties without a break. Hugh felt ashamed when he realized only he had tried to hide in fear. He vowed never to do that again.

All around him, Marines were at work building less technologically advanced defenses. About fifteen meters from him, the Marines threw dirt up in a berm using hand-held pressors, working their way in a circle around the camp. Once he'd been allowed to use one while Dad watched. It slid easily into the ground, but he couldn't lift the dirt out. Only when Dad cut slices all around the piece he wanted had he been able to get it out and up. Dad told him pressors concentrated gravity into a blade and plate. It hadn't made any sense to him, but it seemed to work.

He watched the Marines using them to create an eight-foot-high earthwork all the way around the inner base as quickly as if they were using bulldozers. Unfortunately, they also were cutting off his view of anything going on outside. In the air above the shield, their other seven shuttles continued to fight it out with the rebels. He couldn't tell which ones were on his side, but he wanted to see better.

Hugh glanced back toward the TOC, proud of himself for knowing the military acronym for Tactical Operations Center. He scanned for anyone watching him. Good, he couldn't see Sergeant Daniels or Doña Carlota, which meant they couldn't stop him from finding a better spot. Now he could get a clear view of the fight going on outside.

Spotting a dead, old tree near the shuttles, he began climbing to the top. He'd easily be able to see all around from there; its broken crown stood well above the berm. He saw shuttles fall out of the sky in flames, not knowing which were from his side or the rebels' side. Around the edge of the shield, he could see anti-ship missiles shooting off.

All the action mesmerized him, his position affording him a great view. Then, Daniels called to him, breaking the spell, "Get down here, Hugh!" He shook his head, not wanting to miss anything. Then, an odd motion drew his attention to a quiet sector of the shield. Shading his eyes, he saw it again. He had seen that type of thing before with Dad, a man in nanocamo moving too quickly. He yelled a warning to anyone who could hear, "There's a guy in nanocamo trying to get in!"

He moved across the top of the trunk to get a better look. Suddenly, he felt it giving way. Falling into the rotten core of the tree, his arms and legs scraped against the jagged wood. Worse, as he hit the bottom with a thump, a shower of debris following, covering his mouth and head. Arms partially pinned to his side, he tried to shake everything off. As he did, something wriggled on his face. *Spiders!* Crawling all over him!

"Help!" he screamed. "Help, there's someone out there, coming through the shield." A moment later he added hysterically, "There's spiders in here!"

WARD SAT ON A FOLDING chair in the back of the battalion TOC as it buzzed with activity. After the holodisplay went up without a hitch, he leaned forward to watch. The missileers and shuttles gave good account of themselves, making landing near the shield too hot even for drop ship Marines. Hugh's screams broke his concentration. Dashing out, he saw Daniels desperately trying to find a way through the tough, old trunk of the dead tree near the berm. A dozen Marines swarmed around, some with pressors. Before Ward could get there, a lieutenant, Austin Carhart, started giving orders. "Everyone back."

Ward kept back with everyone else. Ward could feel Carhart had that indefinable something that spoke of command. Carhart approached the tree, before tapping it low to the ground with the butt of his pistol. A solid thunk sounded. He began moving up until three feet higher a hollow thud resonated inside the tree like a drum. Tapping another four feet up the trunk and finding it still hollow, he called out, "This is Lieutenant Carhart, Hugh. Stay low, I am putting a hole in the tree above your head so we can see in."

Hugh's scared voice, muffled by the tree, answered, "Okay. Hurry," he pled, "Spiders are all over me." After a moment, he asked, "Did you get the bad guy sneaking in?"

"Hang on," Carhart answered. "I don't know if we got their scout. Someone will check while we get you out."

Scanning around him, his head stopped, focused on a Marine with a laser rifle. Pointing to a spot on the tree about six feet above the ground, he directed, "Narrow beam, low power, make me a hole." Spotting a second Marine, he ordered, "Fire extinguisher. From a shuttle. Now." He indicated two more. "Set up your pressors as plates to push against the tree on both sides above this spot and hold the trunk steady."

A moment later, a searing bolt of light punched a one-inch hole in the trunk at the spot Carhart indicated. A small flame licked the edges but quickly died with a light spray from the extinguisher. Carhart pushed a skinny eye through the hole and peered for a minute as he manipulated it, impressing Ward with his professionalism and self-possession. *Good man.* Carhart looked up at the tree again, took a step around to the left, and examined it one more time. "Bring me a pressor. You two," pointing at the men with pressors, "move around with me keeping the trunk steady and upright."

Within seconds he had configured his pressor into a scrape field, yellow guide lights on each side showing the width of the gravitonic blade. Sweeping the focused gravity field slowly left to right across the trunk in a three-foot arc at eye level, he removed a thin layer of trunk, then another on the return stroke, followed by a third.

Pressors weighed just five pounds, but even weighing so little, Ward saw Carhart begin to sweat with the effort of keeping it level and exactly on target. After a good three minutes, he broke through the trunk near the center of the swath. Carhart set down the pressor and called, "Hugh, don't get near the hole or you could be hurt. I am making the hole bigger and will get you out. You understand?"

"Yes. Yes, sir," came a shaky answer.

Carhart moved a little faster as the tree above the entry point began to creak. Over his shoulder, he called to the two men with him, "Keep the trunk steadier, and another couple of you men with pressors help out, one above the hole on this side and the rest of you around the other side of the trunk at the same height. Now! This tree could crumble at any time." A rush of men set up a circle around the trunk, causing it to stand rock steady for a moment, until Carhart's next swipe created a quiver as he removed another layer of supporting wood. The tree began groaning dangerously as he went deeper, even though he kept the hole just a foot wide. Putting down his pressor, he pulled himself up on the trunk under the now unsupported side of the tree. Thrusting his head into the hole, the tree shifting and creaking ominously over him, he yelled, "Now, Hugh! Jump up to me."

Between the whine of all the pressors in operation and the wind shaking the tree, Ward couldn't be sure he understood Carhart's words but recognized the urgency. With a tremendous tug, Carhart yanked Hugh out.

Doña Carlota and Daniels now stood at Ward's shoulder watching as Carhart lifted Hugh down. Letting go of Carhart, Hugh ran to Daniels, who began brushing off the harmless spiders still on him. Doña Carlota, however, raged at Carhart. "Follow me into that shuttle, Lieutenant." Ward heard her shouting as the hatch closed, "What were you thinking? He could have been killed!"

In that instant, the tree crashed, collapsing into a pile of kindling. Ward agreed with Doña Carlota, to an extent. What Carhart had pulled off had been very risky, almost as risky as trying to get Hugh out with ropes from the top, because the tree would not have supported the weight of a man up there. Carhart had made a correct snap decision, and Doña Carlota should have commended him instead of chewing him out. Worse, she had not waited to take Carhart aside, but had done it in public. Too late now to change that, unfortunately. He headed back to the TOC alongside Daniels. Hugh ran ahead, no worse for wear despite the harrowing experience.

He spoke to Daniels as they went. "What were you doing when he fell in, Sergeant?" he asked in a neutral voice that those who knew him took as far more serious than it might seem.

In Ward's peripheral vision, Daniels appeared pale, but answered calmly. "Watching him. This kid is always getting into and out of jams. Truth to tell, Top, I had no idea he would fall in when he started yelling about the scout."

Ward interrupted, "What scout?"

Daniels gave him a ghost of a smile. "He spotted a scout in nanocamo trying to breach the perimeter."

"He was the only one who saw the scout?" Ward's anger had begun rising with Daniels' every word, and not just with Daniels.

"Far as I know. When he began yelling, I ran over to the berm to see what was going on. Seems one of Gladstone's scouts had snuck in and only Hugh got eyes on him. I sent two men out to remove the problem. That's when the tree caved in."

Ward felt astonishment. The boy had that much presence of mind? "He ever do anything like this before?" he growled.

Daniels shrugged. "All the time. The warlord thought it showed character and panache, whatever that is."

Ward looked toward the TOC, where Hugh sat eating a protein bar. *This boy just might have what it takes.* Turning back to glare at Daniels, he growled. "This conversation isn't over. If we survive this fracas, we'll continue this counseling session and go over precisely how we keep an heir alive despite himself."

IN THE HOLODISPLAY, WARD SAW a fleet of rebel shuttles dropping toward them. He guessed about forty, which meant some of Gladstone's ships had died during the massacre of the *Quetzal* and her squadrons, or else he might be keeping a few back as a reserve. If all of Gladstone's ships had survived, they could have dropped more than sixty shuttles.

The ops officer, Major Ahu Kalili, shook his head. "Either they have some ace up their sleeves or there are about to be a lot of dead Marines in that drop."

Colonel Gary Garand chuckled grimly, "That's a good thing. For us. I haven't a clue how to operate our remaining seven shuttles outside the shield as air cover." Turning toward his com team, he ordered, "Tell our shuttles that are still alive out there they can do anything they want as long as they shoot down those incoming shuttles."

Their combat shuttles, now lighter and more agile without cargo or Marines, darted toward the incoming shuttles. Missile traces and lasers lit up the display. Ward found himself leaning forward. Three rebel ships disappeared before the formation even seemed to notice, and then five more. Maybe they'd be able to hold the rebels out completely? A moment later, the first of their own shuttles disappeared, and then a second one. A trio of sloops from the fleet overhead made a pass with missiles and lasers and knocked out two more. Three more rebel shuttles fell in flames, the sky now abruptly clear of the brave men and women willing to die to defend the landing zone.

The remaining approximately thirty rebel shuttles spread out in a parade ground-perfect formation around the shield. Each group of shuttles split up into four sets of three and came in hot, combat shuttles in the lead. Ward couldn't believe his eyes. Did the rebels think the Marines would roll over? With no air cover or any attempt to suppress the ground forces, what were they thinking? Ward saw Garand nod to Kalili, and a spread of anti-air missiles sped off from the margins of the shield. In the nearly picture-perfect ambush, seven more shuttles fell and the rest broke for the cover of the surrounding ridgelines. Ward stood to join Garand.

Garand's brow puckered in thought. "Gladstone's got two drop ships, two battalions there, and possibly another scratch battalion or so from the other ships. What do you think, Tiny?" he said, turning to Kalili.

"Probably followed doctrine and put both scout platoons in lead shuttles. Armor in lead shuttles is doctrine, too. That would give him three hundred sixty suits against our eighty that survived to hit the ground."

Garand pursed his lips as he considered the thought. "I've met Gladstone, and he's a psychopath but not stupid. I have no idea whether he'll follow doctrine or not. If he does, they may not have as much armor as us or they may have lost most of it in the dog fight and missile ambush. On the other hand, he may have saved the armor on his ships to keep control up there. Probably trying to cover all the bases by attacking us, while keeping enough suits up there to stop any counter-mutinies. Could be we have the advantage in suits down here."

Kalili shrugged. "Hate to plan on *if,* Colonel."

Garand nodded. "Me, too."

Ward cleared his throat. Garand turned to him. "Thoughts, Sergeant Major?"

"We need some hard numbers?" he asked.

Both nodded at the obvious statement.

"We need to turn off your scout platoons' archeonC so they can't be found by the rebels when they're outside the shield getting that information. At least until they have what we need."

"Why just the scouts? Afraid Gladstone will try to subvert them?" Garand bristled back.

Ward shook his head. "No offense meant. If we leave the scouts' coms active, somebody up there could ping them. Or they could set up a computer monitoring program to track all transmissions in the area, scrub out transmissions coming from their people, and then pinpoint whatever remained. Who knows, he might even have all our information right now and be tracking everything we do anyway. Gladstone likely has access to all Prime Fleet files including Marine communication implants. Or did up until three days ago."

Kalili nodded thoughtfully before answering, "All Marines have an archeonC implant. Simply changing the communications algorithm, we should be able to prevent someone hacking or even locating our people. It should be safe enough, Sergeant Major."

Ward shook his head. "I want those scouts on the other side of the shield identifying where the bad guys are coming from and possibly taking some of that armor out, not dying. It would be very simple for that nova's electronic warfare techs to program their computers to watch for unexplained transmissions. Doing that would locate our scouts. They don't need an algorithm for that. With our ships wiped out, their EW section has nothing better to do to keep them occupied and, since Gladstone is an intel weenie, he should know how to utilize them.

"As for the guys inside the shield, it shouldn't make any difference if they know where we are because they won't have indirect fire weapons that can lock in on us. The shield prevents that, and we need to communicate."

Kalili looked at Garand who shrugged before saying, "He's in charge. If it keeps our people alive a bit longer, it's worth a shot. And it would be helpful to have that intel."

Without saluting, Ward headed for the door. "I'll brief them myself as to what I want and make sure they can reactivate the link when they have the info."

As he left, Kalili softly added, "Cold-blooded guy. Keeping them alive until he has what he needs for the mission."

Garand didn't bother to keep his voice low. "That's what command is all about, Tiny. Just be glad you're not the one who has to send those people out to die."

Galactifacts for Kids 3500

USE OF NUCLEAR WEAPONS ON PLANETS. Regardless of all the other horrors of war, one thing is common throughout the galaxy, no one will use nuclear weapons on planetary surfaces. The reason is simple. Using them inside an atmosphere makes a planet at least partially uninhabitable, sometimes for thousands of years. Destruction of a planet erases the benefits of victory. The only instance where these weapons were justifiably used on a planetary surface occurred in ancient times on Earth, to end the reign of a tyrannical cult. This was before the world understood the full impact of their devastation. Afterward, they were used as a deterrent rather than an active weapon.

After the colonization of the galaxy began, there have been only three recorded instances of the use of nuclear weapons on a planet, all by totalitarian governments in danger of losing a war to rebels. After each instance where they were used, neighboring star systems banded together to hunt down the perpetrators. Their executions have served as a warning that such use will not be tolerated in the future. For this reason, no one is foolish enough to use atomics against planetary targets.

4

Serious Business

Camp Cascade, Deft

1940 Local/1140 BBMT 5 May 3463

A SHARP PINGING SOUND WOKE Hugh Cascade. A second sharp sound almost immediately followed the first. Hugh sat up, rubbing his eyes, trying to see. The purple shimmer in the dark from the shield above him blocked out the stars. "Sergeant Daniels?" he called out tentatively.

"What do you need, Hugh?" Jake Daniels sounded sleepy.

"What made that noise?"

"Just the bad guys testing the shield, seeing if they can overload it and crash it."

"Can they?"

Hugh saw Daniels sit up. "No, Hugh. This is a ground combat shield, even tougher than ship shields. And when the area is limited, the shield's even tougher. That's why we have such a small-sized area to work in."

Small? A kilometer and a half across sounded big to him. "Can they shoot through it?"

Daniels' voice sounded confident to Hugh's young ears. "Not very likely. They'd have to drop a bunch of nukes on us at the same time, but nukes have a problem. If they explode too near each other, they don't work very well, and we are a very small target. That means overloading the shield to get to us is very tough to pull off. Besides, nuking a planetary surface from orbit is something nobody does. So, the short answer is *no.* The real reason they're dropping rocks is to keep us penned in here, preventing a shuttle from escaping with you on it, and also to prevent us from making the shield smaller if they do get in. It's easier to defend the edges of the shield than have a fight inside. But, even if they do get in, you have a whole battalion of Marines defending you, so go back to sleep."

Hugh didn't really hear the explanation. After Daniels had said "Not very likely," nothing else mattered and he drifted off, snoring softly by the time Daniels finished.

DOÑA CARLOTA GONZALVEZ Y RODRIGUEZ del Castillo shifted restlessly on her somewhat comfortable cot. She didn't enjoy camping, preferring her own bed. Outside her tent some of the Marines greeted each other, further disturbing her sleep. Annoyed, she wished they would find somewhere else to chat. *Why can't Ellis be here to shoo them away?* But she had left her majordomo, Philip Ellis, back home to take care of pressing business while she came here. Unlike her family, which had been caught at the palace in the attack, he had been at the estate. Grief filled her at this fresh reminder of her terrible loss, causing her to gasp out a sob before controlling it.

Rolling over, she pulled the pillow over her head, but she could still hear them. Yanking the pillow off, she turned again to her back. Even so, she could still hear them. Why couldn't they go, leaving her to her suffering? Suddenly, the subject of the soft conversation penetrated her pain, catching her attention.

"Why are we here, anyway? It's just an eight-year-old kid, after all. Is he going to be the next emperor? I don't think so."

Someone chuckled. "Nah. He's a spare. But to tell the truth, he's better than the heirs I've met. He's pretty down-to-earth. I was on a protection detail, but I can't tell you who I was assigned to protect. He was a jerk, thought we were there as his personal errand boys. I hated it. Most guys think protection is a cushy gig, but not when you have to put up with that nonsense."

Almost without thinking, Doña Carlota got up and stepped out into the dark. Smoke thickened the air, making it distinctly unpleasant to breathe. Walking around the tent, she found four

Marines barely visible in the star glow. As she appeared, they popped to attention. Smiling, she waved them down before asking, "Could I have a moment of your time?"

One of them blurted out, "We were just shooting the breeze, ma'am. We'll be going now." They made a move to leave.

She spoke quietly, but it sounded like a command. She said, "It would be a favor if you would stay."

All four settled back without answering aloud.

"May I sit, too?" Instinctively, she felt the need to reduce the social distance so they would be honest with her. One of the men offered his helmet as a seat without a word.

"Thank you," she said graciously. "I realized that you deserve an explanation as to why you are being asked to risk your lives. None of you are stupid and all of you probably know by now that the odds are stacked against us. Heavily."

Uncomfortable agreement came from all four.

"I'm sure you are wondering what is so special about this one small boy. To answer that question, let's take a brief look at history. The reason that only children of Constantine Jackson, the first emperor, and Evie, queen of Green Gardens, are chosen is simple but not publicly discussed. Why might you think that only their descendants are chosen?"

One sounded surprised as he blurted out, "Were they real? I thought someone just made up that story."

Relaxing inside, she could feel this going in the right direction. "Yes, it is true. Their son Joe gave his life for the core stars and Jack and Evie set up the empire. They wanted all to be free of the tyranny they saw coming. In fact, Jack and Evie lived apart the last dozen years of their lives as they worked to make a free galaxy a possibility."

Another voice asked, "So why did they set up a monarchy if they wanted people to be free?"

"They decided that if they taught their children right, and picked the very best one, whether man or woman, to rule, they had a good chance. What you don't know is that the new emperor or empress must pass a test where failure is death. I hope you think less badly of the heir you watched over. That is a heavy burden to have hanging over your head."

Mutters of agreement came and another voice said, "I wouldn't do it, not if I had to pay that kind of price. I do terrible on tests."

Someone else added, "You're bad at everything." General chuckles followed.

Doña Carlota smiled thinly, which she felt certain they could not see. "There is no choice; they are picked at birth."

"There should be millions of heirs by now. What makes Hugh so big a deal that we have to face a whole division to save him?"

Doña Carlota shrugged. "There are never more than a few hundred chosen, generally less. We don't have archeonA access now, but before you arrived, I had reports of heirs being killed all over the empire."

"But he's just a kid. I don't think he'd be a good emperor now."

"You're right." Her smile became tighter. "But in another fifteen or twenty years he could be just what we need. Remember— Well, you don't know. No one over fifty, and generally forty, has been asked to take the test. If you take out the old and young, there aren't all that many available at any one time. We want the best."

A very soft voice came back. "Like Benjamin?"

Doña Carlota sighed. "Sometimes we . . . err. We do try to avoid people like him, as well as those . . . less mentally stable."

"That let's all of us out, or we wouldn't be here." General laughter greeted that remark.

She chuckled. "I agree. You did join the Marines, after all." The men all laughed at that. "One thing I'll tell you, anyone who says they can fix anything by throwing out the old system without explaining why their way is better is not being honest with you. 'Just trust me' is what a con man says, not a leader. Or, more accurately, a con *woman*."

"Morgain," whispered a different voice.

"She is one of the people I'm concerned about. The public is enamored of her, seeing only her surface beauty and not aware that she lacks substance."

A voice from the dark added, "I've heard her speak. She's no dummy."

A general murmur of agreement answered his observation.

"True. In fact, she may be brilliant. Certainly when it comes to manipulating public opinion, she has demonstrated considerable skill. She has convinced many that what they have is less than they want, but what does *she* want? How will she provide the masses with this mythical *more* and, most importantly, what will it cost you?"

"She says we'll have more freedom."

"In what way? You are not conscripts. There is no slavery in the empire. Each of you has the opportunity to pursue whatever goals and dreams you have and are willing to work hard to achieve. So how could you be more free? And I will leave you with this thought: If she were in charge, what protections will you have *from her*?"

With the silence, she knew she had planted the seed of doubt. She had said all she could. Morgain's popularity had grown quickly and with it came influence over popular opinion. Counteracting her siren call required people to look beyond the shiny surface and exercise critical thinking skills that seemed more and more in short supply. For now, she couldn't convince them by arguing. She could only try to steer them in the right direction and coax them to think for themselves. "Now I need some sleep. Good night." Standing, she noted that her circle of listeners had grown to more than a dozen while they'd talked. Returning to her bed, she slept soundly.

WARD LISTENED TO THE NIGHT. Subdued sounds of battle provided muffled background music for the activity in the TOC. Out in the night, an occasional ping indicated active patrolling, both sides probing for weaknesses. Two scouts had returned out of the thirty that had gone out the morning before: Abdul Jebet, a huge black man, and Tabitha Fleisch—"just Tabi"—a woman of slightly above-average height, with dark hair and an olive complexion. Both lay sacked out in a corner of the tent.

Even though other things worried Ward, he had ordered these two to hang tight. Frankly, it amazed him that anyone had returned from the scout mission. Jebet reported that the scouts drew straws as to who would reactivate their archeonC first to report in. These two drew two of the shortest straws but had survived anyway. Among other things they'd done, Fleisch had called from inside a cave and Jebet from inside the wreckage of a downed shuttle, both hoping to buy some time before their signals could be filtered out. The others had attempted similar tricks but their luck had run out. Ward wanted to keep these two close. You couldn't count on luck, but neither should you reject it.

Ward caught Colonel Garand glance in his direction for input before making his troop dispositions. Ward simply watched silently. Back on Beacon, this battalion had started with over seven hundred effectives, including the flight crews. As of oh-dark-thirty this second morning on Deft, there were barely four hundred sixty Marines plus twenty surviving crew members from the shuttles. Forty men and women operated the TOC or manned the inner perimeter, so things were a little sparse along the edge of the shield. Things looked tough. Garand moved over to whisper to Ward. "This situation isn't all bad news, Sergeant Major. There are no more than two battalions of Marines and sixty hard suits facing us on the ground. The holodisplay shows only three axes of advance."

Ward snorted in disgust at that. "Gladstone is either an idiot or getting bad advice. Splitting up is a bad thing to do because we can defeat him in detail, one group at a time. On my last swing out there a couple of hours ago, I saw the rebels digging in near the tallest gaps in the shield. They've been very quiet recently, however. That bothers me."

Ward wished the shield could go all the way into the ground, but shields generated by shuttles or ships had to be symmetrical. Shields hogged power even in space, much more in atmosphere, which made generating sufficient power for a shield to penetrate a planet's surface nearly impossible in field environments, except with access to the power supply of a major city. Meaning that until they leveled the ground at the shield perimeter, the lowest point for a shield equaled the highest point on the perimeter. Ward shrugged, with more time the Marines could have either filled in the gaps or lowered the high points, but they didn't have time to smooth the five-plus-kilometer perimeter.

Plus, they needed fresh air, which is why they kept the perimeter so large.

Even though tired, Ward felt confident. "We should be able to do this, Colonel. It's only three-to-one odds. The Eight-Four-Seven should be able to hold out for a week, more than enough time for Davies to get here. A frontal assault, the only possible way to get under the edge of the shield, will be suicidal, so Hugh should be safe."

Of course, if Davies didn't get here in time, they would run out of fuel to power the shuttles, which meant no shield. Neither the super-condensed hydrogen gas to power the fusion generator, nor the fission primer, a cocktail of radon, plutonium, and assorted other radioactives used to produce a nice bang, could be found just lying around. So, when the fuel ran out, the shield would go down, following which, the kinetics would end them. Quickly, effectively, and completely.

"You're doing a good job, Colonel. I'm going to rack out." Ward recognized Garand's greater expertise in battalion tactics, so despite his technically out-ranking him as a major in the Imperial Guard, he'd ceded command of the defense to him. Of course, Ward had taken command back on Beacon so he would be making the hard calls. And that kind of choice could come at any time. As he headed for the door, thirty shuttles appeared on the holodisplay streaking toward the three areas being developed by the rebel ground troops near the shield. Kelili turned toward the com team. "Contact all three companies."

Ward froze and watched.

Garand quietly cleared his throat. "The hard suits out there will slaughter our people if they try and shoot down the shuttles.

They're bait for us to send out our people to die needlessly. Don't send them out."

Kelili nodded in comprehension. "Who, or what, is Gladstone sending down on those shuttles, do you think?"

Ward stepped closer and interrupted. "Gladstone is stripping the ships. He knows Prime Fleet could be here in three days and he understands the odds currently don't help him enough to win. If Davies arrives in force, he is unlikely to get to us before the shield runs out of juice. So, he's sending everyone he can down here. He'll use the spacers as bait and then cannon fodder, and the Marines he has might then be enough to wipe us out. Regardless, shooting down a shuttle or two will slow the sortie rate, and trading one or two Marines for forty is something we can't afford to pass on. Give the order. Shoot down as many as they can." The deaths of those Marines would be on his conscience for the rest of his life, but he had to make this call for Hugh to have a chance.

The blood drained from Kelili's face as Ward spoke, but he passed on the order, "Each company will send out six three-man missile teams and take out as many shuttles as possible."

Ten minutes later, the holodisplay reported missile tracks with three shuttles splashed.

Over half the missile teams made it back inside as the shuttles hit dirt, except in front of Charlie Company. None returned. Ward's knuckles tightened on the edge of the table. He had known his decision might be more costly than he wanted to pay. It had been. Charlie now mustered fewer than one hundred effectives.

The comm came alive. *"This is Charlie. There are hard suits headed our way, lots of them, maybe forty. Lots of troops, too. The CO asks for any help you can send. Our suits are dug in, but he doesn't think they'll be able to hold against this."*

Ward grudgingly acknowledged Gladstone's cleverness. A few suits showing themselves around the other LZs had fooled him into assuming an equal distribution. His assumption had turned out horribly wrong because most of two battalions were charging down on one surprised and under-strength company with just eight suits.

Garand acted even before Ward could decide how to handle this. "Send four suits each from Alpha and Bravo over there and the six-suit reserve. Fall back to secondary position Charlie Three. Order Charlie to begin a move back to three by echelon while maintaining suppressive fire on the attackers. We can't hold the edge of the shield there, so we need to shorten lines. Alpha and Bravo need to pull back also, maintaining a tight grip on the company to either side so no leakers get through." Kelili nodded and briskly went to work.

Ward shrugged. "I didn't see that coming."

Garand smiled sourly. "Neither did I, and I should have."

Ward stood straight and adjusted his gear before looking over at Jebet and Fleisch. As far as he knew, they had been sleeping but now they sat checking their gear. *Smart.*

As soon as they stood, he quietly told them, "Let's go," before jogging out the door toward supply. "Either of you need anything?" he inquired as they stepped up beside him at the tent. They didn't reply as they loaded up on munitions. He appreciated that they were concentrating on business and not chatting.

Ward grabbed four limpet mines. He considered taking a couple of single-man missiles, but they were just too bulky, and you could only carry two. Limpets used a strong magnetic element that let you throw one in the general area of the target and it would do the rest itself as long as it didn't find something even more metallic nearby. Besides, the potential for survival after use of even a single missile in this environment approached zero, as the loss of Charlie Company's six missile teams proved.

Ready to leave, he glanced around at his scouts. They both grabbed a sack of limpets. Together they headed for the sally port, where the earthen berm wall overlapped to prevent a straight shot into the CP from the outside

He waited a moment as two badly injured Marines were helped in by buddies. Passing beyond, Ward activated his chameleon skin and night vision, noting without comment that the other two did as well. This close together, they could see a watery outline of each other but, if they were more than ten feet apart, they would lose each other completely unless they activated the archeonC trace also. "Keep your archeon off and stay close. We are about to inflict a little havoc before the other side gets rolling on this side of the shield."

Both confirmed with a laconic "Roger."

"We should get to the edge of the shield in seven minutes or so if we hustle. Move out." Without stopping to see if they were on his six, he started off in a ground-covering jog. With chameleon skin engaged, he could lose them very easily if he went faster.

Around him near the berm, plants still covered the meadow, war not having come yet except for the trails made to and from the fighting positions prepared the day before. Solitary trees spread their limbs in leafy splendor and, here and there, a cow or two still stood munching with vast unconcern. With grim certainty, Ward knew that would change quickly.

The rattle of gunfire and explosions from missiles suddenly increased. The rebels apparently were inside the shield. The gap between the shield and ground stood fairly high, three feet, in front of Charlie Company. Of course, an unarmored grunt could easily slide through a three-foot gap, but armor must crawl in carefully, making it vulnerable.

As Ward passed the position at Charley Three, he saw men darting and firing, faces toward the shield, but losing ground as the rebels came nearer. He could also see three suits of smoking armor ahead of him nearer the shield. Checking his heads-up display he saw they were from Charley. That left Charley with five suits against nearly forty to hold out until the cavalry got here. With enhanced muscles, the suits reinforcing Charlie should be there about now, but his display showed them still minutes away.

Just at that moment, two rebel armor suits stood up at the inside edge of the shield. The sizzle of a laser rifle blasted one, and the other flew apart as a man-held missile hit it dead center. A barrage of return fire blasted back at the points from which the shots had come, even as three more rebel suits stood up and took fire from Charlie's remaining men.

Stepping close to his trailers, Ward spoke softly, "Okay, there are a lot of rebels inside the shield already. Charlie still has five suits, but a rush could overwhelm them. Let's get to the edge of the shield and take as many suits out as we can before they get really rolling. How many limpet mines do you have?"

The big shadow rumbled, "Eight." The smaller one said, "Five."

Ward nodded, his four giving them seventeen. It would likely be enough to slow down the attack, even if they only got a few kills. Any unexplained explosions should make the rebels cautious, anyway. He smiled grimly. "I'll go up the middle. Fleisch, get around the left flank, Jebet, the right. Don't wait for a signal, just start killing things."

Without acknowledgment, the two shadows flitted away, and he turned toward the shield, not a hundred meters away. He could run it in fifteen seconds but, even in the dark, night vision goggles would note the distortion his camo suit would cause if he moved that fast, making him an easy target.

Regardless, with no time for subtleties, he bent over and began to jog forward. He needed to get there fast but alive to be able to make any difference. Within ten meters, however, he hit the deck and began to low-crawl, the air around him alive with death. Bullets flew overhead like hail. Occasional laser bolts left retina trails as they shot across the dusk. Ward knew the size and weight of the lasers made them less portable, thus exposing their gunners to greater risk. Explosions from grenades added to the din and danger. Ward could have easily launched himself in a suicide run at the incoming troops—would have welcomed the cold embrace of death, if only to put an end to the grief that overwhelmed him in every quiet moment—but he knew he couldn't. Not until he got Trevor Cascade's boy somewhere safe.

In his peripheral vision, he saw a rebel lift his head and sight down his rifle toward Ward's left. Looking that way, Ward saw four other rebels also preparing to fire. He popped a grenade, tossed it on three, then rolled into a depression and covered up.

The ballistic protection properties of a chameleon skin stopped some things, but only went so far.

The grenade explosion rocked the ground beneath him. It must have been closer than he guessed. Worse, a cyclone of fire concentrated on the area around his position, ripping the earth and shredding the little surviving greenery. As the firing lessened, he scuttled away.

Through the wisping smoke, he saw a terrifying sight: a trio of suits heading straight toward him. He pulled out three limpets and set them to blow immediately on contact. Then he activated his Imperial Guard code key. Suddenly his heads-up display went from showing only his men's positions in their nanocamo to a mass of signals, most coming straight toward him.

Ward smiled grimly. *Guess they didn't remember their transponder lockouts didn't work against officers of the Imperial Guard.* Probably didn't expect him to be here, especially not at the sharp end of the stick. Knowing where the rebels were gave him a chance—a tiny one—of surviving this. He, on the other hand, refused to take a chance that someone over there might access the same code key.

He waited for the suits to get closer, almost right on top of him, keeping the limpets on the ground underneath him so his chameleon skin could keep them camouflaged. Rifle ready in his left hand, he decided the order of his targets. Two breaths. And, go! First limpet to the left, second to the far right, third straight ahead. The explosive concussion from the limpets knocked him and most of the Marines nearby off their feet.

Recovering quickly, Ward knelt in order to be in a steadier firing position but still see the men lying on the ground. On semiautomatic, he began pouring fire into the disoriented rebels, but they recovered quickly. Breaking one of his cardinal rules, he flicked his selector to automatic. Spraying the area to his front to keep the attackers' heads down, he hoped help came before he ran out of ammunition. He'd be in a world of hurt if they didn't. Fifty to one were long odds, even for him.

As he sprayed the area, he noted that two of the suits, the

ones to the left and center, had exploded. The third limpet blew up when it hit a rifleman unfortunate enough to be in the way, leaving only pieces of his uniform in the crater. At that moment, his rifle's chamber locked back a second time, out of ammo. Slamming in a third magazine, he continued to hammer the stunned troops on the ground. As he ran out of ammunition the third time, he saw the remaining suit locking onto him, its laser rifle sweeping toward him in what felt like slow motion.

Funny the things your mind picks up on when you're about to die. The man in that suit is right-handed. Makes it tougher for him to bring that heavy laser rifle around quickly.

As the laser swung near him, Ward flattened himself on the ground. Then the suit disappeared in flames. Someone else had gotten him, but he couldn't guess who.

His hearing returned as the action seemed to stop for a moment. The moaning of the wounded, along with piteous calls for help, rose from the field to his front. Lifting his head, he saw the area littered with dead and wounded as men moved to help them. But there were others, too, armed and searching for whoever had attacked them, meaning him. Unless he wanted to actually commit suicide, he could do little more from this position. There were too many of the bad guys and they were too alert.

With only a single limpet left and down to a third of his ammo, what more could he do anyway? With the advance slowed to a standstill, here at least, he had accomplished his mission.

His hands shook as he low-crawled toward Charlie Three, surprising him. After all these years, staring death in the face still rattled him. Just as he rolled through a gap in the line, a series of explosions behind him near the shield's edge told him one or both of his shadows were still busy. A hush fell as firing from the rebels nearly stopped. At least his little diversion had bought some time.

Ward shook his head. He needed to leave all this kind of activity to the young bucks; at his age, he should just sit and watch. Using his rifle as a staff, butt on the soft ground and barrel up to avoid fouling it, he stood and headed, slowly, back to the TOC. Reaching the sally port, he deactivated his chameleon skin. Inside the berm, he uncapped his water and drank the entire quart almost at a gulp.

Combat and stupidity made him thirsty, and his actions over the last half an hour qualified for both. As he stepped into the TOC, the roar of battle echoing off the shield increased again. Twenty minutes later, his two bad pennies showed up carrying a badly injured Marine, not saying a thing except to report. An hour later, the sun came up while the casualties kept coming in.

HUGH SAT ON A BUNDLE of supplies swinging his legs. Sergeant Daniels wouldn't let him go anywhere, he grumped. Right now, things were boring. Earlier he had started to climb the inner side of the berm to see the fighting going on outside, but Daniels had dragged him back down. "Stay down here!" he ordered. "If you get killed up there from a stray bullet, all these good people will have thrown away their lives for nothing." So here he sat but didn't like it.

"Coming in!" echoed from the sally port. Two men and a woman came in running, two carrying a stretcher and one holding up a bag over the man on the stretcher. Hugh stood up for a closer look, riveted by what he saw. The man on the stretcher looked like he'd lost his right arm; blood soaked his uniform all the way down his side. Behind him, the berm shook with an explosion. Startled, he turned in time to see a Marine slide down the berm toward him. The Marine's eyes stared at the sky unblinking, his chest a mass of red. Hugh stood paralyzed until Daniels came and led him to a tent. Looking back, Hugh said quietly, "I should have gone to help him."

Daniels, voice shaking with anger, asked bitingly, "What could you have done? You saw him die."

Hugh's face hardened. "I don't know, but I could have tried." Shaking off Daniels's hand, he marched off, back straight.

An anonymous Marine behind him offered, "That kid just might be just worth saving."

A COUNTDOWN CLOCK READING FORTY-ONE hours, seventeen minutes hung on the wall of the TOC. They had started it originally at seventy-two hours based on the now-dead Pak's estimate of when Davies might, possibly, with luck, get here. Ward privately suspected help wouldn't come in time, if at all. Certainly not in forty-one hours and change.

As he sat, the stickiness of his dried sweat reminded him that he hadn't had a shower since before they had landed two days ago. Rubbing his chin, the stubble irritated him even more. He ignored his discomfort as he had for years past on field problems. Like all the other irritations in his life, he stuffed this one into a box so he could concentrate on what truly mattered. Like contacting Prime Fleet and Davies.

A cruiser only carried an archeonB transmitter, and, because of the distance, contacting Prime Fleet back on Beacon or Davies' supernova-class flagship *Black Hole* required archeonA. Gladstone's nova-class ship, *Emperor Jamal*, a class smaller than the supernova class, carried an archeonA transmitter, but Ward felt quite confident Gladstone wouldn't pass on any messages from them, leaving Deft's planetary archeonA transmitter as their final option. However, if a call from Deft on its archeonA array had gone out, it must have been a retransmission from Pak before her ship blew up because, after hitting dirt, they could only get static on their archeonC from the planetary frequency.

Ward stared hard at the holodisplay, but nothing changed, only a perimeter holding three hundred meters out from the berm.

Standing and hooking up his battle rattle over his chameleon skin, he headed out. Doña Carlota Gonzalvez y Rodriguez del Castillo, nominally in charge of everyone fighting to save Hugh, gave him a nod as he went by but said nothing. She looked drained after the unrelenting pressure of the past two days.

Ward passed Garand on the way out. "Going somewhere, Top?" Garand asked.

"Thought I'd stretch my legs, take some ammo and water to the people at the sharp end." Combat made you thirsty, very thirsty.

Garand nodded his head. "Don't get shot. I don't want to explain that to your boss."

Ward's face hardened as he answered, "My boss, that little boy's father, died in the palace when it went up, along with my son, so I don't think you need to worry." Not waiting for a reply, he activated his chameleon skin. Turning, he noted his shadows following, not saying anything, just staying close. So be it.

At the sally port, he lowered himself to his hands and knees and began to high-crawl before going out. Gladstone's men undoubtedly kept the entry port under close observation, which brought him back to his real problem: How could they hold the perimeter for forty-one more hours?

Jane's Fighting Starships

Appendix D: Imperial Ship Types

Core Navy Cruiser—named for planets

366 meters long, 30 meters high, 46 meters wide, 7 decks

3 hydroponics/life support bays

3 power rooms

Main bridge about one-quarter of the way down from nose in center of ship with dedicated auxiliary bridge two-thirds to rear

Preon drive only

Carries 2 shuttles externally that can carry supplies or personnel

40 Anti-missile pods

10 missile bays

6 magazines, 50 missiles each

2 armories

12 two-man gun pods

12 three-man laser mounts

Kinetic Bombardment Bay: 5 graviton drive weapons

Crew of 498

Communications: ArcheonB

Nose air lock, shuttle air locks, with a double spiral of emergency air locks from nose ending two-thirds down-ship

Carries platoon of Marines with heavy armor for one squad

Max speed inside dense star neighborhood such as galactic arm or core—1.1 parsec per hour

Can accelerate to over 120 parsec/ hour outside galactic arms

5

Paying the Price

Camp Cascade, Deft

0625 Local 8 May/2225 BBMT 7 May 3463

A STRAY BEAM OF SUNLIGHT, false promise of hope on this third new day, momentarily blinded Sergeant Major Sean Ward before he flipped his visor back in place. Another night survived. To an extent, it surprised him that anyone had lived through the night, but he and some others had made it. Behind him, he could see the berm barely fifty meters away. Only one of their suits remained. As far as he could tell, the rebels were out of suits, too. He hoped so, because he had run out of limpets during the night.

The com crackled in Ward's ear, a laser bolt splitting the air overhead creating static and causing him to involuntarily burrow deeper into the torn, black earth. The techies said nothing could interfere with archeon reception, but he didn't believe them. Black holes, large magnetic fields like suns or giant gas planets, and massive energy discharges near enough to cause sunburn, all could disrupt archeon reception; anyone who lived in the real world knew these things from experience.

All of that flew through Ward's mind in a split second as he hugged the dirt. He really needed some kind of distraction and that stray thought would have to do for the moment. That last shot probably passed more than a meter over his head, but it might have been just inches.

If he stood up now, it would all be over in seconds. *Ann Marie, you weren't supposed to go first.* The two of them had always assumed Ward would die first, the way it usually happened in military families. But he had survived instead.

He missed little Rod horribly. He found himself fighting a traitorous thought, a wish that Hugh had been in the Hall of Judgment with his father instead of Rod. He didn't blame Hugh; they sent him here as part of the standard succession plan. Besides which, for the empire to survive, so must Hugh or one of the other heirs. *Surviving heirs.* As chief of the proctors, he knew there weren't so many to start. *Shut up and get the job done. You can die after getting Hugh to a safe place.*

To his left, firing picked up from the encircling troops. Lasers crackled, filling the air with the smell of ozone. The few trees that still stood burst into flames, hellish additions to the cratered landscape. Ward checked his heads-up display. The icons representing the Marines in this sector remained constant, as they patiently waited. When the rebels attacked, it would be time to move, shoot, kill, and maybe die.

Suddenly the ground jolted, bouncing Ward into the air. Explosions, a string of death walking toward his position, told of another attack coming. *Back to business.* Next, more sniping, straight-line missiles used as artillery prep, then another suicide rebel attack, after which he'd pull the survivors back, shortening the line as they lost one irreplaceable man after another.

Ward forced his thoughts back to the current situation and took stock. Artillery, drones, and other weapons designed for standoff capability were at best severely limited inside a shield. Shooting in an arc under the shield generally led to one of two bad results: either the munition exploded on the inner side of the shield, which absorbed the energy and revealed your position, or the munition bounced back at the person firing it. The second potential result discouraged most people, no matter how fanatic. That left Gladstone with a single option: attack straight ahead. The shield delayed him from employing his overwhelming superiority in manpower and equipment most effectively, but couldn't prevent the relentless assault from grinding up Hugh's defenders, one by one. Ward chalked that up as a partial victory. By postponing the inevitable, it gave them a chance.

Unfortunately, other than around the edge, the shield trapped the air inside. With each explosion, more dirt, powder residue, and who knew what else, filled the air. Breathing had become difficult. It also took away one advantage he had used mercilessly the first day: the ability to sneak around wearing nanocamo. The particle-filled air reduced the effectiveness of it to protect a person in motion, producing only a swirling vortex instead, which made a person more easily seen. So, if he moved, he could be located. If he stayed put, he couldn't be found until the rebels hit him with overwhelming numbers. Either way, life could be short. For the moment, staying put gave the greatest chance for survival. And ultimately, revenge.

Move his people or stay put? Counterattack, withdraw, or hold? The choice came down to killing as many of the rebels as possible while keeping enough of his Marines alive to protect Hugh. He just didn't know. He could only go with his gut because the answer to those all-important questions came down to the simplest one of all he couldn't answer: *When will Gladstone run out of troops?* Ward's people killed them and killed them, and still they came.

The Eight-Four-Seven had blunted Gladstone's attack, dying hard to stop him, but the battalion couldn't last much longer. All of the flight crews, including all three women, had died, except for a flight engineer, a guy named Klostermann who would be considered big until Jebet came by, now running the shield generator in Viper One by himself. In addition to the other improbable survivors, his two scouts, Tabi Fleisch and Abdul Jebet, their chameleon skins out of power, were around here somewhere, fighting as a very deadly team. Ward now sent them on suicide missions expecting them not to come back. Surprising him every time, they did. All of Garand's officers, except Lieutenant Carhart, were gone.

Carhart . . . The man rubbed Ward the wrong way. His quick thinking had saved Hugh earlier from the tree, but as his company fell back, the most dangerous assignments always seemed to fall on someone else. Back on Beacon, Ward had rated Carhart highly. He had charisma and knew how to lead. Technically, he did his job well. Unfortunately, Ward saw no evidence that self-sacrifice made up any part of his character. And that made Carhart a liability who would put his safety before his anyone else's. Not a good attribute in someone protecting an heir.

Ward understood Gladstone's reckless squandering of his men. He needed to kill the defenders as soon as possible. If Admiral Davies arrived with the balance of Prime Fleet before Gladstone killed Hugh, there would be a very short battle with no question as to the outcome.

Pulling up his display, Ward located each of his remaining Marines again, the living armor that kept one small boy unharmed and, with it, a hope of a return to peace and order. He'd promised himself he would live until he delivered Trevor's son to safety, then it would be okay to die.

Then, almost before he realized it was happening, total quiet descended. First the rebels stopped firing, and then his people. A voice spoke in his ear through the active com of his archeonC, *"This is the true empress and leader of the Restitution Movement, Morgain uch Roberts."*

The Restitution Movement? Ward recalled hearing something about bringing back the empire as it was at the time of Benjamin, but only a complete idiot wanted that. Benjamin had abused his power and the trust of the people he'd sworn to protect. Corruption had blossomed during his reign. His philandering tore apart the court and proved to be terrific fodder for holodramas long after he'd died.

The only reason anyone would want to return to those times would be to hold power. Not to lead, but merely to have power for the sake of having power. Yes, he could believe that about Morgain. He knew the entertainment streams followed her every move. The youth of the empire seemed particularly enthralled. She promised success without hard work. Everything she said sounded like some kind of fantasy. No government—and no emperor—could deliver what she promised. Unfortunately, she seemed to have co-opted a surprising number of military commanders by tapping into generations of anger and jealously among families that had been excluded or eliminated from the line of succession. Ward knew her father, Robert, to be a loyal officer of the fleet. He couldn't imagine how Morgain had turned out to be the leader of this coup.

"Emperor Cyrus usurped the power that rightfully belonged to others, aided and abetted by the traitors Doña Carlota Gonzalvez y Rodriguez del Castillo and Trevor Cascade, the former who led the witch hunt to eliminate all those Cyrus felt were disloyal, and the latter as warlord, who commanded the fleet . . . to its detriment.

"The Restitution Movement is in the process of rectifying all of that, bringing in a glorious new era of prosperity for all. However, to prevent more unnecessary bloodshed, I have decided that if you bring the pretend heir you are protecting, whoever he or she is, to me, alive, I will let that heir, and you, live." The voice became cold as space, "That promise of safety does not apply to Doña Carlota Gonzalvez y Rodriguez del Castillo, who must pay for her crimes, just as the emperor and warlord did. However, the rest of you now have a choice to make: Join the winning side and save your lives or share the consequences with Doña Carlota. You have thirty minutes to decide."

WARD'S HEADS-UP SHOWED THAT everyone else, with the exception of Jebet and Fleisch, probably because their traces were still off, had received the transmission. Ward figured it for a trick. You didn't cause this much death and destruction and then call a time-out. Suddenly, he saw what the rebels were trying to do. A hole now existed to Ward's left, exactly where that last laser bolt had gone. "L-T," he signaled on the com, "there is a hole between us, three men wide."

Carhart responded. "I see it, Top. You move a man in from your side, and I'll send one from mine. That'll have to do."

Ward carefully checked his Marines, blue symbols on the display. He picked one at random, a female corporal named

Marchetti. Not that he could tell the men from the women anymore, as covered in dirt and blood as most were. "Marchetti, move into the hole. Carefully. They'll be coming through there in a minute."

Ward's heads-up display went red, an alarm showing to his right as Perkins fired at what appeared to be an open piece of ground. Ward caught sight of a disturbance in the smoke and dirt filling the air. *Scouts in nanocamo.* Mines, white symbols on his display, blew, and then the world went crazy. The rebels, green symbols where they could be identified, now attempted to storm through an area they had previously left alone, figuring the line must be extra thin there. Apparently, someone over there had expected their concentrated fire to Ward's left to be seen as the prelude to an attack there.

Ward smiled thinly. A brilliant trap but too clever by half, and the obvious play for which he'd refused to take the bait. Gladstone's men now headed straight into the teeth of the defense, or as much of one as still existed. Ward fired into his portion of the fire plan, anger now cold as space at these men who had helped kill his wife and son fueling him. Bodies began to pile up in the slaughter. A hundred men, maybe two hundred, walked right into a minefield and interlocking fire they didn't expect. And died.

Ward called, "Cease fire," unwillingly. He wanted to keep shooting until the universe ended, but they were running low on ammunition. He checked the traces for a head count. Altogether his company now amounted to fewer than ten Marines on this side of the arc. Looking at the entire perimeter, he saw that very few of the battalion remained. Gladstone must have tried to hit a couple of other spots, too.

Putting up a skinny eye, he examined what he could of the other side. He almost dropped it in surprise as he focused on a man in full armor walking around out there as if he didn't have a care in the world. In that armored suit, it could be Gladstone himself, possibly having come for the kill.

Regardless, Ward smelled a trap. No one could take down

that armored suit without a missile or, if close enough, a limpet. Anyone getting into position to take the shot would be a sitting duck. Suddenly, a movement to the right in his peripheral vision drew his gaze, just in time to see Perkins go down at the intersection of three laser bolts. Ignoring the danger, he had stood and taken the shot, even knowing he would likely die. Too bad it hadn't worked. He had missed, and Gladstone still strutted around over there.

Shaking himself, he called out, "Fall back to the positions inside the berm, evens and then odds." Ward watched on the heads-up display as Carhart and the evens carefully fell back. As they reached the sally port, the rebels opened up. Three of the men in the group were down before a laser rifle spoke from the top of the berm. Ward recognized Colonel Garand's trace. He fired again as all the enemy's ordinance centered on him.

"Eyes front, watch your fire lanes!" Ward ordered. Just in time, the odds turned their attention to the front, opening up on the converging enemy troops. But he didn't have enough people to hold off the attack on this line. "Fall back!" Ward ordered as he continued to fire in his zone. Of his Marines, four fell before they could even try for the safety of the berm. Two more died trying to work their way around to the gate. Only he, Abdul Jebet, Chi Ngaio and Luzia Marchetti made it inside. Tabi Fleisch met them there. Glancing over his shoulder as he ducked through, Ward's last sight of the outside gave him a surge of satisfaction. The armored suit—Gladstone, or whoever had come in it to the battlefield—now lay a smoking ruin. Someone had gotten him, but even so, the rebels kept on coming blindly. Too much blood had already been spilled to stop, the offer from Morgain had been nothing but another trap.

Inside of the berm, grass still grew and the trees stood quietly, a haven separate from the reeking, rotting moonscape outside, peaceful except for the mangled body of Colonel Gary Garand lying on the inside slope of the berm. His heroic last action had allowed these few Marines to get inside. As Ward took stock of the situation, two men came up to him from the generators.

"Top, where do you want us?" asked the big man, Vincent Klostermann. He and the other man, Timothy Kennion, both shouldered rifles like they knew which end of the barrel the round came out of.

"Keep the generator up," Ward ordered brusquely. "You do your job, and we'll do ours."

Behind Klostermann, Doña Carlota and Hugh walked toward them from the TOC.

Kennion, so completely average Ward wondered if he could get lost in a crowd made up of just himself, shook his head. "Just got the call on the shuttle's archeon. Davies and Prime Fleet are pulling into the system right now, and Gladstone's ships are running. We just have to hold out till they get here. On the ground, that is."

Ward stared at him, scarcely comprehending the words' meaning. Ten hours, maybe six if Davies ignored all safety protocols on the way in, and they'd be here. He shook his head to snap himself out of the fog created by too much combat.

"Okay. Klostermann, you guard the sally port. Kennion, you provide overwatch for him." Looking around, he began making assignments. "Take the far wall. Daniels and Ngiao to my right, Appleton and Marchetti to my left. Fleisch and Jebet, reinforce the sally port on both sides. The L-T and I are the reserve by the generator with Doña Carlota and the boy."

He noticed Carhart talking with Hugh. A fist bump, a hair tousle, and a comforting hand on his shoulder. Other than the rescue from the tree, Carhart hadn't shown any interest in Hugh. Ward could barely think straight, but he knew Carhart hadn't suddenly developed a paternal instinct. *What's he—*

Doña Carlota and Sergeant Daniels converged on Ward as he finished his disposition of the remaining people. Ward had never seen Doña Carlota with a hair out of place, never mind as dirty and disheveled as she was now. Bloodstains on her sleeves and pants showed she must have been trying to help with the wounded. Her hair, utterly in disarray, had been pulled back into a ponytail. *A ponytail!* Hugh looked like he'd been tossed in a pigsty, with dirt caked under his nails, his clothes and hair filthy. *Is that blood, too?* His mind reeled at the thought of what Hugh had seen—and done—these past days. Daniels didn't look much better. Sweat had run down his face, leaving streaks in the dirt and blood there. Ward easily read the anger on their faces. Daniels spoke intensely but quietly, "I'm his proctor. My job is to be with him, twenty-four seven."

Ward stared him down. "I know your job, Sergeant. I assigned you to be his proctor. At this moment Hugh belongs to all of us, so the best way to do your job is to be on that wall."

Daniels backed up a moment before nodding. "Aye, Top."

With another hair tousle and a smile, Carhart sent Hugh on his way, followed by Doña Carlota. Ward watched as Doña Carlota led Hugh back toward the deserted TOC. The communications techs had taken positions on the berm, helping to repel the rebels, and paid the ultimate price. Even the medics, having done the best they could for days to help the wounded, had ultimately picked up their weapons, falling back on every Marine's primary MOS: rifleman. There were no longer enough Marines to collect the bodies of the fallen and, as Ward looked around, he saw the dead men and women of the battalion, still where they had died.

Carhart stared at Ward. Just as dirty and disheveled as any of them, Carhart had done his job, though, Ward had observed, he wasn't a *lead from the front* officer. Someone had failed to instill in him that a good officer never sent a man to do a job he wouldn't do himself.

Ward noticed that Carhart held his weapon cradled, finger on the trigger guard, barrel centered on Doña Carlota's back as she walked away. "The boy's valuable," he said to Ward quietly. "Morgain's offer was clearly a trick. No matter. I know you would never turn him over. But Morgain isn't wrong. A genuine heir is beyond valuable right now. You saw how he is with me. The boy's just desperate for a father figure. All we have to do is train him so he'll do what we want. He's Trevor Cascade's boy. The fleets will fall in line if we tell them we have him." He paused.

"With every emperor, there's someone who's the power behind the throne. For years, it's been Doña Carlota, but her time is over. It's just bad luck she didn't die with the emperor. But Hugh should be no different, and we can be there to ensure his success."

Ward studied Carhart. Did he just hear what he thought he did? Did Carhart just suggest they kill the protector of the succession and turn Hugh into a puppet emperor with them pulling the strings? He remained silent, watchful, and aware of where Carhart's weapon pointed. Would he just gun her down right now if he agreed?

"What do you say?" Carhart prompted.

No question, Carhart thought he, Ward, would go along. Ward's rifle rose, tracking onto Carhart smoothly. He growled, "I don't think so." Carhart shrugged, his rifle drifting away from Doña Carlota. "Okay, Top. I get it. Loyalty to the end and all that. Let's just hope we all live long enough to not regret it." With that, Carhart walked away.

Ward's eyes checked the perimeter assignments, his rifle never wavering from the retreating Carhart. He'd have to keep an eye on him. Carhart had proven himself to be the lowest of the low in officers. His only goal: advancement at all cost. He deserved fragging. But they were so shorthanded that Ward couldn't do the universe a favor.

A DESULTORY SILENCE SETTLED OVER the dirt fortress with the occasional shot barking out, but now the cards were all on the table and the pot called. With Davies on the way, Ward had almost started to feel only 99 percent sure they were all going to die.

Ward found some shade next to a shuttle and Hugh came and sat beside him, falling into a fitful sleep, his head resting on some poor soul's backpack. Carhart approached him again, carefully keeping his rifle pointed at the berm. Waiting a minute, he observed in a hushed voice, "The navy will be coming soon, Davies'll be here before you know it, and then this'll be over. All but the dying on every planet in the empire. We can stop it."

Ward could feel anger beginning to rise within him. He could shoot Carhart without blinking and feel no remorse. In a whisper, he demanded, "Say what you have to say, Lieutenant." Intermittent fire hit the berm and crossed overhead. No one fired back, waiting for the attack.

"Don't take that tone with me, Top. The empire's falling apart, and you're throwing away the only chance to save it and all those innocent lives. It's why the Restitution people were able to put together this coup attempt. They know the people need someone who *looks* like an heir, whether or not they are, and tells them what they want to hear. Morgain fits that description, at least for the plebes. But we can position Hugh as the better choice because he's the son of Warlord Cascade, who many in the military loved. Morgain has popularity on her side, and obviously enough military commanders under her spell that she could start this coup, but she has a long way to go to gain the trust of the entire command structure. And the majority of the military is far more likely to get in line behind Hugh than her. We can shut this down in a few days, just by naming Hugh emperor."

Beside him, Hugh squirmed, but stayed asleep. At that moment, Ward saw Hugh as if he were his own son Rod and felt the rage building within him. Ward stood but did not leave Hugh's side. "I can imagine how his training will go under your supervision. If that's what it takes to save the empire, it's not worth it."

Carhart glared. "I would do it for the empire, to stop this madness. He's just eight. From what I've seen, heirs are hardly ever allowed to take the test before age thirty. So, if no one else gets control soon, Hugh won't be able to try for the crown for at least twenty years. What'll happen to the empire in the meantime? Will even one sector hold together that long? You know they won't; there won't *be* an empire by then. We need to put things back together now, and we have a chance with that boy."

Carhart's eyes grew eager. "You've seen the way he is with me. He likes me. I can guide him, control him. You saw the way he did what I told him at the tree, and he *knows* I'm the one who pulled him out as it crumbled around him. As Trevor Cascade's son, if we declare him emperor, it will pull the empire together. We can do it, saving billions of lives. And from there, we can shape him to be the kind of leader we know the empire needs."

There it stood, an offer meant to truly tempt him, giving him the opportunity to *fix* things, avoiding any more death while possibly saving lives. He only needed to commit two capital crimes by killing Doña Carlota and Daniels, because they would never agree. Neither could he, but Carhart didn't understand that or why.

Carhart thought that by using Hugh he could reestablish order, but failed to understand what the empire meant and what made it tick. His ignorance of the proctor's true role in protecting an heir meant he didn't know that Daniels not only wouldn't but *couldn't* be a part of his plot. Nor, as head of the proctors, could Ward. Even if not the case, his oath and what it represented meant more to him than any power Carhart could offer. An empire under Carhart would not be one Ward or anyone he respected could serve.

Trevor Cascade had not only been Ward's boss but also his friend, a friend whose boy he could either look out for or raise as his son. Ward could volunteer for that responsibility, doing for Trevor what he no longer could do for himself. Hugh at least deserved to have someone watching over him, protecting him from Carhart or anyone else who might try to use him for their personal benefit.

Ward kept a steady bead on Carhart. "You don't know what you're talking about, L-T. If you tried to control the throne, you'd die and never even know what killed you."

Carhart glared at him. "I don't believe those fairy stories the proctors tell, Top, and you shouldn't either." A note of fake sincerity came into his voice. "Is one little boy worth the lives of billions?"

Ward snorted. Every life held infinite value, and his honor demanded he do one thing only: keep Carhart as far as possible from Hugh.

Besides, the *fairy stories* were true. As head of the proctors he, more than anyone, knew only how true. What a fool! He'd just saved Carhart's life, doing him a favor, and the man didn't even know it. "L-T, I think you better go help guard the sally port. Send Klostermann back when you get there. The shield generator seems to be running a little rough."

Fire flared from Carhart's eyes. "I know the Creed says 'to the Death,' Top, but that's not meant to be taken literally, you know." Ward stared at him, the look in his eyes making clear just how much he did *not* agree with that. After a moment, Carhart turned and strode away angrily. Ward watched him go the whole way. Klostermann came back and headed straight to the generator without saying anything. Ward had made the only choice he could. Perhaps Carhart had, too. Only time would show who was right.

ANGER SWELLED WITHIN CARHART. EVERY few minutes he looked back from the sally port, only to see Ward or one of his bodyguards, Jebet and Fleisch, watching with a rifle locked on the edge of the entry.

So be it. Activating the little bit of juice left in his nanocamo, reserved in case he needed it, he walked out, being sure to turn off his trace at the same time. Keeping his pace slow and his head on a swivel, he moved carefully until he had passed through the line still held by Gladstone's people. Picking up the pace a bit, he headed toward what he had earlier identified as one of the rebel landing zones.

His mind worked over his number one problem. Number two, really. Number one: get off this rock alive. Number two? How to survive while he found a way to get Hugh away from the sergeant major and Doña Carlota.

Sliding under the shield, he decided he could move faster. No one behind him could shoot him through the shield, even if they could see him.

He could be a pirate, but the danger and unpredictable nature of it didn't appeal to him.

Mercenary? He'd had enough of the military and still unpredictable.

Information? Maybe. In this mess, everyone would need information, not least commercial houses. Knowing what others didn't, but wanted to, had value. And he had a way with people. The Marines had trained him to be an intelligence officer, but the coup had forced him to be a platoon commander. He much preferred to be behind the lines, processing intel and analyzing enemy movements. And now he could put that training to good use.

If he made the right connections, it would also put him in a position to take Hugh away from Doña Carlota and, most especially, the sergeant major.

Crossing a small rise, he saw a rebel corvette, the smallest class of vessel to be considered a warship. Bigger than a shuttle, but not as big as a frigate, it had a crew of about twenty and he would have to convince all of them that he was on their side.

Straightening his clothes and dusting them off, he did his best to look presentable. His trace off and without any other unit identification, the crew of the corvette would have no reason to think he wasn't one of theirs, separated from his unit.

Shaking off his fatigue, he marched over to the corvette, rifle slung on his shoulder. Only one way to play this: as if he had the authority. Hopefully that would be enough, because he had no idea how to get this bird off the ground by himself.

Apparently, his demeanor had the impact he hoped for. The female spacer guarding the entry port came closer to a military stance as Carhart approached.

"Close her up; we're lifting," Carhart ordered as he entered without even bothering to stop or even acknowledge the spacer's attempt to question his right to be aboard. Over his shoulder, he added, "Davies' fleet is in-system and we don't have much time. Tell the captain I'm on the way up."

Crossing his fingers mentally, he relaxed as he heard the hatch cycle closed. That woman seemed to understand what would happen if Davies caught this ship on the ground. Or in space, for that matter. Reaching the bridge, the ship's commander, an angry naval lieutenant, greeted him. "What do you think you're doing?"

Facing the man directly, he felt completely calm. Icily he told the captain, "Lift now; waiting will only get you killed, Lieutenant. Your fleet left you to die, just like the poor suckers still trying to kill that little boy. Davies will be here in under five hours and we need to be headed out-system well before then." He let that sink in. Selling something like this relied upon timing. And truth didn't hurt, either.

The lieutenant didn't seem to be ready to give in, however. "I have my orders to stay and pick up the rest of the ground units after they finish mopping up."

How stupid could you be? "If your men haven't killed the boy and Doña Carlota by now, they won't do it before the heat death of the galaxy. Your little coup attempt didn't go well and now you don't have a home. Get us up, now."

Stepping to the captain's chair, Carhart sat. Serenely he looked around, though inside his stomach butterflies danced madly. If this didn't work, if these people didn't follow his orders, things would get messy fast. He slid his rifle off his shoulder but maintained a grip on the trigger housing. A slight tip up of the barrel, and someone would die. "Now, Captain. Do we have enough fuel to get somewhere safe? Or at least away from this system?"

The ship's captain nodded after a second. "Fueled up just before coming down. We can go anywhere within two weeks' flight."

Carhart considered this as the ship began to rise. *Well, why not?* "Take us to Treadle, Captain. I have an idea that will keep us all alive and maybe even make us rich." After a moment he added something to keep the crew on his side, at least until they arrived there. "Any man or woman who wants off at that point is free to leave."

THE HOURS PASSED IN A series of steadily weaker attacks until shuttles carrying Marines from Prime Fleet dropped around them.

The only ones left alive inside to greet them were Hugh, Doña Carlota Gonzalvez y Rodriguez del Carvalho, Jake Daniels, Vincent Klostermann, Tabi Fleisch, Abdul Jebet, Luzia Marchetti, Tim Kennion, Preston Appleton, and Sean Ward. As the relief marched up, Ward looked around proudly at the dirty, exhausted survivors. All were standing protectively behind Hugh, who waited at attention in the sally port, just the way his father would have expected. These people had become Hugh's family. Ward approved of Hugh and all of them. These, and all the others who had died, proving faithful and solid to the end, all except for Carhart. Sometime during the last of the fighting, he had simply disappeared.

Galactifacts for Kids 3500

The Core Empire. Established in 2587 AD on Beacon by Dave Jackson, it grew to include most of the core and some of the surrounding star systems in the arms. Divided into twenty sectors, it remained the safest and most prosperous area of the galaxy for most of its history.

6

Pygmalion

Supernova *Black Hole*, Gantry System, Prime Sector, Core
0725 9 May 3463

AS LITTLE HUGH CASCADE ZOOMED by down the passageway, Sergeant Major Sean Ward couldn't restrain a smile. Yesterday, he had looked like a tired, dirty eight-year-old with haunted eyes, but today he ran around at light speed, a curious young boy getting into everything. His proctor, Sergeant Jake Daniels, clomping along after him, appeared exhausted. Ward smiled helpfully. "Need some help, Sergeant Daniels? Like maybe a nineteen-year-old girl?"

Daniels stopped and glared at him. "Have one in your back pocket, Top? Or are you volunteering to take over?"

Ward raised his hands in mock horror. "No way, Daniels. Besides," a sly grin replacing the fake shock, "I recall that at the beginning of this assignment a year ago you requested someone easy, not an heir who might be tested at any moment."

Daniels now seemed really put out. "Low blow, Top, beneath even your standards for terrible humor. I said I wanted to help raise an heir who would then have a good chance to pass the test, not someone ruined by another proctor."

A crash from a cabin off the passageway caught both of their attention. "Better see what Hugh's up to before he causes some real damage," Ward suggested.

Daniels didn't bother to answer, taking off like a shot.

A frown replaced Ward's brief smile, mirroring his internal unease as he went the other way. Two hatches down, he stopped and faced an entry guarded by two immaculately turned-out spacers. One knocked, though Ward knew the occupants were already aware of his arrival. The appointed hour for this meeting had struck, after all. Tradition, however, required a knock.

Straightening his uniform, fresh from the ship's stores, he prepared to enter. Although the uniform was clean, his boots still showed the wear and tear from the three intense days of combat. Not acceptable to him, but he didn't want to break in a new pair out here.

Today he faced the first board of inquiry for his own actions, ever. Always before he had testified or sat in judgment from the other side of the table. The deaths of all those people now weighed on his soul. If victory looked like this, he never wanted to be in position to win again.

"Come," squawked the wall box. One of the spacers impassively opened the hatch to let him in.

Stepping through, Ward approached the table facing the hatch, halted precisely four paces in front of it, and saluted crisply. "Sergeant Major Sean Ward, Imperial Marines, reporting to the board as ordered, sir!"

Behind the table, Admiral John Davies, Commander, Prime Fleet, and Doña Carlota Gonzalvez y Rodriguez del Castillo, Protector of the Succession, exchanged glances. Ward recognized something improper here—they needed one more senior officer for a quorum to hold a legal hearing or board—but kept silent.

Admiral Davies leaned back, tapping his fingers together for a moment. "You requested this hearing, Sergeant Major. What exactly is your heinous crime? Protecting the heir in impossible circumstances? Inspiring one of the most heroic actions in imperial history?" he asked sarcastically, but without meanness.

"Austin Carhart, a lieutenant in the 847th Marine Space Assault Battalion attempted to enlist me in using Hugh Cascade to gain power in the empire . . . if I joined him and removed Doña Carlota and Hugh's proctor, Sergeant Daniels."

Admiral Davies merely muttered, "And?"

Doña Carlota shook her head before adding, "Since I am here, you clearly didn't take him up on his offer."

"No, ma'am." After a moment's reflection, he added softly, "I wish I'd shot him then. He is an extremely dangerous individual in my estimation."

"Where is he now?" Doña Carlota asked. "I don't want a man who will play for the highest stakes in the middle of a killing field wandering around. We would not want him to reappear at"—she paused to choose her words—"an *inopportune* moment."

Ward smiled at Doña Carlota's phrasing. She had always been given to understatement. "I only know he disappeared some time before Admiral Davies and the fleet arrived."

Admiral Davies sat forward. "When do you leave to hunt him down, Ward?"

Ward shook his head. "That's a young man's game, and I've given all a man can or should be asked to sacrifice for the empire. It's time for me to retire." He felt a wave of grief wash over him as he spoke. The night before, alone in his quarters, he'd watched the holo of the attack on the palace, seen the explosions that had killed his wife and son. It had broken him. The grief came over him like a tsunami. He had sobbed and raged for hours, not caring if someone in the passageway outside heard him.

Neither Admiral Davies nor Doña Carlota spoke at first, Doña Carlota's expression especially inscrutable. Then, sitting back, she began tapping the table with a nail before asking with some asperity, "That's it? You would selfishly deprive the empire of your services when you are most needed because you lost your wife and son? Most of my family happened to be in the palace also; should I quit? I think not. I need something to keep me going, and so do you."

Davies shook his head. "You may be right about deserving a rest in exchange for services rendered. You certainly deserve it for all the years you've served. Regardless, the good of the empire requires you stay. *Especially* you, Sean. We need you, now more than ever."

Admiral Davies' use of his first name broke through his

grief. Doña Carlota finished shattering his self-constructed prison. "Ann Marie once told me Sergeant Major Ward could be counted on to do what she needed done as long as she carefully defined it."

Ward shook his head. "I'm sure she never said any such thing."

Doña Carlota glanced at Davies. "Once, long ago, I served as his lieutenant. I know he would go crazy sitting and moping." Turning toward Ward again, she frowned. "Which brings us to our real problem: What do we do to keep Hugh alive and hidden while things are sorting themselves out? Equally important, how do you evaluate him while he prepares for the test?"

Ward began to open his mouth, but Doña Carlota raised a hand to stop him. "There are, of course, at least one hundred qualified heirs with their proctors, and Hugh ideally shouldn't even be considered for the test for another twenty years. Nevertheless, I think he shows real promise. He's far braver than any boy his age and his character is beyond reproach. But there are people like Carhart and Gladstone who value or hate him simply for being a Cascade."

Ward broke in. "I agree with everything you just said, having seen him in action personally. In addition, saving him from himself calls for a younger man, because the very qualities that make him a potential emperor could get him killed. Doña Carlota, you are protector of the succession and essential to the survival of the empire, but do you need an old warhorse like me? The last few days have shown me I can't run with the young dogs like I used to. How could I possibly put an heir through the test?"

Admiral Davies gave them both a look. "You both think he has what it takes, even at his age? I'll look forward to reading the reports on him. From both of you." He paused, looking first to Doña Carlota and then Ward. "I need you, so you stay."

Before Ward could react, Davies pointed to a chair and ordered, "Sit!" Ward sat, a look of annoyance pasted on his face. The admiral continued, "Regarding Mister Carhart, he will be sentenced to death for desertion, in absentia, after I convene a court.

"Now, I have been receiving reports from all over the core about heirs and their proctors disappearing or being assassinated, so Hugh may be more of an insurance policy than we would like to admit or rely on. From the interrogation reports on the few captured assassins, it appears they belong to this Restitution Movement."

Ward sat up straighter as Doña Carlota raised an eyebrow, a sure indication of surprise. She looked thoughtful as she spoke. "I believed that Morgain mostly led a bunch of grifters and scoundrels who were out for themselves, like Quadros."

Davies smiled. "You mean the late and truly unlamented *Lord* Quadros. The cruiser he tried to escape on met an unforeseen accident: a spread of capital missiles amidship." Pausing a moment, he asked thoughtfully, "How could a woman as young as Morgain put this together so widely and have so many devoted followers? She's only, what, twenty, twenty-five?"

Ward shook his head. "Twenty-two, actually." Speaking into his com, he ordered, "Bring up Morgain uch Roberts's picture and bio."

A beautiful blonde came up in the holo in the middle of the conference table. Admiral Davies snorted. "I've heard about her from my kids. Doesn't she hang around with the playboy set, actors, actresses, those with nothing better to do than have their picture taken at high-society events?"

Ward shook his head. "As far as her social climbing, you're right. But it's what she's been doing with her contacts out of the limelight that disturbed her proctors. She had three over the four years since she turned eighteen. None of them would stay with her because she didn't even pretend to believe in the Creed. Self-centered, almost to the point of cruelty, she displayed little to no regard for the truth. Her personal life as broadcast core-wide, of course, speaks for itself as regarding virtue. Based on her proctors' reports, she wouldn't come close on dedication, protection, justice, or judgment, much less integrity. Perhaps she's willing to sacrifice for what she wants, but that isn't the point of the test. Her scores did impress me: intelligence quite high, low genius range even. I forwarded the info to Guardian Command. Guardian Command must have agreed with me, because it ordered that she be removed from the pool of potential heirs immediately. Regardless, she is quite dangerous. We'll need to find her and end this threat."

Davies shook his head. "I wish it were that easy. There are several task groups throughout the core that have broken off and there are sectors completely out of our control at the moment. She could be anywhere. I still don't think someone that young could pull this off. Not by herself."

Doña Carlota seemed to be speaking to herself before looking up. "My children heard rumors about her recruiting, but I believed it to be nonsense. What could she do? Without high-level help, anyway? But, of course, those are the kinds of people she spends time with. I want to point out that someone who understands the proctor organization planned that part of the coup very well. Assassins targeted Hugh's older brothers, all four of them, attacking three of them aboard their ships. One is dead, one badly wounded. The other managed to kill the attacker on his ship. My guess is that neither of the survivors will last long because they seemed to be of special interest to the assassination squads. The youngest brother, Drawton, is at the academy on Beacon now and refuses to go into protective custody; hiding, he calls it. Probably because they are Trevor's boys and the fleet loved him, they won't last long. Interesting that they targeted Hugh, too."

Ward nodded. "It appears that Bill Dent's failed coup and execution didn't close the book five years ago. When Cyrus replaced him with Trevor Cascade, who ferreted out over a dozen co-conspirators, most thought the entire conspiracy had been shut down. More than half of those arrested remain in prison and the balance joined Dent in whatever afterlife they believed in. I did wonder, though, if there were more. Clearly, there were, and if Warlord Cascade had cast the net wider, he would have caught more, I'm sure, whether he could prove their guilt definitively or not. In the end, it seems the example

Cyrus made of Dent and the others didn't discourage those who weren't caught; it just made them more careful."

Davies seemed to agree, but Doña Carlota vehemently disagreed. "If judgment and justice in the Creed mean anything, it's that everyone is judged, and punished or rewarded, on facts, not convenience. Our investigation uncovered everyone who could be *proven* to have been involved. Conjecture can't be used to justify an execution. We don't kill people just in case."

Ward bowed his head. "You're of course correct, ma'am. The problem is that Bill had a lot of friends and admirers throughout the core. One of those could have been looking for a front person like Morgain. If she connected with them, that could be what gave her this chance."

Silence hovered for a while before Ward went on. "But none of that matters now. One thing is obvious, they seem pretty focused on removing Hugh. Why else send a task group to take out one little eight-year-old? And how do we keep him safe from here on?"

Davies shrugged. "Bring him into Prime Fleet HQ."

Ward shook his head. "Gladstone came from HQ. We found his people on the ships we used to get here. That's how they knew where we were going. We have no idea how many moles he left behind on Beacon."

Davies nodded. Doña Carlota looked thoughtful. "Beacon might also be the worst place to raise him, always the center of attention, always protected and pampered. He needs to be treated normally, so he can understand what life is all about."

Ward added, "Someplace quiet. We don't tell him that he's an heir, but he needs a first-rate education in case he does become emperor someday."

Doña Carlota smiled beatifically. "I know just the place, an unimportant planet in Sector Seven where there's a preparatory school located out in the country, the Academia Escolastica, which combines an elite education with some military training for those who are interested. It is on the Hacienda Mirabel.

"During the Qabal invasion, Charles Roland built an emergency command center there. We can upgrade the defenses. The children of locally prominent people already are enrolled there. It will explain the heightened security, while giving Hugh a chance at having a normal upbringing. We won't tell anyone who he really is, just the orphan of an old friend I owe a debt to. It is out of Prime and Second Sectors, places where most of his family live and where assassins would naturally look for him."

Davies raised an eyebrow. "And where is this place?"

"On Jeffco, a minor planet in Sector Seven. A distant cousin recently died without children, so the family could publicly give the estate to the planetary government. In private, the fleet would control it. As for me, I can announce I am retiring and going into seclusion because of my grief over my family, without saying where. The estate already has a shield. In a way, we will be hiding him in plain sight." Doña Carlota then focused his beaming smile on Ward. "And you will step down, officially at least, from being Sergeant Major of the Imperial Marines. You will quietly continue as Head Proctor, as well as overseeing Hugh's education, and troubleshoot as needed. We will make sure the fleet knows about your *retirement*, which will make dropping you out of sight easier. Besides, Hugh needs a firm hand. I hear he is well on the way to tearing this ship apart to see how it ticks."

Ward sat stunned. For the last two years he had overseen all the proctors and heirs throughout the empire, and now his main responsibility in the back of beyond consisted of watching over the upbringing of just one little boy? A good boy, for sure, but also a constant reminder of the son he'd just lost. "Hugh *has* a proctor," he protested.

Doña Carlota simply shook her head. "You know as well as I do Sergeant Daniels will only be able to be his proctor for a limited time. In my judgment, Daniels is already getting far too close to Hugh and will surely become even more deeply involved in the boy's life. He will become much too attached to his heir and would never be able to carry out his responsibilities in the event Hugh fails the test."

Turning to Admiral Davies, she asked, "Don't you agree?"

Davies nodded. "This situation is practically unprecedented, such a prominent heir being orphaned this young. Daniels is a fine man, and I'm sure he can help Hugh through his grief and getting settled in his new home, but will no doubt lose his ability to be objective in the process. Ward can keep an eye on things until then, but let's keep that mum for now, especially from Daniels. When Ward lets us know the time has come to replace Daniels, we will go through the regular procedure for choosing a new proctor."

With a sinking feeling, Ward knew there would be no new proctor. There would be him. Worse, he had given them the opportunity to assign him to Hugh by demanding retirement. When would he learn to keep his mouth shut?

The Core Empire

Appendix E: Recently Declassified Imperial Documents

Proctor Training Course—Removal Procedures

When an heir is determined to be unsuitable, a directive will be sent by Guardian Command to the proctor of the heir as well as the removal facility (currently located on Harwell), and Proctor Command. Proctor Command will arrange for transport to the removal facility. All nanites will be purged and the proctor will be assigned to a new heir at this time.

No public announcement will be made as to the former status of the individual as an heir nor of the removal. The number of heirs will NOT be published at any time nor a list of them maintained outside of Proctor Headquarters.

7

Never Disappoint a Lady

Core Naval Spaceship Supernova *Pechnaya*
1200 BBMT 9 May 3463

YEOMAN FIRST CLASS CINDY USSEIN KNOCKED and then entered the command conference room. "Your call, Commodore."

Commodore Brian O'Donnell smiled. "Thanks, Cindy. We'll take it in here."

Beside him, Morgain uch Roberts smiled brightly at the yeoman, evaluating her. *She seems a bit too eager. And he seems too familiar with her. There's something more than professional there.*

Around the table, holograms of the other leaders of the Restitution Movement appeared. Flashing a blinding smile around the table, but most especially at the commodore, Morgain waited to hear what these people had to say as she considered their motivations. None of them she considered a friend, most particularly the commodore. However, she needed him . . . for a while longer.

She didn't miss Quadros, who had considered himself both the smartest man in the galaxy and an irresistible ladies' man. His ego certainly had been easy to stroke. She had met him at one of the many social engagements she'd attended. Her grandmother had taught her that every invitation to a party could also be an invitation to power. Her grandmother had groomed she and her sisters to enter society at the highest level. And they had succeeded, captivating both men and women with their beauty, becoming darlings of the society streams and entertainment holos. Enlisting Quadros in her plans had been shockingly simple. She had merely led him to believe that she was supporting him in his desires for power, while using him to rise to higher circles of society, as well as to make connections among the military. *Why couldn't he have waited to declare himself a sector lord? He messed everything up. After that he had been of no use to me whatever.*

Before that, her media connections had led to interviews about the current state of the government, the empire, and the emperor, and the need to embrace the Restitution Movement. Conspiracy theories about the emperor and the line of succession ran rampant. Had Benjamin been secretly assassinated? Was Bill Dent the rightful heir? Was Doña Carlota a Rasputin-like figure, manipulating the emperor for her own goals? From there, the momentum among average citizens grew and grew, until a large percentage of the empire looked at the attack on Beacon as a necessary evil.

Jeffrey Gladstone had been useful, if not wholly successful. Doña Carlota heading off to retirement counted as a win. And since she had received no report of the survival of Warlord Cascade's youngest son, she assumed him dead.

Now to business; she needed to keep her mind in the game. She flashed another smile around the table in case anyone had noticed that she might have a brain.

Chau Tran, vice admiral commanding Task Force 5-2, spoke first. "That idiot Quadros really messed things up. I warned you, but you wouldn't listen. We weren't ready. As it is, my sector is a mess with most of the major ship and squadron commanders supporting the empire."

Idiot. We were never going to put all the pieces in place to make this a risk-free operation. Morgain feigned concern, so Chau would think Morgain sympathized with her point. Chau wanted an easy path to get what she wanted, which was less than the whole pie, but that would never happen. Morgain did appreciate having Chau as the voice of caution in this group, however; it kept the hotheads in check. In addition to that, when it came to time to remove her, it would be easy. People in love with planning were never ready to move, making it simple to catch them by surprise.

Garrison Traynor, vice admiral commanding Task Force 13-1, would be an entirely different problem when the time came. He wanted everything, no matter what it took. Acidly, he answered Chau, "Quadros, as you very well know, didn't want to be executed, or even in prison, so he took action to avoid that. Anyone with half a brain knew he wouldn't wait on the rest of us to save him. I wouldn't have either."

Commodore, now vice admiral, Miroslav Kučera, who had taken over Twelfth Fleet when the cruiser that had picked up Quadros exploded during his escape from Beacon, sat quietly, trying to remain unnoticed. *Interesting. He likely never expected to have anything and probably only wants to keep what has dropped in his lap.* She smiled to herself. In this shark tank, not drawing attention to yourself would not save you. But that weasel Gene Perdot, who had taken a large slice of Sixth Fleet, also remained silent. *I wonder what he has up his sleeve. Likely trying to decide who to stab next*, she guessed.

Neither of these thoughts applied to Madame Furaki Aswini. She lived on Keep Off the Grass—so named because the first colonists discovered the native grass could be deadly—capital of Second Sector, with no—or in any event known—military support, which had been the table stakes for the others here, other than herself. However, the woman had another kind of power: information. Information that had been extraordinarily useful in setting up this coup. Unfortunately, Morgain had no idea how to get a hook into the woman. Yet.

By this time, the conference had broken into a free-for-all of accusations, interspersed with demands for help against local imperial forces that had held together. No one asked for her opinion. When they wanted someone to represent them, they'd tell her what they wanted her to say.

At least for now. Glancing to her side, she noticed that O'Donnell looked uncomfortable. He truly believed in the Creed. And that she adored him. She had played on that attraction to pull him into the movement, but she wondered about that yeoman. Perhaps her hold over him had begun to slip, and perhaps he had begun to see that the Restitution Movement would not bring back what Constantine Jackson had built a thousand years ago? It would be exceptionally unfortunate if O'Donnell developed a conscience at this point. She needed to speed up her timetable.

AN INCOMING MESSAGE ALERT POPPED up on the com panel in Morgain's quarters. *Who could be calling so late?*

"Accept."

A female tech came on the screen. "Queen Euryple of Green Gardens would like to speak with you."

What now, Grandmother?

"Please put her through." Irritated, she struggled to replace her frown with a smile. She then said sweetly, "Grandmother."

The woman who appeared had a harsh look and steel gray hair. Despite her age, she still looked beautiful. *If ice queens can be beautiful.*

"Morgain, I had expected to hear from you at least a week ago. What has happened? Have you removed Robert?"

Faking contrition, Morgain answered, "No, Grandmother. My team was able to get close, but couldn't kill Robert or my youngest sister."

"But?" Euryple demanded. "I definitely heard a hesitation."

Morgain ground her teeth. She needed to be a better actress. Nodding, she answered, "Mother died in the attack, protecting father's *princess*."

She expected an explosion. Of what kind, she didn't know. *Anger? Grief? Remorse?* Really anything but the cold indifference she saw on her grandmother's face. In a hard voice, Euryple said, "Maude should never have run off with that *man*. You and your sisters should have been born here on Green Gardens, just as I and all our foremothers were. That idiot, Esau Emmanuel, should have sent Maude and Robert back when I told him about their eloping. Either way, she'd still be alive and happy here."

Her voice rose and Morgain heard anger as she continued, "I should have killed Robert years ago, but he had the protection of the emperor. Everything, *everything*, that has happened since then is all *his* fault. And now my daughter is dead."

Then her look of anger appeared to almost give way to something else. For a moment, Morgain thought her grandmother might express actual empathy and perhaps offer some comfort that her efforts to kill her father and youngest sister had only led to her mother's death. But the moment passed.

"When will you finish your little task?"

Morgain waved a hand in dismissal, causing Euryple's jaw to tighten. "I am trying, but things are a little chaotic on Beacon at the moment."

Euryple gritted her teeth as she said, "Just get it done."

Morgain decided that showing a little deference might be useful just now, to help defuse her grandmother's obvious disappointment in her lack of commitment to patricide. *And sororicide.* Not that she was close with her youngest sister. *Mother's "baby girl." Father's "princess."* At times, she wondered if they'd forgotten their three other daughters, so enamored they were with her third sister. "Of course, Grandmother. Nothing is as important to me as ensuring the success of our plan. I look forward to leading the empire with your continued mentoring and wisdom. I could have achieved nothing so far without your guidance."

Euryple beamed. "Of course. It was only right. Being one of Jane's descendants, you should *never* have been removed as an heir. When you came out for your visit, I knew right away you had what it would take to rule over the empire, and they should have seen it too."

Morgain's mind flashed back to that first visit. She knew her mother had both feared and despised her grandmother, but she couldn't say no when Euryple played the lonely grandmother, hoping to get to know her granddaughters. She refused to visit herself, knowing her mother would never have let her return to Robert, but she trusted her not to harm her own granddaughters.

Only a fool trusted an enemy.

Morgain had gone for six months. Not an unreasonable length of a stay, given the distances involved; one didn't just "drop by" Green Gardens from Beacon. Her mother wouldn't send all of the girls at once. Having Morgain, Vivian, and Nimue—her youngest sister still too young to consider sending—all there would have given her grandmother too much leverage. Mother had been too smart to allow that.

But Maude hadn't been smart enough to foresee the queen's grand plan. Morgain had barely unpacked before all of her things had disappeared, replaced with far grander and *royal* attire befitting one of her station. The seduction of wealth and power pulled her in, as her grandmother made it clear she expected her granddaughters to achieve heights her daughter had not. The visit had been like attending a finishing school, complete with history lessons and intelligence briefings designed to make *her place* in the empire clear to her. Lessons in rapport-building and public speaking helped her to understand how she could wield influence. There had even been some rather frank and surprising schooling in the art of literal seduction. How to flirt with people, engage them, and tease them. How to make them want you, to fall in love with you. And even in some of the more intimate skills a woman might use to keep a lover close. And on Green Gardens, it had been easy to practice because men knew their place.

Vivian and Nimue had each followed for their own lengthy visits. Each embraced their grandmother's thinking, but knowing they were not in line for the throne, they took what they learned and applied it in their own ways, wreaking havoc amongst the younger officers of the navy, ruining marriages, and deeply embarrassing their mother, who didn't need to think hard to understand how her daughters had become so *socially skilled* and sociopathic. She had exploded at her mother, forbidding her to ever see her granddaughters again. But the damage had already been done. Morgain had seen real power in action, had lived life as a royal, even if for just half a year, and she wanted that life, no matter what price needed to be paid to get it. She had loved her mother and regretted her death, but her father . . . He'd always been a stranger, off on one mission or another, generally for months at a time. She wouldn't get satisfaction from his death, but understood that it needed to be done to achieve the end goal: Empress of the Core Empire.

Her grandmother had been talking, but Morgain had been lost in her memories. She shook her head to focus again on what her grandmother said, "—but you have exceeded my expectations. It's only a matter of time before an heir of the *right* line is once again leading the empire."

Morgain nodded. "Most certainly, and I will always know how much I owe you for making it possible. But now I need some sleep."

"Goodnight, Granddaughter."

"Goodnight, Grandmother."

MORGAIN SLIPPED OUT OF HER cabin quietly so as not to disturb O'Donnell. She had dressed carefully because this would be a busy day and she needed to look her best. As she stepped out into the passageway, four massive shore patrolmen met her.

Controlling her urge to flash her smile, she maintained a calm face. "Are you ready?"

The lead petty officer, Fernbill, nodded.

"The other ships, too?"

"The *Emperor Wo Han* and the cruisers. You said you'd take care of the colliers and other support ships." He sounded doubtful about the last.

Her face hardened. "Are you questioning me, Fernbill? Are any of you?"

They all shook their heads, two looking scared despite towering over her. *Good*, she thought with satisfaction. *They remember what happened to that oaf O'Donnell had in charge of security. Personally blowing him out an airlock into space without a suit had both removed him as an obstacle and brought the rest into line.*

"And the lovely yeoman, Ussein?"

Here Ferny smiled cruelly. "Taken care of."

Morgain nodded. "Commodore O'Donnell seemed fond of her. Send him to join her." With that, she headed toward the bridge.

As Morgain stepped onto the bridge, no one seemed to notice. Silently she waited until Lieutenant Braithwaite looked up. "Attention on the bridge," she called out. Loudly.

Good. The woman better perform if she wants that destroyer command I promised her. Keeping promises was one lesson O'Donnell had taught her that she had taken to heart. *Too bad he truly didn't see the universe the way it is, and not how he wanted it to be.*

"As you were," Morgain ordered coolly. To the comm section tech—some woman she didn't recognize—she added, "Open a Ninth Fleet-wide link."

The female tech sat still, evidently confused at the change in command. Just then, a movement behind Morgain told her one or more of her enforcers must be there. She heard one of her men say softly, "It's done." *Finally. Now to business.* Impatiently, Morgain signaled Braithwaite as she moved toward the command chair.

"Now, technician," ordered Braithwaite brusquely.

Sitting in the chair, Morgain carefully feigned a look of sorrow.

"Open now, ma'am," reported the tech.

Using the techniques she had perfected during years of public interviews, she reached out with her eyes to her audience, the members of Ninth Fleet, or at least that part she controlled. "I am sorry to report that Commodore O'Donnell is dead. His vision, leadership, and principles will be sorely missed. Earlier this evening, his yeoman, Cindy Ussein, attacked me in a fit of jealously. Commodore O'Donnell gave his life defending me, just as he willingly put his life on the line to bring the empire back to what Constantine Jackson wanted it to be."

Pausing to let a tear drip—just one so it didn't look overdone—she continued. "To honor his memory and his dream, I am taking command and will lead us forward. I expect all of you to do your best for me, the same as if he were still alive. That is all."

Facing the tech, she added in a neutral voice, "Make sure all ships acknowledge receipt and that all crew have seen this by the end of their next shift." Standing, she left, a silence filling the normal buzz of the bridge. Now for the real plan: find an heir she could control, with a willing proctor.

Appendix E: Recently Declassified Imperial Documents

Medical Directive Archives

SENDER: ArcheonA—Guardian One
RECIPIENT: Secure ArcheonB—Imperial Actions Office, Hopewell Medical Center, Faith City, Beacon, Prime Sector
MESSAGE: 3455/4/7-B
SECURITY CLASSIFICATION: Top Secret/Heir Test

Action Alert—Immediate Implementation Required

SUBJECT: Hugh Cascade DOB 4 April 3455
PARENTS: Trevor Cascade/Jane Merriweather
DNA STATUS: Approved, paternal descendant Emperor Allen to Dave Jackson and Crystal Maris, maternal descendant Emperor Esau Manuel to Dave Jackson and Yvonne Sabonnis
AUTHORIZATION CODE: DY233904VV1331
Medbot/commobot package must be placed in approved archeonC receiver BEFORE authorization code input to avoid self-destruct fail-safe. Upon completion of medbot programming through archeonC, the medbot/commobot package MUST be injected within twenty minutes.

Any delay MUST BE REPORTED IMMEDIATELY, and package NOT be injected. Injection in any other individual than subject or delayed injection will result in death.

Activation of commobots in subject must be verified as final step of procedure by pinging the trace using the one-time code unique to the subject included with package. His personal code will then be active. Report completion of procedure as well as any adverse reactions within first 24 hours.

ON BEHALF OF THE EMPEROR CYRUS

8

The Hunt

Snaggletooth Mountain on Rancho Mirabel, Jeffco
1735 Local/1135 BBMT 9 October 3473
Ten Years After Deft

HUGH CASCADE SLOWLY ADDED TENSION TO the bowstring. The lightweight compound structure added many pounds to his pull strength, but he knew that, even with a simple bow, he could shoot and bring down anything he could see within one hundred meters. A bead of sweat trickled down his temple, feeling cool in the crisp autumn air. A big man, especially for eighteen, not overly tall but well-muscled—no one called him an Adonis, but girls didn't run screaming at the sight of him—he had piercing gray eyes that, at the moment, were focused on a magnificent stag in the golden, late afternoon sun. The ten-point buck proudly surveyed his kingdom from a mountain spur one hundred meters away. Hugh knew that a small herd of does grazed in a meadow on the far side of the spur, but only seconds in the stag's reign remained. Hugh let out half a breath and released . . . but the arrow flew through empty space, the suddenly startled buck leaping away.

Hugh quickly began a visual search of the area to see what had caused the buck to bolt. Nothing he could see. But *something* made him jump. *Two hours' work with nothing to show for it!* Shaking his head, he took a step toward the long, tortuous path back off the mountain, westward, toward home. It would have been much worse, of course, with the stag. Plus he wouldn't have been able to start until near dark by the time he finished dressing it. There would also have been the minor problem that, with over a hundred pounds of meat strapped to his back, the trip would have been just a wee bit more exciting in the dark than even he normally liked. He'd never admit to any of that aloud, of course. He needed to maintain his reputation and pride. Being a cadet in the military unit protecting Doña Carlota meant something here on Jeffco.

The academic side had always been less important to him. Nevertheless, somehow he now neared completion of his general course work at Academia Escolatica, the school Doña Carlota Gonzalvez y Rodriguez del Castillo maintained for the children of the local elite, as well as the dependents of the people assigned to her estate. Not *her* estate, really, but she treated it as her own, and nothing else really mattered.

He did well enough in class and on the soccer pitch to enjoy some popularity, though the local girls had their eyes on bigger prizes than the orphan taken in by Doña Carlota. The military dependents were more welcoming, though he often still felt out of place. He felt most comfortable with the actual military personnel detailed to the estate, or alone, as now.

Standing there with the green, pine-clad mountains rising sheer and tall all around him, he felt at peace and one with nature. *What spooked the stag?* He noted a hawk high above, rising on a thermal, but ignored it. The stag wouldn't have fled because of it. The marmots playing about the rocks nearby told him they sensed no nearby threat. They always popped into their holes when danger appeared, but they were happily enjoying the sun, unafraid of the hawk so far away. *What am I missing?* The far ridges were already purple as the sun sank lower in the west behind him.

His training had taught him to be aware of his surroundings without allowing them to distract him. His tactical sergeant, Technical Sergeant Vincent Klostermann, constantly drummed into him to concentrate on the mission in order to survive. Honed by his years here in the wilderness, as well as long field exercises, he almost always maintained a strong situational awareness.

A cool breeze blew and he felt the sweat drying on his brow and across his back. Something felt wrong, but what? Hugh took a second step, pausing to survey the terrain around him. Pines climbed the slopes above him, while aspen, oak, and birch covered with magnificently colored leaves clothed the lower flanks, broken by occasional openings that hardly qualified as meadows, being more vertical than flat. Around him, the trees were mixed. He soaked in the magnificent vista. Tonight, that would be all he took home with him, without the stag.

Suddenly, a stray echo caused him to turn. Startled, he saw a combat shuttle coming in low, sonic boom sending rocks cascading down the cliffs. Frowning, he realized the stag had reacted to the flyer ten seconds before he sensed anything. A flicker of motion in the corner of an eye might have been enough to startle the deer. Or an odd echo. Glancing up as it passed, he saw ordinance strapped to the wings. Wide-eyed, he nevertheless followed his training immediately. Diving, he hit the ground and buried his head under his arms, closing his eyes. This ridge stood sixteen kilometers from the estate, one minute at six hundred knots. Crawling with his butt as low to the ground as he could get, he headed to lower ground with his eyes shut.

A minute later, a flash reflected off the mountain rock, visible even through his tightly closed eyelids, announcing the detonation of nuclear ordinance somewhere near the estate. Without his training, he'd likely be fried or blind. The shock wave hit shortly thereafter, followed by a blast of heat. Hugh felt his skin prickle. The very roots of the mountain shook from the explosion. *Nukes aren't supposed to be used on a planet! Why now? Why here?*

Debris, rocks, and logs rattled down the steep hillsides, dislodged from precarious ledges above by the ground tremors and pressure waves. Waiting another minute to ensure nothing else dropped from the sky near him, Hugh jumped up, already evaluating his options. Twenty minutes away, roughly, west and downhill, he could get to the closest entrance to the secondary facility. Looking that way, he saw smoke rising in a huge cloud above the west slopes. Heading three kilometers straight toward what looked like the beginning of a truly spectacular wildfire didn't seem like a good life choice.

As for door number two, to reach the next nearest access he would have to travel about five kilometers to an upland park south by east and 600 meters higher, easily an hour plus to get there. Scanning the mountainside in that direction, he saw lines of fire on every ridge. Pines blazed on the side exposed directly to the blast. Even as he watched, the fire spread to their neighbors on the backsides that had escaped the nuclear blast. Run uphill into a potential fire sack? Not advisable.

Almost unconsciously, Hugh rejected both options, stepping out onto the trail headed east toward the side canyon leading to the back of the mountain. Twenty-five kilometers away, up that canyon, sat a rarely used secondary entrance. Right now, even though he had complained during training, he felt grateful for all the running he had been required to do as a part of his training. Unfortunately, he would have to beat the fire moving that way, so he picked up the pace. If he hurried, he could be there in about four or five hours over these rough trails. That might be quick enough to get there ahead of the fire. Otherwise, he'd be toast. He smiled tightly at his pun as he hit a level place where the path neared the stream, allowing him to run flat out for several hundred meters before he slowed for another slope. As his body followed its programmed training, he mulled over theories as to why the estate had been attacked.

Cruise missiles and kinetic strike weapons from space were fully defended against. The estate boasted the latest in electronic defenses, as well as a geosynchronous platform in orbit. *Leaving the only way in by a manned stealth flyer.* That seemed to be exactly what had happened. Did the estate's multiphasic shield stop the nuke? The shield could absorb that amount of energy, but had it? Shields weren't perfect. A nuke had gone off, so what did that mean? Nothing good, for sure.

So, why? Who could Doña Carlota have irritated that much?

Truth to tell, she could be smug at the best of times, but who might be angry enough to go to this much trouble? The navy apparently thought it likely enough to have provided lots of protection. The Marine protection detail, a full company assigned by Seventh Fleet, should have been enough to deter just about anybody. A naval detail stood watch in the control center, manning and maintaining the sensors. People in both areas, men and women he knew and liked, had trained him. And they might be dead right now, along with Doña Carlota.

As he ran, Hugh worried about the other Marines and cadets on the estate. Did any of them get out? Emotionally, his world had turned upside down. Were Liz and his teammates at school all right? Bettis and the other cadets? What about Kevin Dunn, his best friend?

Liz, with her blonde hair and blue eyes, a golden girl who considered herself a rebel. The social pecking order at school dictated that the local girls date within their own circle. But not Liz, who had even invited him to her house. He had just been getting up his courage to kiss her when her parents arrived home and sent him packing with orders to never step foot in their home again or they would get him expelled from school. Worse, they must have spread the word to the other parents because, after that, none of the local girls would so much as look his way, and the fouls during soccer games were always from the local boys. Which left hanging out with the Marines if he didn't want to become a hermit.

Not that it really changed anything. After he'd turned sixteen, Hugh had begun spending most of his free time with the combat Marines. He enjoyed their company, but hanging out with them didn't exactly expand his dating options; there were few women in the unit. Worse, the Marines often talked about women in very rough terms that he would never apply to the girls like the ones in his classes.

Sergeant Pete Peterson treated women like they were disposable, while some of the others treated them like they were princesses, at least until they broke up. Neither approach made sense to him, and he knew for sure Doña Carlota would never approve if he acted like that. She showed the utmost respect toward everyone, speaking to them as though they all were her equals socially. Hugh knew if he wanted to meet the right girl, he'd better do the same.

Right now, though, Hugh only wanted to know if all of his friends were okay.

A rock rolled under his foot, giving his right knee a jerk to the left, shaking him back to reality. His boot prevented his ankle from twisting, but it still gave him a twinge. If he didn't pay attention, he could be badly injured, and then he would never get to safety.

High above him, a pine exploded from heat expanding the sap, startling him. It brought him back to that time years ago.

Explosions, people screaming. A colonel firing until a laser cut him down. Cold sweat broke out all over him as the memory triggered a visceral response. Shaking it off, he concentrated on the trail, pushing aside the fear-filled memory. Heavy smoke made it hard to see clearly ahead and any distraction could be deadly.

Hugh caught his breath as he carefully negotiated the edge of a scree field. The sun disappeared behind the high mountain ridges, shadows lengthened, but with eerie gaps from the roaring fires. Hitting a section of trail that led deeper into wild terrain, he started to jog again. At the top of a slope, he stopped again to catch his breath, wheezing. Thick smoke blew down the canyon past him on gale-force winds toward the blast area.

The black smoke summoned another memory. A small group sped with him away from a town or city. Behind them, fire shot high in the air. The attack had come from space. He remembered crying and being so scared. The Marines with him seemed to be scared, too, but they didn't cry; they were just angry. He shook his head to drive the memory away.

Too much burned on the heights, deadfalls and green growth, for the air to clear, even with the strong wind. Tearing a strip from his shirt, he wet it from his canteen and tied it as a mask to filter the worst of the particles floating around him. Worry filled him. He had only come a few kilometers, and things were bad already.

Running on, tendrils of fire began eating their way down the slopes to the north and south of the trail. Glancing back, he noted that a rolling wall of flame now completely blocked the trail with the fire. The mountains' knife-like ridges had initially blocked off the bomb's heat blast from most of the forest, but the full fury of the nuclear weapon had scorched the trees on the top ridges facing the plain. As he ran, he saw lines of fire from those ridges moving closer, entire slopes now roaring with the glee of a devil's pyre. Looking up, he could clearly see individual forest giants roaring in orange and red fury. Hugh could feel his own anger at the attackers feeding on the cataclysm surrounding him, an urgency to escape pounding in his blood.

Atop a sheer cliff just ahead and only 300 hundred meters higher, another huge, ancient pine exploded. Flaming debris flew in every direction, some falling toward Hugh as he ran. A flaming pinecone grazed his arm, singing a hole in his shirt. With a quick swipe, he brushed it off.

More memories came flooding back. Shooting, people dying, and him falling into the tree. The memories almost choked him with fear, bringing out his deepest terror from sleepless nights.

If I die, will anyone know? He pushed the thought aside. If his friends were dead, Doña Carlota gone, no one would remember him. But if he survived, and they didn't, he would go after whoever killed them and make them pay. He could do no less.

The stream expanded into a meadow below a beaver pond. An elk's bugling distress stopped him from getting nearer. The huge animal's alarm caused a flock of grizzlings to break cover, fleeing in terror. Most of the surviving animals must be gathering here for safety, he realized. Stepping out of the trail onto the flanking rocky scree, he carefully picked a way through trees throwing deep shadows. Smoke completely blocked the twilight and early stars. Between the smoke and trees, no light penetrated the densely packed groves.

With frantic animals searching for safety and deadfalls from above clogging the forest floor, Hugh searched the shadows near the water as he carefully made his way forward. He spotted the form of a black bear with her cubs silhouetted against the lighter water of the background. More easily seen out in the water were other animals. A small elk herd nervously watched some moose, also bugling their fear. Hard-shelled peak shoorns circled their young. Mingling with them were deer and a lone white mountain goat with enormous horns.

As he picked his way through the underbrush, a mountain cat's yowl broke through the roar of the fire. He heard the cries of the herds in the water and a putkoff's chortle for its pack. Hugh relaxed when he heard no answering chuff; those critters could be trouble if they caught him alone. *Getting crowded down here.* He hoped all these animals would be okay, that the pond would save them. He hunted them but loved their wildness, the sense of community they gave him as he encountered them in his explorations.

However, at that moment, Hugh wished he could go faster. *A broken ankle would be extremely inconvenient at the moment.* So he continued to step carefully through the dark shadows. From his starting point, he reckoned he might be halfway to the meadow where he would turn south toward the entryway. Unfortunately, the fire crowned the ridges to both his right and left. He hadn't gotten ahead of it yet. To be able to reach the meadow and turn south safely, he needed to arrive before the fire started down the backside of the mountains.

Hitting the trail again half of a kilometer beyond the pond, he dropped into a steady jog. He might need a burst of speed later. Putting his body on autopilot as he ran gave him plenty of time to think, something Doña Carlota had taken great relish in pointing out as Hugh's greatest, but by no means only, flaw. *Well, I am thinking now, ma'am!*

Almost absently, he noted several booms coming from behind him, the kind he associated with kinetic strikes. Booms he heard in his nightmares, booms that left people dying all around him.

But not the same sound. The kinetic strikes aimed at the estate might have vaporized on the shield instead of impacting the ground. The primary shield remained up, apparently, so the main defense array might have been working when the attacker struck, absorbing most of the nuke's energy. *Interesting. If someone was alert enough to bring it up, there will be survivors.* He picked up the pace a little as his hope increased.

His feet pounded as he ran. The booms from multiple kinetic strikes echoed up the canyon behind him, followed minutes later by what sounded like an attempted missile attack. *Shields generally could stop missiles, too, right?* he wondered. Doubt and fear squeezed his heart. A shield in space used enormous amounts of energy and active shields in an atmosphere drank even more, as much power as a large city. Not even Doña Carlota could afford to keep a shield up except in an emergency.

The sound of engines overwhelmed the roar of the fire and his head snapped up. Ground assault shuttles began dropping from the sky, streaking past him toward where home used to be. Apparently, they thought someone still needed killing back there. Hugh smiled grimly. *A good sign.* Or as good a sign as a battalion of shock troops dropping in on you could be. A real mixed blessing. Stopping, he examined the shuttles to learn what he could about the attackers. Although just a cadet, he critiqued the formation. A little ragged, in his opinion. One of Klostermann's scorching remarks about the unalloyed confidence of youth in one's fully formed and inexperienced judgment came to mind and made him smile. He had never seen combat as an adult. He still judged the formation to be ragged.

Mind in neutral as he ran, more random thoughts came to him. He felt very lucky to have been accepted as a cadet. He didn't remember his family well, just his father mostly. A tall man, at least to a small boy. Erect and proud in the white navy dress uniform he almost always wore. Some much older brothers tousling his hair and teasing him but nothing about his mother. She had died when he was very little, or so Ward had told him.

So, what made Doña Carlota accept him as a cadet? Hugh

felt that his dad must have been a very old and good friend of Doña Carlota for Hugh to have been given this chance. Openings like this were few and far between these days, from what he could tell. Few people, since the coup attempt, seemed likely to remember debts, much less honor them. It said good things about Doña Carlota that she would act on the memory of a dead friend to give an insignificant orphan a chance. Staring at those ships roaring in to destroy his life, he felt truly alone. Alone but strong. He would honor his personal debts, too. He pushed on. Once he escaped this attack, he would hunt down the assassins. He would have debts to pay, friends to avenge. And they would b—

Hugh's head snapped back up toward a series of sudden explosions above him. The shuttles began to blow up! He hit the dirt under the torn-up roots of a leaning pine and dragged his body camouflage cover over him. Leaving a space, he peaked out at the action. A flight of space fighters slashed past and through the remaining shuttles, starburst-sevens on the wing flashes of the ships, taking out the ground assault shuttles. Seventh Fleet to the rescue! Cheering loudly for the attacking fighters and each exploding shuttle, he could barely hear himself over the sounds of combat. The fighters left nothing behind before disappearing into the clouds overhead. Hugh screamed his voice raw in the acrid air as the last shuttle hit behind a ridge to the north.

Watching for stragglers, he waited prudently as per his training. Seventh Fleet arriving in the nick of time seemed a bit odd. Not to complain, of course, but it seemed a little fortuitous that the fleet happened to have combat ships near enough to clean up the mess. *More than nearby, because they must have been in-system when it started.*

During his last rotation in the ops center two days before, no one had mentioned any major fleet activity in-system. He tried to remember the intel he had read. Nothing unusual, just the standard depressing stuff. The empire continued tearing itself apart, the loyal fleet units were stretched thin trying to protect too many civilian worlds whose inhabitants seemingly didn't care . . . at least in his opinion.

Hugh's training also included standing watch both in main control and the defense batteries. After countless hours of simulator time, he felt confident he could perform effectively in any engagement. His scores were pretty decent, if he did say so himself. However, Sergeant Klostermann, Sergeant Major Ward, and Doña Carlota all seemed to enjoy pointing out the innumerable times he had died or been less than successful. To encourage greater effort, of course.

Even Kevin Dunn, whom he considered his best friend, rode Hugh when they were on duty together. Although the youngest of the sergeants, he rated Dunn as tough as any of them, demanding perfection, and a bit more.

Like everyone else, Hugh had participated in escape drills, sliding into the shafts that connected to the back of the mountain. That only worked, unfortunately, with enough warning. He hadn't received an alert tone, so this attack might have been a total surprise.

Scanning the sky, he saw nothing. No shuttles, no fighters. Of course, the smoky murk made seeing anything more than a kilometer away, even one hundred meters most of the time, impossible. Still, it appeared safe to continue. Slowly speeding up, he dropped back into his distance-eating trot.

The Core Empire

Part II

The key issues to be discussed in Chapter 3 include the impact on Jack, but more especially Evie, of the deaths of two of their three sons at the Final Battle, the political maneuverings that transformed the Core Confederacy, founded 2475 by Joseph Jackson with forty-three core systems, into the Core Planets with thousands of component worlds in 2490.

The impact of Dave Jackson (2453 to 2531 AD), their surviving son, on the structure of the government and reasons for the creation of the Test of Heirs are included herein.

The Test of Heirs itself, its creation and operation, is discussed in Chapter 5. Because of Evie's central involvement in the creation and maintenance of the test, an in-depth review of the political and military situation on Green Gardens during that period is essential for understanding what led to such a lethal choice. Chapter 4 explains how Evie came to her opinions.

9

Home Base

Rancho Mirabel, Jeffco

Earlier That Day

SERGEANT MAJOR SEAN WARD STOOD, hands on hips, eyes squinting at the mountains towering over the estate. His whipcord leather face and body had picked up new white lines of scars on a dozen worlds over the last ten years. The late afternoon sun, streaming from behind, threw long shadows ahead of him. He stood parade ground sharp and crisp. Of all his many duties on the estate and beyond, disciplining one missing cadet, Hugh Cascade, topped the list. Unfortunately for his blood pressure, he couldn't find said cadet.

He glared across the lush green meadow fronting the manor with its hacienda-style main house. A stream, reflecting the pale blue of the autumn sky in its occasional pools, burbled among the rocks of its bed as it meandered from the canyon. Between the mountain and the manor and its surrounding buildings, reaped golden fields of corn and grain rested in the purple haze of fall.

Six barracks formed a square on the manor's far side. On this side of the manor sat two dormitory buildings, as well as a group of academic buildings in a gothic style, all fronted by the command center that guarded the main entryway. The motor pool sat farther out into the plain to the south, near the power station, shield generator, and air and space defense weapons. In the center of the academic quad, the flag of the empire stirred in the light breeze. Around him, a faint buzz of regular activity arose from the standard comings and goings, military and academic.

Normally, he took satisfaction in everything being ordered so he could concentrate on molding and forming the people under his command. At the moment, though, he felt dissatisfied with everything, even though all around him things were running smoothly, practically to perfection. The naval detachment stood watch in the command center as prescribed, while the Marine duty platoon appeared to be alertly manning its stations in the air and space defense pits. Nothing ever happened here, so undoubtedly the Marines were playing cards or telling sea stories; the kind of tall stories of exploits, both on and off the battlefield, women and men of action share that are not necessarily accurate. In fact, likely aren't anything beyond being entertaining.

But they were where they were supposed to be. So, if something did happen, that would be what mattered. However, as angry as he felt just now, if he walked into those defense stations, he would chew those people out royally. And it wouldn't even be their fault, the real reason he stood out here away from everyone else.

Kids! Why isn't he hanging out with his soccer friends? Or studying? Or, heaven forbid, on a date with Liz or even Bettis? Dating either one would be a headache, opening very messy cans of worms. Different ones, granted, but still lots of problems. Neither did Ward want Hugh to go hog wild, be another Peterson, who constantly created problems for himself and everyone else nearby. However, even with Hugh's native charisma, he acted shyly around girls outside the classroom.

None of that mattered at the moment, however. Ward didn't need Hugh for anything in particular at this moment, but Hugh should have let people know when he left the base. Standard operating procedure—SOP—called for everyone to sign out with destination as well as expected date and time of return. In Hugh's case, when he left, an unobtrusive bug generally tagged along, in addition to the trace, taping what he did for later review. Unfortunately, no bug rode along with Hugh today for the simple reason that no one knew he had slipped away.

For a moment Ward, wryly amused, saw himself as a mother hen. Trevor Cascade certainly had teased him often enough about sweating the details, but sergeants sweated the details so the officers could think they were in charge. At least Ward told Trevor that in response and he half meant it. He missed those days that would never come again. None of that mattered now, of course. He just hoped Trevor approved of the job Ward had done taking care of Hugh.

As for the trace, Ward didn't want to check it for three reasons. First, a chance existed that Hugh would find out if he did ping the trace. One of his friends in the com center might tell him that Ward could find him. Knowing Hugh, that would cause him to wonder about Ward's extraordinary interest in keeping track of his whereabouts. Plus, others would also speculate about Ward keeping such a close eye on a lowly cadet. Third, though less likely, someone else might notice the odd ping up on the mountain and investigate. Keeping Hugh safely anonymous superseded his irritation, except when absolutely necessary.

What irked Ward most at the moment was Hugh acting like a teenager. The mountain Ward stood staring at formed part of the manor, so Hugh technically didn't have to check out as long as he remained less than half an hour from his emergency duty station. Hugh, when challenged upon his return, would feign innocence and say he had always remained within thirty minutes of his duty station the entire time. If pressed, he might admit he measured the time based upon an aircar retrieving him and not foot speed, the way he left, but he would be technically right. By hitting his com, Hugh could have a ride in five minutes and be back five minutes later.

Ward ground his teeth. Hugh excelled at skating on the edge of the rules, something Ward hated. *Too clever by half. Why did Hugh have to act like an eighteen-year-old?* Still, Ward wished Hugh would quit flirting with the line and choose to do the right thing because he wanted to. It would make Ward's job so much easier.

Nevertheless, not having eyes on Hugh made Ward's palms itch. He thought about the bears and mountain lions that roamed the forest. He knew, though, that as of the moment, Hugh was fine. *The Gift*, through Hugh's medbots, told Ward that, so probably he just needed to calm down and not act like an old woman.

Ward's com buzzed. Lifting it to his mouth, he tersely said, "Go."

"Something a little weird on my screen, Sergeant Major. I think you better come take a look." The voice that spoke to him belonged to one of the naval ratings on watch in the command center.

"On my way," he answered.

Ward walked, quickly, toward the command center. It wouldn't do for anyone to see the sergeant major run; it might create a stir and make people think an emergency had popped up.

Sliding his card into the portal reader and placing his fingers in the genetic scanner, he paused for the seconds necessary for security to recognize him. Stepping into the glass booth on the other side of the door, two Marine guards finished the ID procedure. Before the coup, only high-security areas maintained anything approaching this level of caution; back then people took peace and freedom of movement for granted. There were few places today that didn't have a more intense level of protection than before the coup. The pause to be IDed gave him another moment to consider what else he needed to do.

Raising his com, he spoke, "Klostermann."

Within two seconds the com connected him to Sergeant Vincent Klostermann and alerted him. *"What's up, Top?"*

"Hugh's in the mountains with nobody tagging along."

"He's a big boy, Top. Let him have a little fun."

Ward glared at him a moment in the little screen. "Be that as it may, the command center is concerned about some odd sensor readings."

Klostermann snorted before answering, *"I'm sure Lieutenant Commander Morrell will figure it out. Eventually. This could be someone messing with her. You know how she pisses off the enlisted people by never listening to them when they have a suggestion or idea on how to do things better. But it's probably just more sensor ghosts."*

"Sergeant Klostermann, Commander Morrell may irritate you with the way she disciplines her spacers, and I may agree with you, for that matter, but nothing she has done is out of line. She's simply never learned how not to be a one-man band. She is a competent officer, even if neither of us likes her. As for the sensor reports, Barry Wong called me in, and you know how good he is. That means I'm taking this seriously, at least for now. So get an air sled and go find the boy. Or do you need a *please* to go with that?"

Ward easily heard Klostermann's snort on the com. *"Don't get your knickers in a twist. I'm on my way."*

Ward still felt that something just didn't seem right today. All day the command center had reported ghosts, the kind cloaked aircraft might leave. If the manor still relied on the older sensors, they would never have picked up even this much activity, but the new upgrades were specifically designed to find people who didn't want to be seen. Sometimes, though, they found ghosts because the sensors were too sensitive. Ward moved quickly to the elevator, remaining outwardly calm as the car descended thirty meters down toward the heart of the operations center, a white-painted room filled with gray equipment. Of course, it might be that the Seventh Fleet task group, hiding out-system, wanted to play games with them. After a week or two of imitating holes in space, they could have decided to run a few ops to keep their edge. If so, Ward intended to tell Doña Carlota so she could share Ward's dissatisfaction with Admiral Hollister, because having a security force nearby only helped if they could surprise the bad guys. Running around playing sneak-n-peek could get you noticed, even if only accidentally.

If someone has gotten a bright idea to run ops without permission—an involuntary smile broke through his control at the thought—*it won't be pretty.*

Ward negotiated the desks and chairs strewn all around the command center like toys badly in need of being picked up. If he had pushed it, he could have avoided this mess when Morrell decided to set her command center up this way to be more *collaborative.* He preferred functional over touchy-feely. Grudgingly, he admitted it worked well enough. Not that he could object. Doña Carlota had restrained him from getting involved, reminding him that Lieutenant Commander Morrell technically served as the detachment commander and would lose serious face with the naval ratings if Ward told her who really ran things. Ward reflected, once again, on her explanation for this rat's nest, saying it made for "better information flow between her and the techs."

And now I need to make nice. Here she comes to make sure I know this is her house.

"Commander? You have something more on the sensor ghosts?" he asked politely.

She gave him a narrow look before speaking, "I expected Doña Carlota to come down." Apparently, she didn't like him either and saw no reason to hide it. Another mark against her in his book. How an officer treated subordinates meant more than how she got along with superiors. He stuffed his sour appraisal of her in a box for the moment. He needed to work with her, plain and simple.

"She couldn't make it just now," Ward answered respectfully. "She asked me to check it out. She'll be along if it's serious." In truth, Doña Carlota left all of this to him, always.

"Just make sure she knows I asked for her," she snapped at him before taking him to a console.

"Aye, ma'am," he answered, "I'll make sure she knows you're on top of things." *Or actually Barry is.* Around Chief Petty Officer Barry Wong, a series of monitors provided live feeds, showing the manor from every direction, as well as near space.

Barry glanced up tensely as they neared, "Good to see you, Top. After this morning's sensor ghosts, I started looking closer at the activity. A while ago, I noticed there were a bunch of rocks nearing the outer atmosphere, rocks flying in tight formation." He pointed to some objects barely registering on his screen. "That seemed a little odd, so I queried and pinged them with the close-in net. They were much bigger than the sensors showed originally, so I turned a couple of cameras on them. This just came in."

A squadron of shuttles flashed up on the main screen. Ward paled. "How far out?"

"At least forty to fifty minutes if they fire up the engines now. Longer if they wait until the last minute," Barry reeled the data off automatically.

"Anything else?"

Focusing on his board, Barry said, "You always know the right questions to ask." He next brought up several weather satellites that orbited above the manor permanently. At least, they might have been weather satellites if they tracked weather patterns, which they didn't.

Barry leaned into his board as data began to stream in, professionally calm as he reported, "There is a cloaked aircraft coming our way about one hundred sixty kilometers out at just under the speed of sound, about Mach .85. Picked it up by heat from its engine and some wing surfaces. It must have come in over the pole to hide the reentry signature but still hasn't cooled to local air temps." Barry Wong liked to show off his analytic abilities, his smile telling Ward that he had intentionally held back this crucial piece of information for last to show off his expertise.

Unfortunately, Wong's desire to show off, and Hugh messing around in the mountains without a keeper, combined with Morrell being her usual obnoxious self, made Ward want to bite Wong's head off for not following SOP. Worse, Ward just didn't have time to get that satisfaction right now. Barry's ego had almost killed them before they could even take a shot at defending themselves. This happened when a unit went too long without an obvious threat. People got distracted, lost their edge, and found more immediate things to concentrate on when times were quiet. He should have taken that into better account.

Ward leaned forward over the keyboard, fingers flying over the keypad to enter the defense code bringing up the protective shield. Next, he hit the panic button. A siren went off and a red light began to flash. A recorded voice, Morrell's, because she had insisted it would be obeyed better than an unknown person's, spoke in every indoor space including the school and across most of the fields surrounding the manor, "Alert. This is not a drill. Immediate evacuation of all non-essential personnel and backup crews to the beta location. I repeat, this is not a drill."

As Ward stood, he noticed Morrell's furious expression. "Sergeant Major, you've overstepped your bounds. I'll court-martial you for this. Now stand down the alert."

Ward glanced down to see her fingers typing uselessly on her keypad. His code had locked in the alert, something unknown to her until this moment. Only he and Doña Carlota could override it.

"No can do, ma'am," he answered distractedly. Raising his voice, he bellowed in parade ground tones, "Skeleton crew remain and fight the base. Everyone else, evac tubes. *Now!*" From the corner of his eye, he saw Morrell turning almost purple with apoplexy at this additional usurpation of her authority. He felt sorry for her. A pretty good officer, generally fair to the people under her, she just didn't know she didn't know *everything.* Sadly, she simply didn't understand why he needed to act immediately without discussing it with her, and he doubted if she would understand why if he tried to explain. *She'll just have to live with it.*

Panels rose on all four walls revealing the evacuation tubes' mouths and the pile of escape sleds needed to ride them. A queue of naval men and women began lining up at each one, popping in at three-second intervals as the green light blinked *Go.*

As he walked to a tube, Ward called into his com, "Klostermann," to reconnect with him. He followed that with, "Vinnie, get out," before he could be acknowledged. "We'll find Hugh later. We have incoming. He'll have to take his chances just like the rest of us."

Choosing a tube without a line, he turned to survey the room. Four men and a woman manning the defense boards remained with Chief Wong. At the tube across the room, he saw Morrell diving last into another tube. *At least she knows a good officer goes last.* Ten seconds more he waited and watched, staying with these brave people until the last of the personnel were gone.

"Launch, launch, launch," Barry reported with hardly a quiver in his voice. "Multiple bogies coming at us in less than a minute."

Ward still hesitated. Although he needed to either be watching over that boy on the mountain or inside the mountain at the beta command post, how could he abandon these people, his men and women? If the shield failed, these six and the men manning the defenses outside were dead. He owed it to them to stand with them. Unfortunately, his obligation to the empire, as well as to these men and women, required a little more than the empty gesture of remaining physically with them. He must make their sacrifice, if it came to that, worth it.

Barry looked directly across at him. "Doña Carlota's out, and most of the other tubes show all clear. If you don't go now, the tubes'll lock down before you get outside the perimeter."

Ward saw the understanding in Barry's eyes, of what Ward *must* do fighting with what he *wanted* to do. Nodding in agreement with Barry's statement, as well as gratitude for his implicit permission to go, Ward dropped into the tube and onto a waiting sled. It immediately whooshed away at two G's. Here in the tube, the sled rested on air, so he felt as if he were floating. Sliding through the tube, dimly lit with a vague off-white light, felt like falling into a fog bank from a great height, not shot like a bullet through a narrow straw deep inside the earth.

Twenty-three point three seconds after jumping into the tube, he began to decelerate. Forty-one seconds from the start, a five-second chime warned him of imminent arrival. Dropping easily onto a soft pad with flexed knees, sixteen kilometers from the manor under the mountain, he stood without a stagger. Smiling inwardly, he walked off the arrival pad naturally. A small thing, but he hated to ever appear out of control of the situation.

Looking around, he saw Doña Carlota waiting angrily for him. Ward sighed, preparing himself to handle her barely concealed temper. Doña Carlota had aged over the last decade, perhaps more than any of them. Physically, anyway. The stress of being "retired," had taken a toll. Though she still projected an air of authority and had an iron will that no one on the estate would choose to test. Today, she wore her gray hair drawn back into a bun, perfect as always, and was dressed informally in gray slacks, maroon bolero vest, and cream-colored cotton blouse. The attack seemed to have caught her by surprise also, since she hardly ever appeared in public wearing anything less than a suit or dress. Regardless, her demeanor projected her natural command over everything around her. As such, her muttered statement of, "Just a minute, Commander," to Morrell standing at her shoulder, anxiously trying to get her attention, spoke volumes as to who Doña Carlota depended upon.

"What's happening, Sergeant Major?" she demanded. A tremor shook the chamber as she spoke. Ward judged it might have been from a small earthquake under the mountain or a big nuke hitting the estate. He'd lay his money on the nuke, a very big one.

Morrell, at five foot six a woman of normal height, seemed to tower above Doña Carlota. She also kept her figure trimly military. Ward watched curiously as she tried once more to get Doña Carlota's attention. "Doña Carlota, if I could just have a moment?" Ward figured she wouldn't succeed. "I have the full situation report, sir," she hastily spat out, desperate to get control of the situation.

Doña Carlota gave her an infinitesimal glance before answering her, "I hate to be rude, Commander, but I really must speak with Sergeant Major Ward first. It is a matter of some urgency. I will come see you next, in the beta command center. Say in five minutes?" Doña Carlota's polite, mild tone avoided being rude while leaving no question she had dismissed Morrell.

Ward hid his amusement as he watched the color drain from her face at the casual rebuke. There were only a few people left in the tube delivery room, still gathering themselves together after their wild ride, to hear Doña Carlota's summary dismissal, but that would be more than enough for the story to get around the base before the end of the shift.

"Aye, ma'am," she answered, voice not betraying anything of her feelings. She pivoted before scurrying off, the last one out of the area.

"A little harsh on her, don't you think?" Ward inquired mildly. "Hard to command when your people already think her boss doesn't respect her. You should have let her get in her bid to get credit for identifying the problem and sounding the alarm."

"You're right, but I just don't have time to avoid hurt feelings right now. We both know there are more important issues. She is extremely competent, which is why I have kept her on. I'll even give her an award in front of the troops, so they all know I have confidence in her. Later." Doña Carlota sighed before continuing, "So, if she didn't notice the bogies, then who?"

"Chief Wong noticed the incoming bogies, and I sounded the alarm. Over her protest, as a matter of fact. Looks like someone has found us. A good-sized nuke probably caused that shake a minute ago." Ward's tone maintained its neutral tone, but his eyes watched as Doña Carlota tensed and leaned forward.

"Is everyone safe and accounted for?" Doña Carlota's confidential tone sounded more concerned than she normally did regarding accounting for her troops during war, at least to Ward's ears.

"The shield staff, air and space defense crews, and skeleton staff in the main command center were all that was left when I jumped into the tube." Ward felt the tug of Doña Carlota's real question but still didn't elaborate, even though they were completely alone. Doña Carlota could stand a little non-cooperation from time to time, Ward judged. It helped one's humility.

In an off-handed manner, Doña Carlota inquired, "Anyone unaccounted for?"

"We have two details in towns out of the area, sir," Ward answered calmly.

A glint of anger in Doña Carlota's eye told Ward he had almost gone too far. "You know who I mean."

"Hugh went hunting earlier without checking out and is somewhere on the mountain overhead right now."

Doña Carlota's real alarm showed at Ward's report. Quickly looking around, she demanded in a low voice, "Who's with him? Is he safe?"

"He's alone, and I have no idea how he's doing for sure. I intended to send out Klostermann, but Barry called me just before I did. Good thing; he would have been caught in the open when the attack hit. After Barry told me about the attack inbound, I called Klostermann to tell him not to go."

Doña Carlota sagged a bit, something she had done much too frequently the last few years. It genuinely concerned Ward. After a moment, Doña Carlota straightened. "If he dies out there, these last ten years—everything since Deft—have all been for nothing," she said softly.

Ward smiled tightly. "He's alive. Take my word for it."

Doña Carlota gave him a scathing look. "Becoming psychic in your old age, Top?" The sarcasm in her voice could have cut battle steel.

Ward just shook his head. "The boy can take care of himself. But we'll send out someone to pick him up if it makes you feel better."

"Do it!" Doña Carlota ordered.

"That may draw enemy follow-on forces to him if we do," Ward reminded her.

Doña Carlota's face twisted through various emotions before settling into her accustomed one of command. "Good point, but, at a minimum, send a remote. We'll have to trust him to get back on his own until the enemy is mopped up. Let's get to the command center."

IN THE BETA COMMAND CENTER, Ward watched from the far side of the room, leaning against the steel wall. Morrell stood in the central command area evaluating her team as they pinpointed the opposing forces and directed fighters from the formerly hidden task force in to wipe them out.

As fighters slashed in to destroy the combat shuttles, he almost despaired. He knew the real danger Hugh ran just being in the area. A shuttle might pick him up on its sensors and decide to kill the target just to be safe. A fuel tank might explode above him, showering him in flaming hydrogen. Pieces of a shuttle or fighter might rain down on him. Stray ordinance from the fight could easily hit him by accident.

Outwardly, Ward remained calm and fully in control. Inwardly, his helplessness twisted his guts, knowing everything he had done, the sacrifices of thousands of others over the last ten and a half years, could be lost in an instant, become meaningless, through a quirk of fate.

If Ward could have done anything to protect him at that moment, reach out to him regardless of cost, he would have. Having no choice, however, he couldn't deny the inescapable logic that anything they did to protect Hugh could easily draw attention to him. And that *would* get him killed.

When the last shuttle fell, he realized he'd been holding his breath in an anticipation. He let it out, then quietly ordered out drones to track Hugh, even as shuttles with reinforcements approached the mountain. Ward could see from the icons that Admiral Hollister's personal barge flew with them.

Great. I lose Hugh for a few hours, and the whole world comes apart.

Naval Space Training Guide, 263d Edition

Appendix L: Imperial Military Training Standards

Introduction to Military Technology

Shielding

Naval Officers Basic Course issued 3411 with revisions

A thorough understanding of the practical applications of shielding for purposes of ship handling in both tactical and standard situations must be demonstrated by each midshipman to pass this section. In addition, midshipmen must demonstrate a basic level of understanding of the theoretical basis of shield projection to receive a passing grade.

Shielding for purposes of this section is either standard or multiphasic. Standard shielding protects ships against all normal hazards of space travel, both from expected energy exposure up to that of being within fifteen million kilometers or one-tenth of an Astronomic Unit of an F Class star, as well as from contact with matter up to class two meteorites at standard in-system speeds. Once matter exceeds class two, it emits a gravity wave of sufficient strength for detection and avoidance. The automatic detection and avoidance systems built into all ships are the subject of a subsequent section.

Midshipmen must demonstrate proficiency in calculating energy demands for shielding in the following standard situations: Inner star system travel; outer star system travel; Kuiper Belt transit; Oort cloud transit; interstellar travel within the core; interstellar travel within a galactic arm; and inter-arm travel.

Multiphasic shielding provides "onionskin" protection to a vessel in a combat or tactical environment. It is a series of shields of varying frequency nested within one another designed to handle impact from kinetic weaponry as well as nuclear blast from missile warheads. Each layer handles a portion of the impacting matter or energy, handing off to the next layer before overloading. Ship class determines the number of layers due to energy requirements per layer. Midshipmen must demonstrate proficiency in calculating and configuring multiphasic shielding for a frigate-class ship in combat.

10

Decision Gate

Degas Fork, Chelly Canyon, Jeffco

2045 Local/1445 BBMT 9 October 3473

ROUNDING A SPUR, THE trail zigzagged up sixteen meters beside a foaming cascade. Slowing to a walk, Hugh Cascade slogged up and through until he passed opposing cliffs that seemed to form an entrance to a wide mountain meadow of about fifty acres. Jogging sixteen or twenty kilometers in three hours or so uphill over rough trails had taken a toll. Pushing himself to go a bit farther, he reached a deep grassy patch before dropping to the ground, breathing deeply. He took off the bow and quiver so he could stretch and lie down. A stitch stabbed deep into his side. Before he continued, he needed to work it out. Turning, staring back at the mountains facing the plain, the fire burned no closer than a kilometer and a half, more like two, from the meadow. The mountains appeared crowned with coronas of fiery glory. However, fire kept creeping down their back flanks toward him. Behind him, in the safety to the east, he saw no sign of fire yet. The stream coming in from the south noisily ran from a secondary valley to join its bigger sister coming down from the east, before continuing off westward together, downhill to the manor and the plain.

To the south, up the smaller stream, lay duty, possibly a commission. It would be a regimented life, but one with purpose. Did he want that life, really? What if he followed the stream behind him eastward, away from the fire? Thirty or forty kilometers farther through the mountains and over a saddle lay another plain with villages, small towns, and farms. He could report in there and then go after whoever killed his friends. Or build a life for himself. Becca, a waitress at the café in town, might just help him make that happen.

He could go anywhere he wanted to go. Do anything he wanted to do. Be anything he wanted to be. But what did he want to be? Really? He considered the question as his breathing became more regular. The western pyre filled his sight, its roar overwhelming his hearing as it grew nearer.

The whole world seemed ablaze just like the galaxy overhead. If the fire jumped east to the next mountain as he ran the five or so kilometers south to the entrance, he'd be dead. Literally. If he survived and fought for the dying empire, sooner or later he could just as easily be dead, one more unremembered footnote to a lost cause, one more sacrifice no one would know or care about.

But he knew, deep in his heart, if he headed deeper into the mountains and then to the towns on the other side, he would never be happy. He couldn't abandon his duty and be happy. What would Doña Carlota think if he did that? Kevin Dunn and Sergeant Major Ward would be disgusted—worse, disappointed—to know the thought even crossed his mind.

A thought gnawed at the back of his brain. What made a man? The things he did for himself or the things he did for others? "Duty" meant so much more than taking a shift in the control room or serving on a ship. At least to him it did. And it had to his father, he knew. *Doña Carlota could write a dissertation on the subject, I'm sure.*

His breathing back to normal, he picked up his things and adjusted them so they wouldn't interfere with his motion, before going to the stream. Leaning over, he drank deeply before chewing on some jerky. Doing a body check, he felt a little sore in places, arms stinging, legs a little tired but ready for one more push. Almost subconsciously, he squared his shoulders, facing south into the nightmare landscape. Fires, still only halfway down the west mountainside, ate at a steady rate toward the valley floor. Darkness and deepest night reigned still to the east. Smoke hung in a veil, hiding what might be there if he entered.

Setting off at a slow lope, he aimed for the narrow valley opening to the south. His feet pounded out the pace as he pondered, steps automatic, careful, sure-footed, as he kept subconscious track of his surroundings. If the fire jumped to the east side of this small valley, things could get interesting fast. *Too interesting.*

A stream ran through the bottom of the valley, fed by a small waterfall. Walking carefully down to the stream, he knelt for a drink. The water felt cold, icy even against his face and forearms. He realized he had been burned by the nuclear blast. Last, he rewet his face rag in the stream, tying it again around his mouth so he could breathe. Then he set off again at the best pace he could manage.

The lines of fire crawled faster, closer. He felt the first breath of heat from their flames. Slowing to catch his breath again, Hugh took a swig from his canteen. Exhaustion pulled at him. Stepping off once more, he began to stumble occasionally. Tripping on an unseen root, he fell to his hands and knees, painfully scraping his palms. Here in the bottom of the canyon, the air grew stiflingly hot as the roaring fires neared the canyon floor in places, smoke settling into every crevice, making it difficult to see and breathe. His eyes burned.

Finally, staggering with weariness, he reached it: a small, nondescript cave opening just meters above the narrow, noisy stream. Gratefully, he turned aside. He had worried he might miss it in the dark, but the fires chasing him replaced the night, leaving a strange half-twilight in the deep valley. The shadow of the cave mouth easily stood out as a patch of midnight in the reflected fire glow.

Ignoring the sting in his palms, he got down on hands and knees and crawled fifteen meters into the opening until it turned into a tunnel tall enough to stand in. Coughing from the smoke filling the cave, he fought to stand. He dampened the rag once again from his canteen and tied it back over his mouth and nose before going on.

Moving forward, the passage abruptly opened up further, giving him a feeling of greater space above him and to the sides. After a series of S-bends and over a hundred meters farther, he reached a wooden ladder, the only man-made object this close to the entrance. He climbed rung by rung up sixteen meters to another tunnel that went on for another hundred meters. The climb took him twice the time he would have normally taken to go this far in training exercises.

Maybe more. He stopped to rest twice on his way up. He coughed nonstop now as he reached the top of the ladder, the smoke much heavier up here. No metal could be found anywhere in the tunnel this close to the entrance. That included exhaust fans, something an alert sensor crew would look for.

Starting into this tunnel leading even further into the mountain, a sensor-proof roof now covered his head. Hundreds of meters of iron-impregnated granite with streaks of low-level radiation leftover from the formation of these mountains millions of years ago, protected him from the sky, shielding him from anyone trying to scan the area. Completely wrung out and wheezing, he leaned against the wall for a moment.

Twenty-four plus kilometers uphill in the dark in just four hours qualified as decent time under any conditions. Arriving alive through the inferno raging outside? He must have been on fire. He smiled at his black humor, something he picked up from being around Marine combat vets.

A steel door stopped his progress sixteen meters farther in, the smoke filling the tunnel causing him to bend over in another wracking fit. The door blocking him stood blank, plain and forbidding, with no handle, keyhole, or knob. A simple keypad and retinal scanner were inset into the stone wall on the left of the door with no way to short circuit the mechanism from this side.

He messed up the code the first time as another bout of coughing shook him. Hugh entered his code and submitted to scanning. Would it open? Another coughing spasm wracked his chest. If it didn't open, with the fire and smoke having already trapped him . . . *Game over.*

Suddenly the door opened smoothly. Relieved, he took a deep lungful of clean air as he lurched forward. Facing the wide-eyed guard there, he pulled himself together, came to attention slowly, saluted, and stated firmly, "Cadet Cascade reporting," Behind him the door closed smoothly, shutting out the smoke.

As his arm dropped from the salute, he broke down in another fit of coughing, sagging back against the wall to keep himself upright. His bow jabbing into his side reminded him to take it, his bag, and quiver off. He almost melted into the wall with exhaustion and relief. Looking up, as he got his coughing under control, it hit him: this corridor, normally dead quiet, teemed with people he didn't know. So different from its normal skeleton crew status. Somehow, the activity seemed out of place in the light of its cool green hue.

With this many people in this outer corridor, the complex must have been crowded, probably filled to capacity. He relaxed, relieved. At least others had survived.

Private First Class Kirkwood, the door guard, gave him an appraising look after speaking into his com. "Stand fast. Someone will be here to get you in a minute."

Hugh remembered a minor little problem he had forgotten about while struggling to get here. When he had headed out to go hunting, he had failed to let people know where he would be. To be fair, he hadn't known precisely where the hunt would take him. He had often overlooked—intentionally ignored, really—that detail in the past. It looked like that reg might just have caught up to him.

Regulations clearly required that admin be notified whenever he left the estate or planned to be more than five minutes from headquarters. He understood the purpose: in an emergency, the unit could recall its members and find missing personnel. He couldn't see any way the current situation didn't qualify as an emergency. He had busted the reg in the exact situation it had been intended for. As a result, he could undoubtedly expect to get ripped up one side and down the other. He judged it likely he would get a double portion of punishment details as a result.

Hugh asked Kirkwood, "Did Sergeant Dunn make it? And Liz Polchar? My teammates?"

Kirkwood gave Hugh a pitying look. "I heard everyone got out, but I don't think we should be talking. The com center sounded like you are likely to be the center of high-level attention very shortly, and I don't want any of it splashing on me."

Hugh nodded in complete understanding, waiting in a modified rest position, leaning against the wall. Occasionally, a stray cough escaped. Seeing Doña Carlota Gonzalvez y Rodriguez del Castillo hustling up two minutes later, Hugh gathered himself and came to attention.

But Doña Carlota shocked Hugh by not stripping him to the bone immediately as expected. More surprising still, Doña Carlota didn't say anything at all for a long moment, just stopped suddenly a few feet in front of him and looked him over. She paled. Hugh glanced down to see why.

Soot and dirt covered his woods clothing except where mud splotched them from splashing through mountain streams. His arms below the short sleeves were a flaming, sunburn red. Several small holes from burning cinders peppered his shirt and pants. Minor burns, nothing more. But he could see why Doña Carlota appeared shocked by his appearance. Hugh looked worse than he felt.

Oh joy, here comes Sergeant Major Ward. Ward now reached out with an arm to support Doña Carlota. "It's all right, ma'am. He's safe and sound. I told you not to worry."

Doña Carlota nodded, recovering her composure. "I just wanted to make sure for myself," she answered Ward without taking her eyes off of Hugh. Standing as tall as she could, she gave herself an almost impossible-to-see shake, then turned to a navy lieutenant, trailing along almost unnoticed, in their wake. "Inform the admiral, personally, that he is accounted for and safe. Courier only." The lieutenant saluted and left for the lift at the end of the corridor.

Hugh's confusion about all this now peaked. *The admiral?* An admiral needed to know his condition? Hugh barely noted the strangeness of a serving officer saluting his guardian in the midst of all the other odd occurrences piled on top of this extraordinary day, but it didn't escape his notice either. Doña Carlota distracted him before he could consider the meaning of the salute by doing what Hugh had expected in the beginning.

"Mr. Cascade," she began astringently, gathering her normal mien and attitude. Her voice carried the upper crust snobbery found in entertainment broadcasts, but from her it sounded natural. Combined with the easy, natural carriage of a manor-born aristocrat, she was a woman not to be trifled with.

Hugh thought he had come to attention when Doña Carlota first arrived. He realized his mistake as his automatic reflex brought him to an absolutely motionless and erect full brace.

"Where were you today without leave?"

Hugh responded, "Ma'am, hunting on the estate during my off-duty hours. Ma'am!" Strangely, from the corner of his eye, he seemed to catch a brief smile from Ward.

"Did it occur to you that you might be needed for something? You are an officer cadet! Why did you not log out? We might have assumed you were somewhere in the blast zone; someone might have been killed or injured trying to find you during the evacuation or a dangerous rescue might have been initiated."

Hugh maintained his brace. "Ma'am, I recently became aware that a locating tracker often follows me wherever I go, so I assumed you could find me. Ma'am!"

At this, Doña Carlota truly blew up, something she had been obviously faking to this point. Hugh definitely could tell the difference. What a huge mistake he made with that last flippant remark! Doña Carlota's tone could now chill metal like liquid nitrogen, her green eyes becoming spears that pierced Hugh's soul. "*Mister* Cascade. Perhaps you are not aware that even in the fleet, officers, commissioned as well as noncommissioned, often have a locating tracker assigned to them? They are still required to keep the logs accurate as to their intended location and activities. Perhaps you no longer wish to join the Imperial Fleet? You no longer wish to be a cadet?"

At this threat, Hugh's marrow almost froze. "No ma'am. No excuse, ma'am!" came his almost panicky response. A corner of his mind noted he at least sounded composed.

"You are on probation! Remember this conversation, Mr. Cascade. I have been training you in remembrance of your father, a truly great man. Do not cause me to regret my decision in this matter!"

Hugh noted that Ward seemed completely unperturbed by all this; in fact, he acted almost amused. He *never* undercut others' authority, especially regarding discipline and, most particularly, in anything regarding Doña Carlota. *Odd.* Hugh remained facing front as he shouted, "Ma'am, yes, ma'am!" Of course, Ward wouldn't lose anything if Doña Carlota carried out her threat and took away Hugh's life-long dream.

"Dismissed!" Without another word, Doña Carlota spun about and headed for the lift.

Hugh sagged back, surprised to feel cold sweat all over his body. Ward gave him a silent examination, then added, thoughtfully, "Nice sunburn."

"The heat blast, Sergeant Major," Hugh uttered without thinking of possible consequences. From past difficulties, he knew the truth avoided all kinds of problems. Shading sometimes helped, but he never, ever, outright lied.

"Thought so." In a conversational tone, he continued, "Did you remember that EMP from nuclear detonations could knock out trackers outside an exclusion zone? We would have been blind and couldn't have informed Doña Carlota of even where to start looking. It can even temporarily block archeon trackers implanted in Marines and others. You really worried her. Don't scare her like that again; her heart can't take it. Until you showed up here a few minutes ago, nothing I said made her feel any better."

Hugh wondered exactly what Ward told Doña Carlota to comfort her. *Don't worry, ma'am, no great loss*, maybe?

Ward concluded more severely, "Almost her entire family died in the assassination of the emperor, so you are the closest thing she has to a grandson."

"I . . . understand, Sergeant Major." His surprise at this news showed both in his voice and raised brows. Strangely, a warmth and strength stirred inside him at the sergeant major's words. *Like a grandson?*

"Better make sure you didn't pick up radiation. Wait here until Sergeant Klostermann comes. He'll go with you to decontamination. You need to be cleared before you can report in for duty."

"Aye, aye, Sergeant Major." Hugh suddenly realized he had forgotten to take any precautions against fallout. He might have died as a result. That would have seriously put a damper on his day. *Oops!*

Saluting, Hugh waited until the sergeant major disappeared around a far bulkhead before sagging back against the wall in almost total exhaustion. He tried to order his thoughts but couldn't keep them straight. He pictured, with great effort, the missed shot as the starting point of this journey, but his memories quickly dissolved into a blur. In the past, the sergeant major had impressed on him the need to review and analyze an operation as soon as possible. He liked to say that the human mind acted more like a sieve than a basin and couldn't hold much for very long. Accurate analysis being essential to improved performance, or survival, a Marine needed to review what happened so as to learn as much as he could to better deal with future life-threatening events. Hugh smiled at the total illogic that he might soon be facing more life-threatening events, but his thoughts wouldn't focus, floating instead in a mist through his mind.

He suddenly felt Kirkwood shaking his shoulder.

"Wake up. Klostermann's in sight."

He'd drifted off to sleep leaning against the wall? He felt worse than when he came in, the momentary nap having awakened his body to its crying need for rest. Forcing himself up, he stood erect when Sergeant Vinnie Klostermann hurried up. Hands on hips, Klostermann slowly surveyed Hugh.

"Let's go, Joe the Ragman," Klostermann ordered. Hugh's jaw

fell open. Klostermann always kept himself strictly professional, Joe the Ragman, being the worst thing he ever called anyone. Klostermann went on, "We'll save our counseling session for another time."

Oh, joy.

"Sergeant Major tells me Doña Carlota has already torn a bloody strip off you tonight. Plus, we need to make sure you'll live long enough for me to get my piece of you. So, off to decon." Klostermann turned toward the medical section, forcing his way through the unusually crowded corridors.

Hugh gritted his teeth, grabbed his things, and shoved himself off in Klostermann's wake. You could count on Vinnie Klostermann to be a fair man, but his bite really did hurt worse than his bark. Hugh heaved a sigh of relief, though, that Klostermann appeared to be waiting to take his bite out of him until a later date. Although Klostermann tried to walk quickly, the crowd in the corridor made it tough to go faster than a crawl. Hugh asked, "Did we lose a lot of people?"

"Not many, maybe five or ten. We're still looking for a few strays." Giving Hugh a sidelong look, he added, "Like your buddy Peterson. He apparently went on a date when this went down. Sergeant Major has already counseled him, too."

Peterson being with a girl, no surprise there. Hugh didn't really like Peterson all that much, but Kevin hung out with him, so Hugh tolerated him. He asked his most pressing questions, "What about Dunn? And Liz Polchar?"

Klostermann gave a thin smile. "They're fine. Dunn wanted to go look for you as soon as we got here. Sergeant Major almost needed to tie him up to keep him from going out against orders. Ward said something about bad pennies always showing up, but Dunn didn't find that very funny. He and most of the other guys are fine. The students, too, from what I hear."

Hugh let out a sigh of relief. A warm feeling of appreciation and brotherhood filled him, knowing that, at just five foot six, Dunn wanted to stand up to the whole world to go look for him in the middle of an attack.

Entering the pale, yellow-painted medical office, they stepped to the reception window. Several Marines and spacers sat waiting on chairs around the wall. The duty corpsman yelled at Klostermann and Hugh, "Get out of here. The smoke is bad for the patients. Come back when you have a cleaner uniform."

Klostermann shoved his face into the corpsman's grill. With a hard squint, he growled, "Doña Carlota wants him decontaminated immediately. So shut up and do it."

The corpsman, though bigger than Klostermann, blanched before directing them back to the main medical bays.

"Take your clothes off in the sensor booth and toss them out here," the corpsman, Rodney according to his name tag, directed.

Hugh dropped his bow and other things at the door before walking into the standard four-by-four exam sensor booth and closing the smoked-glass door. Sinking to the slat protruding from the wall that served as a chair, he almost collapsed completely. But rousing one last effort, he began by pulling off his boots. They were special hiking boots purchased six months before, costing almost a full month's pay. They were pretty hashed, he judged. It would take some work to fix them back up. Next came the torn pants. They weren't worth saving. The shirt and hat came last. Tossing them out, Hugh yelled, "Where can I get the boots and shirt cleaned?"

"Orders are everything coming in from outside must be destroyed to avoid radiation contamination. I'm tossing them down the chute now."

Hugh burst out of the booth, buck naked and furious. "You do and you'll follow them. The jacket in my bag and those boots cost me almost two months' pay. And don't even think about touching my bow!"

Vinnie Klostermann sat grinning at the confrontation from a chair across the examination foyer. Rodney stood uncertainly for a moment, flabbergasted at this cadet—this *naked* cadet—challenging him.

"Check Hugh and his things for radiation," Klostermann suggested. "If they're contaminated, down the chute." Here he shot

Hugh a hard, unwavering look demanding Hugh's agreement to his solution, to which Hugh unwillingly nodded. Klostermann gave a hard smile in return. "If not, we'll get them cleaned."

"I've got my orders," bristled the corpsman. "It's standard operating procedure."

"Doña Carlota will back me up on this exception. Check with the sergeant major if you have any doubts."

Rodney turned almost as white as his medical scrubs at the mention of the sergeant major getting involved. "Fine," he snarled. Tossing Hugh's things back at him, he directed him back to the sensor suite. "Stand in the middle and don't move." Hugh gathered the bow and quiver, his bag, the boots, pants, and shirt, taking them back in with him. A minute later, Rodney reported, "No radiation. Drop the things out here and I'll run them through the ozone chamber to get rid of the smoke. You step into the shower."

The corpsman's threat to his precious possessions, some of the few things he really treasured, had given him a jolt of adrenaline that lasted long enough to get him into the shower, but two minutes of warm water washed that burst of energy completely away. Stepping out, he saw that, while he showered, the corpsman had run his things through an ozone screen that pulled out the worst of the smoke. Pulling on his ragged and burnt clothes, he almost tipped over as he picked up the bag, bow, and arrows. Barely able to keep his eyes open, he asked Klostermann, "Where to?"

Sergeant Klostermann directed him out the door and through a series of hatches and open steel stairwells until he reached a row of doors. Opening one, he stepped out of the way allowing Hugh to stumble in. Hugh dropped onto the bed before he realized something odd: no one else shared the room with him. "What's going on?" Hugh demanded leaning on his right arm. He didn't have enough energy to even sit up straight.

Klostermann just smiled thinly. "We'll talk about it later. Get some sleep. You have duty in four hours." He shut the door, a bit surprised that he wasn't sharing the room with three other guys. Hugh set the alarm sitting on the top of the bedside table, before lying down. Light still on, his first snore erupted before his head hit the pillow.

NAVAL SPACE TRAINING GUIDE, 263D EDITION

Appendix L: Imperial Military Training Standards

Introduction to Military Technology

Ship-Based Archeon Communication

Naval Officers Basic Course issued 3411 with revisions

Simultaneity communication, better known by the basic particle that makes it possible, archeon communications, is essential to fleet operations. This section will require midshipmen to demonstrate understanding of ship design that makes archeon transmission possible by archeonA stations that include supernova- and nova-class ships as well as planetary arrays, and archeonB stations for most smaller classes of vessels. Specifically, understanding of frigate, cruiser, and supernova design parameters must be demonstrated to pass this section. Basic proficiency in theory, not to include Twi of Namib's integrated theoretical calculations, must be demonstrated. Finally, a midshipman must send a message from the base of training to archeonB and archeonA receivers designated by the instructor.

11

Duty Stations

Fleet Emergency Complex Beneath Snaggletooth Mountain, Jeffco
0135 Local 10 October/1935 BBMT 9 October 3473

CADET HUGH CASCADE SAT HUNCHED FORWARD IN his dove gray uniform, scrounged from a storeroom full of uniforms and equipment kept stocked for such emergencies. Fresh from a plastic wrapper, it appeared sharp and crisp, other than the creases from where it had been folded in the package. As a cadet, he rotated regularly through the various posts, including the skeleton staff kept here, for training, so he knew his way around the vast underground labyrinth.

Rubbing his eyes, he forced himself to stay focused. The few hours of sleep after his visit to decon helped, but not enough. Regardless, he had appeared for duty at midnight anyway. Being on probation, he didn't need any more black marks. Normal training rotation brought him, tonight, to watch the electronics defense board with Noor Bettis. He envied her looking so fresh and alert, much better than he felt. She looked especially pretty today, the cadet gray setting off her athletic build, olive skin, and dark, exotic eyes. As a rule, he didn't even think of her as female. He decided he must be noticing her because of his near-death experience.

Normally this duty bored Hugh to tears. It required nothing but keeping track of merchant ships and space junk, and he thought it should be closed down and the personnel better utilized elsewhere.

Today, however, aside from wanting to be directly involved in the fight, he had no desire to be at any other station. Riveted, he watched the fleet action above the planet unfold. He still searched for space junk, because it could be a kinetic weapon disguised as an asteroid. The secondary control room sat so deep in the mountain only an asteroid could kill it. So, despite his judgment as to the usefulness of the post, he continued checking the board from time to time for any kind of space debris, whether on a collision course with the planet or not.

Still, even the space battle raging in his backyard couldn't keep his full attention. Additional personnel with shoulder flashes from various Seventh Fleet ships kept coming through. For what, he didn't know, but they seemed to be everywhere, which made Hugh wish for the open spaces on the mountain.

Out of the side of his mouth, he asked Bettis, "Why are all these fleet types here?" The question nagged at him on top of all the other mysteries of the last two days. "Doña Carlota must be extremely valuable to someone at fleet headquarters."

Bettis answered back just as quietly, "Shut up, Cascade. You're going to get us in trouble. Again. Morrell jumped a rating just before you came in and she doesn't look happy."

"Why is she sore this time?" Hugh asked with genuine curiosity. Lieutenant Commander Veronica Morrell seemed to delight in giving the cadets, especially him and Bettis, a hard time.

"I heard Doña Carlota ignored her after the attack, and she's been pissed off since." Hugh saw her eyes flash up and then back to the board. "Here she comes. Now you've done it." Hugh studiously kept his eyes on the board, even as he felt a presence at his back. After a few minutes, it went away. He sagged a bit with relief. Another demerit from Morrell would have made the start of a new day perfect. He kept silent from then on as he and Bettis traded breaks.

On one such break, in the mess, no one could provide an explanation, satisfactory or otherwise, as to how a Seventh Fleet battle group just happened coincidentally to turn up, flipping a potential massacre into an ambush of the attackers. He listened hard, hoping to pick up something that made sense about the situation, but heard nothing.

When he came on watch he had noticed Scottie—Petty Officer Third Class Scott G. Frampton—talking to two of the strangers. Asking Scottie for scuttlebutt, he'd just shrugged his shoulders and mumbled something about standard operating procedure. Obvious red flag. *Scottie knew something he wouldn't tell.* Sailors and Marines always gossiped about everything. This quiet made him nervous, suggesting deep, dark, shoot-you-in-the-head-if-you-talk secrets. Or very bad things in the offing.

As he kept an eye on his console, it suddenly hit him. Unlike the older equipment in the manor's control center, here he had a new fleet-standard station. Trying out some of the enhanced capabilities, he found himself able to zero in on various parts of the battle, something the manor's equipment couldn't easily do. *This must be how God sees the battlefield.* The screen gave him unbelievable range and definition with silver, red, and black icons on the lilac-colored screen. He loved working on this upgraded machine!

Two hours into his shift, he'd become fully engrossed watching Seventh Fleet surround the enemy, executing a classic englobement. When a force found itself overmatched, it had better run. For the attacker, creating a sphere of fire around that force prevented the smaller force from leaving, while allowing for destruction in detail by coordinating fire from all ships in the larger group for maximum effect. On the other hand, chasing a fleeing force pitted the small, fast ships of the pursuers against the slow, heavy ships of the pursued; not a good match. Small, fast ships could also get away while the big ships acted as a roadblock, but catching and surrounding a smaller force could be done.

Almost forgetting their need to remain silent, he and Bettis exchanged excited glances, coming close to cheering the action as if they were at a sporting event, instead of witnessing the actual deaths of thousands. Corvettes and frigates, silver like the other fleet icons, harried and wounded the major enemy units in red, delaying them and slowing their acceleration as the larger fleet units caught up with and surrounded the intruders.

The major ships remained outside missile range, but not the frigates and corvettes. To slow down the enemy's drives, they needed to come almost into range of the enemy's anti-missiles.

A truly aggressive commander might employ his combat shuttles, which were short-legged but very fast, in a system like this. Whoever commanded this attack force had clearly decided to throw everything at the defenders, making the action thrilling and foolhardy but essential. Without risking so many lives, he wouldn't have a chance to create an englobement.

All defense modules tried, generally not effectively, to translate communications within the opposing fleets. Hugh's station reported its progress in a sidebar as Battle Group 7-3 (Heavy) tried to maneuver the opposition into a sack without the benefit of them responding to any inquiries as of yet. Frustratingly, only class and type of the attackers' ships showed on his screen, but not who they were. Suddenly, an aspect change reduced electronic security on the fleeing force, bringing up enough info to allow a determination of who these strangers really were. He intently began an analysis and comparison of known fleet units that were now part of rebellious groups.

"What are you doing, Cascade? You're going to get us in trouble!" Bettis hissed.

He ignored her. Behind him, he heard a gasp. Hugh watched as a ship identification popped up on his screen. *Adelon.* The name screamed at him. Nova *Adelon* belonged to—in fact, *led*—Task group 1-12. Prime Fleet anchored those loyal to the empire and this battle group should have been leading the protection of the Protest Star Group. What just happened? One of the strongest and most important parts of Prime Fleet couldn't be out here!

Hugh had been keeping half an eye on Seventh Fleet's communication traffic because it made him feel like part of the action or even out there running the show himself. Three seconds after the ship IDs downloaded, the task group's communication code changed, locking out Hugh as well as *Adelon*, from knowing Seventh Fleet's plans. Hugh smacked the console.

In shock, Hugh realized Seventh Fleet had used a private code! Fingers flying, he began running a diagnostic to see if he could decrypt some of the information flow. His station locked down as he entered the final command to begin the diagnostic. Looking around, he saw Lieutenant Commander Morrell headed his way. Red hair flaming as if she were on fire, her green eyes appeared to be lasers aimed right at him. He hated coming to her attention.

Now I'm in for it. Fleetingly, he wondered why.

"What are you two doing?" Her over-loud tone ensured everyone looked at them.

Hugh braced to attention in his seat. "Bettis had nothing to do with it, ma'am. I enabled the console code diagnostic mode so I could continue reading the traffic, ma'am!"

"Were you ordered to do that?!" Morrell demanded even more loudly.

"No, ma'am! Trying to stay ahead of the tactical situation, ma'am!" He needed to act like a bright new penny whenever she addressed him. She seemed to delight in dropping demerits on him whenever he didn't. Plus, as commander of the navy detachment, she would endorse, or veto, his request for commission at the end of his cadet tour.

"Are you aware that, if you break the fleet's code, the intruders might, and I reiterate might, piggyback on your work, thereby reading our internal traffic? They may already know what we are saying because our codes are similar. They could analyze our new codes based upon our traffic with the fleet and break it." Hugh paled. His actions had almost betrayed his side to the enemy.

She turned to the screen, hands behind her back, shoulders pensive. "These ships won't get away. But, sure as Earth is lost and can't be found, they will have a ship hiding out that will take all intel they can get back to their headquarters."

Pivoting back toward Hugh, she continued with a minor sigh. "So, think! It is not a good idea to help the other side, even accidentally. I didn't want you on this board tonight, but certain people insisted." Her eyes flicked toward Ward standing quietly to one side. "Said Barry had earned his pay for the week, staying at the manor and leading the fight there, as if doing your duty should cut you any slack. But here you are, so measure up!"

Hugh judged that being told who would be manning which boards, much more so than his troublesome initiative, had kicked off her tirade. No matter, a warning sign flashed brilliant orange in his mind indicating utmost caution; no clowning, no subtle jabs allowed. "Yes, ma'am!"

Morrell's eyes narrowed, judging his response, obviously weighing it for a smart-mouth factor. "At ease, Cascade. Back to work. You, too, Bettis."

In unison, they answered, "Aye, aye, ma'am."

As Morrell wandered away, Bettis murmured, "Idiot."

Hugh felt grateful things hadn't turned out worse because Bettis and Morell were right. Being relieved from duty as a cadet could likely be the death knell for his hopes of being commissioned. As he returned to analyzing his screen, he noted that Seventh Fleet had sent out a general band call to the intruders to surrender, even before any major fleet units had fired at them. He wondered why? These marauders had attacked using a nuke, making them outlaws. They would be hanged if they surrendered, so why should they? Their response didn't surprise him: a full missile salvo from the major units. He saw that all of the ships had now shifted from local control of their own anti-missile defenses to an interlaced grid, preventing missiles from getting through. *Smart move.* Then he noticed something else odd going on out there. His board reported a bleed picked up from a light speed com laser caught by a sloop. The transmission seemed to be organized strangely.

Hugh frowned as he ran a diagnostic. The message time stamp preceded the firing by the main body of enemy ships by 2.5 seconds. Why were they the ones reacting to the code? He back-traced to the sender. It had originated from a cruiser on the fringe trying to edge out and escape, 2.5 light-seconds away from the main ships.

He hit an attention signal to bring back Morrell, although,

after her last visit, he had no desire for more personal time with the commander. An involuntary chill shivered through his core as he chose to bring himself to the attention of higher authority in a battle situation. His call additionally alerted several other stations both here and in the task group. Taking an involuntary breath, he highlighted the cruiser, tagged the intercepted code group, and rapidly entered his conclusion. *Slave commands to major units from this cruiser. Cruiser might be trying to slip out while we are concentrating on fleet action.*

As he looked up, he found Morrell's frozen features staring at him from two feet away. How had she gotten back over here so quickly? Had she been watching him that closely? Inwardly, the single icy shiver turned to something approaching real fear. *She must have been watching me, waiting to pounce.* Bettis came to attention at a rigid brace in her seat.

In a politely curious way, he asked, "Ma'am?"

"Are you sure of this, Cascade?"

"Yes, ma'am. The pattern is unmistakable. Slave commands from that cruiser to the major units."

"You know that slave commands generally go from major units to smaller ones?"

"Yes, ma'am, but there is no doubt these are slave commands. The major units are being run by this subgroup, ma'am."

Leaning over, she ran a quick series of commands on the screen. Concentrating, she ran another set, getting a high-speed review of the last hour of maneuvers. Making an almost unnoticeable nod as she finished, she typed a brief series of commands. Her sure actions impressed Hugh. Whatever his opinion of her failings, she knew her stuff. Her signal brought an acknowledgment from fleet, then nothing more. Morrell nodded again absently but said nothing to Hugh, no praise, no instruction, nothing. She just walked away.

"She is highly irritated. Twelve on a scale of ten," Hugh judged quietly to Bettis. "But then she didn't ream me out. I don't get it."

"Good job, genius. You were just lucky this time. But now she'll really be watching us, so keep your head down."

Shaking his head again, he paid closer attention to the screen. At first, nothing seemed to change. Outgoing flights of missiles, aimed at the enemy's capital ships, kept accelerating, as a few ships, including the mystery cruiser, began to set themselves up to exploit gaps and escape in the mayhem. Suddenly, a pod of missiles skewed toward the cruiser, surprising him. The pod spread out, also targeting the frigates and destroyers in the cruiser's vicinity, blasting through their limited defenses. The best defense for small ships in a fleet action came from being locked into a capital ship's defense grid, or running away, thereby avoiding being identified as a primary target. A flare of energy erupted in the middle of the group, quickly spreading outward before disappearing.

Apparently, being out on the edge and away from the defenses protecting capital ships has its downside, Hugh observed.

All craft around the cruiser disappeared in an instant, wiped clean in a moment of ravening fury. The screen flickered, as it always did in simulations when reporting that much subatomic destruction. On the other hand, all the remaining missiles passed the slaved units without engaging. Hugh raised his eyebrows. Those other missiles reoriented, heading for rendezvous with small craft all around the englobement.

Well, waste not, want not. Especially when you started with so little. Missiles you didn't use now would be available later. Seventh Fleet's defensive network took on the inbound missiles. A few missiles ignored the recall instruction, injuring a nova, while completely obliterating a cruiser and two destroyers covering major ships.

Bettis murmured, "Well, can you believe that?"

Hugh leaned back, a stunned gasp escaping his lips. The remaining attackers were dropping their shields and killing their drives. The battle ended just that quickly, as no missiles followed up the initial exchange after the attacking ships' clear token of surrender.

"What just happened?" Bettis muttered. "Why are these people surrendering? It doesn't make sense." Hugh noticed Morrell grudgingly favored them with a thoughtful look from across the control room before turning away. Bettis slapped him on the arm. "You were right! Good job. That cruiser and its group *did* control the rest of the fleet. But why?"

Hugh shrugged. "No idea." He continued to scan for anomalies throughout the solar system.

Excitedly, Bettis said, "Look there! I've got something."

One of the anomalies on their consoles flamed to life! A ship slipped from behind a gas giant before accelerating for deep space. Throughout the fleet, alarms went out, but no one appeared to be in position to give chase. A solar system, being a very large place, provided lots of hiding places, after all. He hit the console hard, a sour look on his face. He should have caught it first, and early enough to put someone in position to stop the courier.

"One for you, Bettis."

Smugly, she grinned at him. "We're even now. Let's see who gets the next point."

He felt irritated and good at the same time; irritated that she had found the next one, but happy about their success. He smiled back and said, "You're on."

His console noted a message from the task group on narrow beam going to a blank area of space. Concentrating on the target area of the message, he noticed a shimmer, then nothing. He logged the shimmer and ran another diagnostic. Nothing wrong. Another mystery his tired brain couldn't sort out.

That shimmer could only come with firing up an anti-preon drive, but his board didn't show any ships in the vicinity. Tightening up the focus from wide scan to narrow, he reran the shimmer's data back through his console at half speed. Now he didn't see just one large shimmer but five small ones, none of which would have grabbed his attention by themselves. Forwarding the info to Commander Morrell, he whispered from the side of his mouth to Bettis, "My game. Found another one."

Bettis bit her lip. "Fine, Cascade, you win today." He smiled. Tactics being his game, he carried out his duties through the end of the shift in only a light fog.

Walking off duty toward the mess to get a bite together, he caught a motion in the corner of his eye. Turning his head slightly, he saw Morrell giving them another thoughtful look. Potentially not good, but what could he do about it? Just doing his duty. As they entered the mess, Bettis waved at a group of cadets at a long table. "You'll never guess what Cascade did to get Morrell's attention this time," she called cheerfully. The anticipatory looks and catcalls from his fellow cadets normally would have revved him up, but his lack of sleep had suddenly caught up with him. Grabbing a sandwich, he said, "I'm beat. See you later." Bettis gave him an inscrutable look. *Is she annoyed I'm leaving?*

Heading wearily down the corridor toward the berths, he unhappily saw Ward loitering at his door. Ward straightened from his slouch in a single fluid motion as Hugh approached, then motioned for Hugh to follow him. Hugh fell in.

Suddenly Morrell's explanation as to why she put him on the board instead of Barry hit him, starting a blinding chain of understanding. Actions by estate personnel, unusual and out of the chain of the command, became clear. Then those anomalies niggling at his subconscious for some time fell into place.

No matter what happened, Ward always seemed to be more in charge of the estate's military than any of the officers nominally assigned. Their commands often sounded like suggestions when directed toward Ward. On the other hand, his suggestions were always treated by the recipient as orders, officers included. Mystified by this observation, he put it aside for later reflection.

Ward rarely said much except when Hugh screwed up. He always seemed to be there, just in the background, terse, succinct, and specific in his comments. On only a few memorable occasions had Ward truly exploded, expressing his disgust with having been cursed with the misfortune of associating with such a lower-level life-form impersonating a cadet such as one Mr. Cascade.

After the last time, Hugh had promised himself to try very hard not to bring himself to Ward's attention again in quite that same way. It *had* been a prank. Nothing too serious, he thought. He'd arranged for a skunk to set off the intruder alarm in the alert platoon barracks. A little over the top as far as most pranks went, but not life-threatening, just smelly. But afterward, Ward explained in excruciating detail what could happen should an attack have occurred with the alert platoon off-line. The potential consequences for the estate, should the duty platoon be delayed in carrying out its assigned tasks, could have easily been catastrophic.

The memory of his spectacular crash of a ground speeder brought another involuntary shiver. First, somehow he had escaped certain death or dismemberment by the merest thread of fate. Then, an icy, enraged Ward stood him tall before tearing a bloody strip from his hide. Ward's precise stiletto-like phrases regarding Hugh's disgracing Doña Carlota and his training had laid him open like a carving knife. He still remembered the words cutting deep, how he didn't deserve the energy and nutrition his existence consumed that would have been better employed growing amoebas or even viruses. However, Ward's certainty of the shame his deceased parents undoubtedly felt in the afterlife from his lack of self-control and Ward's own disgust with training such an utter black hole in the grand scheme of things had cut the deepest.

Ward considered recklessness and stupidity intolerable. That ten minutes had seemed like an eternity, and he still recalled, vividly, almost every single one of Ward's words. He felt Ward might have gone over the top with that particular tongue-lashing. Admittedly he *might* have been going a little fast for the road and conditions; one hundred forty-five kilometers per hour in a fifty zone, actually, about ninety-five kph over the limit in that mountainous area. But he had driven *almost* that fast there before. And he *had* been in control! Mostly. Then, coming around a curve, a strange shimmy had begun, and then the undercarriage had come apart, sending him hurtling into space. So, really, it hadn't been his fault. Luckily, the speeder had come down more or less right side up, and he had then managed to slalom to the bottom of the canyon despite the foam and airbags doing their best to keep him from controlling the car.

Ward knocked on a hatch as they reached the command suite, interrupting his woolgathering. It suddenly registered on Hugh where Ward had brought him. *Oh no! I've really done it this time.* The door slid open, followed by a peremptory, "Come," ordering them in.

The Core Empire

Part IX

Following the federalizing of the empire by Charles Roland in 3308 during the Reconquest (see Chapter 27), the transition of power upon the deaths of the immediately following emperors remained relatively tranquil, as opposed to the legitimacy disputes between the descendants of Crystal, Yvonne, and Elsie in Chapter 9 and the series of assassinations in Chapter 24.

That changed with Benjamin's ascension in 3380. A descendant from the house of Elsie Paracletes, the surviving daughter of Joe Jackson, he carried out a campaign to destroy all potential rivals. Chapter 30 gives indications of how the test began breaking down, as well as how Benjamin sowed the seeds for the coup of 3463.

12

Volunteering

Fleet Emergency Command Complex, Jeffco
0820 Local/0220 10 October 3473

CADET HUGH CASCADE CAME TO PERFECT ATTENTION behind an empty chair at the foot of the onyx table. A surge of adrenaline shot through him as he evaluated the scene in front of him. Holograms occupied all but three of the seats around the space-black table, Doña Carlota Gonzalvez y Rodriguez del Castillo and Sergeant Major Ward being the other two live participants. The projections of naval officers filled eleven of the fifteen seats, a Marine general and an army brigadier sat in the other two. He knew he had screwed up, but did they need to embarrass him in front of so many officers.

"Cadet Hugh Cascade reporting, sir," he barked out as he saluted the head of the table and the flag. Nothing else gave any color to the otherwise bland room. Doña Carlota sat in the chair to his right and Ward settled into the chair to his left.

For an instant, Hugh focused on the flag hanging on the wall behind where the admiral's hologram appeared to be seated. A green and blue orb occupied its center, which most people thought of as Earth, surrounded by a golden corona. A tall and narrow four-pointed star edged in purple ran from the top to the bottom. The crimson of the St. Andrew's cross ran from the corners behind the star. A black field spangled with constellations, each constellation representing a sector, completed the flag.

The hologram at the head of the table broke Hugh's concentration on the flag. "Let's start this properly, in light of what we are here to do. Junior man leads us in the Creed."

Hugh identified the speaker as Admiral George Hollister, a leonine man, blond and tanned, with a huge frame, the man trying to keep back the tide of darkness in Seventh Sector.

As a cadet, Hugh served under him, so far beneath his lofty and exalted status that he had never seen him before, other than in videos. The possibility that his actions might have brought him to the attention of the admiral almost terrified him.

The sergeant major's bark broke Hugh's train of thought, "Cadet? The Creed!"

They all stood as automatic reflexes kicked in. He barked out the Creed, one part at a time to allow the others to repeat it after him, "Protection . . . Integrity . . . Judgment . . . Justice . . . Sacrifice . . . Virtue . . . TO THE DEATH!"

Hollister, reseating himself, shook his head. "Doña Carlota, you chose a Marine to train him. Why?"

Ward snorted with amusement at the admiral's comment. *Bad Idea, laughing at an admiral.* Doña Carlota answered the admiral, "As you know, Admiral, no proctor may serve for more than five years at a time, so they don't become overly attached to their charges, in the event the test . . . goes badly. Sergeant Daniels exceeded that, as you may recall. When it became clear that Daniels had grown too close to his charge to perform his duties any longer, you told me to pick the best. Having personally suffered the ministrations of Sergeant Major Ward, beginning as a naval lieutenant, I just thought it seemed like the best option, seeing how I turned out. Plus, we couldn't find anyone else to replace Daniels. The training program has . . . lagged."

What in the starless dark is a proctor? Hugh focused on Doña Carlota, watching her expression as Hollister spoke. Hugh's survival might depend on some minor nuance of the situation, so he paid the same kind of attention he would on the hunt. He noted that Doña Carlota's face remained perfectly bland and mild.

Surprised, this alerted Hugh to the fact that, first, Admiral George Hollister, Seventh Fleet, Commanding, in no way intimidated Doña Carlota and, second, that she seemed truly amused by the admiral's question, a small smile tugging at the corner of her mouth. This thoroughly confused Hugh. Doña Carlota and the admiral must be old and good friends to talk to each other like this. He couldn't figure out what all this meant nor had he any idea why either of them wanted him here. The proctor comment should have given him a clue, but he simply couldn't make any sense of it.

A commander down the table, someone much too junior to normally speak amidst such high-ranking company, much less commit lèse-majesté, shook his head. "Please, Doña Carlota. Once a Marine, always a Marine?" Hugh realized all of these people knew and had good relations with Doña Carlota, which made Hugh readjust, radically, his opinion of her importance to the empire.

His focus on Doña Carlota broke when, out of the corner of his eye, he saw Ward nod firmly before saying, "Oorah."

They all laughed at Ward's response while shaking their heads. Before the laughter died out, however, Admiral Hollister cut through the noise, "Put Mister Cascade at ease, Sergeant Major, and seat him at the table so we can take care of this business."

Hugh's view of reality barely began processing the fact that the sergeant major belonged at the table just as much as Doña Carlota when Ward ordered, "Cadet Cascade, at ease and be seated."

Hugh sat but did not relax. He knew that, when the hammer fell this time, it would really hurt. Could trying to decode Seventh Fleet communications have been that big a deal? Could he be tried for treason? Did his failure to log out before the attack merit this kind of attention? What about his noticing the stealth ships? These all seemed minor, in the extreme, something a few extra hours of guard duty would resolve, nothing a sector commander should ever be concerned with. He held himself straight and still, a model of polite and focused interest in the proceedings. He allowed nothing of his internal turmoil to show; he had his pride. *No matter what, you show a strong face, all the way to the firing squad.*

Looking right at Hugh, Hollister announced, "Before we get started, Mister Cascade, I wanted to compliment you for the good work you did spotting those slave codes. A couple of other ships caught it also, but good work, nonetheless."

Hugh felt a little better getting that commendation from the admiral.

Admiral Hollister turned to Ward. "Well, Sergeant Major?"

"He's old enough to know the truth, I think, George," Ward confirmed confidently.

Several of those present looked concerned, Vice Admiral Duong Ngaio certainly appearing to harbor disagreement with Ward's assessment. *Of me?* But most, Hugh judged, were leaning forward, barely suppressed excitement evident in their faces and postures.

Doña Carlota interjected, "I agree, Admiral." Hugh saw her give Ward a warning look that seemed to have remarkably little effect on the sergeant major. Shock coursed through Hugh when Ward grinned back at Doña Carlota, who added, "And, really, Top, calling him *George*?"

Ward shot back somewhat smugly, "Doña Carlota, you know that George and I have known each other since he wore a single gold bar and my duty consisted of keeping him alive during piracy patrols. Besides which, as an heir's proctor, I am somewhat out of the regular chain of command."

Hugh's mental antenna went up. *Heirs have proctors? Good to know. The sergeant major being one of them also raises interesting questions: I wonder who his heir could be? It's not Noor Bettis, she's from outside the empire, but could it be Liz Polchar? Probably not, she's rarely around Ward. None of the other students either. One of the other cadets? Wouldn't they know if they were a prince or princess or whatever you call an heir? It certainly can't be me. The way he's treated me the last ten years, it's obvious I'm not an imperial prince!*

Hollister shook his head with a mournful look on his face. "I can see by Mister Cascade's confused look that neither the irrepressible Sean Ward nor the tight-lipped Doña Carlota has explained anything to him, so we should do that before we go any further." Gazing straight at Ward, the admiral went on with a frown, "I would have preferred for him to come to the meeting with some idea of why, but he has been, as we noted earlier, in the care of a Marine. Marines, after all, need to have things explained to them in small words and great detail."

Ward's grin disappeared. "Kept him safe while the whole galaxy tried to kill him," he muttered loud enough for Hugh to hear. Ward apparently found nothing amusing in the admiral's little witticism. Hugh wondered what they were supposed to have told him. It seemed preposterous, all this talk about heirs and proctors.

Without answering Ward, Hollister nodded at his adjutant.

The hologram, a Commander Friedman, stood. "Sergeant Major of the Imperial Marines, Sean Ward, you are ordered to perform the duty of Proctor to the Heir Apparent and carry out the test as of this date if the heir agrees to the test. By order of the Imperial Chief of Staff, Doña Carlota Gonzalvez y Rodriguez del Castillo, Companion and Protector of the Succession, Order of Earth, Vice Lord of Sector Seven."

Ward now held himself rigid, radiating anger. "You two sandbagged me! I thought we were just going to let him know the reason for the attack so he could protect himself. I *agreed* that he is ready to know. I do *not* think he is ready for the test yet," he barked. Hugh couldn't help himself, he wanted to keep facing front, but almost involuntarily turned to stare at Ward. Ward looked as angry as he'd ever seen him; he didn't even try to hide it. Glancing around the table, he saw several of those there, including the vice admiral, clearly showing their displeasure with Ward's response, although most of the others were keeping their expressions guarded.

Admiral Hollister chided, "You should have added a *sir* to the end of that sentence, Sergeant Major." Then completely serious, he went on, "I understand your concerns, Sean, but what choices do we have? The first indications point to this raid having one purpose, kill Mister Cascade. I would like there to have been more time to prepare him, but as someone from Earth named Napoleon once said, 'Ask anything of me but time,' so here we are. What other options do we have, Sean? Hide him again?" It almost sounded to Hugh as if the admiral really did want Ward's agreement before going forward.

The raiders attacked because of me? Impossible! Ward got his anger under control and slowly nodded in reluctant agreement, while Doña Carlota gave a palms-up gesture and shrugged.

Hugh noted that the others all nodded their consent to whatever the admiral planned to do. Agreement became unanimous when the sour vice admiral also nodded. Hugh's confusion turned to dread. What couldn't possibly be true might just be fact.

Hollister smiled, if a little grimly, before leaning forward toward Hugh, "Right. Now all we have to do is tell the guest of honor what he just got volunteered for."

Those around the table dutifully chuckled at the admiral's somewhat poor joke. Ward didn't laugh, and Doña Carlota just wore a pained expression. Hugh didn't feel like laughing at the joke either, at least not until he knew what the admiral intended to do with him. Picking sides, he decided to stay silent with Ward and Doña Carlota.

Hollister pointed back at Doña Carlota, who nodded before standing. Facing Hugh, he addressed him. "Hugh—Your Highness," she said, "I, as well as others here, are guilty of not being completely truthful with you. Like millions of others, some around this table, you are descended from the House of Jackson. However, in part because of your father, Warlord Trevor Cascade, and for other reasons we do not know, the Guardian Program chose you at birth as a potential heir, along with a few hundred others over the last fifty years. Following an heir's selection, a special nanite package is implanted. Only those who have been implanted can take the test or become emperor or empress. Unfortunately, during the coup, most of the Guardian facilities on Harwell were destroyed and no additional heirs can be implanted. As far as we can tell, the majority of those others who have received the nanite package are dead. Those two facts told us there were individuals still working in the fleet for the other side. To protect you, we have kept secret the truth of who you really are."

Your Highness? The universe has officially gone crazy.

Over the last ten years, Sergeant Major Ward had trained Hugh hard to hide his thoughts and feelings. Among other experiences, Hugh had traded with nomads for life essentials while on survival treks, played cards with some of the sharpest poker players on the estate, as well the planet, and thanks to Pete Peterson, he had even found himself in extremely awkward social circumstances involving young women and very protective guardians with sharp knives. That had led to Hugh learning to keep a cool head and straight face at all times. Always.

But his poker face almost broke down in the face of such a ridiculous idea. Fighting to keep his jaw from dropping, he took a large breath and said, in a reasonably calm tone, "Really? Go on."

Although focused on Doña Carlota when he answered, he noted from the corner of his eye that Hollister seemed to be amused by something.

Doña Carlota explained, "Well, Your Highness, you are still Hugh Cascade, but we kept from you the rest of the information regarding your past. To our knowledge, you are the only surviving great, great-nephew of Emperor Esau Manuel, the predecessor to Emperor Cyrus. Your mother and Cyrus' wife, Sythia, were sisters, grandnieces of Esau Manuel. Your father, Trevor Cascade, was a fifteenth great-grandson of Emperor Allan."

"Nephew to an emperor and a however-many-greats grandson to another?" Hugh asked, trying to follow the list of ancestors and relatives.

"Yes. Following the murder of his wife and family, Emperor Cyrus almost constantly worried about the succession. He insisted, from that point on, that several heirs be kept in safe locations during public events, with their assigned proctors and security. At the time of the coup attempt, the Succession Council chose to send you off-planet on a fishing trip with your proctor and security team, while your father attended the session of the Lords."

Deft! The smell of fresh-caught fish cooking and the sound of soft wind in the trees came back to Hugh. And more . . . but he quickly shut down that memory.

Doña Carlota didn't pause, "Twelfth Sector and some of the other fleets were not responding to imperial communications and your father thought Quadros responsible. He claimed to be part of something called the Restitution Movement. A woman—a very young woman at the time—called Morgain uch Roberts, appeared publicly as the leader of the group, but we all questioned if that were true, given her age. She has since taken effective control of Ninth Sector, causing us all to reevaluate our estimates of her abilities. She even tried presenting a false heir, which blew up in her face. And ours, unfortunately. She keeps trying to expand, but so far with no luck. Gene Perdot now calls himself an admiral and has made a mess of Sixth Sector and Vice Admiral Garrison Traynor has more ships than our loyal forces in Thirteenth Sector, but it's something of a stalemate. These are the biggest individual problems, but the other sectors not under loyalist control are also nightmares.

"As you know, Quadros' ordered his fleet, including one Prime Fleet cruiser he had suborned, to attack Beacon, and started the coup to avoid trial, but he didn't act alone. Cunning but stupid, he couldn't possibly have put the coup together by himself, which is why his actions pretty clearly blindsided his friends as well as us. He didn't even have a decent escape planned. We gathered lots of information on the coup after Davies and Prime Fleet wiped Quadros off the face of the map and captured the data core of the cruiser that had picked him up. He died on the cruiser that had delivered the kinetic strike on the Imperial Palace. After he died, his chief of staff, Miroslav Kučera, took the remainder back to Twelfth Sector and hunkered down. He controls the sector but Kučera doesn't seem to be interested in spreading out or working with the others, so we're leaving him alone for the time being." Old grief bled through Doña Carlota's recital. Hugh couldn't remember ever seeing such pain on her face before, this woman who apparently had sacrificed everything to protect him.

Admiral Hollister leaned forward, causing the leading edge of his hologram to fuzz and disappear, and continued, "You probably don't remember much because you were so young." His narrative of Deft brought it all back, though. Flashbacks of a whole planet dying in the coup because of him overwhelmed his mind. Ward and Doña Carlota had defended him there, along with a Marine battalion and Sergeant Daniels. After Deft, when the nightmares came, Sergeant Daniels had been there, always ready to comfort him. He knew Daniels understood because he had stayed with him while almost everyone he knew, and hundreds of Marines he didn't, died just to keep him alive. At that moment, the memories threatened to engulf him in remembered terror.

Hugh reflected on Doña Carlota and the grief on her face. Her entire family had died in the coup, but she couldn't have been sure, not at first, that they were all dead. Strange things happened in combat, like eight-year-old boys surviving a planetary bombardment followed by a ground onslaught. Doña Carlota had stayed with him, done her duty even as her heart must have been breaking. Tears prickled at the edges of Hugh's eyes. *And Ward, too. Daniels had told him, years after Deft, how Ward had lost is wife and son, also.*

Hugh fought back the tears. He couldn't let anyone know he wanted to cry like a child, like he had when they'd told him he'd never see his father again. Hugh examined the admiral, really seeing him as a man for the first time, then looked searchingly at Ward and Doña Carlota, realizing at least some of the sacrifice these men and this woman had suffered on his behalf.

Hollister concluded, voice a bit husky, "Since then, as far as we know, every other heir has either been hunted down, gone missing, or died attempting to pass the test to become the new emperor, hoping to reestablish good order in the empire. More than a dozen men and several women have tried and failed."

Hollister let it sink in for a minute. So, what did they want from him? Did they really think he could succeed where so many had failed? The admiral didn't leave him in doubt for long. "Cadet Hugh Cascade, you are the only remaining heir we believe can take the test and restore the empire. If you accept this burden, Doña Carlota and Sergeant Major Ward will give you more information. If you decline, no one will blame you or hold it against you. It has to be your decision, taken freely. We'll give you twenty-four hours to consider it." Ward stood and the other holograms did also.

That quickly, the meeting ended. His mind raced. *What to do?* He felt the weight of the decision they had just placed squarely on his shoulders.

Suddenly, he jumped to his feet and stood at attention, startling everyone in the room. "I don't need twenty-four hours, sir," he stated firmly. "I'll take the test."

Hollister's image remained rock steady, examining Hugh closely. Hugh couldn't remember ever being under such intense scrutiny before in his life, not by Klostermann, not by Ward, not even by Doña Carlota. He stood silently, proudly, gazing back into the admiral's eyes. After an eternal moment, Hollister stood in the hologram. "Hail the heir, Hugh Cascade," Hollister trumpeted, saluting with his right fist over his heart.

The others joined him, repeating, "Hail the heir, Hugh Cascade." Their salutes, with looks ranging from exhilaration to tentative hope on their faces, were firm. They began clapping, even the sour vice admiral, Ngaio. Hugh felt a sudden surge of emotion, not knowing what to say. They thought he could do it and were placing their lives in his hands, he realized.

Hollister broke through the noise, "Your Highness, we'll meet again tomorrow at this hour. We need time to prepare a plan to support your test. Is that satisfactory, Your Highness?"

Momentarily flustered, Hugh nodded. "That will be fine. Tomorrow at six hundred."

"And people," the admiral went on, "keep this secret."

A chorus of, "Aye," answered him. The holograms congratulated Hugh one by one before leaving. He noted that the three women present, as well as some of the men, appeared to have tears running down their cheeks or glistening in their eyes. After a few minutes, only Doña Carlota and Ward were left.

Galactifacts for Kids 3500

Nanite technology. At the far end of the technological spectrum from terraforming are the miniature machines that make much of our world possible. They are used for everything from utility maintenance of our cities to safety. Medbots are used in limited situations to repair serious injury and medical problems. They read the genetic code of the patient and stimulate proper healing.

Commobots help keep children safe as tracers and let the elderly call for help in emergencies. A simple archeon signal pings off the individual code of the person's archeonC commobots that answer with the person's location. Both are installed by a simple injection.

They are even used by the military for their uniforms. Camouflage has been used since before space flight and the first chameleon skin uniforms were in use before the first interstellar flight in 2077, but nanotech made camouflage so effective when introduced in 2109 that the military has abandoned all other methods for making themselves unseen. Uniforms are impregnated with nanites that together act as a supercomputer to read the light frequencies coming from various directions. They then emit a simulated pass-through light, creating the illusion that there is no one there.

13

The Oath

Fleet Emergency Command Complex, Jeffco

0855 Local/0255 10 October 3473 AD

HUGH CASCADE TURNED TO LEAVE, BUT Doña Carlota placed a hand on his arm, stopping him. "Please administer the Oath before we leave, Sergeant Major," she requested formally.

Sean Ward thought for a moment before replying, "Ma'am, the charge is normally done in private, just the proctor and his or her heir should be present."

"But I am the protector of the succession, so I know about not only the charge but the fact that Hugh will now receive it. If Hugh needs to ask any questions, I can answer them for him. Besides which, I'm the closest thing he has to a parent since the warlord died ten years ago." Doña Carlota's tone remained reasonable, but Hugh judged it would be easier to budge the mountain they were sitting under than get her to change her mind.

Ward responded with perfect outward calm, that hallmark of every high-ranking NCO, but Hugh could almost feel him deciding exactly what he should do. Nodding, Ward asked simply, "The Oath Ceremony can be potentially dangerous to anyone in the room, even the heir and proctor. Are you sure you want to be present?"

Doña Carlota shrugged urbanely. "I've been living on borrowed time for ten years. Please proceed."

Uncharacteristically, Sergeant Major Ward formally faced Doña Carlota, bowed, and stated firmly, "Do you fully accept the risk to yourself that your presence may cause?"

Doña Carlota responded in a similarly firm voice, "I do so accept the responsibility." Sinking back into her chair, she asked a bit impatiently, "Can we begin now, please?"

Ward's hard-planed face gave away nothing of his inner feelings as he turned back to Hugh and brought out a curious-looking bag. It didn't look like wool or cotton or any synthetic material he recognized; it seemed almost alive. As he watched, it constantly but subtly changed shape and color. It didn't even seem to have an opening but appeared to be a completely closed sphere. Speaking now to Hugh, Ward formally began, "Hugh Cascade, remain standing." Hugh suddenly felt apprehensive. Slowly, he came to attention, not sure of the proper etiquette in this situation. "Hugh Cascade, being the heir apparent, only known living heir in the line of succession to the Throne of Constantine, Emperor of Beacon and the Core Empire, you are about to embark upon the Test of Heirs. Do you swear on your honor to keep everything you are about to hear confidential? Access to this information is limited to those who embark on this test and those administering it."

What have I gotten myself into? After a moment, Hugh took a breath before stating firmly, "I do so promise."

Ward smiled briefly. "Thank you. The purpose of the test is to determine if you are worthy to occupy the Throne of Constantine and to rule the Core Planets. If you succeed, you will receive the Galactic Starburst. You have seen pictures of Emperor Cyrus wearing a large, jeweled representation of the galaxy on his left breast; that was the Galactic Starburst."

"Different from traditional gems, those in the Galactic Starburst have a joint function. When in physical contact with the emperor or empress, such as if a hand is placed on it, it acts as a master key to all ship and planetary defenses. The Galactic Starburst's signature is hardwired into every ship's and every planet's command-and-control systems. If someone were to attempt to cut off communication or take the system off-line without proper authorization, a series of fail-safes would activate with consequences designed to ensure any such attempts not only didn't succeed but that those attempting it never tried again. Because the attacking ships were not stopped cold the day of the coup, we know he did not activate the Galactic Starburst. Why, we don't know. Regardless, only the emperor can alter the consequences."

Hugh's eyebrows went up. "Consequences?"

Ward nodded. "There are multiple levels built-in, ranging from crippling a ship to shutting down life support to full autodestruct. For a planet-based facility, they include temporarily shutting down a planet's power grid to generating an electromagnetic pulse that would do more permanent damage. In extremis, planetary defense systems can be used against the rebellious forces, effectively turning their own weapons on them and laying waste to the planet."

Hugh's mouth hung open. He suddenly realized how much planning must have been done, and how many traitors enlisted, to execute the original attack to ensure the throne remained empty. *The rebellion must reach the highest levels of the government. Food for thought. For later.*

Ward waited a moment, allowing Hugh to digest what he'd just been told. Then he asked, "Do you wish to proceed?"

Hugh didn't pause, saying without hesitation, "I do."

Ward nodded his acceptance. "To pass the test, you must prove your worthiness and understanding of what it means to rule. Recite the Imperial Creed."

Hugh momentarily froze. The Imperial Creed? He had been reciting it almost mindlessly since age twelve and just led it minutes ago, and now he couldn't remember it at all. He felt himself flush and then suddenly, like an involuntary muscle reflex, said loudly, "Pro—Protection, Integrity, Judgment, Justice, Sacrifice, Virtue, to the Death!" Hugh could have sworn Ward almost smiled as he finished. Almost.

Waspishly, Doña Carlota commented, "Couldn't you have taught him to do that in a more normal volume when there are just a few people present? My ears are ringing."

Ward gave Doña Carlota a severe look. "He did it the way Marines do it. The right way. No further comments will be permitted."

Doña Carlota looked like she wanted to add another comment; in fact, she appeared as if she could barely contain herself. In Hugh's experience, Doña Carlota *never* denied herself the pleasure of expressing any of her valuable opinions. Returning his gaze to the sergeant major, Hugh realized that the bag or sack, or whatever, now lay open on the table, flat as if made that way. But this oddity barely registered as he took in the seven objects lying on the cloth. Seven exquisite, breathtaking gems lay jumbled together. The sergeant major waited patiently as Hugh examined the beautiful gems lying before him. Finally, Hugh glanced up at the sergeant major's impassive face.

"Hugh Cascade. The seven gems you see before you represent the Creed you have just recited. Each is impregnated with nanites programmed specifically for you. As you pass each portion of the test, you will receive the nanogem it represents and complete activation of the nanites it carries. Only you or I may ever handle the gems and you only when given them by me. If you handle them at any other time or if any other person does, that person will die, killed by the nanites. Do you understand this restriction?"

Hugh thought about that a minute before nodding in agreement. "One question, Sergeant Major. Why can you handle the bag with the gems?"

"The nanites on the bag are attuned to the proctor; in your case, me."

Another question, unbidden, entered his mind. *Why do I need something that will kill me or somebody else even by accident?*

Ward continued, answering unasked questions, "The nanites in the gems are integral to the functioning of the Galactic Starburst. They interface with the biological nanites with which you were injected at birth. They are deadly to any unauthorized person who tries to use the Galactic Starburst."

I've got nanites in me? Hugh's head spun with the realization that he had been a part of the succession since birth.

Ward didn't wait for Hugh to come to terms with the idea of miniature robots running around in his body. "A new Galactic Starburst must be manufactured because the coup destroyed the last one. Originally the emperor used the one handed down from Dave, Constantine's son. That one disappeared when the Qabal invaded. Charles Roland replaced it with a new Galactic Starburst brought back from a secure manufacturing facility."

"The gems, once paired with a specific emperor or empress, remain active only until the moment of his or her death, at which point they deactivate and, upon removal from the starburst, self-destruct and are reduced to slag. They are replaced by the gems of the new monarch. A Galactic Starburst cannot be activated until after you qualify and the nanites on the gems interface with your nanites. The gems can then be placed in their proper places in the starburst by you and you alone.

"One more thing about the Galactic Starburst: it activates or deactivates all imperial ships and installations, specifically their shield, weapons, and propulsion systems, through Trojan horse codes hidden in these programs. Before you ask, the codes are virtually undetectable due to the immense size of onboard programs. However, these hidden programs are not infallible. Given enough time, programmers undoubtedly could find and bypass our codes, so you should only enable the code when loyal units can take immediate control, unless you order the self-destruct."

Hugh's eyes widened at the thought of such terrible responsibility. With a mere keystroke, he could kill hundreds, thousands, maybe millions or more.

Ward went on, "The self-destruct is embedded in the maintenance nanobots essential to the functioning of every imperial ship. They will blow every air lock and warhead. Now, a further word of caution: once the gems are placed, they are still deadly to any other person who touches them. In addition, the nanites, being attuned to the emotions and mind of their carrier, can detect an attempt at manipulation if the bearer knows he is being coerced in any way. The results can be . . . unpredictable, from what I understand. Do you understand and consent?"

It hit Hugh: If he said yes, he agreed to a deadly game with only one of two outcomes possible for him: success or death. If he said no? The empire crumbled but he would live a normal life. The moment stretched, and he could see the tension on Doña Carlota's face grow. But only he could make this decision. He knew, though, he could only give one possible answer and could imagine giving no other. Firmly, he stated, not overly loud, "I do." Doña Carlota sank back into her chair, as though a great weight had been lifted from her, but Ward remained unmoved.

"Pick up the purple amethyst," Ward ordered.

Slowly, Hugh reached out with his right hand to pick up the deadly beauty. He knew—or assumed—it wouldn't harm him, but Ward's warnings about the potential lethality of the gem to others tempered his enthusiasm to touch it.

Hugh's hand paused again briefly over the amethyst before he picked up the clear, deep-purple stone, clutching it in his right hand. A tingling warmth immediately filled his palm before running up into his hand and arm. The soreness from his scraped hand instantly vanished! He realized he couldn't let go of the gem now even if he wanted to. Which he didn't. He and the stone had become melded into one.

Ward spoke firmly, a voice of doom and charge, "As explained, these gems, as well as the bag, are covered in nanites. Only those they are programmed to accept may handle them. The medbots within you protect you and keep you safe, helping to heal you if you are injured or sick. Now, holding the gem in your right hand before you, repeat after me: I will provide Protection to the weak as well as to every citizen."

The words were familiar. The Full Creed or Emperor's Creed vibrated in his chest as he spoke it with a new and more personal meaning, "I will provide Protection to the weak as well as to every citizen."

"Place the gem back on the cloth and take the topaz with your left hand."

Reluctantly, he stretched out his hand toward the bag. That purple gem seemed a special part of him now. He forced his hand open, dropping the amethyst back onto the table. With his left hand, he picked up the topaz. The same amazing warmth now filled his left hand and arm as if it were made of sunshine.

"Holding the gem before you, repeat after me: My word is unquestioned because Integrity is the bedrock of my being."

Confidently now, Hugh recited, "My word is unquestioned because Integrity is the bedrock of my being." He thought he could see the golden glow of the topaz blazing in agreement through the skin of his hand.

"Every citizen, every person in the galaxy, must be able to believe that if you promise protection, you will protect, if you promise destruction, you will destroy. Every word you say must be true. Place the gem back on the cloth and take the sapphire with your right hand."

He replaced the golden stone and picked up the rich royal blue sapphire. But he felt nothing special. Looking up at Ward, he thought he saw a glint of amusement. Why?

"Taking the stone, touch it between your eyes, repeating after me: I seek always to exercise true Judgment in all of my acts."

Carefully placing the stone between his eyes, he felt sudden coolness spread through his forehead, behind his eyes, all the way to his ears. His headache, silently pounding from lack of sleep, seemed to melt away. Speaking confidently, he responded, "I seek always to exercise true Judgment in all of my acts."

"Clearness of sight, depth of understanding, true hearing, all are required to act well. Wisdom is more important than learning. Place the gem back on the cloth and take the emerald with your left hand."

After a moment, he placed the sapphire with the topaz and amethyst, taking the emerald with his hand.

"Taking the stone, touch it briefly to your lips, then repeat after me: I will administer Justice that is stern, fair and impartial, fearing no man's censure, taking no man's gift."

Eager to see how this stone would affect him, he touched his lips with it for a moment. Disappointed, he didn't feel anything different. "I will administer Justice that is stern, fair, and impartial, fearing no man's censure, taking no man's gift."

"Doing what is right is more difficult than knowing what's right. You will often not know if you have acted correctly, or at least not until well after the fact. You must have a deep, securely anchored, sense of right and wrong to judge in the face of dissent and criticism. Be firm, be fair, be consistent. Place the gem back on the cloth and take the ruby with your right hand."

Hugh traded the stones and looked up.

"Taking the ruby, touch it to your shoulder, repeating after me: I fear no Sacrifice necessary to uphold my oath. I will carry every burden of my office, whatever the price."

As he touched it to his shoulder, the bloodred stone seemed to burn him to the very core, searing his flesh! Focusing on Ward, despite the pain bringing tears to his eyes, he spoke, "I fear no Sacrifice necessary to uphold my oath. I will carry every burden of my office, whatever the price."

As he finished speaking, the stone ceased to burn, a strange sensation of strength replacing the pain.

"All burdens exact a price. Know this as you take up this test. They also grant great strength. Place the gem back on the cloth and take the diamond with your right hand also."

Somewhat leery, he wondered what the diamond would do. Not all the stones seemed friendly after the ruby. Nevertheless, picking up the diamond, he happily let go of the sacrifice stone.

"Taking the diamond, touch it to your heart, repeating after me: Perfect Virtue is unattainable, but I will seek it as my goal in all I do."

Almost reluctantly, Hugh placed the diamond over his heart. Suddenly an elation mixed with bottomless sorrow swept through him. He understood! The price and the reward, the reward being worth much more than the price. Each stone's nanites told him how they would help him. "Perfect Virtue is unattainable, but I will seek it as my goal in all I do."

"Virtue brings both deep temporary sadness and overwhelming joy. Whether fearing the sadness or choosing wrongly, either will deny you the joy that knows no description. Place the gem back on the cloth and take the onyx with your left hand."

Hugh wondered what he would learn from this last gem.

"Taking the last stone, hold it in front of you as you would a sword haft, repeating after me: I will fulfill my oath to the citizens of the empire, to the death. So help me God."

"I will fulfill my oath to the citizens of the empire, to the death. So help me God."

Somehow, Hugh knew these nanites would hold him to his promise if he ever sought to betray his oath. Silently, he vowed they would never have to.

"Place the gem back on the cloth."

Hugh did. As he released the onyx, the cloth folded back into a bag. Ward took the bag and put it in his pocket.

"Do not seek the stones until and unless I release them back to you. They will kill you if you do. Do you understand?"

"I understand," Hugh answered firmly. As he stated his understanding, he felt the strength he gained from the nanites begin to ebb away, returning him to where and who he had been just a few minutes before, almost. He understood, he must carry out the test without them. Most of life would be like that, he guessed. Help always near but hidden.

Doña Carlota stepped up, tears streaming down her cheeks. "Congratulations, my son. Your father would have been so proud."

And, shocking Hugh speechless, Doña Carlota Gonzalvez y Rodriguez del Castillo, Companion and Protector of the Succession, Order of Earth, Vice Lord of Sector Seven, hugged him, weeping openly. Hugh, somewhat carefully, returned the hug, feeling as he did, a genuine love and affection for this lonely old woman. Glancing at Ward, as he hugged Doña Carlota, he saw what looked suspiciously like a tear in his eye, too.

After Doña Carlota finally let go, Ward politely continued, "One more thing, Your Highness. All heirs have the Imperial Trace, an archeon trace, injected at birth, similar to what Marines have implanted. As a proctor, I also have a way to determine your well-being, called the Gift, that is tuned to you as long as I am assigned to you. It works through your archeonC. That is how I knew you were okay on the mountain. You also have a Marine Commando trace so I can find you that way also, if necessary. Before the attack hit, I didn't use either one. After it started, I delayed pinging the trace until afterward, afraid that activating the trace might have called attention to you."

Doña Carlota's tears dried quickly, anger rising to the surface. "You knew and didn't tell me?" Hugh felt similarly outraged. *An air sled could have been sent to pick me up?*

"Doña Carlota, I did tell you I felt finding Hugh could wait until later. I couldn't say anything more."

Turning to face Hugh, he continued, without giving him a chance to express his anger, "I let you go on without rescue for several reasons. First, I literally couldn't explain then how I knew where you were. I can only discuss it with you now because you have taken the oath, and with Doña Carlota because she is the protector of the succession.

"A rescue would have raised questions, yours and others. You now know the answer to those questions and why the ability must remain secret. Plus picking you up might have gotten you killed by drawing attention to you. I did send out drones after the attack, but only to monitor for later evaluation as to how ready you were for the test. As you would guess, the Imperial Trace lets me and others find you. Even though only a person with your personal code can ping you, that doesn't mean others can't see someone has been pinged, so we will be careful with that. Because I have a military trace, you can also find me. We are tied together by the nanites of this bag.

"Next, the Gift. It allows the proctor during the test to gain an emotional reflection of *why* an heir does something, not just what. The longer a proctor is with an heir, the more he understands him or her. Even before you committed to the test and took the oath, fully activating your nanites, I have occasionally known some of what you were feeling. It is another reason why proctors are rotated out, as we did with Sergeant Daniels. He grew too close to you, with or without the Gift being a part of it. Saving you on Deft and then helping you handle the nightmares and the rest of growing up, becoming a surrogate father . . . He could never have administered the test. He knew you too well and loved you too deeply."

Pausing to make sure Hugh understood, he continued. "Things were so intense for you out there that I felt some of the emotions you were dealing with. I sent the drones to observe, nothing more. You will face serious problems taking the test on our way to retrieve a new Galactic Starburst. I cannot interfere. You must make your own decisions." Grinning a little crookedly, he ended, "But I did have an air sled standing by just in case the fire got too close."

Slightly stunned and suddenly upset at Ward's cold-bloodedness, Hugh clamped his jaw shut. He didn't have to run all the way in? Ward could have gotten him any time? He felt a chill. Ward meant it when he said he would administer the test regardless of any other consideration.

Doña Carlota's left eyebrow twitched, indicating her likely unhappiness with Ward not keeping her completely informed, before placing a hand on his arm. "One more thing, Your Highness. At this moment, the fact that you are an heir remains a secret, but we will be unable to keep that secret for long. Hence the urgency that you are on your way as soon as possible. And before that secret becomes public knowledge, we should discuss your interest in certain young women."

Hugh began to color. He didn't need a speech about the birds and bees.

Doña Carlota smiled. "This is not about what you think. You are a healthy young man and as such you have both sought and received the attention of certain women. Some of those interested, I dare say, you have remained shockingly ignorant of. But let us focus on the others.

"Senorita Elizabeth Polchar's father has come to me on several occasions to have you kicked out of school, or at least kept away from his daughter. He felt you were not of the same social class and didn't want anything to happen to his priceless princess.

Unfortunately for him, he couldn't force me to comply. That said, I agree with him." At this, Hugh's eyebrows went up.

Doña Carlota continued. "You are not of the same social class as his daughter, just not in the way he imagined. Liz is not marriage material for the emperor. Although sweet, she is used to being catered to. Also, despite being relatively smart she is somewhat lazy and lacks the social skills to deal with the pressures of an imperial household. It takes a certain type of temperament and she, unfortunately, either has not been blessed or cursed with it, depending upon your point of view.

"That goes double for your friend, Becca, in Robertson. Becca is a lovely young woman, but neither she nor Liz is a woman of the type you need." Hugh felt an angry defensiveness rising within him. He understood he'd committed to success or death, but he hadn't even passed the blasted test and Doña Carlota was already picking out his wife?

"That leaves Noor Bettis," here Doña Carlota raised her hand to stop Hugh from jumping in with an obvious denial. "I know you're going to say you don't think of her that way, but she is one of the women who *does* think of you that way."

Noor? Noor likes me? And like an idiot, I didn't notice? Doña Carlota doesn't miss a beat.

"Nice young woman but, for various reasons, it wouldn't do her any favors to get her involved with you." *Why not? Sure, I'm leaving to take the test but if I pass, why couldn't I come back to Noor?*

Doña Carlota went on. "The woman for you must be worth any sacrifice, and she will support you in all things. The last empress, your Aunt Sythia, met that standard. Before her death, the emperor performed his duties in a manner some might describe as competent, but no more than that. Empress Sythia made Cyrus a better man in almost every way. Her death left him without a rudder and directionless. Without strong leadership from him, others began jockeying and scheming for power. I mean Emperor Cyrus no disrespect but, before the coup, he had frankly lost control of the empire.

"I do not believe you suffer from the same weaknesses as Cyrus, but I do believe you would best serve the empire with the kind of woman by your side who has similar qualities to your aunt. Alas, Noor does not." She paused and smiled, "But you don't think of her in that way, so I'll stop blathering on."

Hugh felt blindsided. In the space of three minutes, he'd both discovered he had a shot with Noor and lost it.

"As far as matters of importance go, specifically regarding saving the empire, first you must pass the test, something many have died attempting over the last thousand years. Second, I will help you find the right companion. All else falls in line from there." Doña Carlota bowed, not waiting for a response. "Now I beg your leave to retire, Your Highness." Hugh nodded, not sure what he should say. Doña Carlota left Hugh with Ward and shut the hatch behind her.

Ward chuckled. "Not what I expected her to say, either. As far as I'm concerned, I expect you to ignore all thoughts of girls until you pass the test. Let's go, Your Highness."

The Core Empire

Chapter 5

Previously in Part II, Chapter 3, we discussed Dave Jackson's near-obsession with leaving a strong and moral leader behind him as emperor. In Chapter 4 we concentrated on Evie Jackson's gradual loss of control of Green Gardens to her granddaughter, Boudicca. Chapter 5 will show how these two strong emotional and psychological streams converged to create the Test of Heirs.

In fact, the Test of Heirs designed by them became so draconian that Dave did not impose it on his own successor but acted as proctor to name his son Marvin directly to the throne. No other heir in the long history of the empire escaped the test, although several, Benjamin most notably, seemed to have been able to avoid meeting the standards while technically completing it.

The test itself required several items to support its administration. First, a corps of trained proctors to administer it. Second, an infrastructure to train proctors as well as produce the gems and medbot/commobot injections. Third, an imperial culture that accepted without question what is essentially trial by combat to prove one's worthiness to ascend the throne. Fourth, and perhaps most importantly, an objective check on the normal tendency of mission drift from the original purpose, in this case the Guardian Program. Each of these will be discussed in depth, except for the Guardian. The full treatment of the Guardian is reserved for Chapter 39 in Part XII.

14

Introspection

Fleet Emergency Command Complex, Jeffco
0930 Local/0330 BBMT 10 October 3473

STEPPING INTO THE CORRIDOR, SEAN Ward motioned to the guards standing beside the conference room door. "Dunn, Klostermann, on His Highness. He needs some rest, so get him safely back to his room."

Kevin Dunn stepped out first to lead Hugh, chuckling at Ward's words. To Hugh, he said, "Wow. You must be some special kind of special to have earned that new nickname. 'His Highness?'"

Klostermann glared at him and a look of confusion crossed Dunn's face.

Ward's eyes flashed, while his voice became even quieter, its scathing tone bit bone-deep. "Are you hard of hearing, Sergeant? He is the heir apparent. Now get your act together. Imperial protection detail protocols are in effect until you are relieved. Now!"

Hugh Cascade, still numb after the oath and trying to catch up emotionally, felt just as confused as his friend, Kevin. *Protection detail?*

Their chorused, "Aye, aye, Sergeant Major!" echoed in the corridor. Turning, they took up positions front and back and walked off with rifles ready. To Hugh's eyes, his best friend looked stunned. Klostermann, Hugh's boss not an hour before, didn't blink an eye. To Hugh, he even seemed a tad smug. Just days ago, he had assigned Hugh to stand guard at a side gate for four hours as a punishment for not having his duty boots sufficiently shined. Hugh had performed the punishment detail just like every other scut assignment he had received over the last five years, smiling on the outside and grumbling on the inside. Then, just last night, he had promised Hugh a "counseling session" for not keeping his whereabouts current when he left the manor. *But now a smile? Why? Had he known?*

Kevin asked from the side of his mouth, "You really going for emperor?" He added, "sir," as an afterthought.

"Yeah, Dunn. Lucky me, I'm the savior of the universe. Or supposed to be."

Kevin shook his head. "I don't believe it . . . sir."

Klostermann, pulling trail, hissed at him. "Dummy, he's the heir apparent now. You call him 'Your Highness' or 'sire' and you don't just talk to him. He has to speak first. Don't you remember the classes on this?"

"I thought it would never happen without an emperor to guard," Dunn answered as they moved down the corridor, "especially not with a friend of mine."

Klostermann hissed back at him, "Well it has–or is. And it's for real. Fleisch, Kennion, Jebet, and Peterson were with him on Deft. We've always known. It's the reason none of us have ever rotated off Jeffco. You think we were going to leave him after that? Before we knew all of those sacrificed that day had been worth the price?"

Hugh suddenly saw Klostermann in a new light. He had always known? His mind raced as he tried to do math. Most enlisted and NCOs served twenty years . . . if they survived that long. It had been ten years since Deft. That meant that nearly all of these men were near or beyond retirement. And still on Jeffco. Despite the need elsewhere for experienced NCOs to help train new recruits and keep what was left of the empire secure. *That's certainly not SOP.* And they had stuck around to see if he succeeded? If he became emperor? His mind reeled at the implication that hundreds had died on Deft to protect him and these men had stayed with him for the last decade to make sure those deaths had not been in vain. He felt a lump in his throat and swallowed hard.

Then Hugh backtracked mentally. *He knew, but he treated me just like everybody else?* He couldn't quite decide how he felt about that, then decided he should be glad. Without a doubt, if the circumstances had been different, he wouldn't have been one of the guys.

Meanwhile, Dunn hissed back at Klostermann with some outrage, "You could've told me!"

"You know Sergeant Major. He said not to. Would *you* ignore him?"

To Hugh, this felt more like being under guard than protected. People they passed in the corridor gave him the hard looks more associated with someone under arrest than what he imagined royalty would get. On top of which, Dunn and Klostermann were ignoring him as they chatted, and that made it worse. He understood it, though. He had been trained to treat the assignment of guarding the emperor the same way. His life represented the empire, everything else about him being secondary. *A very strange feeling to be the package.*

Dunn and Klostermann's heads swiveled, constantly watching ahead, behind, and into every door and side corridor as they talked. Kevin muttered something under his breath about being left out of the loop, but not loud enough that Hugh had to notice it. Hugh suddenly realized he would have to decide whether he *heard* certain things from now on, because what he heard and thought about things mattered, since he was now the boss. *Of everyone.*

Hugh answered the sentiment, "Don't sweat it, Kevin. I've only known for an hour or so, and it still hasn't sunk in with me, either. Until Klostermann mentioned it," Hugh relished calling his former drill instructor by his last name for the first time, "I forgot I need to start every conversation. What a nightmare! I liked being a cadet better. Won't even be able to be alone with a girl without everyone knowing I'm holding her hand."

All three of them laughed at this partially true amusement, but it also sounded like the type of laugh Hugh had heard Admiral Hollister get for saying something only remotely funny in front of his subordinates.

A further troubling thought came to mind. He recognized that, from now on, there would always be distance, a wall, however invisible, between him and every other person he talked to, every other person he met. As heir apparent to the empire, the most powerful man in the galaxy, he could never be just one of the guys ever again. Something else to think about, worry about. In many ways, he would live more alone than if the attack had killed everyone he knew. In that case, he could have made new friends. But now? He would always be a man apart.

Reaching his room, Dunn stopped Hugh from entering while he checked the room for threats. Hugh demanded, "Is this necessary? We're in our home base."

Kevin just gave him an odd look, but Klostermann answered, "Your Highness, we're expendable. Kevin, me, the entire fleet, if necessary. You're not. Besides being the leader of the empire, you represent everything we're fighting for. That makes you irreplaceable right now. There's no one else I know of to take your place. If you die, the empire is dead, just waiting to be buried. So, let us do our job, which is to keep you safe and alive. That means here in the base as well as anywhere else, Your Highness."

Hugh colored as Klostermann spoke carefully and precisely. His excruciatingly polite tone, one designed to not give any hint of insubordination or insolence, struck deep. His obvious, long-suffering patience shamed Hugh to his core. Although Klostermann didn't sound like Hugh's tactical supervisor, a position he'd held until less than an hour before, the exquisitely careful wording nevertheless delivered the message loud and clear. "Thank you for the protection, Sergeants, and the reminder."

Klostermann graciously replied, "No worries, Your Highness. We'll be right here when you need us."

Hugh said, "Thanks," before closing the door. Then it hit him. As if he were sixteen again and come in late from curfew, Ward had just sent him to his room. A sudden heat rose on his neck before the ridiculousness of the situation hit him. *Heir apparent and still sent to my room!* He started to chuckle, then guffawed, and finally fell back on his bed helplessly unable to stop the gales of laughter rolling forth. As the fit passed, his stomach growled. He needed food.

Opening the door, he saw Dunn and Klostermann pop to attention. "Let's go get something to eat, guys," Hugh suggested.

Klostermann deferentially suggested, "What about having it brought here, Your Highness? It's safer."

Hugh considered that. He didn't want to make their lives tougher but didn't like being cooped up either. The thought of freedom won. "Let's head to the mess," Hugh stated, quickly starting down a light blue corridor before they could come up with an argument he might have to consider.

"Excuse me, Your Highness," Dunn said. Hugh stopped and turned to look at him. Kevin, poker-faced, pointed the other way, saying, "The mess is that way, Your Highness."

Hugh colored before performing a U-turn. Being the heir apparent didn't suddenly make him infallible, unfortunately. He saw a slight smile on Kevin's face as he passed him. Well, he'd have to think of something to do to get even with Kevin. Not something using his new position but something truly, diabolically, clever. He just couldn't think of what that might be just now. *But I will.*

Hugh became intensely aware of the looks he received as they passed people in the corridors. Once they reached the mess, most people just ignored him. He became just one more person in the crowd. Getting a tray just like everyone else—*just like normal*—he remembered that senior officers either received their meals in their quarters or ate in private dining areas. This most likely would be one of the last times he could eat like this, mostly anonymous, still one of them. Sitting, he looked around as he ate, trying to sear every image into his mind. After a while, he caught his eyelids drooping.

Dunn, standing to his left, bent down to whisper, "Don't you think you ought to sleep in your quarters, Your Highness?"

Hugh's head jerked up when Kevin spoke. Now he owed Kevin two. But for the moment, a bed sounded wonderful.

Standing without acknowledging Kevin's breach of protocol, he headed back to his room. He noticed Kevin grinning. *Expect some payback*, Hugh vowed.

WARD OBSERVED THE MIDDAY SHIFT in the command center carry out its duties calmly and professionally with silent efficiency. He smiled to himself as they studiously ignored him. Today's orderliness stood in marked contrast to the confusion and chaos caused by the attack, as well as the excitement of the space battle. Subconsciously, he soaked in the quiet, while reviewing data on routes and available ships in the area for tomorrow's meeting with Hollister. Chief Wong maintained confident control under the nominal command of Lieutenant Sobieski. Thankfully, Commander Morrell seemed to have more important things to do. In his opinion, things just seemed calmer without her.

He focused on the list of ships available for the mission. He really needed a stealth mission ship, but Hollister believed in overkill and had assigned five stealth ships to follow the rebel messenger yesterday, stripping the system of that option. The remaining list consisted of ships either too large, such as destroyers and the other major ships out there guarding Jeffco openly now, or lacking in firepower to cover themselves on a long mission without stealth, like the frigates. Any of those drawbacks could get Hugh and his entire security detail, including Ward, killed, which he would just as soon not happen quite yet.

A rating tapped him on the shoulder. "Archeon transmission coming in for you, Top," he said.

"Thanks, Archer," Ward answered absently, "I'll take it here."

Petty Officer Second Class Griff Archer shook his head. "It's coming in from the supernova *Andromeda* with a secret classification. You'll have to take it in the secure com room."

Ward scowled, tired from lack of sleep and irritated after the meeting. With a limited window in which to find transportation so Hugh could take the test, he didn't have time for whoever thought their rank entitled them to his services. Probably someone who wanted his help managing Doña Carlota for a promotion or some other nonsense. Forging through the command center much like a fast-moving storm front, he entered his code and submitted to the retinal scan so he could enter the secure com room. "Ward," he stated brusquely after entering.

Suddenly, the hologram of a pleasant-looking female commander of about forty with gray streaking her red hair appeared. Smiling, she cheerfully chided, "Well, if that's the welcome you have for me, I'll sign off now."

Irritation subsiding, Ward ruefully shook his head. "You could have told them to tell me you were calling. Are you okay? I heard you barely made it back in one piece."

Gail Felt, commander of the *Ambrose B*, just smiled wider. "I didn't tell them so I could see you as your charming and natural self."

Ward quirked his mouth into a half frown. "Sometimes your sense of humor leaves something to be desired, Gail. But you didn't answer my question. How did the mission go?"

"No one injured and the ship's fine, though it got interesting a time or two. Almost got nailed by Twelfth Fleet's 3d Task Group, but *almost* only counts in horseshoes and hand grenades, as you've told me more than once. Worse, we didn't find any trace of Carhart. We missed him. Again. He seems to have intel resources better than our own. He knows whenever we're onto him. Anyway, I'm told we get six weeks of rest before the next one. I look forward to seeing you as soon as we refuel and restock here. Day after tomorrow at regular speeds."

"I won't be here. They decided to tell Hugh who he is *and* send him on the test. As soon as I have a ship, we'll be out of here. Tomorrow, I hope."

Gail looked concerned. "Will he pass?" Her brow furrowed, telegraphing her real concern.

"I don't think he's ready. He'll give it his all, no question about that. You wouldn't believe how strong the reflections of his feelings are now that he's taken the oath, but he just doesn't have the maturity. He's six months shy of nineteen, for pity's sake. As for the fleet, what do you think will happen if he fails? That will leave us worse off than before," Ward stated, emphatically, as if it were an obvious truth anyone should be able to recognize. "But my opinion apparently doesn't count. Doña Carlota and Hollister decided he has to do it, so we're off." Anger lent added volume to his words.

"You don't have to bite my head off," Gail answered with some heat, eyes narrowed. "Besides, who else can they send? If we don't get an emperor soon, it won't matter anymore."

Ward knew deep inside that Gail understood the situation perfectly. People were forgetting, losing faith. He just didn't want Hugh to fail and die. Not receiving an answer for a minute, she went on while giving him a searching look. "You know there isn't anyone else. Hugh has to take the test," she stated, almost gently.

Ward jerked a nod in reply. "Clarence Martinez seemed like the best prospect and he disappeared years ago. Your heir, I can't remember her name, died on that mission to Ararat. I can't think of more than three or four others that I don't know for sure are dead. What about your friend, Priscilla Jenks, and her heir?"

With sadness in her eyes, Gail answered, "Anna Beth Fitzgerald, my last heir, could never have passed the test; just too sweet. I loved her just the same. As for Priscilla and her heir, I'm pretty sure they're both dead. I heard they flew off into the middle of Thirteenth Fleet's mess five years ago, or something like that."

Ward nodded. "What about Art Nouvelle or Ceacescu or Nbele? I haven't heard anything since they left to take the test some time ago."

Gail just shook her head. "Don't know, but they should have been back by now and are undoubtedly dead. You know that as well as I do. So, do you need me to take Hugh out? We can be there in twelve hours once we've refueled," she asked eagerly.

"No, I don't want you with me," he stated harshly. "This is a suicide mission no one is likely to survive. You've already been on enough of them without going on this very long shot. I doubt even you have many lives left." His voice softened as he finished.

Gail visibly bristled. "We're the best there is, and you know it. If it's as tough as you're saying, you need me and my crew."

Ward nodded, but his face hardened. "Fortunately, you aren't here and aren't likely to be ordered to fly like a crazy woman to get here in twelve hours. Which means I'll see you when I get back."

Gail just stared at him for a moment. "I see there's no reasoning with you. I'll see you when I see you, then."

A moment later Ward stood staring at blank space. Gail had cut their transmission. After a minute thinking, he turned and left. *Well, that didn't go well.*

HUGH'S EYES OPENED TO DARKNESS. A faint glow came from the clock on the desk, but otherwise he saw nothing. *What a weird dream.* Then he realized how amazingly good he felt for having run so far just a few hours ago, almost as if he'd gotten a full night's sleep. *Yikes!* What about his duty shift at twelve hundred? If he had missed it, Morrell would have him drawn and quartered.

That thought shot Hugh bolt upright. Staring at the clock clearly for the first time, he read twenty-two hundred, ten p.m. civilian time. *What day is this?* he panicked. He remembered dropping into bed about ten hundred. Did he miss his duty entirely, sleeping the entire clock around? Flipping on the light, he hurriedly showered and dressed but didn't shave. Usually, he could go a couple of days if he didn't have time to worry about it. Like today, unless he had reached tomorrow. He couldn't shake the feeling that his dream might be real.

Opening the door, he saw Dunn and Klostermann standing there, rifles shouldered. *Maybe I didn't dream the whole thing.* "What day is it, Kevin?" he blurted out.

"The eighth, Your Highness," Kevin said with exquisite politeness. Hugh's refusal to accept Dunn's statement must have been evident on his face because Dunn went on, "The attack happened yesterday, and your meeting with the admiral has been moved back to oh nine hundred tomorrow morning."

Hugh sagged. *Rats!* Not a dream but a full-fledged nightmare. What did he know about being emperor? He'd said yes this morning mostly because Ward had taught him to run straight at problems and volunteer for everything he knew he should do. *How do I get out of it now?*

Klostermann spoke up from his other side, "Want to go for a walk, Your Highness? Sort this out?"

Hugh turned to face him. "Can't you just call me Hugh or cadet? I'm not ready for this *Your Highness* stuff."

Klostermann shook his head. "If you don't get used to it now, you never will. Besides which, Sergeant Major would skin me alive if he heard me doing that."

"I could tell him I ordered you to," Hugh added, hopefully.

Vinnie Klostermann just shook his head. "Truth to tell, I wouldn't want to do it. I've waited too long for this day."

The meaning of that took a second to sink in. Ten years since Deft. After surviving that, if Klostermann wanted to call him "Your Highness," Hugh couldn't tell him no. He had earned the right. Slowly, Hugh nodded. "Fine, Sergeant Klostermann. You call me anything you want to. But I'm hungry, so let's get a snack and find somewhere we can talk and think. Tomorrow's likely going to be worse than today."

Dunn suggested, "We can talk in the gym. Things have quieted down and most of the fleet people have headed back out to their ships, so it should be pretty empty."

"Good idea. Lead on, *Private* Dunn," Hugh said with a straight face.

Dunn came to a complete stop. Turning slowly and fixing Hugh with a hard look, he muttered, "Low blow, Your Highness, even for someone with your sense of humor."

Hugh smiled back like the cat that ate the canary. "I still owe you one more, so be warned."

Dunn glowered at him a moment before leading on. Hugh felt content. All felt right with the world. Kevin remained his best friend, and he got one back. "Sergeant," he asked Klostermann formally, "how come you two are still on guard at my quarters?"

Klostermann smiled. "We're pulling four-hour shifts, but only people the sergeant major can depend on to keep their mouths shut have the duty. Kennion with Peterson and Fleisch with Jebet are the others. We just came back on an hour ago. Didn't expect to see you up until tomorrow morning, actually. After your workout yesterday, duty in ops, and then that little meeting with the admiral, you looked pretty beat."

Hugh noticed that he failed to mention the oath. If Klostermann knew about it, he must have recognized it should be kept private. If he didn't, Hugh shouldn't just go blabbing about it all over because need-to-know applied. A lot of people had died proving the truth of that.

Dunn apparently felt the conversation had returned things to normal enough so that he could add a little something. "There's a rumor going 'round that you're the new emperor," he said evilly, looking for payback. "A few people saw you go into the situation room with the holo-conference and guessed."

Hugh groaned but didn't answer. *Can't anyone keep a secret around here?*

Dunn went on, "There is another rumor out there claiming you are being tried for treason and are going to be shot. Your run-ins with Morrell, as well as Kirkwood passing on the tale about your dressing down by Doña Carlota, make that the odds-on favorite, when added to the several hundred people who saw you under guard in the mess earlier today. I've laid a few quiet bets about that with those poor benighted individuals who think Morrell has any pull with Doña Carlota."

Hugh snorted, "Is it too late to choose that option? I think I'd prefer being shot to what I'm going to have to do. What do I know about running an empire?" It was a question he'd been thinking about. He'd never really thought too hard about the fact that the sergeant major had often taken a direct interest in his education, an education different from other cadets, always being pushed to examine the why of the way things worked down through history. It made him think he might have a chance, if only a small one, to succeed.

Walking into the mess, he pretty much could choose to sit anywhere. *Of course,* Hugh groaned to himself, *one of the few people in the mess would be Lieutenant Commander Morrell.* He watched her carrying a full tray toward the door, likely headed either to her room or ops. He ignored her and went for the pile of sandwiches and juice bulbs sitting on the serving counter. From the corner of his eye, he watched as she almost dropped her tray before spinning to intercept him. Just before she reached him, though, Klostermann stepped in front of her. "No speaking with the prisoner," he gruffly stated. Even Hugh would have believed him if he didn't know better.

Bafflement briefly crossed her face before she spoke in a quiet, firm voice commanding, "Belay that, Sergeant. I know what's really going on. I have friends in fleet ops, and they are moving heaven and earth to get a certain secret project set up no later than oh nine hundred tomorrow."

Hugh kept quiet, waiting. He had never really liked Morrell, and nothing had changed that. Taking the oath changed his perception of the galaxy a bit, but not so much that he now saw things through rose-colored glasses, just the opposite. Her sudden friendliness most probably arose from one motive, in his opinion: brown-nosing. She looked at him, took a small breath, and said, formally, "Your Highness, congratulations. You were one of my best watch standers. I wish you good luck in taking the test. Are you headed to Beacon first? I understand most tests start there."

The change in their relationship had his head spinning. A day ago, he'd been terrified she would ruin his chances of ever joining the fleet and now she stood here congratulating him. He struggled with how to reply. *Emperors probably deal with lots of people they would rather have shot.*

"Thank you, Commander. I'll do my best for all of us out there. I'm not sure exactly where we're going, yet." It sounded lame and evasive to him, but Morrell's face beamed at that.

"I'm sure you will, Your Highness. Thank you for trying." Not knowing what else to do, Hugh took her hand and shook it before heading on to the sandwiches.

Dunn whispered to him from the corner of his mouth, "Can you believe her? For a minute I thought the wicked witch might melt into a puddle right there when you shook her hand." Hugh swallowed a laugh. He thought so, too, come to mention it. To be fair, thinking back on it now, he couldn't decide if she had been brown-nosing, pumping him for information to make her look more important by being in the know, or honestly wishing him well. Whichever, he didn't want to do that again anytime soon.

Grabbing food, they sped off before anyone else could corner him. Approaching the gym, he saw only a few people, none of whom he knew well. *Hopefully, they'll leave the prisoner alone.* Hugh sat down on a bleacher near the empty basketball court as Dunn and Klostermann took up overwatch positions. "Have some," Hugh offered.

"Can't," Dunn said regretfully. "You know the rules. Besides, Sergeant Major gave us all a quickie refresher about how to do this. Seems the admiral caught him by surprise."

Hugh smiled at the memory before launching into an edited version of the meeting for their benefit. It felt good to review it and share it with someone.

When he finished, Klostermann just shook his head. "Sounds like you handled it well."

Dunn jumped in to offer his support. "I don't know anyone who can do the job better." Kevin's support genuinely boosted his self-confidence.

Smiling, Hugh stood. "What about a little game of horse?"

Both his guards shook their heads regretfully. "No can do. You know the rules," Klostermann reminded him.

Yes, I know the rules. They were already starting to feel like chains binding him down. Heading for the weight machines, he hoped to clear his mind. Tomorrow he needed to be sharp for the conference. Focusing on lifting, curling, concentrating on using proper form, allowed him to avoid thought and tire himself out. At the same time, he could work muscles not abused on the run up the mountain.

But the thoughts wouldn't stop, continuing to gnaw at the corners of his mind like mice in the woodwork. He felt the weight of the world—no, the empire—on his shoulders. He appreciated that growing up on Jeffco had given him as close to a "normal" life as possible, but it had also done nothing to prepare him to be emperor.

Or did it? He thought about the oath he'd just taken, and the Creed. Certainly the Creed had been drilled into him over the last ten years. Before that, really. And he recognized that between Doña Carlota and Sergeant Major Ward, he had a clear sense of right and wrong. A strong moral compass, some might call it. He didn't just recite the Creed; he *understood* it. And, yes, he believed in it. But would that be enough to let him succeed and to become the emperor that so many appeared to think he could be?

As he chewed endlessly over those questions and more, twenty minutes became an hour, and then two, before he headed back to his room tired enough to ignore them and get some sleep.

The Core Empire

Part VIII

This part encompasses perhaps the most fascinating episode of the entire history of the empire, Charles Roland. Chapter 25 in Part VII ended with the death of Emperor Bert in 3271 as he attempted to rally the fleet in Sector Sixteen at its capital of St. Augustine. Chapter 26 begins Part VIII with a discussion of the attempts to find an heir by the proctor Jeremy Dansforth and the three failures he personally terminated, which almost ended in his own death.

Chapter 26 will then focus on Charles Roland's test and coronation on April 1, 3276 AD in the smoking ruins of Harwell, the Marine training planet. Chapter 27 will examine his campaigns of the next twenty years to restore Sectors 1 through 16, leaving 17 through 20 for his heirs. Chapter 28 explains the federalization of the empire he brought about in the final twelve years of his life and how this differed from the structure set up by Emperors Jack and Dave eight hundred years earlier.

15

Revelations

Fleet Emergency Command Complex, Jeffco
0615 Local/0015 BBMT 11 October 3473

BEFORE DROPPING OFF, HUGH CASCADE had set the alarm for seven but found that he couldn't sleep past six. After thrashing around for fifteen minutes, he got up and shaved to kill time, even though he didn't think he needed it. As boss, couldn't he decide whether to shave or not? He didn't want to push it and find out, though. Besides, as boss, whatever he did, or didn't do, became either the standard or excuse for everyone else.

Six twenty and nothing to do for more than two and a half hours except think some more. If he went back to the gym, maybe he could find something to do for a while. He found the olive-skinned woman named Tabi Fleisch and Abdul Jebet, a huge coffee-colored mountain, on guard when he came out. Fleisch stood five foot ten, but when paired with Jebet, she looked tiny. Jebet towered over most people at six foot eight and weighed well over three hundred pounds. As a bodyguard, Hugh figured, his size alone should keep people away. "Let's go to the gym, you two," he said cheerily. He felt surprisingly good this morning.

Without a word, Fleisch took point with Jebet filling the corridor behind him. Pushing the pace, they were almost jogging by the time they reached the gym. Hugh's smile of anticipation as he entered the gym kept him from looking like a prisoner to anyone who saw him.

Standing in the door surveying the crowded place, the mass of echoes from all the activities created an almost ear-shattering din. People were using the stationary bikes, weights, various types of treadmills, and other equipment. The racquetball, handball, and squash courts were full, with lines waiting to play. Through a set of doors on the far side of the gym, Hugh could see the pool. A track full of runners entered from the wall behind the near end of the swimming pool, ran along the outside walls of the gym, and disappeared behind the far wall of the pool. As he looked that way, he caught sight of Noor Bettis diving from the springboard. She looked rather good in her black one-piece. His mind drifted back to Doña Carlota's evaluation of her . . . and the news that she liked him. He half considered going over to say hello, then realized that he'd have an audience of at least Fleisch and Jebet. *This situation does not bode well for my love life.*

Surveying the scene with new eyes, Hugh stood drinking it all in, savoring just being with all these people. Even though they didn't know it, he felt responsible for their safety. He now owned this gym, and these were his people. After his talk with Klostermann and Dunn, he felt not only anxious but excited. The anxiety made him want to get on with the test. He probably needed to work off his excess adrenaline before the meeting. Running or swimming. He stepped toward the pool.

Stopping him, Jebet whispered, "This is way too dangerous, Your Highness. Let's go where there's less chance of getting you killed."

Hugh just shook his head; he knew these people, and they knew him. "I can't imagine anyone here has it out for me."

Jebet looked thoughtful. "Almost half the fleet participated in the coup. Are you willing to bet your life that everyone here is loyal? Or could some of them believe that the Restitution Movement was right? Some of these people grew up watching Morgain on their holoscreens, preaching the evils of the empire. Who know knows how much of her twisted logic made an impression?"

Hugh blanched. If they threatened him here, could he ever be safe? No. But he also refused to be a prisoner of his new role and responsibilities. He considered the options. Swimming, pass. Racquetball, tennis, or handball? The lines were too long. He'd worn himself out on the weights last night and wanted a change. That left basketball. Not his favorite, but some banging and running wouldn't hurt him at all. "Let's play some b-ball," he directed.

Jebet stepped in front of him. "Are you sure, sire? I've seen you play and, well, you're just not very good."

Hugh smiled up at Jebet. "Correction, Jebet. You've played against me and you know I'm terrible. However, I'm not going to play against any giants."

Jebet thought for a minute, "Wouldn't you rather just enjoy a long, slow breakfast in your room, Your Highness?" he suggested.

"Running laps?" Hugh countered, looking over at the crowded track.

"B-ball it is," Jebet agreed.

Jebet and Fleisch followed Hugh to the court. A couple of corporals, one from Fleisch's platoon, were picking sides as he came up. Both captains ignored Hugh. One ended with four players and the other, five. Hugh walked over to the captain of the team with four. "What position do you want me to play?"

The corporal, Alvarez, gave him a dismissive look. "Don't want you, *cadet*."

Hugh couldn't figure out what to say to that. The admiral wanted his situation kept quiet, so he shouldn't say anything. Last night, he thought he preferred the possibility of custody to taking the test to become emperor. But now, faced with the reality of being treated like a prisoner, he didn't like it. In the least. The very thought made him angry. Before he lost his cool, however, Fleisch put her nose an inch from Alvarez's face. "Corporal, I suggest you change your mind," she whispered intensely, but so softly no one else but Hugh could hear her contralto voice. "Do you understand me?"

Hugh had never seen Fleisch mad before. Several times she had worked with him in hand-to-hand training, and he found her to be cold, often utterly ruthless, but never angry. If he had been Alvarez, Fleisch would have frightened him. The corporal must have agreed with Hugh about not messing with Fleisch because he turned green around the gills. "Sure, Cascade can play on my team."

"Thought so," Fleisch said, still too quiet to be heard by anyone else.

Hugh settled for saying, "Thanks, Sergeant," before stripping off his T-shirt. Basketball turned out to be perfect. Running, guarding, getting knocked down by the big guy on the shirts team, in moments a huge grin came over his face, and within minutes sweat began running off him in sheets. Forty-five minutes later he carried a series of bruises accumulated in the rough and tumble of playing with essentially no rules, as well as a slight limp in his left leg from taking a hard foul. He felt wonderful.

Jebet got his attention. "Let's go shower, Your Highness. Doña Carlota wants you to have breakfast with her." Jebet couldn't speak softly to save his life. The words *Your Highness* echoed through the room. Alvarez's head snapped up, his eyes wide, and then he smirked. Some of the other guys were laughing, probably thinking Jebet had just made a joke at his expense. A few others had curious looks, wondering why Jebet had said that. He agreed with Jebet, though, that he better go get ready if Doña Carlota wanted him.

Pushing through the doors out into the corridor, Hugh demanded with a false frown, "So why weren't you guys protecting me? They were fouling me all over out there."

Fleisch quirked her lips. "Says you, Your Highness. From where I sat, you were the one doing most of the fouling. Wouldn't you agree, Jebet?"

"Definitely," Jebet rumbled. "You were a wild man, the way I saw it. I stopped counting your fouls after ten."

"Hey," Hugh cried, "whose side are you on?"

Fleisch, totally deadpan, answered, "Truth, virtue, and honor, sire. Isn't that the side you're on?"

Still laughing as they arrived back at Hugh's room, he felt great. Bantering all the way to the room, he felt ready to take on the universe.

The shower gave him time to think. The question, *Why does Doña Carlota want to see me before the meeting?* looped in endless variations through his mind. He didn't know the answer, and none of the options were pleasant to contemplate. The most worrisome possibility revolved around them changing their minds, deciding he didn't measure up.

On his way to breakfast, he hustled between his two guards, both of whom kept their weapons up, looking very serious indeed. Naval and Marine personnel stood aside as they passed, most eyeing him speculatively. Between his thoughts and the bubble he seemed to be living in, a very somber mood had enveloped him by the time they reached Doña Carlota's suite. Jebet knocked and Doña Carlota's majordomo, Ellis, opened the door. Not one to smile, the somewhat pudgy man bowed deeply. "Welcome, Your Highness," he said simply in his mellow tenor.

Ellis's greeting, more than anything else that could have happened, threatened to make Hugh break. In Hugh's opinion, Ellis always presented the very picture of decorum, always saying and doing exactly the right thing. By calling Hugh *Your Highness*, he had put Hugh's greatest fear about this meeting to rest, that he might have been about to lose the opportunity to take the test even before he started. Hugh swallowed the emotion, saying simply, "Thank you, Ellis."

When Ellis looked up, Hugh saw what looked suspiciously like a tear in the old man's eye but couldn't have sworn to it. "Doña Carlota is waiting in the breakfast nook, Your Highness. It will be just the two of you this morning."

Hugh nodded, not having any idea what the proper forms were in this situation. He followed Ellis with Jebet and Fleisch right behind. It seemed *just the two of you* meant bodyguards and servants didn't count. Hugh felt decidedly odd about that, having gone from nobody to the most important somebody around.

Reaching the breakfast nook, a dining room capable of seating fifteen, Doña Carlota rose and inclined her head. "Your Highness, did you sleep well? I hear you were wandering the halls till the early hours," she added with a glint of humor.

"Good morning, Doña Carlota," Hugh answered in a perfect mimic of her upper crust accent. "I slept very well, thank you. And yourself?"

"Very well, Your Highness, thank you for asking. And, if I might be so bold, I can't sit until you do." A definite twinkle glinted in her eye as she pointed the proper protocol out to Hugh. Doña Carlota glanced at Ellis who immediately began the breakfast service. Toast, juice, fruit, eggs, every possibility Hugh could think of, came rolling off the carts wheeled in by silent servants. Hugh couldn't decide what not to eat, so he took some of everything. Looking at the loaded plates set in front of him, he realized he'd never be able to eat it all and felt guilty for the waste.

Distracting him, Doña Carlota commented, "You always did have a way with mimicking people. I hadn't realized until this morning just how well you do *me*, Your Highness."

Embarrassed at being called on his mimicry but delighted at the compliment, he answered in the same tone, "Why, thank you, Doña Carlota. I always try to copy the best around me."

Doña Carlota laughed. "You always were a scamp. You so often said the right thing to get yourself off the hook that I worried you'd become a first-rate scoundrel instead of the fine young man you are." More seriously, Doña Carlota continued, "What makes it even more impressive is that you are able to be your, shall I say, normal, irrepressible self, in the face of such enormous pressure and change. I find that truly remarkable."

This sincere compliment and her obvious concern touched Hugh deeply. Never having suspected the depth of Doña Carlota's feelings toward him, he suddenly discovered some difficulty in swallowing his mouthful of omelet. He just nodded, rather than say something sappy.

Doña Carlota smiled fondly at him for a moment, then chuckled, "The only thing that seems capable of upsetting your equilibrium is a sincere compliment." Her grin betrayed her equal enjoyment of the moment.

Searching for small talk, Hugh asked, "So where is the sergeant major this morning?"

The twinkle in Doña Carlota's eye grew even brighter as she answered, "A special ops ship came in unexpectedly after midnight, and he wanted to debrief the captain as soon as possible. I told him he wouldn't be needed until the conference at nine. I may have neglected to mention my invitation to you for breakfast, but I'm sure Ward won't mind.

"So, on to business. Here we are before your great quest to save the empire. I wanted to explain a few things before the meeting because George Hollister hates background briefings on areas he already knows about. These are things you should certainly know."

Looking at Ellis, she ordered, "Make sure the servants are not where they can overhear us, if you would." Ellis silently bowed and left. Jebet and Fleisch remained standing in opposite corners, silent as posts.

Doña Carlota gave a slight smile in response. "Remember yesterday, we explained the importance of the Galactic Starburst? It's not a weapon alone, although it does give the emperor the ability to shut down, power up, or destroy every military ship and installation in the empire. You can also use it to try and talk rebels into surrendering or speak with your commanders."

She frowned. "Cyrus was killed in the first strike before Charles Roland's Galactic Starburst could be used. If he had been wearing the Galactic Starburst, he could have shut down Quadros' ships before they attacked."

Hugh asked thoughtfully, "If I get one, I can stop the rebellion, right?"

Doña Carlota nodded, "To an extent."

"So, how do I get a new one? Where do I go and what do I need to do?"

"There are several things you need to understand, Your Highness. There were over fifteen hundred star clusters in the empire at the time of the coup, about one in every thousand habitable systems in the galaxy. The first major expansion from Earth ended in a massive war throwing humankind across both spiral arms into barbarism. Some planets were bombed into oblivion, others lost the ability to sustain human life entirely. On some, the atrocities from one or another extreme form of political theory brought the people to a savagery hard to understand or even believe."

Doña Carlota paused for Hugh to acknowledge he understood before going on. "Constantine Jackson founded this empire to avoid all of that. He felt Plato's philosopher kings, people with absolute power to control the lives of everyone else, were generally a bad idea. The reason is simple. A good king, who knows he isn't a god, will focus on his subjects' needs and pour out his life for them.

"Unfortunately, an egomaniac knows, is absolutely sure, that what he wants is best for everybody else. So, Emperor Dave came up with an idea to save what he could while avoiding turning it over later to an egomaniac: require each emperor pass a rigorous character test and then have him, or her, confirmed by the representatives of the people of the empire before he could rule."

Hugh, confused, asked, "Confirmed by the people? How is that done?"

"Good question, which we'll get to in a minute. As for the character test, he set up proctors with deep programming to examine the heirs and find the best one to be emperor. Dave still worried about the potential of power corrupting after a person passed the test, so he limited the emperors to one duty with the power to carry it out: defend the empire internally and externally, which Charles Roland changed, unfortunately.

"Everything else in the empire is supposed to be carried out by the people's elected representatives. Dave also wanted to keep the power hungry away from the throne. The imperial purple is limited to members of his family; no one else can ever be recognized, so it discourages most would-be usurpers. In the usual course of events, an emperor or empress passes the test that allows him or her access to the Galactic Starburst. After which, he or she must be confirmed by a vote of two-thirds of the sector lords chosen by their sector senates. The thing preventing your confirmation is that there are not enough sector lords available; the whole system has broken down. You can thank Quadros and the Restitution Movement for that. Sector lords are chosen by the council of planets in each sector. Quadros, Sector Twelve's fleet admiral at the time, brought about the crisis by usurping the position of sector lord, essentially a rehearsal of the military coup he'd hoped to use to overthrow the emperor. Guns and the lack of scruples can be effective. In the short run."

Riveting his attention solely on the names Doña Carlota now brought up from myth, explaining their importance for him today, Hugh was stunned. He was descended from Constantine, the emperors were his family, a family chosen to serve the empire forever?

Doña Carlota continued on as if she were speaking of the most ordinary things. Hugh didn't understand why it didn't electrify Doña Carlota the way it did him. He meant something! No longer would he be just an orphaned cadet. "So, can we get nine sector lords, elected by their sector senates, who can be called upon to confirm that you are qualified? No. Sector One is still functioning as it should. Here in Sector Seven, we are also. Sectors Two, Four, and Fourteen also are functioning to an extent, but that is it. To make matters worse, we were keeping your existence a secret. Only the fleet admiral of Sector One, Davies, knew about you besides us and we haven't been able to contact him since the attack on Periastron, so he's probably dead. We kept your survival such a secret because heirs were being hunted down ruthlessly all over the empire, your brothers among them, and even people not on the official list of heirs."

Sadness filled Hugh. He didn't remember his brothers well, but nevertheless felt their loss.

"Leaks of top-secret data kept popping up, so we limited information about you to a small group. That means, even among the loyal fleets, only we know who you are, only five votes can be counted. If the empire is considered just those sectors, we might get Sector One and Seven to vote for you, but I doubt Two, Four, and Fourteen would agree to elevate you after all this time."

"So that's that?" Hugh asked.

Doña Carlota shook her head. "Fortunately, if the full test is required, activating a new Galactic Starburst acts as the sole qualification. Two hundred years ago, when the Qabal invaded, many heirs attempted the full test before one succeeded. You see, qualifying for the Galactic Starburst tests you mentally and physically. But even more, the full test reveals your character completely, almost cruelly, exposing who and what you are."

"But why won't the other sectors vote for me?" Hugh wondered.

Doña Carlota's face became grave. "That is thanks to Ninth Fleet. Morgain uch Robert, a member of the imperial family who rose to prominence in certain social circles, and used popular opinion and her own charisma and guile and, I hesitate to add, feminine wiles, to take command of Ninth Fleet. Within the first year of the coup, she put forward a pretender of the first order. When the pretender was discovered to be a fake, the backlash spread throughout the core, creating distrust between the sectors and undermining cooperation between them. While trade for essentials continues, politically the empire is fragmented. Only the presence of loyal military forces in various sectors provides cohesiveness.

"The one positive result of the disaster came from being able to prove conclusively, if any doubt existed before, Morgain's involvement at the center of the coup. Her attempt to take over the empire settled that question.

"We removed her as a possible heir years before the coup, as we did most of her sisters, based upon the recommendation of their proctors, as well as, unusually, their father, Robert Ap Morgan. Robert's loyalty to the empire has never been in doubt, but his wife came from outside the empire. She was a princess, and related to the emperors, but she never made a point of that. The gossip must have affected her daughters, though. Regardless, the oldest daughters debuted at court. All great beauties who were immediately the subject of enormous public attention. They did not . . . *benefit* from this attention. It highlighted a psychopathy in them that their proctors and the Guardian Program had already identified. And their father's absence over the years in service of the empire meant that he couldn't counter the negative influence of their grandmother and the attention of those they associated with.

"Now let's return to the Restitution Movement. What do you remember from your classes in school?"

Hugh paid little attention to politics, so he just shrugged.

Doña Carlota gave him a moderately severe look before going on. "The Restitution Movement began with several families who felt unfairly treated after being removed from the succession. Many, but not all, of the Restitution Movement families, believed that only a direct heir of Emperor Benjamin should rule and that then prosperity would return to the empire. Complete nonsense, of course, especially since their figurehead, Morgain, is not one of Benjamin's descendants. Worse, he can only be described as an utter disaster. Anyway, five years before the latest coup, some of their relatives tried to take over the empire and we executed them for treason.

"My role as protector of the succession involved me directly. The executions weighed heavily on Emperor Cyrus; he hated ordering the deaths of people he knew and, at one time, trusted. Over time, he refused to even consider the penalty, which may have led directly to our situation, as several members of the movement were sentenced to prison, instead of death. In time, they were released, either pardoned when they claimed loyalty to the empire, or through technicalities embraced by judges who may or may not have been members of the movement themselves. We may never know. Regardless, these people feel entitled to the throne with or without the test and Cyrus's unwillingness to make them pay the ultimate price for their disloyalty allowed them to foment greater dissatisfaction in certain circles, creating the environment in which the coup plotters were able to succeed.

"Now back to Morgain. She wants to be the power behind the throne if she can't be empress herself. Nine sectors were still cooperating at the time when she introduced her pretender, and that made a hash of everything, as I said. Her stunt blew up on her and her fleet. Ninth Sector is still overrun with every kind of barbarian and rebel unit left over from the breakup of its fleet."

Something else bothering Hugh made him speak up. "This sounds like an unfixable problem. The sectors don't trust each other. Many have no leadership or a stabilizing military presence. Forces loyal to the empire are—correct me if I'm wrong—barely holding on. So, even if I succeed in passing the test, how do I restore order?"

Doña Carlota nodded. "A concise and astute summary of what you've just learned, Your Highness. The answer to your question is the Galactic Starburst. With it, you can, in a sense, 'reboot' the empire. You can shut down or destroy the disloyal ships and use it to take back control of the rebellious systems."

Several long moments of silence passed as Hugh considered what Doña Carlota had just said. Then he spoke, choosing his words carefully, "It seems to me that what you've just described is at best a temporary solution, even if it works. Yes, rebellions can be crushed using military force. And the starburst is the ultimate form of that, effectively allowing me to kill an entire ship—or a fleet even—systems away for being disloyal. Or attack a planet using its own defense systems, forcing it to come to heel or face complete destruction. But how does that bring these ships and planets back to the empire? How does it restore loyalty in those who are being cudgeled into submission?"

Doña Carlota's eyebrow rose. Behind her, Fleisch glanced over at Jebet with a barely perceptible grin. Doña Carlota sat back and looked appraisingly at Hugh. "Questions like that would have helped you earn higher marks in your studies, Your Highness." She smiled. "The answer is that it will not. One cannot beat loyalty into a person. One can only inspire fear. And there are no leaders who rule by fear; they are simply dictators. One of the purposes of the test is to determine your leadership qualities and whether you will have the wisdom and character to use the Galactic Starburst only when all other options have been exhausted.

"Do not forget that many citizens of the empire remember what it was like when everything worked. When there was peace and general prosperity. And they want a return to those times. They are living in fear *now*, never sure if barbarians will storm their gates or if the food will run out. They *want* leadership; they crave it, like a person trapped in the desert craves water. That have been without it for, really, two decades. It is my sincere hope and genuine belief you can provide that." Her voice broke as she finished the sentence, took a sip of water, and cleared her throat. "The Galactic Starburst is not a cudgel. It is a sign, a validation of your ability to lead, as only a true leader can pass the test. Can it help you to break a rebellion? Yes. But more, it will show the people that you have what it takes to lead, that you have the qualities of an emperor, qualities that some of us have seen in you for some time now." Her voice had become husky and her eyes glistened with tears. Hugh heard Jebet cough and clear his throat. Embarrassed by this powerful expression of faith and confidence, he looked out the window, then asked, "So where do I go for the Galactic Starburst?"

"Where do you go to *manufacture* a new one?" Doña Carlota corrected. She paused for a moment, gathering her thoughts, then went on. "We don't know everything about it, even those of us charged with protecting the succession. When the Qabal attacked and killed the emperor, they destroyed Constantine Jackson's starburst that he had brought with him when he founded the empire. As a result, the heirs went looking for a new one outside the empire. There is a legend floating around, a pretty accurate one, I believe," Doña Carlota smiled thinly at her statement, "that a new Galactic Starburst for the heir can be found on Lost Earth. Not strictly true. Emperor Dave, Constantine's son, set up a facility there to make a new one if needed.

I believe it is protected by nanites like those you received when holding the gems. When your nanites are fully activated, you will be able to access the manufacturing facility to create a new Galactic Starburst. As for why on Earth? Dave believed that in the event of destruction, no place within the empire would be safe for hiding such a facility. He put the replacement machinery in a place he thought no one would look for it: a tired, ravaged old world. Two hundred years ago, a number of heirs, all fine officers of the fleet, Marines, and army, tried to go there to find it. I have no idea how many altogether. All but one died or disappeared searching for it. Charles Roland survived and brought a new Galactic Starburst back. So, when Twelfth Fleet destroyed the Charles Roland Galactic Starburst, the heirs began looking outside the empire again. As far as we know, everyone who tried is dead."

Silence descended until Hugh thoughtfully asked, "So, I have to make a controller in a facility that can't be found? And in the process, I have to demonstrate that I'm a leader who can reunite the people of the empire?" Doña Carlota nodded. Hugh pondered for a moment. "Sounds simple enough. Let's get going," he said brightly.

Doña Carlota shook her head, "Always the clown trying to hide your real feelings. You can't hide from yourself forever, so it is better to not get in the habit of trying to." Hugh's face went blank at this all-too-accurate assessment of him. Speaking to the thin air, Doña Carlota went on, "Ellis. Please have the servants clean up breakfast."

"Yes, Doña Carlota," Ellis replied.

Hugh looked down at the table, suddenly aware that nothing remained in front of him except the plates and silverware. He must have been hungry after all. Checking the time, he saw just fifteen minutes remained before the conference. "Just about time to go," he murmured.

Doña Carlota agreed. "After you, Your Highness."

All of this protocol is going to take some getting used to.

NAVAL SPACE TRAINING GUIDE, 263D EDITION

Appendix L: Imperial Military Training Standards

Introduction to Military Technology

Astrogation Part I

Naval Officers Basic Course issued 3411 with revisions

Critical to the military mission is arriving at the right place at the right time with the right force in condition to fight. Emperor Charles Roland propounded this to his forces in the Reconquest and it is still true today. Astrogation provides the commander with the tools to know what he can and can't do, which makes the astrogation officer key to mission success.

Matter and energy density calculations within systems, as well as various core, galactic arm, and interarm regions, are the subject of Part II and essential to successful interstellar transits. Part I is limited to basic course computation for three standard scenarios based upon average matter and density factors: transit within the core; transit between the edge of the core and a point of reentry to the core; or transit between a low-density area of a galactic arm to a point of entry to the core. A midshipman must pass this section with 90 percent proficiency before continuing to Part II.

16

Situation Room

Fleet Emergency Command Complex, Jeffco
0900 Local/0300 BBMT 11 October 3473

HUGH CASCADE AND DOÑA CARLOTA arrived precisely at nine so as not to embarrass anyone. Outside the conference room, guarding the door, stood Sergeant Major Sean Ward with Sergeants Kevin Dunn and Vincent Klostermann. As Hugh and Doña Carlota arrived, Sergeants Abdul Jebet and Tabi Fleisch peeled off. *Must be end of shift.* Steeling himself, he walked in. All the holograms stood to attention as he entered. Sitting, he ordered, almost hesitantly, "Be seated."

Mentally he kicked himself, the right thing to say but the wrong voice. Intellectually, he knew he must say it, but it felt odd with all the brass standing around the table. Unfortunately, one more thing he didn't feel ready for. "So, what's the plan?" he asked with a little more confidence. Since they had put him in charge, he might as well sound comfortable, whether true or not. Speaking in a command voice made him feel more like he should be sitting here. Settling back into his chair, he waited.

Admiral Hollister answered. "Please give us an update, Ngaio."

The little, bald vice admiral, Duong Ngaio said, "First, I would like to tell His Highness that my brother who died on Deft would be proud of you this day. My entire family is honored to serve you." Continuing, he said, "Our situation is this: Admiral Davies is likely dead, and Prime Fleet doesn't know you're alive, which means we're on our own. Commodore Moboto has the details about the *Adelon* and the remnants of Battle Group 1-12 we fought with yesterday. Commodore."

Even as a hologram, Commodore Moboto towered over the others. Jebet beat him, but not by more than an inch and twenty pounds. Moboto spoke with the clipped accent common to the planet Kilimanjaro, "Apparently, the rebels surprised Battle Group 1-12 during a maintenance period at the base on Periastron. As far as can be determined, Perdot's men overran the entire base. Almost half the crews were killed during fighting on Periastron when some of the spacers rebelled, trying to join the rebel Perdot. He put all of the surviving rebels on a few ships that were to rejoin him after this operation, so we can assume all the survivors are loyal.

"He planned, from what the commanders of the ships tell us, to create confusion among the loyal fleets. Stupid, not likely to happen, but Perdot has never been the smartest tool in the box. After losing the control ships you identified, Your Highness"—he bowed to Hugh—"he has very few ships left and we are tracking them now."

Hugh acknowledged the compliment before watching to see who would speak next. *Better to be thought a fool by keeping silent than open your mouth and remove all doubt.* He saw Admiral Hollister purse his lips.

"Fine," George Hollister said. "We can always use another battle group or return it to Prime Fleet, whichever seems best. Keeping those ships raises the question of where we might get enough trained spacers to fly them. Recruiting and training are not easy to ramp up. That, of course, assumes the recruits will be loyal to the empire, let alone us." Hollister waved his adjutant back into her chair as she tensed, apparently preparing to speak up in response. "I know. Training Command is doing its best, but we also are barely keeping up with repairs and replacements on the units we're losing in combat. No criticism intended.

"Does my suggestion meet with your approval, Your Highness?"

Another shock. His opinion mattered on a fleet level, something he knew he had no qualifications to make. Ready to blurt an agreement, he made a conscious effort to settle back and think as Ward, on countless occasions, had tried to get him to do in the past before he did or said something stupid. These people wanted to believe in the empire and, right now, that consisted of one very young and inexperienced Hugh Cascade. Whatever he did, he needed to reassure them.

If he just went along, would he become a figurehead or considered one? If he said something stupid, he'd likely lose their trust. Which left going with his gut and trusting the men protecting him all these years so he could become emperor.

Taking a surreptitious breath, he sat forward. "Talk to Prime Fleet and go from there. Use your own discretion as to what is best once all the facts are in."

The admiral nodded. "Thank you, Your Highness. I will ensure your trust is not misplaced." Looking back over at Moboto, he asked, "So how did they know where to find the heir?"

Hugh suddenly wondered about that, too.

"From Admiral Davies, probably," answered Moboto flatly. "He happened to be on an inspection trip to Periastron when Perdot attacked. He may have been captured."

"So, who is in charge of Prime Fleet now?"

"Braddock. Solidly loyal, but he reached his present position after the coup killed so many of his superiors. I don't think he knows what a fleet commander should know about most things, which unfortunately includes His Highness."

Doña Carlota broke in at this point. "I reviewed the rest of the strategic situation with His Highness before we met here to save time. As I see it, we have three choices, Admiral."

"Only three, Doña Carlota?" Hollister responded drily. "We must really be in trouble."

Doña Carlota smiled back thinly. "Well, these are the three *best* choices, anyway. First, we can ignore the rest of the old empire and build something new here. Unfortunately, because they all have the same tech base we do and they outnumber us, it would just mean we would be the primary target for all of them, having an heir as we do. At least, we would be the target until we run out of ships and troops. At which point, the civilians would be at the mercy of whatever pirates, barbarians, or despots drop in to pick up the pieces."

"Lots of downside," George Hollister agreed. "Not much upside. We have discussed it thoroughly before, and it didn't appeal to me any better the last time. Next."

"Second choice, we announce we have the heir and try to rally the other fleets. Unfortunately, they may not take our word for it. Anyone disagree?"

Hugh figured that, because of Morgain's attempted deception and the disastrous blowback, it didn't stand much chance for success. Hugh felt the tension mount as Doña Carlota waited for someone to speak. No one did.

Doña Carlota nodded before continuing, "That just leaves the Galactic Starburst." Murmurs sped around the table, but Doña Carlota waited for quiet to return. "Some of you may not believe in it, that it's just a myth, but it's not. Those of you who know about the Galactic Starburst may think it disappeared, destroyed in the palace with Emperor Cyrus. That is true. Charles Roland's Galactic Starburst no longer exists, which means Hugh Cascade will have to go where a new one can be made."

The murmurs became louder and went on longer, so long that Admiral Hollister rapped for order. "Are we a military unit or a garden club?" he asked acidly. Hugh would have dearly loved to say *garden club* just to see what would happen, but he kept his mouth closed. Out of the corner of his eye, he caught Ward also warning him silently. Hugh smiled roguishly but still kept quiet. *Best not to wake sleeping dragons.*

Doña Carlota went on when things were completely silent. "His Highness can manufacture a new Galactic Starburst by following the alternate or full test route." Looking now at Hugh, she went on. "Charles Roland took the test at almost age thirty. With you, we had planned to wait a little longer until you reached your mid-twenties, at least, and gained more maturity so you would have a better chance. We can't do that now because the secret is out that you're alive. Davies, or someone, must have talked. Regardless of how the rebels know, however, you will be the target for assassins as well as hostile fleets."

Now Hollister spoke. "Without an empire and fleet to protect you, you won't survive. Without you, civilization won't survive. Our best projection is that, without restoration of the throne, we can put off the total breakup of the remaining sectors for several years at most, maybe ten. That will be followed by a night of total barbarism throughout the galaxy."

Things are so much worse than I ever imagined. "Admiral, I just need to be clear. There is no way to save even one sector and rebuild from there?"

"No, Your Highness. Eventually the fleet units that have been taken or rebelled will combine with new ships that can be built, overwhelming us. But it is more than that. People are losing their faith in the principles the empire stands for. Without people willing to sacrifice for those principles, then ship by ship, star system by star system, we will lose. We need a living symbol of what those principles mean, and that is you."

Another thought struck him. "We can't just up-ship our families, head out to the wilderness, find some backwoods systems, and set up again where fleet-quality units won't catch up to us until we're strong again?"

Hollister and Doña Carlota exchanged a look before Doña Carlota spoke up. "We discussed it with the other fleet commanders back when there were nine loyal fleets. You know the fleet motto."

"Life and freedom," Hugh answered promptly.

"Correct. It means the lives of citizens of the empire and their freedom come before anything else. If we went off into the blue, could we take the billions upon billions we are responsible for? No. Just a few hundred thousand, a few million if we commandeered every merchant ship we could find, and then, when we got to a suitable star system, we would have to take over someone else's home. What right would we have to do that? Any at all? We decided it would be a violation of every principle we have sworn to uphold, everything we believe in. We are no more than what we believe and uphold. We frequently come up short, but our ideals determine what we try to be and what our society will become, what we can achieve."

Doña Carlota heaved a sigh. "Fifth Fleet rejected our decision and headed off into the unknown. The little information that has trickled back has not been pretty. On a practical note, the technology base would be insufficient to keep our units functioning for very long. Regardless, the rest of us rejected that option and we have been fighting a rearguard action ever since," Doña Carlota sat back, concluding, "waiting for you."

"So, as I said yesterday, I'll take the test," Hugh said, his face hard with decision. "Where do I go?" Hugh noticed that Ward's expression changed the moment he asked this question.

Admiral Hollister examined Hugh carefully, making him feel very young and untried. "Well, there's the problem. We don't know, not exactly. So, you're going to have to find your own way."

Ward cleared his throat once, then again, more loudly, to get the room's attention. After all eyes turned to him, he raised an eyebrow, looking for permission to speak. Hollister waved an exasperated hand for him to go on. "Actually, I know where His Highness needs to start."

At this, Admiral Hollister's face became an astonishing shade of red and Doña Carlota's cheek began to twitch, something Hugh only remembered seeing once before when Doña Carlota had been unbelievably furious. Hollister burst out, "You *knew* and didn't think we should be told? Sergeant Major, I will have you keelhauled at light speed for this!"

Ward went on, not in the least apologetic, "First, I couldn't remember this particular piece of information because of nanite memory blocks that guard it. His Highness's request for the route just removed this initial set of blocks. Besides which, and with respect, Admiral, you didn't have the need to know. Within the Imperial Guard, a small group of proctors received additional knowledge for just this contingency. We trained the other proctors so they could carry out the mission of giving the normal test. Our special group, named the Implacables because of what Dave Jackson demanded of us, keeps that information secure to keep the empire safe for just this contingency."

Hollister nodded slowly. "I've heard rumors of the Implacables, but mostly just thought of them as only that, rumors."

"We're not. People know about us mostly because of Charles Roland. We gave him, and others at the time, a very special, more in-depth test. It is more thorough than emperors normally face, but the test must necessarily be given this way when the emperor does not have two things: an existing Galactic Starburst and the consent of the governed at the enthronement. We Implacables are sworn by solemn oath, reinforced by nanite mental block. We can only reveal what is necessary to the heir directly. I have always believed Hugh might be one who could complete this most difficult of all tests, though I expected to have more time to prepare him. Now that he has asked for the test—agreed to this test specifically—he must proceed to take it regardless of what I think. It is essentially a contract between him, Dave Jackson, and death."

Taken aback for a moment, Hugh recovered to give him a sharp look. "So, where am I going?"

Ward gave him a crooked smile. "*We*, Your Highness. I go with you, since I know what you must do and must determine if you pass. In addition, the parameters allow for twelve companions, and believe me, from what I now recall with the first block removed, you'll need every one of them, plus maybe a couple of thousand more."

Hugh felt himself rapidly losing a grip on his temper. "Fine. Where are *we* going?"

"I am required by my instructions to only tell you once we are on the way; it's the only way to maintain security. If we succeed, the empire may need it again."

Hugh colored slightly. "I suppose I should have thought of that myself. Fine." Looking around at the conference table to Admiral Hollister, he asked, "Anything else? How much time do I have to get this done?"

Hollister shrugged. "As soon as possible. Sixteenth Fleet is cut off since Eighth Fleet fell to the barbarians and Ninth Fleet fell into dispute, with Morgain effectively ruling the largest part of the sector. Fortunately, communications still operate throughout the empire. We'll use it to let people know you're seeking the crown. I hope the news you exist will strengthen the defenders and make the rebels and barbarians nervous, maybe even cause them to back off for a while. We want them to think the entire Imperial Fleet is on the way over the event horizon of the galactic black hole with you leading it. Good luck."

Hugh nodded to the admiral, "Please keep me informed about what's happening back here, and I'll hurry to finish the test as quickly as I can."

Hollister shook his head. "Hurrying is certainly a good idea, but I can't keep you informed. If I sent you on a supernova or nova we could stay in contact, but I can only send you on a small ship in keeping with the sergeant major's limitation that only twelve companions accompany you. Because only a planet or a very large ship can maintain an archeonA communications field, we won't be able to communicate with you. Just get there and back fast."

"Can you tell me how far we have to go, Sergeant Major, since time is critical?" Hugh asked.

Ward thought for a moment. "Normal preon polarity drive would take two, three months each way. Graviton drive twice, three times as long. A really fast ship, two months each way. Can we have a fast ship?" asked Ward looking at Hollister. "Everything I could find that's available is at least two days away."

Hollister smiled. "Amazing coincidence you should ask for a fast ship; one just popped up very early this morning. It's perfect for your purposes."

Hugh interrupted, "Just so I understand, I am going off into the unknown to take the test that has killed a good number of very able men and women. While I am gone and out of communication, you are going to tell all the people of the empire—what remains of it and what was part of it—that I will be back soon to save the universe. I can die, which means everyone here will likely die, too. If I succeed, it may be too late and, if I get back in time, lots of people will still die." Hugh paused a moment and then added, "Nothing like an easy mission."

Ward shook his head, then said, "His Highness has pretty well stated my assessment of the situation. Lucky for him and the rest of the universe, he'll have a team of Fleet Elite Marines with him when he goes off into the great unknown. That should even the odds, or put him ahead."

Across the table, Jim Inman, a previously silent army brigadier snorted. "Haven't gotten any humbler, have you, Sean?"

Ward smiled thinly. "Unlike the army, the Marines have little to be humble about, sir."

The brigadier just shook his head. "Always protecting that blind spot, aren't you? Everyone has one, and your faith in the Corps is yours." He held up a hand as Ward prepared an obviously devastating retort. "However, not to worry, Sergeant Major, your pride will not be your downfall. The fast ship the admiral mentioned will help you get the job done. It has a five-member Amazon flight crew from the army experienced in handling all kinds of contingencies. One you know well, as a matter of fact, Lieutenant Commander Gail Felt. Keeping this mission in the family, so to speak. She should keep you out of trouble."

Ward's eyebrows shot up. "They just got back. They were almost killed—again, I might add—and were promised leave." He gave the brigadier an angry look. "On top of which, what if I don't *want* Commander Felt and the *Ambrose B* going on this potential suicide mission? *Sir.*"

General Inman just smiled. "As I am over special ops, it's my call. You also know why I chose this flight crew. If anyone can keep you and your merry little band of bandits in line and out of harm's way, it's Felt. Besides, they volunteered."

Inman's smile grew wider as he dropped the last point on Ward like a bomb. Addressing Hugh, he continued, "Her black ops team is cross-trained in intel, so you get three for the price of one, a good deal, for you and the empire, one that improves the odds considerably. A good deal for the sergeant major, too, since it has been quite a while since he's spent quality time with his—What is the status of your relationship these days?"

Hugh watched Ward's face go through a range of emotions. Clearly Inman had information Hugh didn't. *Ward has a . . . a what? Girlfriend, wife, partner?* Ward took a moment, obviously struggling to get his anger under control, before he answered, "Jim, I'm glad you're finding something to entertain yourself with in the midst of all this Sturm und Drang, but for the sake of those of us who will actually be risking our lives to save the empire, maybe you should find other sources of amusement." He turned to Hollister. "Sir, with all due respect, and nothing against Gail Felt, for whom I have genuine respect and admiration, but she and her Amazons are worse than most of the special operations cowboys I've worked with in the past. That is just one of the reasons I don't want her out there, Admiral."

Genuine respect and admiration? Hugh didn't know that he'd ever heard Ward speak that way about anyone, not even Doña Carlota.

Hollister just shrugged as Inman didn't give an inch, his smile even more shark-like as he continued, "Between her crew and your six-man team and you, that makes twelve, Sergeant Major, unless Marines count differently than the rest of us. Plus, they're all women, so you'll have to act like a gentleman. She also outranks you, so you have to listen to her, which makes she and her crew perfect from our point of view."

Ward's jaw clenched for a minute before growling out, "This is a low blow, even for the army."

Hugh broke in, "I realize I don't know where we are going or what we will need when we get there, but I think having all the help I can get would be good." Here, he took a deep breath. "Let's take this Commander Felt if she's that good."

Inman gave Hugh a tight-lipped smile of triumph. "She's that good, sire. Ask the sergeant major."

Turning to Ward, Hugh asked, "Is she that good? Can you live with her, Sergeant Major?"

Ward evaluated him thoroughly for a moment, as if grading Hugh once more as a cadet. In a slightly quieter tone than earlier, he answered the question. "Yes, Gail Felt is the best, Your Highness."

The others chuckled, but Hugh sat up straight in response, face completely serious, as he directed a response to Ward, "Then let's get this show on the road, Sergeant Major. Yesterday!"

The faces of those watching this byplay showed a mixture of elation and dread, as the full import of this last scene hit them. They no longer considered him just a kid being called the heir apparent and feeling his way. For better or worse, no one could misunderstand that Hugh accepted his responsibilities, as shown by this act of taking the bit in his teeth. He had become the next best thing to emperor, *their* emperor, even if one only in testing. Everyone around the table stood and saluted Hugh, their right hands over their hearts. Hugh stood, soberly receiving the honor.

Everyone remained still for a moment before Hugh mentally slapped himself on the forehead. Then he, as the highest-ranking person present, turned and headed out the door so the others could go, too.

Appendix D: Imperial Ship Types

Core Empire Stealth Ship—Class is designated by a first name and initial. No picture available. All information is based upon non-official estimates including reported sightings, may not be accurate.

Specifications: Best estimate 140 meters long, dual-purpose atmosphere/space. Reported extendable delta wing. 20 meters tall, 60 meters wide wing tip to wing tip, and 23 meters wide in body only. Approximately two-thirds of ship dedicated to engines and fuel. Probably has three decks, maybe two or four. Based upon missions attributed to stealth ships but not confirmed, a ship of this class may carry an insertion team and usually presents itself as a fast passenger liner or high-value cargo freighter for entry into hostile zones.

Speed and Range: Within dense star lanes probably capable of three parsecs/day although information not published. High probability that use of stealth mode requires much slower speeds. Estimated endurance is two weeks extended ops at high speed based upon expected capacity of fuel tanks.

Outside of galactic arms estimate stealth speed at 110 parsecs/day, cruising speed 300 parsecs/day but range limited based upon fuel consumption.

Crew (estimated): Captain, copilot, engineer, two crew.

Drive (estimated): Multi-drive preon and gravitron.

Communications: Likely archeonB com system, possibly only archeonC due to limited space within ship for array.

Armament (estimated): No confirmation, but some reports indicate use of single missile bay hidden amidships in belly.

High confidence of three retractable laser gun turrets. Single crew in each turret for independent operation but likely to have slave capacity to command console.

Internal Configuration: (based upon best estimate, low

confidence) Access to lower two pods likely at end of single, central, lower corridor near engine bulkhead. Access to upper or dorsal gun pod most likely through dropdown ladder in single, central, upper corridor also near engine bulkhead.

Upper corridor accesses direct vision lounge forward, with stores and mechanical rooms along central corridor. Lower corridor similarly provides access to stores and mechanical spaces including environmental.

Main deck probably consists of bridge forward with captain's quarters immediately behind and to port. Likely to starboard is circular stairwell leading to upper and lower corridors. A likely cross-corridor along the central block leads to twin corridors. Central block would include mess/gym, water storage, and shower facilities.

Along either corridor outboard would be two three-by-three-meter cabins and additional stores and mechanical spaces. The central block is likely 30 meters long and a cross-corridor connects up the longitudinal corridors. A likely single corridor leads aft. The engineering cabin would probably be located here, as well as an additional stairwell. The engineering spaces can undoubtedly be accessed by this end corridor.

17

Liftoff

Fleet Emergency Command Complex Jeffco
0950 Local/0350 BBMT 11 October 3473

SERGEANTS KEVIN DUNN AND VINCENT Klostermann smoothly fell into position before and behind Hugh Cascade as they returned to his room. Sergeant Major Sean Ward marched beside Hugh until the first corridor intersection, before halting abruptly. They all stopped with him. "Your Highness, I need to get some things together, and these men need to get packed. If you'll gather your things, they'll take you to the ship. At that point, I'll meet you and let them get their duffels together."

"Our bags are packed, Top," Dunn volunteered. "We talked about it last night and all of us on the team are ready to ship out with the kid—I mean, His Highness." The look on Dunn's face made it clear he hadn't misspoken.

Hugh's heart soared in hearing that Dunn, Klostermann, and the others wanted to go with him. He felt so great he almost missed Dunn's sniping comment. Almost. "That's two I owe you, *Private*," Hugh said sternly.

Dunn, face innocent as a newborn, asked, "Oh, are we starting over?"

Klostermann chuckled. "That's three, Your Highness. Do you want me to keep score or have Jebet do it? I understand he counted all the way to ten before losing track this morning."

"Yeah," chimed in Dunn. "As for shipping out, we're all set."

Hugh shook his head. "I'm glad you're ready to go but I want you to know you're all in trouble. Keeping score? I'll keep my own scores and settle every one of them, too." He let that sink in before going on. Unfortunately, neither of them looked in the least bit worried by the threat. *They should be.* "But apparently we need to get moving. Correct, Sergeant Major?"

Ward nodded, face hardening. Hugh gauged that Ward took the addition of Captain Felt and her Amazons to their mission personally more than professionally.

Ward said to Klosterman and Dunn, "As for you two, I'll have the others grab your gear. See you on the ship, Your Highness." He saluted. As Hugh returned it, though, he detected a slight start of surprise before Ward headed off down a side corridor. Ward's hesitation reminded Hugh that in all of the historical footage he had watched of the empresses and emperors, he could not recall them ever returning a salute. That might be proper protocol, but he had decided that as for himself, he would salute. He had been taught in military etiquette classes that salutes represent a courtesy, and, after growing up in the military, it felt natural acknowledging them. Besides which, unlike the almost god-like figures in the videos, he *knew* he wasn't some kind of higher being, and didn't intend to try and act like one.

Hugh pointed toward his quarters, Dunn leading off. Hugh wanted to luxuriate in that little private room that would still be his. For the next ten minutes, anyway. He'd been in small ships and he couldn't remember one with cabins as large as his tiny hole in the wall here.

Reaching it, Dunn checked the room, again, before letting him in. Grabbing a bag, he stuffed in his jacket, boots, and the few other items he had had with him when the attack hit. As heir, he probably could afford much nicer boots and jackets than these, but he'd sacrificed a lot to buy them. They would always remind him of his trek through the fire and the mountains. His other mementos and clothes were on the estate where he couldn't get them, so he, the heir to a significant portion of the galaxy, owned what could be easily packed into one small rucksack consisting solely of his personal possessions and two uniforms. Turning to leave, he skidded to a halt. Spinning back into the room, he grabbed his bow and quiver of arrows. Though not a practical weapon in the far reaches of space, his bow had significant meaning to him, a reminder of his days when he was just Cadet Cascade and he could run off into the woods without a platoon of Marines.

Settling the pack on his left shoulder and the bow and quiver on his right, he walked out into the corridor and turned toward the lifts leading to the hangers. "Onward and upward, gentlemen. The sooner we go, the sooner we're back."

Hustling together, they almost jogged to the lifts, followed by a ride up three levels to another series of corridors and stairways that led to the huge dock and hanger area carved out of a massive cave near the command center. A force screen and camouflaged doors protected the outer entrance to the cave. Hugh noticed a sleek dual-purpose atmosphere/spaceship with the name *Ambrose B* in simple script on the bow. A glass dome covered a knob above the nose and the bridge could be seen below it through small windows. Not much different looking than a standard aircraft, Hugh thought, although almost twice as big as most civilian planes. Hugh took a step forward to hurry across the hanger floor but ran into Dunn's back instead. Dunn remained still, scanning the huge cavern. Klostermann watched the rear. Dunn spoke into his lapel com, "Sergeant Major, we could use a larger detail at entry point three."

"Proceed to the *Ambrose B*, Sergeant. His Highness has not been announced, so we should be able to get out with a low profile."

"I think you should look out here, Top. The rumor mill seems to have kicked into high gear since yesterday. Where are you right now?"

"On the *Ambrose B* getting squared away. I'll be out in a minute. Hold fast."

Hugh had pushed around Kevin by this time. He stopped, too, stunned at what he saw.

A large crowd surrounded *Ambrose B*'s boarding ramp. Hugh guessed that almost every off-duty person on the base must be there, as well as many who technically should have been somewhere else. Plus, with all the people not in uniform, most of the civilians from the estate seemed to have gathered, too. With that many people, the crowd noise bouncing off the stone walls and ceilings pressed physically in on him from every side. Dunn stepped in front of Hugh, pushing him back from the cavern, a look of true concern on his face.

They are here for me, Hugh realized, the overwhelming sound they were making bringing home to him in a real way how, to the galaxy at large, he would soon be emperor. *Kevin is concerned one of them might want to hurt me?*

In one way, the gems made him aware of his potential to become emperor, but internally, *personally*, only. As for Dunn and Klostermann, having known him for years, their acceptance calmed the nagging doubt that he couldn't cut it, that Admiral George Hollister had made a gigantic mistake. But this? These people, most he didn't know, seemed to *want* him to be emperor, needed him to be emperor, even without knowing him. He found that faith in him both exhilarating and daunting.

Dunn released the safety on his rifle, eyes nervously flitting around. Hugh could feel his anxiety level rising. "Relax, Kevin." Hugh almost needed to shout to be heard. "It'll be okay."

On a sudden impulse, he stepped out and around Dunn, catching him and Klostermann by surprise, before striding forward, waving. As he did, the crowd exploded in cheers, surging forward in an instant toward him.

LOOKING OUT OF THE COCKPIT, Ward understood immediately. He knew that the amount of time information could be kept confidential to be inversely proportional to the number of people in the know. Thirteen people had attended the meeting yesterday, in addition to himself and Hugh, and to put the gears in motion to get Hugh on his way, had required more be told. Plus with Hugh being marched around the base with a security detail calling him "Your Highness" every other sentence, they might as well have sent out a memo. And with the assistance of archeonA communication, half the galaxy might know by now, or likely would within another twenty-four to forty-eight hours.

STEPPING FORWARD, HUGH FELT the crowd's overwhelming excitement as it surged toward him, then engulfed him. The press of the crowd caused his quiver and bow to bite into his back and arm. He pushed on, even as the rucksack became tangled with people, slowing his progress.

A brief memory of some historic video showing Cyrus, the last emperor, walking out into a crowd during some holiday or other, shaking hands, and speaking with citizens, came back to him. Hugh started shaking hands, greeting as many by name as he could remember in the spur of the moment. It seemed that everyone also wanted to say something. Instinctively, in response to their wishes of good fortune, he answered, "Thank you, very much" time and again.

Astounded by their apparent need to see him, touch him, the press of bodies overwhelmed him, almost suffocating him. As he looked into their faces, some familiar, others those of strangers, he drank in their hope and elation, a mixture immensely intoxicating.

He also saw what looked to him like fear in many of their faces, the same fear gnawing at him. If he failed, destroying their hopes, what would happen to the empire? In fighting the long delaying action, so many had lost hope. Hugh remembered hearing them talk, listening to them during the long watches in the dead of night, as they saw no end but death and failure. But here, suddenly, in front of them, stood an heir, someone they could touch, rekindling a flicker of hope.

And they were crushing him as their hope grew. *How funny,* he mused, *if I were to die like this.*

Halfway to the ship, he came face-to-face with Noor Bettis in her cadet gray, her dark hair in a tight French braid and pinned up in back. *How come I never noticed how pretty her eyes are?* A bit awkwardly, she reached out to hug him, then yelled into his ear, above the din, "Good luck, Cascade. We're counting on you."

"Thanks, Bettis. I'll do my best."

She let go, then smiled crookedly at him and said, "You better, or I'll kick your butt."

Hugh laughed. "One time, one time, and you won't let me forget it."

She punched him in the shoulder. "Of course, that's my job. Can't let your head get too big now that you're going to be emperor. Crown wouldn't fit." He barked a short laugh before moving on and losing her in the press. No matter what Doña Carlota thought, he couldn't help but think he would someday look back at Noor Bettis as the one who got away.

Holding onto his bow, quiver, and rucksack with difficulty, Hugh could barely breathe by the time his protectors, shoving and prying with their rifle butts, opened a small space for him to stand in. After a minute, they restored enough order for Hugh to continue shaking hands and speaking into the ears of these people. *My people.*

Mrs. Kvorth, one of his history teachers, pulled him close, hugging him tightly. Before letting him go, she shouted in his ear, still barely audible in the echoing hanger, "Good luck. I always liked you. Now make us proud."

As he continued to shake hands, suddenly Liz Polchar and her friends, Svetlana and Aiysha, suddenly stood in front of him. He froze when Liz grabbed his arms, leaned up, and briefly pressed her lips to his, blushing as she leaned back. A thrill shot through him but, before he could react, she disappeared into the crowd like a frightened fawn. Both of the others did the same, following Liz just as rapidly, giggling as they went.

In a daze, he moved on toward the ship. Other women, civilian and military, followed Liz's example, most giving him just a peck on the cheek, but he occasionally got a full smack on the lips. *Being heir has its upside, after all, except for the whole victory or death thing.* Smiling at his private joke, he slowly pressed ahead.

Finally, he reached the entry ramp to the *Ambrose B.* Glancing up, he saw a fuming Ward waiting to chew him out. He knew being heir apparent wouldn't save him from a reaming, but deep down he felt greeting the crowd had been the right thing to do. As he glanced around, he noticed Doña Carlota waiting also, her face unreadable. Taking a breath as he let go of the last hand, he stepped onto the entry ramp. The two guards on duty, Abdul Jebet and Tabi Fleisch, snapped to attention and saluted. Hugh saluted back. He looked them fully in the face and knew from their lack of expression that they expected him to get a royal chewing out.

Taking a deep breath, he stepped beyond the threshold, realizing he had told himself a joke without even trying. *Royal chewing out.* Smiling almost against his will, and certainly contrary to his survival instincts, he walked straight toward Ward.

Ward straightened, obviously preparing to bellow, and opened his mouth only to be preempted by Doña Carlota, "Welcome aboard, sire." Then, surprising everybody, the short, elegant, and imperturbable aristocrat threw her arms around Hugh for the second time in twenty-four hours, crying just as hard as after the Oath Ceremony. Taken aback, Hugh managed to return the hug a little more comfortably than the first time. Doña Carlota never displayed her emotion, which made all these hugs even more unnerving. Not wanting to hurt Doña Carlota's feelings by breaking it off early, he stood there for another minute while she held him.

Doña Carlota finally let go. "I'm sorry, sire, but seeing you with those people, people who so very much need you, brought back memories of Cyrus. He drove his security people crazy all the time, but the common people loved him." She wiped her eyes before drawing herself up and regaining her composure. "You have the gift to reach them and, I believe, the strength to be who they need and want. To us, you represent the hope that we can rise to greatness again. To them, that there can be sanity and peace in the galaxy. Thank you." She gave his arm a final squeeze and left before Hugh could think of anything appropriate to say.

Ward, clamping his mouth firmly closed, nodded to Dunn and Klostermann. They saluted and fell in around Doña Carlota as she headed back down the ramp. Ward motioned Hugh forward into the corridor. "We'll be taking off as soon as those two get back here and your admirers clear the area, sire." Ward spoke in such a carefully neutral tone that Hugh felt the chewing out even as the sergeant major controlled his choice of words and tone. "We arranged for some additional things you might need to be put together for you while you were on your way here. Fleisch here will take you to your cabin to stow the gear you brought with you."

Hugh stared at Fleisch's back as he got ready to walk the short distance to the new cabin. *Here is a woman who has almost died for me once already*, Hugh realized. Fleisch carried the look in her eyes of the real spec ops veteran, someone ready at a moment's notice to do whatever needed to be done to protect the empire. Her willingness to again go into the unknown with Hugh spoke volumes about her character.

Before they left, though, Hugh needed an answer to one question. Turning toward Ward, he asked, "Sergeant Major, you were about to chew my rear off for jumping into that crowd. Why didn't you?"

"Well, Your Highness, you certainly didn't display a great deal of forethought—calling it *stupid* might understate it a bit—walking into the crowd like that," answered Ward, with a penetrating look. "If there had been an assassin out there, you and a lot of good people would be dead."

Hugh nodded, then added, "But?"

Ward shrugged, "But the hardest thing to teach young Marine lieutenants is leadership. You have to know when to make yourself a target in order to accomplish the mission, and when to keep your head down. That can't be learned in a classroom. You've got to be able to feel it and you did. Seeing the look on Doña Carlota's face made me realize you instinctively made the right choice. I decided it would be, well, counterproductive shall we say, to chew you out for sticking your neck out at the right time to inspire the troops. Besides, this is the test, and you have to be allowed to fail if you are to have the chance to succeed."

"Thank you, Sergeant Major, for something more to consider. My rear end also wishes to express its appreciation for not being bitten off. But you did just ream me out, if ever so politely."

Ward nodded. "Just a reminder that what you just did could have ended badly. You need to make a conscious choice to do things like that, not just act on instinct."

Hugh nodded. "I'll try and remember that, Sergeant Major." Calling Fleisch back, he asked, "Where's my cabin?"

Hugh felt Ward's eyes on him as he moved off to the left into the corridor. Fleisch led him around two right turns and then to the second door on the port or outboard side. She opened this door, looked carefully around, then said, a bit grandly, "Your cabin, Your Highness."

Hugh entered the modest-sized, ten-by-ten cabin and stood a moment scanning it before tossing his bag on the bed and propping his bow and quiver against the wall. Turning back to Fleisch, he said, "Let's head to the bridge, Sergeant Fleisch."

She blinked. "Sire?"

"The bridge, Sergeant. I've never been on one during liftoff, so let's go."

Fleisch gave him a look of on-your-head-be-it but led off anyway. Reaching the bridge bulkhead at the end of the corridor, she rapped, then opened it. "His Highness on deck!" she bellowed.

Ward, sitting on the jump seat behind the pilots, whipped his head around, growling, "Belay that! No distractions on the bridge." Standing, he changed his focus from the guard to Hugh, asking, "Why are you up here, sire?"

"Never seen a liftoff and thought it would be interesting. That okay with you, Captain?" he asked politely.

Gail Felt, head turning half around when Fleisch announced Hugh, absently nodded before returning to the board. "Just be quiet. Sire."

Hugh noticed the captain's petite build, her red hair streaked with gray and plenty of fine wrinkle lines had him guessing her to be in her forties, easily. Her number two wore her brunette hair in a bob and looked much younger, with nice green eyes and average height. He could see the engineer on the monitor, the darkest woman he ever remembered seeing. Likely, she came from Sector Fifteen, probably Kilimanjaro or somewhere similar. Her hair lay very short and curly on her head.

Gail spoke softly into the intercom, "Okay, Sheila. I see Dunn and Klostermann dashing out of the tunnel toward us now. As soon as they get here, we'll launch. Everything ready to go down there?" On the screen, the engineer gave a thumbs-up. Flipping a switch, the captain spoke into the intercom, "Okay, two minutes to lift. Everyone into lift position." Switching off the intercom, she half turned her head toward Hugh. "That means you, too, sire. You three sightseers need to get out of here." Ward nodded and edged toward the door.

"I would prefer to stay, Captain," Hugh tried to say very politely, but with the firm I-will-be-obeyed tone he admired in Doña Carlota and the sergeant major.

Gail gave him a quick look and simply shook her head. "You're the boss and can do what you want but, being here, you could be a distraction in an emergency. You might do the wrong thing, and I would prefer you in a safe place until we get going."

Hugh nodding, conceded to the reasonable request, returning to his cabin slightly chastened. How did Ward, and now Felt, manage to always make him feel like a little child demanding to get his own way? Even worse, they were right and he knew it. Fleisch helped him hook up before connecting into a second chair in the cabin. Flipping her com, she reported, "His Highness is ready to go."

Hugh reached over to a computer, bringing up a series of views on the screen. He also brought up a status board for the ship. All showed green, ready for lift. Hugh didn't feel anything as they lifted, no acceleration, nor a change of any kind. To an observer on Jeffco, after the ship left atmosphere, the ship would appear to exceed the speed of light very quickly.

And *Ambrose B* had been built for speed. Hugh knew being able to go fast really helped when you needed to go a very long way or to be someplace yesterday. Of course, he had no idea where they were going except possibly to Lost Earth, which, as the name said, wasn't in the navigational database. That put Earth in the same category as all the other mythical things hidden in fairy tales. *Why on earth*—he smiled at his pun—*would anyone hide something like a facility to make a new Imperial Galactic Starburst so far away that it would take months to fly there?*

Without an answer, he watched space shift to red on the light speed monitor as they accelerated outward from the planet. The view on the monitor suddenly adjusted to a view of the universe he understood, computer modifying the real-time feed to a virtual view of space to show the red and blue shifts, ahead and behind, as something recognizable. He noted on a side display that they were being followed outward by a cruiser supported by a flotilla of destroyers.

"*Meeting in the mess in five minutes,*" came an intercom call, breaking in on his thoughts. He couldn't place that voice, yet, but with a ship this small he would soon know everyone.

Galactifacts for Kids 3500

Gravitonic Drive. Most spaceships use gravitonic drive both within solar systems as well as between stars. Only the Core Empire has what they call a preon drive that is discussed in that section.

Gravitonic drive, or more properly gravitonic/ magnetic flux inducing dark energy propulsion, is an example of serendipity, an accidental discovery. Beginning in 2016 AD, scientists on Earth attempted to tap inexhaustible sources of clean energy thought to be available in dark energy found throughout the universe.

Rutherford Nance, PhD, postulated in 2046 AD that, by applying an oscillating magnetic flux to a multi-ply lithium structure from specific angles, immense energy would be released that he believed to be pent-up dark energy. Dr. Ishihara Kaga followed up this postulate in his lab in 2055 AD with a brief burst that went uncaptured. Setting up a massive capture field in Tonopah, Nevada, the only location with sufficient isolation for a permit to be issued by the Department of Energy in the country then known as the United States, he initiated a larger release on July 4, 2059 AD as symbolically freeing humanity from energy dependence on fossil fuels.

As he cycled the initiating energy through a series of vectors aimed at the lithium, he stumbled across an immense trigger point. The resulting intense gravity surge created what became known as "The Hole," a crater sixty kilometers in diameter where Tonopah used to be. Before the wave dissipated, however, readings showed that the lab itself experienced no change in gravity, only the surrounding area. Based upon these observations, control of gravity in starships became possible.

Further research led to a method to use this gravitonic surge, allowing a ship to essentially surf through the galaxy from one gravity wave crest to another. Because the ship is essentially the reference point around which the universe rotates, this limits the negative aspects of Einsteinian time and space relativity to ships and other objects under Newtonian reaction drives.

The first gravitonic ship left Earth orbit in 2075 AD.

18

Breakaway

Ambrose B, Longview System
0450 BBMT 11 October 3473

HUGH CASCADE, WITH TABI FLEISCH standing quiet at his elbow, studied the ship diagram on the bulkhead as he waited to be the last to the meeting. Standard layouts made things easy once you familiarized yourself with them, and *Ambrose B*'s layout appeared to be pretty normal for a small ship based upon simulations he'd completed. He wondered how they would split up six cabins between seven men and six women, especially since protocol required one of the men to have a cabin alone. Him. If he took one, the remaining twelve people did not divide evenly by five, not even close. At least he didn't have to figure out the sleeping arrangements.

Hugh understood that, when *Ambrose B* carried its crew of five women and a six-person insertion team into a hot zone, two per cabin worked easily with no infringement on the captain. Ships normally didn't require a huge crew because of automation. Most things, like the engines, just needed to be watched until something went wrong. Hugh knew from sims that when things went wrong, life became very exciting for everyone, passengers and crew alike. Having Marines on board would help if that happened because they were trained in weapons and damage control.

Okay. Time to start. Opening the hatch to the mess, he walked into a crowded space. Designed comfortably for six, there were eleven after he came in with Fleisch, which left two, undoubtedly one on the bridge and another in engineering. It seemed even more crowded with the captain and Ward facing off angrily. Kevin Dunn bellowed, "His Highness on deck!" which shut everyone up.

Hugh felt ten pairs of eyes on him. Struggling, he tried to find the right thing to say. After a moment, he clearly and carefully offered, "At ease."

What now? Being in charge he should say something more because nothing could happen until he gave the go-ahead. *Every one of these people has much more experience than I do.* It hit him hard; most were at least twice his age. Fortunately, his poker face in social situations helped.

Glancing at Vincent Klostermann, he saw a shadow of a smile. *He's enjoying watching me twist in the wind here.* Klostermann knew him too well. He'd incessantly drummed into him the old adage, *In a firefight, the man who freezes, dies. Always move forward.* So, he charged ahead.

Taking a short breath as he looked around for a chair, Hugh sat and then asked, "Sergeant Major, Captain? What seems to be the problem?"

Sean Ward snorted as Gail Felt answered, "Just sorting out where everyone is going to sleep. I reasonably suggested that you share a cabin with one of the sergeants. Lieutenant Sheila Kirk is the engineer," she pointed to the black woman on the split screen. "She normally has a cabin by herself, but that isn't possible with all this crowding. I am having Petty Officer West," indicating the tall, thin woman with a too-innocent expression and twinkle in her eye that immediately tipped Hugh to her probably being a prankster, "share her quarters because Sheila needs to be next to the engine spaces. Three in a room is just not possible for the safe and efficient operation of the ship if it can be avoided. You met Lieutenant Carr," who nodded from the other side of the split screen. "Lieutenant Carr will share with Petty Officer Hall," a short Asiatic woman who gave him a sardonic smile, "because Sally has to be as close to the bridge as possible since she's copilot. Normally, we don't have officers and petty officers share, but the devil is driving the details on this flight." At this point, she gave Ward the stink eye.

Ward didn't look any happier as he stepped in, "Sire, you have a cabin because there is no way the heir can share with a noncommissioned officer. That leaves two cabins for the other five men besides Fleisch. Three is ridiculous for men as big as we are and four, impossible."

The moment of silence grew, while neither Hugh nor Captain Felt asked the question Ward seemed to be fishing for regarding her crew quarters. He continued, "What is left are storerooms, this mess area, which would impede access of the women to the showers and heads, and the weapons pods where we could sling a hammock each." After another moment, he went on, "The best we can do is to put our gunners into the weapons pods: Fleisch, Kennion, and Dunn. Jebet could take a storeroom because there's no way he can share a cabin or take a pod. Peterson and Klostermann will share a cabin and I will take one so I can carry out my duties as proctor." Looking at Gail Felt, he asked, sounding aggrieved, "Happy?"

Gail shrugged. "It'll work and we are all sacrificing a bit for Cadet Cascade."

Dunn cleared his throat. "Please refer to him properly, ma'am. He is the heir apparent, so he is *sire* or *His Highness*." Hugh turned to look at Dunn. His words, delivered in a calm, even, low-keyed voice, had a powerful impact on Hugh. It indicated that Dunn accepted Hugh as his personal sovereign lord. More importantly, Dunn demanded that Captain Felt, and everyone else aboard, also accept Hugh as the sovereign. Silently grateful for this sign from his friend, he felt his confidence grow deep inside where he kept everything he believed and doubted about himself safely locked away.

He looked around the room. These men had known him—all but Kevin—since Deft, when it seemed like the whole world wanted to kill him. They had in the most literal way *raised* him from a small boy to the man he was today. Yet they were treating him as the rightful ruler of the Core Empire and thousands of systems. He didn't know whether to laugh or cry or cheer. Hugh watched a small but significant change of posture and expression come over Gail. He knew that over the last ten years she, like everyone else, had watched impotently as so much of the empire fell to rebels and barbarians. She had fought hard and watched friends die. Now, she confronted the choice of whether to hope, to accept him as emperor, or not. Hugh wondered what she saw. A fairly good-looking, straight-backed, and physically imposing young man? Did he look like his father to her?

Hugh watched thoughts he couldn't read crossing her face, and then some kind of startling realization must have hit her. Her demeanor changed. Her pause to regain her poise stretched on to almost twenty seconds, which felt much longer. Suspense tied his stomach in a knot; what would Captain Felt do or say now? "Captain?" he prompted her.

"Sire. We are honored to be able to assist you." Facing Ward again, she asked in a still-aggrieved tone, "Sergeant Major, can you tell me now where are we going?"

Ward answered formally, "Ma'am, I can tell you we are on our way to Earth, heading out away from the core. Until we are out of archeon range of planets in this sector, as well as our escort, I can't be more specific."

Gail Felt started turning red again as she answered, "Who here is going to tell anyone, Sergeant Major? *No one knows* where Earth is because over the last thousand years its relationship to the core has changed, which is why I asked for directions. Besides, we don't have long-range archeon and are accelerating constantly."

"We're being followed by a cruiser escort until we reach the core boundary and might be able to call them until then, so I must respectfully decline to give out any further information until they are beyond our archeon range."

Gail snorted in disgust, "I would like to put us on the right heading, at least. We could end up dozens of parsecs or more from where we need to be when we cross the boundary if we don't make corrections now. That could put us days or weeks away from where we need to be. Admiral Hollister told me personally that this mission is time-sensitive, so give me a break, Ward. Where should I point the nose of this scow?"

Ward smiled thinly. "I would think that pointing us out at the last known coordinates of Earth would get us fairly close, within several trillion kilometers anyway."

Gail threw up her hands. "You have always been a pain in the posterior, Sean Ward. I remember the first time my ship took you and your merry outlaws on a mission, you almost got us killed."

"Captain Felt, I remember that mission just a little different than you do." Hugh noticed a brief glimmer in Ward's eyes before he continued, "But I am sorry to say you may be wrong. This mission might just be a lot worse than that one."

"Worse?" murmured Pam West, the tall blonde. "I've heard the captain go on at length about some of your missions. *Impossible* didn't describe most of them. As I recall, on her first mission with you, she lost one of the two ships she has survived having shot out from under her. Unless those were just space monster tales?"

Ward's face became innocent as a babe's as he answered, "I would never impugn the integrity of your captain." Hugh almost busted out laughing as he saw Gail cross her arms and give Ward a severe look before he continued, "Especially since she's driving."

Gail smiled sweetly. "You want to walk instead of doing it my way?"

To Hugh, there seemed to be something unsaid between them in the back and forth. *I wonder what that's about?* One thing he knew, people who had seen combat usually didn't say anything or joke about missions with outsiders. *It must have been really hairy.*

Ward, however, didn't take the bait, allowing Felt to follow up, "So, back to the current situation, when will you tell me where to go?"

Everyone, including Hugh, smiled at that ill-chosen phrase. Ward managed to maintain a straight face as he answered, "If we fly max out and leave our escort in the dust, two days. A week if we fly with them to the boundary."

"I'll hold you to that, Sergeant Major, or I *will* put you out and make you walk, and you know it."

Ward nodded mournfully. "I have learned by sad experience that you never bluff."

Gail Felt did smile at that. "Glad you learned that lesson," she said with a trace of satisfaction and, after a long moment, added, "Finally."

Ward growled, but Hugh saw a twinkle in his eye. Suddenly it struck him, *Is this what it looks like when Sean Ward flirts?*

Galactifacts for Kids 3500

Preon Polarity Drive. The Core Empire discovered and then kept preon polarity drive a military secret for 350 years. The fact that it existed, permitting CNS vessels to travel at three times the speed of gravitonic vessels, became apparent to all other star systems shortly after deployment. The physics and theory, however, remained closely guarded until recently.

Preon polarity drive uses the difference in energy potential between our universe, normally identified as sidereal, and the dark matter universe. The dark matter universe contains four times the energy found in ours. In 2581 AD, Franz Bowdoin and Heidi Metzinger on the planet Jenna Jorgensen, the capital of Sector Ten of the Core Empire, theorized that the differential between the energy states could be used to achieve almost inconceivable speeds.

The emperor of that time, Ian, slapped a ban on any research regarding preon polarity except in imperial high-security facilities. As a result, no one achieved much progress until 3144 AD on Harwell, the Imperial Marine training planet in Prime Sector. From 3150 AD on, all imperial ships included preon polarity drive.

A simple, nontechnical, and somewhat incorrect explanation is that the drive opens a rift behind the ship into the dark matter universe. To determine speed, a wave of varying heights is built up that the ship slides down like a surfer on a wave of water. A limit to speeds achievable exists due to the need to use gravitonic particles to avoid the effects of inertia within the ship. Speeds exceeding three times the ship's maximum gravitonic speed may result in catastrophic graviton overload with immediate and catastrophic effects.

19

Buildup

Ambrose B, Longview System
0520 BBMT 11 October 3473

"YOUR HIGHNESS," SEAN WARD BEGAN after the crew left. "We are going to be on this ship for several months, probably." Looking at the others, he added, "That means, because of the ship's size, we'll suspend the protection detail. Any questions on that?" No one answered, so he continued. "According to my information, we are going to need refueling four times before we get to the neighborhood of Earth. Flying at full speed for two weeks will use most of the fuel we've got, which means at least three months each way. That's the bad news. The good news is that we have plenty of time for training. We'll use the mess for a gym; it's about thirty by fifteen including the kitchen area. With your permission, Your Highness," which he said without any trace of irony as far as Hugh could tell, "I'll set up a schedule including all the ship's weapons systems. This way, we can make the best use of all our extra hours. We're going to have lots of them, so let's use them wisely." Hugh nodded apprehensively in agreement. *What did I let myself in for?*

Ward stood up, looking around the small mess. "Dunn and Klostermann, disconnect the tables from the deck and move them against the wall. Peterson and Jebet, go through the storerooms and find some padding for this place. When one of the storerooms is empty, you can use it for a bedroom, Jebet. Fleisch and Kennion, get the equipment. We need to warm up before we work out."

Hugh shuddered as he heard those words, having participated in these almost-sadistic activities five to six days a week since he had turned sixteen, and sported the bruises to prove it. Besides which, although not nearly as tired as yesterday morning before the Oath Ceremony, he still felt drained. However, he knew from experience that complaining, especially to Ward, just made the workouts worse. So, putting on an expectant look and trying to appear eager, he waited to see what Ward would assign him to do in preparation for the fun and games. Ward stared back impassively until Hugh suddenly realized he now gave Ward orders, not the other way around. He self-consciously smiled and then stripped off his shirt and shoes before stretching.

Hugh remembered Ward's scathing comments regarding second lieutenants not knowing their heads from a hole in the ground and that, *If you want to find a second lieutenant, just stand still and wait. He'll show up sooner or later.* Ward also liked: *The difference between a second lieutenant and a puppy is that a puppy is cute.* Well, he had become, in effect, a second lieutenant, only a thousand times worse, as heir apparent.

No wonder Ward and Doña Carlota had wanted so badly to let him mature a little more before telling him. *Too late now. So, I better get my rear in gear if I want to be worthy of this job.* If he couldn't hack it, even if he did succeed, people would stop believing in the empire, which meant the whole galaxy would be up a creek without a paddle. The entire galaxy depended on him to grow up fast, so, no pressure.

Sobered by that thought, he stood aside while the team set up the padding in the gym. Looking over at Ward, at the moment actively inspiring the team to get done faster, Hugh asked, "Sergeant Major? What are we going to do for running? The corridors are just a tad short for working up a sweat."

Ward gave him a devilish smile. "Not at two G's, sire."

Hugh saw the hardened members of the team shudder at this and joined them in their dread at the prospect of this particularly evil twist Ward had just sprung on them. Adjusting the internal corridor gravity so a man weighed two times as much as normal took no technical wizardry but using it made it blindingly obvious that Ward intended to reach, and likely exceed, his training objectives. Whatever those might be.

At two G's, you got many times more than twice the benefit for the distance. Once around those off-white main corridors measured almost ninety meters. At two G's, with the increased stress on the body, a standard eight-kilometer run would be about eighteen laps. Maybe they could paint scenery on the bulkheads or project a countryside or something to avoid boredom.

Around him, the others began pulling on their specialized pressure suits for running that forced blood out of the extremities and allowed their lungs to fully function. Hugh grinned as he thought about that. After all, their brains did need oxygen to survive, even Kevin's. Muttering to himself, he got ready, too. Hanging the oxygen mask, essential for forcing air deep into the lungs, around his neck, he stood up feeling decidedly uncomfortable, knowing this experience would be very interesting, and painful, for everyone involved.

An odd thought popped into his head. All the gear being on hand and ready indicated Ward had prepared for the training well in advance. If Ward went to this much trouble over the training regimen on a ship that had remained in port less than twelve hours, Ward undoubtedly must have thought out and implemented a training regimen for him to make him at least a passable emperor from age eight, ten years before. Since molding Hugh into a fair emperor seemed to be much more important than not losing muscle tone over a few months, Hugh hoped Ward had indeed been running him through an emperor's prep course. *I might actually have a chance of surviving if that's true.*

Hugh leaned against the bulkhead as he thought. Straightening up, he motioned to Ward to follow him out into the corridor, which he did. "Question, Sergeant Major."

"Yes, sire. Of course, because you are the senior officer, you can call me Ward, if you desire." As he responded, Ward stood in the position mislabeled *at ease* by Marines, actually a very slightly modified parade rest, with legs slightly apart, hands clasped firmly in the small of his back, posture ramrod straight, with just his head tracking Hugh.

"Fine, Sergeant Major. I'll do that just as soon as you assume the position of *rest* while we talk."

Hugh felt Ward's eyes, his will beating down on him, attempting to bend Hugh to his desire. Hugh held Ward's eyes firmly for ten seconds until Ward relaxed. Ward gave him a half smile as he did and prompted, "Sire?"

"Thanks . . . Ward," hesitating on the name, tasting the feel of calling this fearsome legend by his last name. He still felt intimidated, he realized.

"So," he paused as he regained his train of thought. "Without any time lost whatsoever you hit us with a complete training program to keep us in shape. That made me think, maybe you might just have run up a training program for a minor problem like preparing an eight-year-old to become an emperor. True?"

Ward examined him for a moment before responding. "I did not prepare a training program for you, sire."

Hugh remained unconvinced. This required a little more prodding. "*But*, Sergeant Major?"

"There has always been a training regimen for heirs to the throne, men and women. Male heirs were trained by the Imperial Guard and Imperial Marines, females by a special branch of the army."

"Captain Felt represents the army's side?" Hugh guessed.

"Yes, sire."

"You were in charge of the males?"

"Yes, and no, sire. The Imperial Guard evaluated the men, which gave me responsibility for the proctors. Unfortunately, most of the trainers were killed in the coup or soon thereafter. After your proctor, Jake Daniels, completed his five-year tour and then some, Doña Carlota drafted me. We didn't have any other choice."

"How is Sergeant Daniels?" Hugh asked warmly. Jake Daniels

had been his solid rock during those early years when the nightmares had been especially bad. When he had left, Hugh had keenly felt the loss, still did a bit. But transfers were a fact of life in the military, so he'd sucked it up and driven on, as the saying went. The military expected you to do it and didn't show any sympathy if you didn't. He hadn't heard from Sergeant Daniels in a couple of years, but sometimes the mission made it impossible to stay in touch. But now that he was heir apparent, he could get back in contact.

"He died two years ago fighting off a raid from Sector Three, I'm sorry to say, sire." Ward truly looked sad for his loss. "I counted him as a friend, too." Hugh felt both sorrow and anger at this news. "Is there a reason, *Sergeant Major*, that no one shared this information with me?"

Ward actually looked uncomfortable. "You'd already lost one father. There had been no communication between the two of you for some time. It seemed the easiest thing to do was to leave sleeping dogs lie, rather than share news of the death of someone who had been as close to a father as you'd had for years, sending you back into an ocean of grief."

Hugh's jaw tightened as he processed the realization that his communications with Daniels—with everyone, probably—had been monitored for . . . his entire life? And when Daniels died, someone—Ward, Doña Carlota, Hollister, or Davies?—had decided not to tell him, so that he wouldn't have to experience the loss? The invasion of his privacy and the withholding of the information made his blood boil. He wanted to hit something. To rage against the system that had taken so much from him. He hadn't chosen to be born into the emperor's family. He hadn't chosen to be the son of the warlord. Everything—and he was starting to realize just how encompassing that word was—had been chosen *for* him and had been done *to* him. From the nanites injected into his infant body to the murder of his father and brothers, from hiding his true status to withholding the news about Daniels from him. All of this had been out of his control.

And as all of these thoughts raced through Hugh's mind, he seized on that last word, control. He had had no control. He currently felt out of control. And with that, he made a decision to *gain* control, of himself and the situation. He took a deep breath and consciously unclenched his hands. He needed to let the anger go and push whatever feelings of loss he had for Daniels down into a box, to be processed later. Right now, he had one job: pass the test. And he intended to do it.

"Sergeant Ma—Ward, at some point in the not-too-distant future, you and I are going to have a counseling session to discuss some issues of personal privacy and your own . . . reluctance to share the news of Sergeant Daniels's death with me."

Ward's eyebrows went up, clearly surprised by the idea that *he* needed a "counseling session," but he straightened up and just said, "Yes, Your Highness."

Hugh nodded and then said, "So, Sergeant Major, tell me about the program."

"No can do, sire. You have not yet *completed* the program. It would be counterproductive to the ultimate training and evaluation goals of the imperial training regimen if you knew more. In taking the oath, you received complete information regarding what is expected of you but not when or how. That is all I can give you at this time."

"Fine," Hugh bit off the word. "But you can at least tell me how I'm doing."

Ward looked him straight in the eye before saying in a firm voice, "You're still alive."

This truly shook Hugh to his core. Ward obviously had not been melodramatic back at the base in stating the options. This training program, the test, could kill him, just like the gems. *Will Ward kill me if I fail?* That seemed to be the clear implication.

"What if I decide not to complete this test?"

"You'll never be emperor, sire. Refusal to proceed is an option. Unfortunately, at this stage, to fully withdraw, you would need to undergo a nanite cleansing procedure. I know of no facility that can perform it at this time, leaving only option B with regard to quitting."

Hugh nodded. "Got it. Succeed or die. This program will prepare me to be emperor?"

"It will determine if you are *worthy* of it, sire," Ward answered, more softly. "It has been used successfully for a thousand years. I've been working as hard as I can for the last ten years to prepare you."

Hugh's entire conception of what being emperor meant changed, again. He thought for a moment, memories flooding back. A furious Daniels standing over a ten-year-old Hugh holding an apple he stole from a market stall. Coldly marching him back to the vendor, Daniels made him pay double from his meager allowance. Twelve-year-old Hugh, crying, petrified, at the edge of a deep mountain canyon. Behind him, Klostermann, by degrees bullying and encouraging him to walk across a tree bridge spanning the gorge, one he could fall off of if he took even a single misstep. Doña Carlota ordering a severe punishment, outside guard duty in driving sleet, after catching him in a modification of reality, otherwise known as a little white lie. Other scenes whizzed by, always situations designed to make him stronger, tougher, more reliable, and honest. Or wash him out.

Ward really had trained him to be the best. In the past, Hugh had often wondered why the other boys his age, whether locals or his classmates, were allowed to be less dedicated than Ward required him to be.

Now he knew why. If his performance hadn't measured up all those years, would he have died then? Or just never been given this chance? Hugh really didn't know the answer to that question and it really didn't matter. He had done then what he needed to do and now stood taking the test. Ultimately, duty mattered most, or his oath, because of who he wanted to be, and he refused to settle for anything less. Realizing Ward still stood waiting for him to process all of this, he ordered, "Continue the training, Sergeant Major. I'll join you shortly."

"Aye, aye, sire," Ward snapped with a salute. He performed an about-face and reentered the mess.

Mulling over the series of scenes as they had flashed through his mind, Hugh wandered toward the bridge. He remembered additional trips and experiences obviously aimed at improving his character more than his physical abilities. Emperors exercised almost god-like power. They needed to know how to do so wisely and not selfishly.

He thought again about control. *To govern the empire, I must be able to govern myself.* He began to think of the test as far more than a series of exercises to complete, or achievements to attain. The test, this journey, these people with him. All were a part of his becoming emperor, but to pass the test meant so much more than checking boxes. To pass the test, he needed to *become* the emperor, to remove all doubt in Ward's mind, in the minds of the others on this ship, and ultimately in the minds of every citizen of the empire. And to do that, he needed to take control of his own fate in a way that he never had, in a way he'd never been *allowed.* Having reached the bridge, he knocked and waited.

A moment later the door almost burst open. Gail stood there looking up at him. "Your Highness? You don't have to knock; you're the heir apparent."

"Thanks, but I'll continue to knock. It's just polite. Having said that, I would like your team to train me in the various systems of the ship."

"Sire? Aren't you going to be a little busy with the sergeant major's training?"

"I'm sure I will be very busy, but I still need to understand as much as I can about every job on the ship."

Felt looked thoughtful, clearly evaluating Hugh. "Sixteen hundred be a good time to start, sire?"

"Let's try eighteen hundred. The good sergeant major is going to start physical training, including a two-G run around the ship. It may take me till then to recover."

Gail Felt smiled. "You're probably right. See you at eighteen hundred, sire."

Hugh turned back toward the mess for the run and the bruises likely to be received.

Ambrose B, Approaching Limit of Longview System
1210 BBMT 11 October 3473

WARD STOOD WATCHING HUGH CHATTING with the team as they ate, before slipping out of the gym, which had again been reverted to its function as a mess. He carefully stepped into the corridor just to make sure the gravity held at normal. Falling at his age in two G's could be really serious, something he would just as soon avoid. Turning toward the bridge, he saw Gail watching him with amusement. "Something funny?"

Gail just smiled even wider. "Nothing at all. Just watching a decrepit old man trying to get around, an old man who should have retired several years ago, if I may be so bold as to mention."

Ward's mouth became a thin line. "No, you may not mention it, especially as I am creaking up-ship to speak to you. Your cabin?"

Gail chuckled as she led them back to her hatch and then waved Ward to a seat. "You know he's signed on for ship systems training on his own initiative?"

"I guessed he might. He's pissed at me, though. He straight out asked me about Daniels and I had to tell him. I thought he might take a swing at me for holding that back so long, but he reined himself in. Would you believe he told me to expect a counseling session in my future?"

Gail's eyes went wide, as Ward continued. "He's on track, surprisingly, since we only told him yesterday. So far, he uses just the right touch of command, showing he knows his position, while mixing it with deference to experience. Tough for anyone, extremely surprising in one his age," Ward observed smugly.

Gail shook her head. "Don't be so falsely humble. We both know how you feel about the boy, and you are just about busting buttons, you're so proud of him. Did you notice he sounds like Doña Carlota half the time? And you the other half," she teased.

Ward tried to look offended, but inside a warm feeling grew. Gail approved of Hugh, as well as his training of him. Her positive opinion meant a great deal. Relenting a little, he agreed, "He didn't turn out half bad."

Gail nodded thoughtfully before a glimmer of a smile started. "I agree. So, now we run him ragged?"

Ward's smile answered hers. "Now we run him ragged. My favorite part of the whole program."

Supernova *Pechnaya*

1930 BBMT 13 October 3473

PLACING ASIDE THE COM PAD, Morgain stared with distaste at her escargot in garlic butter and the rest of the special meal she had been promising herself for weeks. The food smelled wonderful and undoubtedly tasted just as amazing . . . but she had lost her appetite. Why couldn't Gladstone have at least gotten one thing right?

When Jeffrey Gladstone had managed to take over a full task force of Prime Fleet undetected until the coup, she had hoped that she might soon be on the throne, as he had promised. This should have assured their success despite Quadros' ham-handed behavior. With his task force holding the edge of surprise in the Centrum GY system over Beacon, the rebels had the advantage. The takeover should have been easy . . . and the death of Doña Carlota assured.

But no, the others had completely forgotten their promises to her, not even consulting her before sending Gladstone to Deft. Even after that, who would have expected it to be so hard to kill one middle-aged woman? He should have been back in under a week. And the mission was a total failure.

Picking up the com pad again, she spoke to the technician who had delivered the report, "Thank Madame Aswini for the information." She would have preferred to strangle the tech, but it was not his fault and now she could repair the oversight.

"Contact all Ninth Fleet commands as well as my agents in

the core and outside. Tell them that Hugh Cascade, the surviving son of Trevor Cascade, is taking the test. He has a proctor. He is to be stopped at all costs. The proctor," *and his bag*, she didn't add, "are to be brought to me without delay."

"Yes, ma'am," the tech replied before she closed the channel.

The dinner began to look edible again. She smiled as she took a bite.

Appendix E: Recently Declassified Imperial Documents
Decree in Council—Proctors

January 1, 2491 AD
Faith City, Beacon, Prime Sector
Classification—Top Secret/Succession
Subject: Requirements for Proctors to Administer Test of Heirs

Purpose of position:
1) Train heirs in character development;
2) Ensure heirs can discern individuals' motives with whom they come in contact;
3) Train heirs to standards as set out in Basic Course for midshipmen or cadets; and
4) Be able to terminate heir, should an heir agree to take the test as outlined in the basic materials.

Decree in Council—Test of Heirs Regarding Criteria for Assignment of Proctor
1) Proctor who matches the gender of the heir to facilitate general access;
2) Men five years minimum service with special forces units, women with clandestine service, any branch;
3) Proficient with personal weapons;
4) Complete practical Test of Heirs examination with 90 percent or better;
5) Personally meet standards as set out in Basic Course of midshipmen or cadets;
6) Meets special unit physical fitness standards; and
7) Demonstrate ability to lead, ideally under combat conditions.

20

Step One in Training an Emperor

Supernova *Rift End*

0250 BBMT 14 October 3473

THE CREW OF THE ESCORT ships watched as *Ambrose B* disappeared in a haze of space dust. On the bridge of the cruiser *Rift End*, Captain Madampe Pryantha nodded. "Maximum coverage formation."

All his ships gradually spread out in a disc as they slowed to better cover the back trail. Preon polarity drive left a disturbance wake of subatomic particles that dissipated after about a day. At normal drive speeds, that meant up to about a parsec of travel. A task group in a hurry could easily do three parsecs per day. At the speed at which the *Ambrose B* traveled, it took only a few hours to cross parsecs.

His intel officer said, "The track of *Ambrose B* is no longer distinguishable from the background, sir."

Pryantha nodded. "Notify all units to remain alert. We will remain on station one full day as per Admiral Hollister's instructions."

Rancho Mirabel, Jeffco

0930 Local/0330 14 October 3473

DOÑA CARLOTA SAT IN THE glassed-in observation area with Admiral Hollister, where they could watch the main command center without being heard or disturbed as they worked. She saw Chief Wong sit up straight before quickly typing a message out on the secure printer. A single sheet came out that he sealed into an envelope marked *Top Secret—Urgent* in red, front and back. Waving to a nearby cadet, he handed him the envelope. The cadet marched off quickly. Approaching the door, the cadet knocked smartly.

"Come," called Doña Carlota into the com panel. The cadet entered and stepped over to Doña Carlota's desk. "What do we have here, cadet?" asked Doña Carlota.

"Message from Chief Wong, sir."

Doña Carlota extended a hand and, after receiving the envelope, immediately tore it open. "You're dismissed, cadet."

As the cadet slowly closed to the door, Hollister asked, "What's up?"

"*Ambrose B* has safely crossed out of the sector without anyone tracking them."

Hollister nodded. "Good. Now we have about a thousand other things to worry about."

"I leave those to you, Admiral. I'll continue to worry about Mr. Cascade."

Ambrose B

0445 BBMT 14 October 3473

AS *AMBROSE B* CROSSED THE ill-defined boundary out of the core into the thinly starred region between the core and the arms, Hugh sat gingerly in the copilot's seat on the bridge watching the sensors for any indication of a bogie. He hurt all over. Ward's workouts were objects of dread even among Fleet Elite types who were known for their mad-dog attitudes. This one, the second of the trip, had stepped it up a notch even by his standards. Back home, he had never thought it possible for Ward to create more intense workouts, but he now knew Ward could, and would, do the impossible.

Hugh sensed Captain Felt's eyes on him, studying him carefully, before giving Sally Carr, the ship's jack-of-all-trades, an amused look. Hugh tried to ease himself more comfortably on the lightly padded jump seat before turning to Gail and asking, "Can I ask a few things before we get started today?"

Gail grinned, the first time he had seen her do that. "You're the boss, Your Highness. Ask anything you want. I may not answer it but, before you ask, may I say it looks like Sean has found muscles to abuse you didn't know you owned."

Hugh nodded, noting in surprise the warmth in her voice when calling the sergeant major by his first name. "He definitely is meeting his duty to get me into better shape, and the team is enthusiastically helping. I thought I could hold my own in hand-to-hand, but Jebet used moves I've never even dreamed of, which is where most of my bruises came from today. I understand Peterson is tomorrow and Tabi Fleisch and Timothy Kennion, after that. I am lucky to have such loyal subjects who want me to be ready for anything."

Sally and Gail chuckled at his joking tone before Hugh added, "Now, back to business. I've been thinking a lot about different things since finding out I am the heir apparent and several things are gnawing at me. For instance, both your crew and the sergeant major's team are older than I am, quite a bit older, if you don't mind me saying so. Why is that? Why aren't there more young recruits who've joined up since the coup? Wouldn't they be better able to handle the rigors of something like this?"

Gail's grin faded. "That's a question I didn't think you would get to for a while. The fleet, army, and Marines are generally not as old as we are, of course, but the average age *is* much higher than it used to be. Men and women, mostly men even then, used to volunteer and serve for four to six years. Many would stay on active duty longer, but it remained a generally young force. They joined for the high-tech training, the travel, sometimes the adventure. Ten years used to be the average time in service. The empire always found itself in some little brushfire somewhere inside or outside, so those that craved action got it, but mostly things stayed quiet. Then came the coup. It didn't take long for both barbarians and rebels to realize that if they could knock out the empire's manpower pipeline, they might just knock us off. A series of raids attacked training facilities throughout the empire. They killed lots of cadre as well as recruits.

"In addition to that, there is the horrible attrition as we fight to hold onto planets that often don't want to remain part of the empire, or think that, if they could just be left alone, things would be fine. Most people and planets feel that way and definitely don't like the idea of kinetic weapons dropping out of the sky at a moment's notice. Neutrality is popular with people who don't think things through. Neutrality, though, is ignored by rebels or barbarians when it suits their purposes. It only works when there's someone big enough and strong enough around to enforce it. So, lots of planets keep opting for neutrality, continuing proof of hope triumphing over common sense and experience. That behavior also strangles the empire's ability to protect them. The empire kept the peace, making life easy for so long before the coup that many citizens didn't feel any responsibility to defend themselves. Peace came to be considered a right, not something that must be fought for.

"The direct result of all of those things has been recruiting dropping off and real difficulty in completing recruit training once we get them. Plus, the recruits we get are often suspect as to what they are really fighting for. Too many are in their mid-teens, just running away from home. Look at you, Your Highness. You started basic training when you were barely twelve, an age when a kid should still be having fun. At sixteen, it became more than a part-time job. What we see as time goes on is the young recruits are less and less likely to have loyalty to an empire they barely remember. The special units have been even harder hit because it takes years to develop and train special operators like us, and we're the ones everyone needs. The *Ambrose B* may not look like much, but it can almost disappear when it has to, although going the speed we are right now is like flashing a strobe light in a dark room. My crew has survived two other ships that couldn't be salvaged and we've been together for years now."

"Do you . . . have families?" Hugh asked hesitantly. He didn't want to seem nosy but wanted to know these women who were risking their lives for him.

Gail's face briefly became sagged before answering, "We did once. All of us."

Her pain struck a chord deep within himself, his own emptiness that could never be filled. From the corner of his eye, he saw Sally's face freeze into a mask of hate. Hugh realized even an emperor shouldn't pry too deeply into certain things, this apparently being one of them. *What could possibly have happened to her to make her react like that?* Mentally shaking himself, he said gently, "Thank you for explaining that, Captain. Let's get started, shall we?"

Yesterday, he'd only spent a few hours with the women in the crew, a relatively light day. He assumed Captain Felt needed a little time to create a full training plan. Apparently, last night she had worked hard to correct that shortcoming, because she handed Hugh a completed class schedule. Six days per week, he found himself scheduled for astrogation, ship handling, maintenance (from the dirty end of the rag to controlling repair droids), weapons systems, logistics, and the various systems in engineering for an hour each. Not including study time. Overwhelmed by this unexpected tidal wave, he didn't know what to say but numbly nodded to begin.

THE NEXT MORNING, HUGH dragged himself into the mess still nursing bruises from the prior day's training with the Marines. He fervently wished he could get just a few more nanites helping this morning. *If I ask, I wonder if Ward will let me hold the gems for a few minutes?* Noticing Ward's smile as he examined Hugh, he decided not to ask.

"Your Highness," Ward asked brightly, "how are you this beautiful day?"

Hugh, easing onto a chair, spoke around a puffy lip now much worse since he'd slept on it, "Fine, Sergeant Major. What light entertainment do you have laid on for my imperial enjoyment today?"

Ward bowed and smiled as he handed Hugh the Marines' training schedule. "If Your Highness will approve the draft plan for the week, we can get going."

Focusing on the three-page printout, Hugh noted that Ward planned on running him ragged a solid eighteen hours per day, every day but Sunday. "This is fine, Sergeant Major. Please modify my participation to allow for six hours daily of training with the ship's crew."

Ward became visibly irritated. "You won't be part of the team or ready for every contingency if you don't train this much. Sire." Ward had nearly forgotten the last part, Hugh realized.

Patiently, Hugh answered, "Sergeant Major. I will be as ready as I can be, but I am not going Fleet Elite." Ward began to speak, but Hugh held up a hand for silence and held Ward's eyes until Hugh saw he would be listened to. A very satisfying feeling, he decided. "Now, can you explain to me why I need to dedicate all my time to prepping to assault a fleet command center with a nail file and a flashlight? If not, I need to spend some time on other things. I need to know what the ship's crew is doing as much as I need to gain deep recon skills." Seeing that Ward could barely contain himself, Hugh explained, "You taught me to think before I acted. I recall a little incident where I jumped off a cliff twenty feet into a swimming hole without checking for hazards. At the time, you wondered aloud about my sanity or simple lack of the brains to close an air lock before taking off a space suit." A small smile crossed Ward's face at being reminded of that incident, before he regained his stoic composure.

Hugh went on, "Judgment, I believe, is the appropriate word for what I should have exercised then and am honor bound to use now. So, exercising some judgment, I checked out the Fleet Marine training program for recruits, and this isn't it. This would prepare me to be a Fleet Elite Marine if I dedicate the next eighteen months to this alone, which I definitely can't. To qualify in any of the specialties Captain Felt and her ladies are working on with me is at least ten months each, if not double that. I have a training schedule here that will require five and a half years to complete, but we are only two months or so out from Earth. Based upon your estimates, anyway." Although surprised a bit when Ward didn't jump down his throat and still a bit unsure as to his right to act this way, Hugh waited to make sure Ward agreed with his assessment.

Nodding after a moment, Hugh summarized, "Last night, as my aches kept me up after the workout, a nasty suspicion started gnawing at me. After checking the various training programs involved, I came to a tentative conclusion. I kept it tentative because you taught me to keep an open mind. Now that I've seen your training program, I'm sure. You both are intentionally setting me up to fail and see what happens. Sergeant Klostermann taught me to always pace myself for distance and only sprint for the finish line. This training is definitely for distance." Hugh's face remained bland as he closed the trap. "Am I right, Sergeant Major?"

Ward chuckled. "Klostermann did a good job in training you to look at the reason you were doing things, not just how to bull ahead and accomplish the task at hand. Tough to teach that to young officers, almost impossible to do with teenagers. I'll have to commend him for that. It generally takes an imperial heir quite a while before they begin to tumble to the fact that there are only twenty-four hours per day and they need to decide what's important. Then most, according to the records, grumble, complain, or simply refuse to do it, rather than figure out what is happening and how to fix it. Good work, sire. What really tipped you?"

"I can count, for one thing. Based upon your first two days' training and what Captain Felt gave me, I extrapolated. As you so astutely pointed out, there are only twenty-four hours per day. I *know* Captain Felt can count and, though you are only a Marine," he added with a smile, "it is *likely* you can, too. Also, I am absolutely sure you would never intentionally allow scheduling conflicts to arise between the two of you. That meant you were messing with me to see what I'd do. Then, after establishing the plain impossibility of coming anywhere near completing these courses, I thought about why you would do something like this. The answer? The test."

Hugh looked straight at Ward. "Our little conversation back on Jeffco came to mind about that time. Please integrate the training schedules, Sergeant Major."

Ward stood and saluted, "Good job."

Hugh stood also, holding back a smile in response to the compliment. "Thank you, Sergeant Major."

Ward, his lips in their trademark thin line that passed for a smile, said, "Being able to prioritize, determine what is important, then stick to those things is probably the easiest and most difficult thing you'll have to do. Successfully passing life's big tests depends upon what you decide beforehand. Good choices lead to good outcomes." An evil smile crossed Ward's face as he finished. "And now that I have satisfied your curiosity, the boys are ready for our little warm-up for today."

Hugh groaned as he saw Ward's sadistic smile. However, being a good little absolute monarch-in-training, he hid his trepidation as he headed back into the corridor, prepared to enjoy the two-G run.

A ROUTINE SOON SET IN, which struck Hugh as anything but routine from his past experience. The schedule repeated, but the intensity exceeded anything he had ever done. Physical training first thing every day included the equivalent of an eight-kilometer run in full gear. Weapons familiarization and marksmanship (on a simulator) followed and then a ground tactical problem. Physically wrung out by this time, he caught his breath during a break for astrogation.

After the first couple of lessons, it became obvious he possessed little or no aptitude for higher math, but he definitely needed the break, so he kept it in his schedule. Captain Felt's space tactical problems, which came next, completely fascinated him, however. He figured he might even have some talent in the area because he only died about half the time, even with the difficulty level increasing.

Hands-on maintenance of the actual ship equipment came before recon team planning sessions, based upon various scenarios that were difficult or impossible to accomplish. In between, he ate a few quick meals and crammed study time in before bed. Not a naturally gifted student, he decided to force himself to put in the time rather than just hit the sack.

About a week after they left the frontier behind, Hugh had the dream for the first time. Slogging uphill with a massive pack under what felt like two G's, he moved slowly forward. *Gotta reach the top!* The clock kept running down, ticking inexorably toward zero, and he knew he couldn't make it in time. Still, he kept going. If he didn't make it, everyone would die! He knew it. Then a nuke went off behind him just like on Jeffco, only this time destroying everything, waking him up. That first time he woke in a cold sweat, remaining sleepless for an hour before drifting off again.

The next night, it came again, but before the explosion, he saw the faces of some of the men and women who'd died protecting him on Deft, saving him so he could try and preserve the empire. Nuclear fire wiped them away. He didn't get back to sleep at all that night, choosing to study instead of seeing their faces melt away.

The images began to haunt him day and night. Nightmares from his childhood, reawakened by the fire in the canyon, mixed with new ones. In them, everywhere he looked, people kept dying. The faces changed, but no one survived. His friends became the most frequent victims. To avoid the dreams, he kept himself awake as much as he could. The third night, he tossed and turned, unable to drop off until almost three, too exhausted to worry about the nightmares. It didn't matter, they returned to haunt him near dawn anyway. Now he studied late every night, so he didn't have to pretend to be sleeping, but he stopped really learning. His brain became too fuzzy to remember things. No matter, he preferred staring at pages he couldn't comprehend to dreaming.

GAIL WATCHED HUGH ALMOST FALL asleep as he tried unsuccessfully, again, to calculate a simple course between stars in Sector Seven. Glancing at Sally to take over, she slipped out and into her room. Hitting her com, she called, "Ward, we need to talk."

A knock came thirty seconds later, not terribly fast to cover the thirty-five paces between their cabins unless you were trying to appear like you weren't in a hurry. Slipping in quickly, he sat without being invited. "Planning the scenario for later today. What's up?"

Gail's eyes expressed the worry pressing down on her. "Something's wrong with Hugh. He isn't getting the sleep he needs. His grades are getting worse, even on the things he likes. He isn't a great math student, not because he can't, simply because he doesn't think he's any good; now he's terrible."

Ward nodded somberly. "I've noticed the same drop-off in leadership; he's trying to be a one-man band. He did better as a cadet."

Fear clutched at her gut. "Is he having a breakdown?" If he did, there could be only one result.

Ward shrugged. "Maybe. Probably. You know I can't discuss what he's feeling but he's in trouble, and I am not quite sure why."

Gail smiled. "Remember he's young, too young, really. Keep that in mind."

Standing, he said, "I'll see what I can do."

Gail nodded and stood, too. "Good luck." Her voice choked up as she spoke.

"I'll do what's best, Gail," he answered, gently.

Gail nodded, placing a hand on his forearm. "I know you will, you always have. Just don't be too hard."

Ward nodded and left.

ARMY SMALL-UNIT TACTICS HANDBOOK—INFANTRY PLATOON AND SQUAD

Appendix L: Imperial Military Training Standards

Core Army Cadet Training Course

The primary military skill every cadet must learn is leadership. Protecting and guiding the people under their command until they are needed is essential. Regardless of the ultimate specialization of the cadet, after commissioning as an officer of the Core Empire, leadership, not management, is the measure of success. Becoming proficient in small-unit tactics has been found to be the best way to identify, develop, and hone leadership skills. A cadet must therefore demonstrate the ability to lead and motivate others in a variety of scenarios. Failure to complete this module washes the cadet out of the program.

21

Responsibility

Ambrose B

1450 BBMT 23 October 3473

HUGH CASCADE SIGNALED SERGEANTS KEVIN Dunn and Tim Kennion forward. Night insects sang, as well as a bird in a bush to their right. Hugh carefully examined every square foot within a range of one hundred meters, then searched for general indicators of potential problems beyond that. The air felt sticky and hot, no one and no thing moved. Sweat dripped down his hairline and off his chin. His palms sweated, clammy inside the thin shooter's gloves. The standard 95 rifle he'd decided to use for this mission did not have the stopping power of a laser rifle nor could it shoot through walls. It did have a real virtue, however. In its silenced form, it couldn't be detected beyond ten meters when fired, which he sincerely hoped he wouldn't have to do.

Behind him, Vincent Klostermann and Tabi Fleisch watched the back trail while covering the escape route. Abdul Jebet and Pete Peterson were spread out to the right, ready to open the door after clearing the path. Hugh couldn't see his team in their chameleon skin uniforms and camo-sprayed faces and hands but knew they were there by their icons on his helmet display. As for the bad guys spotting his team, no one should be able to see them in these visibility conditions.

Cloud cover blocked out the star-filled sky above them. This close to the core, the stars shone as brightly as moons on other worlds farther out along the arms, although this planet's sky didn't compare with Beacon, where it never truly reached complete dark at night. Essentially, he and his team were undetectable.

But they needed to achieve two goals. First, grab the port's archeon control room to contact Admiral Hollister and let him know their progress. Second, blow the archeon net so no information about them could be sent ahead.

At the spaceport, *Ambrose B* sat refueled and ready to leave Nighthawk. Sean Ward needed to complete some business in town, looking for info about the next leg of their journey, so he had tapped Hugh to lead this mission. Dunn and Kennion reached the door and disabled the guards. Hugh motioned Jebet and Peterson forward. Crawling to the entry, Jebet slapped a shaped charge to the lock. After he backed off, Hugh fired the charge. And they all died.

Automatic weapons opened up from all sides, ripping their virtual bodies to bits. The psychic pain from the sudden disconnection from the scenario pounded inside his head, and Hugh tore the helmet off, throwing it as far as he could. It bounced against the wall undamaged, which made him even angrier. Hugh sat up in disgust; it should have broken. *At least then I'd feel a little better.*

This made three training scenarios in a row in which no one had survived. Constant failure undermined the team's confidence in the effectiveness of his leadership, to say the least.

As the others left, Ward entered the gym, stooped to grab the headset, and handed it politely back to Hugh. "You dropped something, sire?" he suggested courteously.

Hugh snarled, "I threw it and I'm sorry it didn't break. Don't be nice because I blew the mission."

"Impossible missions have that effect on us, sometimes," Ward observed.

"Impossible?" Hugh's volume doubled as he stood, his face quickly turning red and threatening. "You set up an impossible situation? How am I supposed to learn from a scenario that's impossible?" Ward simply stood there, waiting. Hugh yelled louder, "Well?"

Ward continued to wait without reacting, which infuriated Hugh even more. With a monumental effort, he stood back, trying to get control so he could understand this incomprehensible information. Lowering his voice, although it still quivered with energy, he asked again, "Well, Sergeant Major?"

"Please sit, sire. We need to have a counseling session." His voice neither cajoled nor pleaded. Regardless, Hugh knew a directive when he heard one, even when couched as a request. Letting out one more breath, Hugh sat back down on a hard-backed chair. A sudden vision of his last counseling session suffered at Ward's hands came to mind, Hugh standing tall in the sergeant major's office. The impressive volume as well as creativity of that dressing down, had been ingrained indelibly in his memory.

Hugh now noted a difference in Ward's demeanor. This counseling session apparently would be much different. Outwardly, at least. Plus, the alternative to a counseling session consisted of failing the test, so he could live with counseling no matter how tough. Literally.

"Go ahead, Sergeant Major."

"Sire. What is the purpose for training?"

"Get things right on a mission, Sergeant Major."

"Partially correct. Would Your Highness care to add anything?" Ward asked politely.

Hugh looked sharply at Ward for a moment. He inhaled and held it a second, trying to control the frustration he felt about the scenario. *Control.* Taking another breath, he relaxed just a bit more, concentrating. He noted in passing that Ward sat focused on him, observing him impassively. Hugh thought for several minutes, the silence stretching on. As he became more used to being deferred to in his new position as heir apparent, he no longer felt uncomfortable when others were silent. He noted that Ward gave no evidence of nervousness either, just attentiveness. Giving him a sour look, Hugh clipped out tersely, "Prepare for the unexpected, so the scenarios are opportunities to handle the unexpected."

Ward nodded. "Part of the answer, of course. Anything else, sire?"

"Stress the participants to see how they handle it?"

"Yes. And what else, Your Highness?"

"Test the leadership qualities of the team members."

"That would be the same thing, sire."

"I can't think of anything else, Ward."

"Well, sire, it is obvious you needed to be exposed to this kind of stress. What I have here," Ward showing him the datapad, "is the metric for how you reacted as team lead. You failed. Miserably."

"Everyone died, so that is obvious, Sergeant Major. Our team screwed up."

"You all die in this scenario, regardless, sire. No, I mean that you, personally, failed. You failed to delegate any authority to the two-man teams. You failed to seek input from their scanners and observation. You went on point more than once. You, sire, were a one-man show, who made it clear to your team that they were only pawns you were moving around the board. You didn't rely on them or trust their skills."

Hugh prepared to answer angrily but bit his tongue instead. *Did I do that?* Yes, and it embarrassed him. He had excluded his team in the planning, simply told them what they would be doing. In fact, he hadn't discussed a thing with them. He shook his head at his own failure.

Being in charge and responsible for the success of the mission, he knew he must lead. *If they died it would be my fault.* Of course, he trusted them. *They know that. Don't they?*

"The thing that concerns me, sire, is why you did this?" Pulling out the pad again, he scrolled back to earlier exercises. "As we began these sessions over a week ago, your use of personnel initially improved tremendously, but the metrics are definitely going the wrong direction now. You have gone backward, trying to carry the whole load yourself. A team leader shouldn't do that, although it's possible to succeed despite the misallocation of resources. But an emperor literally can't. There is simply too much going on in too many places. So, what's going on with you?"

Hugh thought before answering. If he told the truth about having nightmares, would Ward count that against him in the test? Carefully, he answered, "I have to succeed. If I fail, civilization dies and a new dark age arises." He felt old and burdened with the weight of the galaxy. "I can't share that responsibility with anyone else."

Ward smiled sadly. "I have felt your anxiety, which goes along with the answer you just gave. Plus, your bioscan indicates excessive fatigue. That alone would explain your progress, or lack thereof, on the ship side of things. You aren't sleeping well, which tells me you are wrestling with how you think you should be handling things. The toughest critic you'll ever face is yourself, which may be why you're demanding too much of yourself. Feeling responsible is essential for a good emperor, as is being able to handle that sense of responsibility so that it doesn't eat you alive." Ward paused and sat watching him.

Hugh thought about what Ward has said. *How can I be emperor if I'm constantly doubting myself? And now my body betrays me through the bioscan?* But none of that mattered, because Ward told the simple unvarnished truth: If he were ever emperor, he would have to be able to let go, allow others to take over problems all of the time.

"How do I let go of actual life-and-death decisions?"

Ward shrugged. "You can't do it all yourself. No one can, and you're not expected to. The fleet, army, and Marines all make decisions based upon the direction of the emperor and the council. These directives, since they come from mortal men and women, are almost always flawed. Often badly. But we assume people are doing the best they can. People still die as a result. Headquarters issues orders, the people assigned attempt to carry them out. Mistakes are made because people are only human, but again we do our best. The civil bureaucracy does the same with similar results. The decisions are made with massive amounts of input from innumerable people, but still they often get it wrong. It happens. Generally not from a lack of desire to do the right thing, but simply because we are all human."

Ward leaned forward a bit, examining Hugh intently, before going on. "There are three major types of failures as emperors: Type one is lazy and doesn't do his job. He just expects it to be done. Emperor Allen, who died in 2928 AD, is a good example of that type of man. The result is the accumulation of power where it doesn't belong: among the ambitious and corrupt. The empire begins to decay from the head. It may run on for years or even centuries because of inertia and lack of an external challenge. But people lose their rights and freedoms to internal oppressors just the same as if someone invades and conquers them. True growth is lost.

"The second type wants to control everything and everyone. He literally sucks the freedom and life right out of the universe around him. He is a tyrant that destroys men's souls. The empire falls internally to revolts because he imposes what cannot be borne: first mental, followed by physical, slavery. Benjamin exemplified that just fifty-odd years ago.

"And then there is type three. Well-meaning, but unable to let people do their jobs. Everything is so important that they insist on being involved in everything. Their approach leads to resentment and ultimately anger and frustration because they can't do anything, much less everything, well and won't let others do their jobs without interference. Denying people the opportunity to act tells them the emperor doesn't trust them. That sours all relationships and reduces the chances of success of even the most trivial of policies. The emperor is not loyal to his people, and so his people are not loyal to him. Esau Emanuel acted that way trying to fix the problems Benjamin created.

"It is a truism, sire, that each of us have only so many burdens we can bear because we are human. Think about what happened in your second meeting with Admiral Hollister. You got the best help you could, made a firm decision, and moved on."

"I think I see that. So, what about Emperor Cyrus?" Hugh wondered aloud.

"The most tragic kind, Your Highness. One that doesn't fit into any of these and that I hope you never become. He lost hope, which caused him to doubt every choice he made. At the end, he no longer believed in himself. He loved the people but not himself. A good man with good intentions but no will is worse than a tyrant."

"So, what kind am I?"

Ward smiled thinly. "The question isn't who you are, but who you can become. It is possible to be one who represents the best in us and trusts those around him or her to do the same. Just remember that Klostermann, Fleisch, and the rest of the team here on the ship know you better than anyone and are behind you a hundred percent. You can rely on them."

"That makes a difference." Hugh nodded. "So . . . I should get some sleep now and let you handle the world's problems for a while?" A small smile crept across his face, a relief he hadn't felt in days. "See you later, Sergeant Major." Hugh stood and walked to the door, already half asleep.

"Good choice," whispered Ward.

The nightmare came again that same night. Twice. But in his dream, someone now tried to help carry the load. It seemed better.

Galactifacts for Kids 3500

Oort cloud. Almost every star system is surrounded by a thin sphere of ice and rocks called the Oort cloud, named after Jan Oort of Earth, who theorized its existence before space travel began more than fifteen hundred years ago. An Oort cloud generally extends from about 0.8 light-years from the central star out to as much as three or more light-years, to an extent dependent on the star density of the neighborhood.

The cloud is filled with comets that pass through solar systems regularly, as well as a variety of wandering planetoids captured by the system's star and many smaller bodies. Although it is sparsely filled, the Oort cloud is dense by interstellar standards. Luckily, all starships carry avoidance and detection equipment that automatically change their course so there are no impacts with these bodies.

22

Lacuna

Ambrose B

0525 BBMT 24 October 3473

AMBROSE B SLOWED TO MAKE a safe passage through the Oort cloud surrounding the Nighthawk system. Slow, of course, relative to their usual speed while traveling interstellar on preon drive. Still, it far exceeded what anyone could have imagined during the age of Einstein. Gail Felt, with Sally Carr as her number two, carefully threaded past pieces of planets discarded early in the development of the system, as well as planetoids, ice balls that fell through the solar system as comets, and rocks of various sizes which, if dislodged, would become meteors, showering down as they fell inward toward the local sun in random patterns. Hugh thought of the difference between interstellar space and the Oort cloud as the difference between driving on a deserted country freeway versus negotiating downtown traffic. The Oort cloud could even be like rush hour if you were going fast enough to get anywhere in a reasonable length of time. *Slow seems to be the better choice.* Hugh loved speeding along at max, the faster the better, but he admitted they were currently going as fast as they should to avoid the large asteroids suddenly popping up ahead out of nowhere. Plus, they were keeping their preon ability as an ace-in-the-hole by relying solely on their gravitonic drive. Unfortunately, this limited them to entry within seventy degrees of the ecliptic, since gravitonic drive couldn't be used within the solar vortex, the thinnest part of the Oort cloud. Hugh remembered from his astrogation study that the solar rotation created vortexes of gravitational energy beginning as fairly narrow cones at the solar north and south poles. They expanded as they approached the limits of the solar system. Simply put, Gail had decided to limit *Ambrose B*'s options to access the system to the normal lanes of travel.

Hugh watched as the automatic evasion equipment kept them away from rocks big enough to get through their shields—everything larger than a pebble. He realized how ticklish this could be as Gail and Sally sweated their flight into the Oort cloud while they watched for really large chunks of matter. *This is why they say there are old pilots and bold pilots but there are no old, bold pilots.* Gail and Sally were careful, but calling either of them old seemed to be the likeliest way to guarantee he never reached his next birthday, so he kept this observation to himself. Hugh silently admired Gail and Sally's virtuosity from the jump seat. His secondary controls were locked out but, as part of his training, he continually updated his own navigation solutions.

It really didn't hurt his feelings that, as they ran toward the inner system, the shields and evasion systems ate the power necessary to crank up the deck plating to two G's. Besides, with no one available to conduct physical training with him anyway, it didn't matter. Everyone had a real job to do today, everyone except him.

Tabi Fleisch, Pete Peterson, and Tim Kennion manned the gun pods while Abdul Jebet and Vinnie Klostermann covered the missile room. Pam West helped Sheila Kirk on the engines and mechanical systems, an unusual luxury from what he understood. That left Sean Ward, Karen Hall, and Kevin Dunn on standby in the missile room, making them also available wherever else they might be needed.

Hugh examined their course, an arc along the system's solar ecliptic through the thickest part of an Oort cloud.

Of course, the other alternative to this poking along would require them to go in cloaked, one of *Ambrose B*'s specialties. Except Hugh knew both Captain Felt and Sergeant Major Ward preferred to always keep tricks in their bag no one knew about. So, in they came, sneaky instead of stealthy, giving Hugh ample time for the training opportunity of joining Gail and Sally in working out the details of the flight without being able to do a single thing about it. Regardless, he wanted to be ready if needed, plus actually understand the problems if—*when*, he amended to himself—he sent someone in harm's way like this. The reality of that possibility grew with each passing day, and he wanted to avoid snap decisions that got people killed.

Ward's little talk the day before and fourteen hours of uninterrupted rest had helped, too. After sleeping on that talk, he knew better what kind of emperor he wanted to be. Only now did he understand how many ways existed to foul up, and he felt sure there were more he couldn't even dream of yet. Every man and woman who served him and the empire would pay a price for his decisions, his judgments, some with their lives. Some were suffering and dying even now somewhere behind him to protect the empire, many not even knowing he existed, just hanging on. For him, he only saw two choices in handling the blood debt and associated guilt this suffering and death could bring him: either become callous or do the best he could. For him, the only option that might give him peace was doing his best.

In front of him, Gail and Sally spoke mostly in single syllables or grunts, everything in terms of up/down, left/right. In space, despite there being no up or down, left or right, forward or backward, people still needed the world to make sense as they understood it, so they adjusted space to fit them. Everything really did revolve around people.

"A little more to port and down," Gail suggested, eyes glued to the scope. Thoughtfully, she added, "The cloud seems unusually thick up ahead and to starboard."

Hugh watched the data flowing on the screen as the ship headed toward an apparently emptier area of space. Probing to the sides as they did, a frown creased his brow. Odd. The sensors couldn't be right. Running a diagnostic, he confirmed the initial solution. Rocks and ice of varying sizes appeared to be moving, actually closing in around them. Not perpendicular to the line of travel but sloping in from all sides toward an opening not far ahead. As a member of the crew currently working for the captain, and not her head of state, he addressed her that way, "Ma'am, it looks like we're moving into a pocket of some kind."

Gail just nodded. "Sally, extend your sensors. If we're moving into a pocket, it could be a pain getting out again. The densities are pretty high around the edges." She busily ran interrogatives through her sensor net, also.

Sally suddenly sat bolt upright. "It can't be!" Hugh saw her hand move, indicating she had sent data, likely to Gail.

Gail's head came up sharply from the board, having quickly reviewed Gail's data. She slammed the intercom button and shouted, "Everyone strap down. Weapons pods, power up. Missiles, get a round in the tube. We may be maneuvering violently, so hold on." Without looking at Sally, she continued, tone suddenly the bland professionalism used in truly desperate situations, "Go dark, now. As soon as our stealth drive is up, corkscrew Z: 270 X: -50, at half-light, ten seconds and stop." Sally sat frozen for a moment, staring at Gail. "Now, Sal gal, now," Gail urged with quiet intensity.

Hugh felt completely helpless as he watched, seeing everything they were doing but having no idea why. In less than thirty seconds, Gail changed them from standard operating to stealth, something he *knew* they were trying to keep in reserve. Venturing to speak after several long, tense seconds of silence, he asked, "What happened, Captain?" He thought using her rank hit the sweet spot between his cadet status on the bridge and being the heir apparent who could demand answers.

"Not now, Hugh. Trying to keep us alive." The fact she'd used his name showed her total focus on the instruments. A moment later she muttered a soft but emphatic, "Lacuna."

Lacuna? She obviously referred to those rocks out there, but what? Whispering to Sally, he asked, "What's a lacuna?"

Without looking at him, Sally hissed, "A trap. Now be quiet; we've got to concentrate."

He began running back the data, trying to figure out what had spooked them. A sudden power loss stopped him for a moment before the drive came back up. The drive and the ship felt a little different than moments before. Or it might just be his imagination. His station came back up with a flashing caret. Hugh immediately noticed he now only received passive sensor data. *No active transmissions at all.* Fitting the reduced data flow to a corner of his screen so he could follow it as he ran his queries, he began a search of the data from their entry into the Oort cloud. Running the data at high speed, he didn't see anything odd at first. He started it again, then a third time. The edge of his consciousness noted Gail began to fly the ship in a totally unpredictable pattern before coming to rest slightly offset from the middle of the pocket where they sat. Then, the screen absorbed his attention completely.

He couldn't believe this. *It can't be!* But his eyes didn't lie. Behind them, they had flown into a rough funnel that led them into the opening he'd noticed earlier. Now that he found it, it became surprisingly easy to see. The sides of the cone were dense, much denser, than the space in the middle of the fairway, as spacers called it. And then he picked up something completely out of place. Small shimmers appeared on various ice and rock bodies in the cloud in an unpredictable pattern. It seemed obvious now, the ice and rocks had been moved into a sort of conic alignment. Keying the cameras, he focused on the areas inside the funnel where they were now, since they were moving slowly enough to be able to interpret objects in real time, something they rarely did except near a planet. Generally, they flew so fast that optics were useless at faster-than-light speed since data otherwise would be months or years out of date and, therefore, irrelevant to current tactical situations. But here, being essentially stopped and so close to the sides, they received close to real-time images of objects just light minutes or light hours away. What he saw made him cold. The end wall almost entirely blocked the light from the local sun. He couldn't remember ever hearing of such a thing this far away from a star, and it still seemed impossible even as he saw it with his eyes. If they had continued at their prior speed, they would have slammed into that wall almost without warning. Hugh reflected it would have been like running into a planet. *Not good*, as Marines referred to events like that. "Ma'am. I am seeing a semi-solid wall up ahead."

"Seeing?" Gail sounded intrigued.

"Yes, ma'am. Seeing."

Gail looked at Sally. "Do the visual sensors work out here?"

Sally shrugged. "Guess so; they probably should." Her fingers ran quickly over the keyboard. "Interesting," she murmured. "The sensors are picking up the remnants of ships all over that area ahead. Definitely set up as a trap. I can't see how people like those up ahead in Nighthawk could put something like this together. They're barely spacefaring from what we've heard. To put something like this together would be extremely expensive."

Going on, puzzled, "It would be tough for Seventh Sector to set this up around just a couple of planets. Besides, what would be the point? Core military vessels, all preon polarity drive ships, come in from well above the ecliptic to avoid just the normal higher densities in the Oort cloud. Yet here is this trap, no doubt about it."

The ship hovered in silence while Gail thought, looking up at Sally after a minute. Hitting the intercom, she called the engine room. "Sheila. Why would someone big and nasty come in generally along the ecliptic?"

After a moment, Sheila answered. "Some reason for asking, Skipper?"

"We are looking at a trap, a very elaborate trap, but it's aimed only at ships coming in along the ecliptic."

"Any ship with a graviton-based drive would prefer to come in on the ecliptic, which includes all non-Core military and raiders. It is difficult, if not close to impossible, for them to come in any other way at high speed. But Core military comes in from above to avoid this mess."

"Hmm," Gail voiced, checking her screens again, "There seem to be gravitonic drive units out here positioning pieces of rock and ice to create this trap, and likely others, in the Oort cloud.

There are also pieces of broken ships strewn across the rock up ahead where people hit pretty hard."

"Okay." Sheila didn't answer for a while, and the silence dragged out. "Well, it is easier, not easy mind you, but easier, to build lots of graviton drives than preon drives to do this. If you wanted to discourage an unfriendly low-tech group in the neighborhood, then this would be a good way to do it. Very expensive, though. I'd build ships instead unless for some reason you couldn't or didn't want to build lots of ships. Either way, someone would have to be a real pest to make doing this worthwhile."

Gail gimbaled the ship to face the opening and took them out. Slowly. Passing the heliopause into interstellar space, she set off on a circuit of the Oort cloud along the ecliptic, sensors set to identify more potential lacunae like the one they'd just escaped. Opening the general com channel, she let everyone know there would be a general council while at their duty stations.

After they signed in, Gail, as captain, led off. "I'm opening up this council because we have run into a major unforeseen situation. As per plan, we were making a gravitonic insertion through the Oort cloud along the ecliptic. As we moved in, we found a gap leading to a void in the cloud, an intentional gap. At the far end of the void, we found a much denser area of material than normal, covered with the remains of several ships that had suffered the misfortune of not finding out about the wall soon enough to avoid it. Fortunately, we didn't join them."

Hugh wished the captain had told everyone he'd found the trap but kept silent. A good officer never blew his own horn, which went double for emperors. "So far, while circling outside the cloud on the heliopause, we've identified several more gaps. The gaps change as we approach, drives moving the rock and ice to meet and direct us. Something like this is very expensive and must have been intentionally set out as a "Do Not Disturb" sign. From what we know of Nighthawk, their government is corrupt and unlikely to spend the money this would take. What would be in it for them? Also, this trap seems to be designed to catch only gravitonic ships. So, I called this council to get ideas before we proceed, since the initial plan is out the air lock. We need to refuel soon, though we could use the ice balls out here if we really got desperate. What we will be short of, though, is rations, if we go much longer before reaching a friendly planet. Navy tradition says junior man first. What do you think, Cadet Cascade?"

Hugh opened his mouth as Gail and Sally turned to look at him, prepared to answer, when it hit him. In this situation, he must act as the heir and not a junior crew member. "I'll go last, Captain. I'd like to hear what everyone else has to say first."

Gail's face revealed nothing. She simply nodded and answered with, "Sire. So, which of the Marines wants to go first?"

Peterson spoke up. "Although Dunn is the newbie, I'll go next."

Dunn muttered, "Five years service, smart mouth. Not so *newbie*."

Ward growled, "Get on with it, unless you want to repeat boot, Peterson."

"Aye, Sergeant Major," Peterson answered without any hint of worry in his voice. "What kind of serious threat would it take to make a star system use its tech base like this? I mean, gravitonic ships could navigate slowly through it if they couldn't just fly around it above the ecliptic."

Gail answered, "Good point, except there are some strange holes in the walls of the lacunae. Holes that look for all the world like what would happen if someone tried to sneak through slowly and ran into something unfriendly, like a nuclear mine. I decided not to experiment, since a positive result couldn't be used to our benefit."

Chuckles came from several of the crew and team, including Peterson. Gail continued, "As for how serious a threat would have to be to cover an area this way, I believe it would have to be something worse than Captain Jolly Roger, Bane of the Space Ways."

Everyone laughed at her comparing the children's tale to the real-life problem, but they got the message.

Fleisch jumped in, "Let's just evade and avoid; it's not our fight. The clock is ticking on getting His Highness through the test and back home. We need to finish before there's no home to go back to."

Jebet and Klostermann agreed with her. Karen West jumped in, "But we have no idea where this problem came from or how big it is. If we don't find out what the folks on Nighthawk are afraid of, we could walk right into it on another planet. This problem might be ancient history we just stumbled into, then again, maybe not."

Sheila Kirk, the engineer, agreed. "Good point, and I need to check an engine tuning problem if they have a good space yard."

Sally snorted, "Sheila, you're always fussing over those engines. If there is something seriously wrong, it would be the first time."

Sheila responded hotly, "And it would be the last time if it were serious and we needed the engines when they weren't up to it."

"Now, girls," Gail soothed, "let's keep our attention on the problem."

Ward cleared his throat, which bought a moment of silence. "If this were a fleet exercise, they'd send in the *Ambrose B*, all stealthy, to check things out before the task force dropped in to chat."

Sally responded, "But you may have noticed we're all the task force we have. So, if we get into hot water, there'll be no space cavalry riding over the hill to the rescue, or even Commodore McQueen, true, noble, and brave, to help us out."

Gail interrupted, "As far as we know. It's been a while since the last fleet task group came this far out, quite a few years before the coup, actually. There might have been some sweeps out here since then, but nothing logged into the fleet database. We have nothing in the navigation system for the area."

Ward answered, "Maybe. And maybe the report is too highly classified for the general instructions. Remember, Thirteenth Fleet covered the area out this way and they went down over three years ago. Only a few task groups came out of the fighting intact, excluding all of the intel nodes. All their intel units either went with the rebels or died stopping them."

Hugh remembered hearing some of the rumors about the brutal fighting after the vice commander of Thirteenth Fleet killed the fleet commander and many of the major unit commanders before declaring himself emperor. Since then, that sector had fallen completely into chaos. After that, none of the surviving fleets remained strong enough to protect the entire sector while still covering their own areas, so the sector had become a shambles with barbarians swarming in. Things there could best be described as *not good.*

"We really need to stop here on Nighthawk," Ward insisted without explanation, "So, sound off. How should we get the mission accomplished?"

He really wants to go into Nighthawk. His hint about highly classified information and reference to Thirteenth Fleet having a standard mission in this system probably means it involves the test. That means we'll stop here. "Sergeant Major," interrupted Hugh.

"Yes, sire."

"Here's what I think we should do and why. If a serious threat exists out here, we need to know as much about it as possible. So, we go in fat, dumb, and happy as a small merchant ship, hiding our stealth and speed advantages. Or, perhaps pretending to be refugees from the empire might be better. Regardless, we go in and check things out. We need to know where the safe havens are out here, and they should know their neighborhood. If they have archeon capability, so much the better. We can find out where things stand at home if they do. Comments, Captain? Sergeant Major?"

Hugh used a natural tone of voice, conversational actually, to get their attention. But, if he were ever to be emperor, he must make choices like this because he, ultimately, held the responsibility. With all the unknowns they could talk forever without understanding their options any better than they did now.

"No, sire," they both answered.

"So, plot us a course in, and let's find out what's going on."

Appendix E: Recently Declassified Imperial Documents
Naval Board Decision Paper

June 7, 3150 AD
Subject: Update of classes and naming criteria
Reason for change: Classified modifications to propulsion systems fleet-wide
New classes: Supernova and Nova
Discontinued class: Battleship

Class	**Missile Bays**	**Naming Convention**
Supernova	40	Destructive Force, natural or man-made
Nova	24	Emperor or empress
Cruiser	10	Planet
Destroyer	6	City
Frigate	3	Battles, famous ships, and heroes
Corvette	2	Miscellaneous
Sloop	1 External	Sector name and number
Fleet colliers	2	Virtues
Combat shuttle	0	Mother ship's name, number followed by letter A
Support shuttle	0	Mother ship's name, number followed by letter B
Special ships	1	First name, male or female, and single initial

23

Unexpected Welcome

Nighthawk/Stave System
1505 BBMT 24 October 3473

HUGH CASCADE SAT UNEASILY IN his cabin watching the approach. Ward insisted on sitting in the bridge jump seat running gun and missile plots while Gail and Sally flew, which left Hugh odd man out. Ward did have much more experience in tactical situations, and this one might just call for his ability to keep everyone alive if things got dicey. Everyone else held down real jobs, positions they'd earned after years of hard work. Except him.

He sat here all duded up in the height of empire fashion as a superfluous, rich, young merchant from Feldspar, a world not far outside the empire, supposedly out looking for new markets. It hid a deeper cover story that, after rogue units of the Imperial Fleet invaded his home world, he'd fled with his wealth.

The rest of their cover certainly did not come even close to telling the truth, but as far as being superfluous, it felt close to the truth right now. The clothes he needed to wear for his cover felt funny on him: a light, loose shirt of yellow silk, loose, baggy pants of thick lime-green silk tucked into soft, brown leather half boots. He stood and tried, again, to get comfortable. Karen and Pam had chosen the outfit out of the mission supplies. Apparently, they often needed disguises on their missions. That having been said, he had a sneaking hunch they chose this costume as a prank. With those two you could never be sure, but Ward had signed off on it so it might have been a serious choice. *Maybe.* Ward could be awfully devious. Hugh's usual uniform of fitted gray shirt and pants over black boots had become a second skin. He'd feel much more comfortable in that than these fancy clothes. This felt like a costume. Which, of course, it was. He just couldn't let it look like it felt that way.

Watching the sensor net as they neared the planet's heliopause, that area between deep space and the local sun's domain, Hugh concentrated on learning as much as he could. Nighthawk consisted of a nondescript little mud ball of the standard blues, greens, browns, whites, and yellows. So far, nothing about the planet told him much of value. He couldn't say the same for the Stave system itself, though. Something serious seemed to have happened here, something nasty. Approaching from eighty degrees above the ecliptic and directly over the planet gave him a panoramic view of chaos. Shattered facilities lay scattered across the meteor belts, interspersed with active operations. Ships sped from point to point at unusual accelerations and decelerations for in-system transits. *Using lots of fuel. Looks like a kicked-over beehive.* He signaled for Ward on a private line.

"Yes, sire," Ward answered with some asperity.

Hugh smiled. If he didn't know better, Ward apparently wanted, very much, to discourage him from calling. "Have you observed the traffic, Sergeant Major?"

"Yes, sire. We were just commenting on it."

"So, you also are discussing the shattered facilities in the meteor belt?"

"And around the major planets and habitable moons."

"I didn't get to those yet," Hugh admitted. Forging on, he continued, "What I take from all this is the original owners are still at home and feeling anxious."

"Yes, sire," Ward answered with exaggerated patience.

Hugh continued doggedly, "So if they are in a world of hurt, they need ships and crews. If we show up as refugees, what is to stop them from attempting to commandeer us and the *Ambrose B*?"

Ward suddenly sounded more intent. "Good point, Your Highness. I tend to think in terms of being blown up as the worst thing that can happen and then only when we open the festivities. Generally, people just back down because we're an Imperial Fleet unit."

Hugh added, "But out here there is no fleet. As far they know."

Ward agreed, but modified the thought, "Out here there is no fleet."

Hugh repeated, "As far as they know."

Hugh could almost feel Ward's evil smile. "As far as they know," he agreed. "Sire, please change back into your cadet issue. To make this work, I think it would be best if you were Mr. Cascade for the remainder of our stay in Nighthawk."

"Aye, Sergeant Major."

Ward hailed *all hands*. "His Highness will be *Mr. Cascade* while we are on Nighthawk, and we are the *Ambrose B* from Thirteenth Fleet. Acknowledge."

Everyone called in, acknowledging the changes. Some grumbling in the background, sounding suspiciously like Pam and Karen, complaining about him not wearing their carefully chosen disguise, reminded him that decking him out in this outfit might really have been a prank after all. Klostermann muttered, "Can you believe it? Thirteenth Fleet. Why couldn't we just stay lucky Seven?" Peterson and Kennion both muttered agreement.

Sally sounded particularly unhappy, "What do I do with these false papers I ginned up? I stayed up all night getting them ready."

Gail took over, "That's enough! If any of you have further complaints, you can talk to me later, privately. In the gym."

A series of, "no, ma'ams," and, "aye, ayes," came in immediately.

Ward shut off the general circuit and came back to him alone. "Here's a new cover story that should work. Thirteenth Fleet is pursuing mutineers and we are part of Admiral Dieter Spitzbergen's task group. They are coming on right behind us. This is your training cruise to qualify as a naval ensign. Use your real name, but you are simply related to former Imperial Warlord Trevor Cascade. That makes you unimportant enough to not be prime kidnap bait if they're desperate enough to try and force the fleet to help them, but prominent enough to leave alone for every other reason."

"I am amazed at your ability to write fiction on the fly, Sergeant Major," Hugh stated with mock admiration.

Ward responded drily, "Certain exalted persons, when they were younger, were extremely accomplished at making stardust up out of pure vacuum, sire. Together with that experience and in training Marine boots, I have a fair amount of insight into how successful covers are created."

"I'm glad you have such a store of knowledge. I'm also gratified I could have been of some small help in your education."

Ward chuckled. "More than a little, sire."

Hugh chuckled back. "I do recall receiving stern admonishments by certain narrow-minded and inflexible older persons, who shall, of course, remain nameless so they don't earn the imperial disfavor. I took those lessons to heart and am now a pillar of virtue and rectitude."

Ward, more drily, answered, "Really? I'll have to take that under advisement, but it is provisionally accepted."

Hugh chuckled at the banter. He had never been what one might call *at ease* in Ward's presence. Ward had hovered over his world, sometimes more, other times less, visible on a day-to-day basis, but always looming as a formidable, sometimes terrifying, apparition. Now, he seemed to be turning into a confidant as Hugh felt his way into his role as heir apparent. "So, what *is* the plan?"

"We come in as Imperial Fleet. Even here, a thousand parsecs from the empire, our reputation means something. Up to a dozen years ago, we regularly sent recon out this way. We refuel, get intel, stock up on perishables, make a call to Admiral Hollister, and get going. The mere thought that a powerful unit of the fleet is in the area giving them hope that the cavalry is on the way or descending in clouds of glory to punish the wicked if they should fall into transgression often keeps people on the straight and narrow."

Signing off, Hugh considered the plan more carefully. As he did, he began to feel troubled as another thought bubbled up:

raising false hope felt wrong. What risks might the people of this system take if they thought the Imperial Fleet owed them protection and had reneged on the deal? How would they feel when it didn't show up? What would happen if *Ambrose B* came back here on the way home?

As emperor, after he passed the test, how would he feel with people lying in his name? Did he want to rule this way? Did he want his agents acting like this, setting up people for disaster for expediency's sake? Would he want to be responsible for the results? Possibly a charred and lifeless world welcoming him when he came back? And then there were the ripple effects from lying as policy. He couldn't see how any of the results could be good. As he considered the effects of his lying to avoid punishment or responsibility, he felt ashamed for taking the easy way out too often in the past.

Life had seemed simpler as a cadet, learning hard and fast rules to accomplish the mission: follow orders, when in charge give orders that could and would be followed, know what the ultimate effect of your orders would be, and then live with those results. He also knew that sometimes people died following orders, which meant the objective must be worth the price.

An early memory came to mind. His father standing tall in a crisp, white uniform telling a man to take his ship into the wilderness to do something. He told the man he might not come back. The man just nodded, saluted, and left. Back ramrod straight, uniform perfect, he marched out to do his duty.

Hugh could tell, at the time, the man had appreciated his father's trust. Hugh asked later what had happened to him and his father said he ran into a trap that destroyed his ship. No one survived. Grief tore his father's face as he told him, but no tears came.

For years Hugh had wondered about that: his father's stern face and the heartbreaking words. He thought he now understood, at least to some extent. His father could never let anyone go in harm's way without knowing the dangers.

True understanding of the responsibility he must bear for the life and well-being of hundreds of billions of people or more began to grow clearer. He also saw that anyone harmed by his orders would weigh heavily upon his soul, especially if he caused it by making bad choices. Which meant expediency could kill his soul just as surely as a bullet could kill his body. Ward had drummed into him from an early age to do the right thing for the right reason.

Thinking again of his dad, he decided that might be why, ten years after Trevor Cascade's death, people were still trying to serve him. Trevor Cascade represented integrity itself, never wavering in his commitment to his people. His people knew he'd never asked them to do anything dangerous unless absolutely necessary and had explained the risks when he did. Hugh decided that he, too, would do the same. Always.

After several minutes of silence, Hugh called Ward back to suggest thoughtfully, "Sergeant Major, a slight change to the cover story. We can't tell them a task group will be coming through here. It could give them the kind of false hope that might get them all killed by taking foolish risks."

"Your safety is paramount, sire," came the prompt hard reply.

"My self-respect is worth more than that. I seem to recall a conversation or two in which you tried to make that minor point. And there is the oath, specifically integrity, Sergeant Major. Always."

Ward hesitated for a beat before answering, "We could say a task group might come this way, which is always possible."

"Improbable, Sergeant Major," Hugh said firmly. "But, if we can be out here, someone else might be, following us to protect us, perhaps. Or hunting us for that matter. The modified cover story isn't true based upon what we know but it isn't necessarily untrue either. It will work. For now."

Ward gave an aggrieved sigh. "So much trouble over little white lies."

"We are what we say and think, Sergeant Major," Hugh intoned.

Ward laughed. "Oh, how much sharper than a dragon's tongue is a child that is ungrateful, or worse, remembers what he has been taught."

Hugh smiled. "What goes around, comes around, Sergeant Major."

Ward continued, "Cadet Cascade, get changed and start following the plot from the bridge. I will monitor the exercise from my quarters."

"Aye, aye, Sergeant Major! I'll get to my station right away, Sergeant Major!"

GAIL LOOKED BACK OVER AT Ward as he signed off. "You really do like him, don't you?"

"Too much," he replied. "I hope he succeeds; I wouldn't like to have to fail him."

Gail's lips tightened with concern for Hugh and Ward. "At least you're admitting it now. I hope you won't have to, either. For more than just the reason that he is likely the last hope for the empire. I read history, and the last time the line almost died out, things got dicey for a long, long time. Sectors Seventeen through Twenty never returned to the empire. More importantly, I know what it will do to you if you have to fail him."

Ward nodded. "Don't worry about me, I'll be fine. You're right about the last time things were this bad. We still don't know how many heirs failed taking the test back then, before Charles Roland passed. Charles Roland's proctor personally failed three or four other heirs before passing him. It was a chaotic time, to put it mildly. Even before the Qabal raised its ugly head, two empresses and an emperor were assassinated by partisans for other heirs in the five years before Emperor Burt took the throne. He died three years later in the invasion by the Qabal. They overran almost everything before Charles Roland passed the test and pulled the empire back together. But not even Charles Roland could get things patched together in an instant."

Gail didn't have time to answer as a knock on the hatch interrupted. "Come," she called over the com.

Hugh barked loudly, "Cadet Cascade reporting."

"Don't push it, sire," Ward growled as he opened the door to leave. "This is a cover story, after all. That said, get your butt in the seat and go to work, Cadet."

"Aye, aye, Sergeant Major."

Gail laid in the course swiftly.

Ambrose B flew in stealth a parsec out into interstellar space, well beyond the detection range of even most imperial units. From that point, she then turned around and hit max acceleration until achieving normal interstellar speed. Reaching the heliopause at full speed ensured they would be seen. They were.

"Unknown ship, standoff. Nighthawk is under military access control due to hostilities with the TechMech Alliance."

Gail nodded at Sally who responded, "Nighthawk, this is Core Naval Ship *Ambrose B* on recon."

"You're *who*?" came an incredulous reply.

Sally carefully enunciated again for the dense or merely surprised tech on the other end. "CNS *Ambrose B.* We are scouting for Task Force 13-6. We would like entry as a neutral power for refuel and provisioning."

"Wait one and hold at the heliopause," came the reply.

"This ought to be good," Sally whispered.

Gail began decelerating to bring them to a stop at the one-light-year limit from the local star, the recognized territorial limit of any star system.

Two minutes passed before the communicator came back on. "Can you prove who you are, *Ambrose B*?"

"We could wait for the task group to arrive and blast their way in but thought the friendly approach would be better. We are asking nicely, after all." Gail sounded as irritated as she felt about this nonsense.

"Wait," they were instructed unceremoniously.

HUGH BUSIED HIMSELF IDENTIFYING AS many ships as possible in the system. They were close enough now to get good solid readings on ship types, good enough to even identify ships individually if they were in the database. Coming in near solar north gave him a panoramic view so he could carry out a careful scan. There were two methods of doing this. Most instructors preferred to concentrate on the nearest neighbors because those were the people who might start shooting at you first. Then you looked progressively farther away until you covered the entire system. Because systems were very big places, that could, and would, take days, especially with lots of system traffic around.

He noted that Nighthawk seemed busy but with oddly limited traffic. All the ships he could find just happened to all be moving. He began a standard search pattern but ignored everything small or operated robotically. This prioritization allowed him to note three powerful ships leaving planetary orbit and heading for the system's south pole. Focusing on them for details, his eyes widened in surprise. He immediately sent the data to Gail.

Gail gave the sensor data a quick once-over before muttering. "Three Imperial Fleet ships—cruiser and two corvettes—headed out away from us. I wonder what that means?"

Hugh now altered the scan with a focus for other fleet drive signatures. Five more quickly came up, a destroyer and four more corvettes. He forwarded that to Gail also. She didn't seem to notice. Head bent over her panel, her fingers flew, being rewarded shortly thereafter with a flow of data over the com panel.

"Oh my," she murmured.

Sally, serious, asked, "Ma'am?"

Gail ignored her, calling Ward, "Sean, get up here right now. We have a little problem."

Hugh, glancing at his timer, saw that more than ten minutes had elapsed. He began to say something when Sally noted formally, "Long time with no answer, ma'am."

"That's because there are Thirteenth Fleet units in this system, which means they likely know we're not," Gail answered. "Maybe we should have stuck with the other story."

Ward walked in at that moment. "Or not. First, they would have known we are fleet just by our emissions. By saying we're civilian we would have raised all sorts of unpleasant possibilities, including mutiny."

"Which these people may have committed, anyway," replied Gail.

Ward nodded and agreed, "Which these people may have committed, probably did, to be way out here." Turning to Hugh, he asked, "Could I have your station for a few minutes, sire?"

Hugh nodded and stood. Ward sat and Hugh watched as Ward's fingers flew over the keypad. He seemed to be looking for something. Data soon flew back.

Gail arched an eyebrow. "King's code?"

Ward nodded in agreement. "King's code."

Sally in a hushed voice whispered in awe, "I thought somebody just made that up; it's real?"

"Real as they come. Now, don't disturb us for a while. We need to know how these ships ended up out here," Gail ordered.

Hugh slipped over by Sally and whispered to her, "What's King's code?"

Sally gave him an astonished look. "You're going to be the emperor and you don't know?"

Hugh gave her an exasperated look. "The list of things I don't know about my job would fill terabyte files. So tell me, what's King's code?"

Sally just shook her head. "Similar to the Galactic Starburst that lets you control all imperial ships and weapons, King's code is supposed to allow the user to access all information in Imperial Fleet databanks. Queen's code does the same for civilian government databases."

"And they didn't tell me because . . . ?"

"Ask them," Sally nodded toward Ward and Gail huddled tightly over the screen. "I'd guess, though, that they didn't think it would be useful to tell you about that because of the extreme unlikelihood of running into any imperial databases out here. As for why they aren't consulting you now, in dangerous situations they're used to making split-second decisions by themselves."

"Probably right," admitted Hugh. "So, King's code is a backdoor? Wouldn't rebels just find it and close it?"

Sally shook her head, her attention focused on Ward and Gail. "Do you have any idea how many lines of code are required to make even a small starship function? Even if they were looking for a backdoor, it would probably take a great coder his lifetime, maybe longer, to find just one. And if more than one backdoor exists? As for rewriting an entire ship's code? The danger of creating bugs that would kill the ship is something no sane person would even consider. So, when you build a new ship, you import the code for the systems wholesale. Anyway, that's what they taught in the introductory courses to ship handling back when there were schools for that stuff."

"Got it." Hugh considered that for a moment before going on, "I think. So, are you following those three ships that are slipping toward the south system pole?"

"Probably messengers," Sally muttered as she refocused on the three ships. "Of course, you don't send cruisers on messenger duty." Distractedly, her fingers flew over the console, soon making the sensors do things Hugh could only dream of.

He watched the small group of ships power down their drives, but they were definitely starting a loop that would bring them in behind the *Ambrose B* in about a day at most. Being sneaky meant low power and slow speeds. Relatively slow speeds. The fleet units still in-system seemed to be setting up a net to catch the *Ambrose B* after it began running when those looping in showed up. After a few minutes, he slipped out, hardly breaking Ward and Gail's concentration. Coming back twenty minutes later, he brought Sally a drink and a snack. With plenty of time until that attempted trap became imminent, neither Sally nor Hugh interrupted Gail and Ward as they reviewed terabytes of data, looking for the critical facts. Hugh felt sure they wanted to know if these were rogue fleet units or not. What happened next depended almost entirely on the answer to that question.

"My goodness," Gail said with some amusement an hour later.

Ward shook his head at her. "That is an understatement. Who woulda thunk?"

"Not me. Of course, he always did have the ability to survive anything. I remember at the Commander's Academy on Gilthorpe he almost got himself thrown out several times. Still, he graduated in the top 1 percent."

Hugh interrupted with some impatience, "Just curious as to when I became a passenger? Who are you talking about?"

Ward and Gail both looked at him as if coming out of a special place in the past together and a little embarrassed because they had neither deferred to him nor included him. Ward answered, "Hamilton Pogue, Your Highness."

Patience definitely thinner, he asked, "And he is . . . ?"

Gail shook herself and sat up straighter. "A real question mark. He's a legend in the fleet. Up till now, I figured he had joined the other dead legends or the other side. Apparently not."

Ward nodded, agreeing, "Apparently not. His methods were always to stomp on things that might be a threat, hard. We currently fit that to a tee since we are definitely not Thirteenth Fleet. He knows that because his units are Thirteenth Fleet. Or were. So, how do we avoid the undoubtedly deadly trap he is setting for us?"

"Call him," Gail said with a shrug.

"Really?" Ward said repressively. "Just like that? You're not setting up a drinking party between him and his buddies and your girlfriends, you know."

"Don't be jealous, Sean. That happened a long time ago, and things have changed."

Gail's assertion didn't appear to appease Ward, but he nodded curtly, letting her go ahead.

Gail called the cruiser, setting the snare, "CNS *Bring It*, this is CNS *Ambrose B.* Please patch me through to Fleet Captain Pogue."

A startled voice came online. "*Who are you, and how did you know who we are?*"

"Bad com procedure, spacer. Now either patch me through to Pogue or a duty officer who can. This is Fleet Commander Gail Felt, on imperial business."

The rating on the com started to sputter, *"You have no business on this net and are unauthorized to call this ship!"*

Another voice came on the line, cutting off the spacer, *"This is CNS* Bring It*'s com officer, Lieutenant Albans. Can I help you, ma'am?"*

"Hamilton," Gail answered gushily, obviously recognizing the voice, "I thought you were dead. We all did after you disappeared into that mess in Thirteenth Fleet. As far as helping me, none of the memories I have about your so-called help on Gilthorpe would lead me to believe that accepting your help would ever be a good idea." Hugh knew Gail well enough by now to hear the absolute insincerity in her response, but had no idea why she answered this way.

Pogue's laughing response indicated he didn't know Gail as well as Hugh did. *"You're Gail Felt all right. Or at least an excellent simulation. You maintained the same untrusting attitude at Commander's Course, as I recall. Got close to lots of your girlfriends, but never you."*

Gail gaily laughed right back. Although certain she was faking it, she really sounded authentic to Hugh. She answered quickly, "And I am still a good girl, Hamilton, so play nice. Please call off that little group trying to get behind us so we can talk. Also, please encrypt this com channel before we go on."

A moment passed. *"Done. Now, you did say imperial business?"* he asked seriously.

"I thought that would get your attention. Those ships will be in a position in about twelve hours to cause me anxious moments, so every minute they move forward makes me a wee bit more antsy. Be a good guy and call them off. Now, please."

Silent for a moment, Pogue came back on, *"Should be seeing them turn around any minute. So, while they do that, could you explain how you knew about me here?"*

Ward broke in. "King's code, Captain Pogue."

Pogue sounded genuinely surprised as he asked, *"Is that you, Sergeant Major?"*

"Yes, sir."

Pogue continued after a moment. *"King's code? If it exists, don't you need the emperor or an heir to use it?"*

"Pretty effective for a rumor," responded Ward. "And we have an heir aboard, but you need to keep that quiet. According to your log, Fleet HQ—what remained after the coup—tasked you to support Thirteenth Fleet against possible mutiny actions. You took an intel group out in a cruiser with no other supporting vessels and arrived just in time to run into the rebellion. Your group managed to peel certain elements off of the mutiny, enough to prevent its success throughout the sector fleet but not enough to keep that fleet together as an effective force.

"However, you seriously irritated a certain task group commander, Garrison Traynor, who apparently made it his life's mission to kill you and your people. Something about blowing up his brother's ship plus leading him into a trap that wiped out half his ships. As a result of his homicidal intentions, you started running. Two years later, you ended up here. You walked in on a nasty local version of barbarians at the gates with the TechMech Alliance playing the part of Attila the Hun. You chose sides and stayed. Now you're afraid Fleet Rear Admiral Traynor has found you again. About right?"

Silence, then Pogue spoke. *"You really have a package onboard?"*

"A package is on board."

"Is he better than the last couple, Sergeant Major?"

Hugh could clearly hear the intensity of interest in Hamilton Pogue's voice.

"He is alive, sir."

"That speaks highly of him and you, Ward. Well, come on in and we'll help you on your way."

Ward answered for them, "One thing, sir. People shouldn't know who he is until we're gone. Call him Cadet Cascade until then."

"Cascade? One of his sons?"

"The only son, now," Ward's tone was grim.

"Everyone thought all of the boys were on Beacon during the coup or killed shortly afterward. Amazing."

"We'll see you in a bit, sir," answered Ward, without directly answering the implied question.

"Bring It, *out.*"

THE CORE EMPIRE

Chapter 32

Completing Part IX, this chapter examines the rule of Emperor Cyrus, beginning with his virtuoso performance in passing the test and the initial hopefulness of his reign. The impact of the death of his wife Sythia and their children and the resulting spiral in governance will be discussed. The Pilgrim's Cove conference in Sector Twelve by the prime movers of the coup, Wilby Dent, Fleet Admiral Jill Efron, Sector Lord and Admiral Bartleby Quadros, Morgain uch Robert, Fleet Commander Jeffrey Gladstone, and others receives extended and detailed coverage. This chapter and part end with the coup, which sounded the death knell of the empire as it existed under the Jackson family.

24

King Maker

Cruiser *Bring It* and Stealth Ship *Ambrose B*

1840 BBMT 24 October 3473

AFTER HAMILTON POGUE SIGNED OFF, Ward looked thoughtful for several minutes, wrapped deeply in meditation. Hugh did not interrupt him, just leaned against the bulkhead. Gail turned to concentrate on flying the ship, while Sally showed the good sense not to intrude either, so the silence deepened. Apparently shaking off his introspection, Ward began searching once more through the data unlocked by King's code. Gail flew calmly, not appearing to be in a hurry getting to *Bring It.* The silence gradually became oppressive before beginning to rise to a crescendo.

"What do you think, Captain?" Ward asked breaking the silence unexpectedly.

Gail turned around to look at Ward, as if she'd expected the question. "About what in particular, Sergeant Major?" Ward raised both eyebrows, a sure sign to Hugh that he didn't appreciate her stalling. Ward didn't say more. Gail gave an exasperated snort. "Don't try your little tricks on me, Sean. We've known each other too long."

Ward gave a short laugh. "You know exactly what I want to know, Captain," he said in a neutral voice, "so please don't change the subject, ma'am."

"Whenever you start acting with full military decorum, things are really going out the air lock without a space suit. What's raising solar flares this time, Sergeant Major?"

"I always act appropriately, ma'am," Ward responded with a slight twinkle in his eye, deflecting her question.

"Mm-hmm," Gail answered back. "Sure you do, and I am the Grand Duchess of Central Core. So give, what is bothering you?"

"You really intend to avoid my question, don't you, ma'am?" Ward tried one more time.

"Rank hath its privileges, Sergeant Major. I outrank you *and* I captain this ship."

Ward's face became serious once again. "But I'm the proctor."

"Granted," Gail agreed with a brief nod. "Two out of three for me, though, so I win."

Ward shook his head but spoke anyway, "Not really the way it works in this situation, but as I am a gentleman . . ."

People rarely got the better of the sergeant major. *Gail must really be enjoying this*, Hugh decided, listening to the verbal sparring from the background. He paid careful attention, trying to understand the nonverbal subtext of the discussion. Sally's broad smile indicated her enjoyment at being a spectator to this heavyweight bout. For Hugh, however, watching Ward and Captain Felt both seek the advantage of being the decider, without inflicting damage to their personal or professional relationship, gave him new insights. He needed to learn how to do this because an emperor's counselors, if they were worth having, would be people of strong will.

Gail snorted. "On Nebo, I seem to recall, you weren't so picky with your language."

"Extenuating circumstances. You needed straight talk, as I recall." Gail snorted a second time before Ward continued. "Now, as you were about to say before we got off the subject, tell me what you think. I really must insist." Ward leaned back expectantly. Hugh's face mirrored his surprise. Ward's verbal jujitsu perfectly reversing the positions of the two with almost effortless ease.

Gail raised her hands in surrender. "Okay, I give. But can you tell me what's bugging you, first?"

Ward shrugged. "The ships' logs are too perfect. Not just day logs or navigation logs but all of the admin logs, engineering logs, the whole bunch. No late entries, no mistakes corrected later, nothing."

Gail nodded. "*Impossible* might be too strong a word to explain it, but highly improbable is an understatement. Plus, Hamilton gave the distinct impression of being happy to see us. So, things are just a little off-kilter. Hinky, even. I always considered him a sleaze, which is why I never went out with him after my husband died. He struck me as a little too eager to comfort grieving widows, to put it politely, after the massive deaths from the fighting. Beds still warm from the dearly departed and all that."

Sally looked as repulsed as Gail. "What a dirtbag," she said.

Gail gave her a girl-to-girl look. Continuing to Ward, she said, "If I were to venture an opinion . . . I think he might try to grab Hugh and become the power behind the throne. Describing him as ambitious, arrogant, and narcissistic would be gentle, even when he occupied a spot lower down the chain of command. Being on his own for the last few years won't have made him more humble. That's why I think they intentionally went deeper into the wild instead of coming back. In my opinion, that's not what a loyal officer would do."

Ward nodded. "My reading of him, too. He always wants others to think he's the sun, moon, and stars, so he's careful not to act too blatantly in his own self-interest in public. He's probably not aware that I personally caught his attempted sabotage of some of his competitors for top honors at Commander's Course. In fact, only his surprise when the others scored well, despite his corrupting their data and notes before the final exam, let me know who rigged it. Otherwise, I still wouldn't have been sure."

Gail nodded. "That sounds like something he'd do."

Ward nodded agreement. "So, we agree that Captain Pogue is not a good guy, and likely a rebel. The question is, does he know that we know he can't be trusted? He certainly seemed to expect we'd trust him, given the way you two were flirting"—at this, Gail rolled her eyes—"so I think we play it that way. We act as though we trust him and believe he's still loyal.

"Your Highness, with your permission?"

Hugh looked intrigued, but inwardly a quaver of uncertainty hit him. This being his test, he gave the final word. Shouldn't he come up with the plan after being formally briefed? On the other hand, he trusted Ward. He raised a hand palm up and shrugged. "Your show, Sergeant Major, go for it."

"Sally?" Ward looked at her, getting her attention, "We need to keep them off-balance. Could you lead snake pit?"

"Oh, no," she moaned. "Please give this to someone else for a change."

Ward shook his head. "Limited number of players, so everyone gets their own bag of snakes to handle. Yours is running snake pit. We need them to underestimate you, thinking you're just crew and easy pickings while you're getting our supplies. We only need to keep them off-balance for a few hours. If we don't, the snakes in the pit kill us; if we keep them off-balance and charmed, we may get through without being bitten."

After a moment, Ward added, "You get Pam and Karen. Tabi and Sheila will take care of refueling and the ship, while the rest of us go with Hugh."

Sally nodded.

Ward continued, "Good. We might have fair warning if you play this right. The alternative is the opposition takes us all out and grabs Hugh. I want a chance to survive and still save the empire."

Hugh interrupted at this point. "Wouldn't it just be better to run for another star?"

Gail took over, "We can get fuel in the Oort cloud but not more food. The same situation applies as when we started coming in: we don't know who's hostile, where they are, or how many. Besides, if we run, Pogue will try and catch us, and a stern chase can be a dicey proposition against a motivated enemy that outguns us at least eight ships to one. All their ships are bigger, although I think we're the only one with stealth. However, for stealth to be effective, it is better that they not know where we started from, since they can still follow our preon trail if they can find it. So, we need to run snake pit instead, Your Highness."

Hugh nodded. "What is my part in this little morality play?"

"Well, sire," Ward answered, "if you could be big, dumb, and happy, it would be safer for all of us." Hugh began feeling mutinous. "If you do, they'll treat you with contempt and say things they wouldn't otherwise say in front of you. That gives us more ears on the ground. It also helps this work, since a dumb, loyal kid won't even understand what's going on. A dumb kid may do something bad to them if his friends are killed. On the other hand, a smart young man is likely to do exactly what they want in reaction to a bald threat. You're no use to them dead or uncooperative, which, in turn, keeps them off-balance if you're playing a stupid hick from the back of beyond. Hamilton Pogue is smart, capable, and ruthless. However, he also never moves until all the pieces are in place. Add to that his opinion of himself as the smartest man in the universe and it makes him pretty easy to predict. Which brings us to the emergency code to break and run if I'm wrong. *Deft* is a good word. Pogue should know it's in Hugh's background and shouldn't get suspicious if we use it."

Hugh didn't care how much it helped; he didn't want to do it. When he had given Ward permission to set out the plan, he hadn't expected public humiliation to be part of it. Sally leaned over and patted his arm where he stood. "You'll be fine as a big, dumb ox, Your Highness."

HOURS LATER, HUGH WATCHED AS the autopilot slid *Ambrose B* to a stop relative to *Bring It*, just eight meters off her bow. He noted Gail didn't look at all comfortable having turned her ship over to a computer, but they had to link up. Hugh carefully examined Pogue's ship. CNS *Bring It* carried two shuttles snugged to her sides attached externally to the cruiser's standard docking collars. This meant that, for any other ship to dock, it must be at the nose entry port. *Ambrose B*, moving in synchronicity with *Bring It*, waited for the extension of a hard tube from the nose to its own docking collar at the entry port. Small spacecraft could have pulled up to the nose for a lock-to-lock hard attachment, but not a ship the shape and size of the *Ambrose B.* After matching speed, direction, and spin, something only computers could really do, a docking tube extended. If either ship changed course while hooked up like this, well, Hugh didn't want to be in the tube without a space suit when that happened.

Ward stood next to the docking port's hatch as the crew formed up in class B uniform, which meant no one sported ribbons and medals. Even so, they looked sharp. No one could complain about simple fleet blue for the women and Marine green for the men. Only Hugh looked unique in his dove gray cadet uniform. Ward ran a practiced eye over them before adding a last word, "Snake pit, keep it simple. Don't try too hard. Let them come to you. If anything smells bad, shear off and act like happy campers. In either case, get our fuel, the supplies, then back here."

"Aye," came from the six doing snake pit. Behind them, Sheila stood watch on the bridge, with Tabi Fleisch in engineering and Vincent Klostermann in the missile bay controlling the weapons pods. The other ten waited for the dock to clang and seal. Once a positive pressure seal showed, Kevin Dunn undogged the air lock on their side. Stepping off in line through the docking port, they entered a narrow passage that looked remarkably like a hallway. Ward led as they approached the entryway to *Bring It.*

Two steps out, Hugh laid his hand on the sergeant major's arm. "I better go first, don't you think?" he asked.

Ward stopped so quickly, turning to look at Hugh, that Gail jostled into him and the others came to a boxcar-like, slow-motion jam. No one fell, there not being enough room in the connecting tube to really fall down sideways, but they experienced a moment of extreme awkwardness just the same. After a moment, Ward nodded his head and then barked softly but sharply, "Dunn and Kennion, imperial security detail. Take post front and clear the chamber of threats. Sidearms out and up. Impress them."

Surging into *Bring It*'s entry port, Dunn and Kennion certainly looked like the imperial bodyguards they were. Quickly and efficiently, they made sure there were no threats in the area. Without orders, Peterson and Jebet took out their side arms, up and ready to take post to the rear after all cleared the tube. Ward motioned Hugh forward, following to his right rear.

Ward whispered in Hugh's ear as they stepped into the other ship, "Good thinking, sire. I almost blew it, focused too much on that weasel. Pogue will expect at least minimum security for you. Let's go."

Hugh sincerely doubted if Ward would have allowed him to step into the entry port without ensuring his safety. He hoped the security glitch just constituted a test to see if he had been paying attention. The possibility of Ward making a mistake, however, shook him. He desperately needed something to depend on.

Hugh straightened his blouse, stepping forward with Gail beside him. Ward slapped him on the right shoulder as he strode into the entry port. Immediately behind Ward came Sally, then Pam and Karen, with Peterson and Jebet bringing up the rear.

A dazzling sight met Hugh's eyes as he stepped out, a row of officers in dress whites with an extremely handsome man standing at the left in a fleet admiral's uniform. The medals, ribbons, and sashes he wore almost seemed like an attempt to hide the whiteness of his dress uniform. Beside him, Gail tensed almost imperceptibly.

Ward, on the other hand, seemed almost completely loose. The few times Hugh could remember Ward being in truly dangerous situations back on Jeffco, he had become extremely loose. Ward's reaction here caused Hugh to tense, all senses alert, though not sure why. If Ward thought things carried the potential of going downhill fast, maybe he needed to improvise. Again.

Pushing that out of his mind with an effort, he put on his game face and his most dazzling smile as he stepped forward. "Admiral Pogue, thank you for greeting us personally."

A moment of panic passed behind Pogue's eyes, but he recovered immediately. Apparently, he intended to walk the fine line of properly welcoming and schmoozing the heir apparent, while telling his people some fairy tale. "Of course, Your Highness. It is our pleasure to greet you in the name of the Nighthawk Republic and our squadron of the Thirteenth Sector Imperial Fleet."

"Quite right, of course," answered Hugh, suddenly taking on the mannerisms that Doña Carlota Gonzalvez y Rodriguez del Castillo, Lady Protector, and all her other titles, used when greeting an especially pompous landowner or self-important industrialist.

Having watched it happen often enough, he had it down pat. When he'd mimicked Doña Carlota for the other cadets, he'd gotten a laugh every time. Very useful to know how to do, like now, when dealing with people who needed to be kept off-balance and who he didn't really trust.

Nodding toward Gail and Ward, he went on, "You know Lieutenant Commander Felt and Sergeant Major Ward, I understand. They mentioned they were acquainted with you when informing me of our good fortune in finding a fleet unit here in the deep Barbaricum, as they say." Now he sounded like a particularly spoiled, and none too bright, rich young man from a sector capital. He wondered if any of the others would laugh out loud or whether even someone as self-absorbed as Pogue might catch on.

Glancing over Pogue's head, he caught sight of Dunn standing in front of a far bulkhead. His stunned expression answered that question. Fortunately, Dunn managed to keep his mouth shut, barely, but Hugh's act apparently surprised him. His eyes gave him away to Hugh. Hugh didn't know anybody worse at poker than Kevin, and it showed now. He hoped neither Pogue nor any of his people looked at Dunn's face. *It might give away the whole game.* Hugh reflected he might be laying it on a little thick but, *in for a penny, in for a pound.* Whatever that meant. He forged ahead, seeing if he could appear even more self-absorbed than Pogue seemed to be.

Hamilton Pogue turned to introduce his officers, but Hugh cut him off, "Yes, yes. All in good time, Admiral. I'll be happy to meet all of your officers at some gala or soiree of some kind later. In the meantime, though, I hope you have a suite ready for me, appropriate to my rank?" Pogue could only nod, dumbfounded. "Good," said Hugh. "Please take me there so I can relax in a bit of comfort. The *Ambrose B* is a nice little ship, but after I complete this small test formality, I shall insist on only traveling by supernova, or nova at the least."

Then, pausing, he looked at Ward. "Sergeant?" he asked.

Ward's face carried the perfect courtier's expression, a completely obsequious one of adoration and obedience. "Your Highness?" It almost shook Hugh to know Ward could fake something like that, much less don it with less than a minute's warning. Ward did that very well. *When else has he been acting in the past?* Putting that thought aside, he continued, "You can send the crew along to take care of the supplies you were bothering me about."

Turning back to Pogue, he continued, "You'll make sure someone helps out with that, won't you, Admiral? My girls will require some help."

Hugh could clearly see that Dunn still looked poleaxed, only beginning to recover. What he had just done effectively jettisoned the original plan out of the air lock. Dunn knew him well enough to know that when Hugh ad-libbed, he needed to follow Hugh's lead. Hugh felt an itch between his shoulder blades, the kind he got sometimes out in the mountains telling him to watch for another predator in the area. He needed backup, which meant the Marines must be with him or on *Ambrose B* manning the weapons systems. He fervently hoped he had made the right play, since he had just called an audible at the line with a score, and maybe the game, in the balance. He also hoped fervently that the rest of them were not giving away the game like Dunn almost had. From what he could see of the stunned expressions in front of him among *Bring It*'s crew, he figured so far so good, regardless of what any of his people did. But it wouldn't be long before that changed. *The only safe direction now is forward.*

A flash of memory gave him an inkling of a plan. Hugh had once watched a con artist swindle a crowd in Frail Wolf when he'd accompanied some of the guys on a supply run. The man had spoken passionately and moved people right along to the point where they'd all willingly given, in fact, had forced him to take, money for a very worthy cause. Everyone but Hugh and Kevin. As a matter of fact, Kevin had stopped Hugh from pulling out his wallet, clamping down on his hand. When Hugh had glanced up at him in surprise, Kevin had simply shaken his head fractionally, but that small movement let Hugh know something smelled about the whole deal. Kevin might not bluff worth beans in poker, but you couldn't swindle him either.

Later, Hugh had heard the man had lifted off-planet with a fortune in stellars before anyone even thought to check on his story of a relief effort on the plague-hit world of Sumner's Crossing. Unfortunately, no world named Sumner's Crossing existed anywhere in the galaxy, as far as anyone could tell, much less in the empire. Later Hugh had asked Kevin how he knew.

Kevin had just shrugged before answering, "Don't know, but everything he said just seemed too pat. He had all the answers ready. The truth is always messier than that."

As for Hugh's current scam, Pogue seemed to have finally shaken himself out of his momentary daze, Hugh noted. Nodding to a commander, Pogue said, "Leslie, see to the heir's request and expedite." Pogue's voice and manner came across as a little pompous in assigning the job to the commander, which indicated Pogue felt he needed to make an effort to assert his authority. Hugh's act must have successfully put Pogue a little off-balance, which pleased Hugh.

All for the good. He hoped. However, Hugh decided he might have pushed the envelope a little too far if Kevin Dunn still showed amazement at Hugh's act. Even with Pogue trying too hard to appear to be in command, he still might figure out the scam. "Please lead on, Admiral," Hugh said a little less imperiously, but not much since he needed to maintain his persona.

Pogue led him down-ship with Ward and Gail two steps

behind. Peterson and Jebet blocked Pogue's four-man security detail while Dunn and Kennion took the front until they reached the flag cabin. Entering, Hugh observed that, although Pogue obviously lived here, it appeared clean and neat, decorated in extremely expensive materials. Hugh glanced around in disgust. *Only the best for Captain Pogue, even here at the back of beyond, apparently.* Obviously, Captain Pogue planned on receiving them here in any event. Drinks stood on a bar on the side of the room. Dunn and Kennion entered first, giving the suite a once-over before allowing Hugh in. Peterson and Jebet took the corridor side of the hatch while Sally, Pam, and Karen followed the commander. The other officers had just disappeared when Hugh failed to invite any of them along. All except the exec, Commander Bhat, who remained at Pogue's right shoulder.

In the short walk to his quarters, Pogue seemed to have recovered his poise as well as acquiring a bit of anger at being treated lightly on his own ship. Hugh had seen enough self-important people lose their tempers in his life to know the signs. Amusingly, they thought they possessed some inherent right to get angry, which justified everything they did. Still, Hugh admired the way Pogue kept his anger firmly under control, even though Hugh could tell he dearly wanted to throw a tantrum.

After graciously sweeping Hugh and Gail into chairs, while obviously leaving Ward without a seat, Pogue sat also. Bhat stood slightly behind and to the left of the overstuffed armchair that Pogue chose.

"Pretty good act, Sergeant Major. If I didn't know better, I'd say he really is one of Trevor Cascade's boys. Unfortunately, they died either on Beacon or shortly thereafter."

"You seem pretty certain of that . . . Admiral?" He emphasized the last word just enough to question Pogue's "promotion."

"Yes. Admiral. Seemed appropriate since I am keeping these people alive. The TechMech Alliance is real and worse than we ever saw coming from outside the empire. Forced marriage of underage girls and slavery are just some of their delightful cultural norms. They also practice an eye for an eye when it comes to crime. Chopping hands off criminals and such things."

Gail leaned forward. "You seem confident he's a fake. Why is that, Hamilton?"

Pogue's face colored a bit as he answered, which did not make him attractive at all. "*Admiral* Pogue, Commander." Being able to snap at someone seemed to relax him a bit, allowing him to swallow his choleric expression. "I've seen footage transmitted at the time of the coup. It shows the events in real time until the feed cut out. One can see little Hugh there, standing proudly beside his father as the first strike came flaming in. No one there could have survived," he stated flatly.

Ward's face turned to granite as he spoke, "You may have noticed my Ann Marie standing right behind that boy as the strike came in. You remember her? The warlord had invited my wife and son to be there since I needed to be away on a training assignment. Following protocol that at least some heirs always be away from a central gathering, Doña Carlota took Hugh off-planet. My only surviving son, Rodney, took his place that day."

Listening carefully, Hugh felt Ward's pain at losing his son. Sons. Ward had lost three of them altogether, one to cancer and one in an accident, in addition to Rodney.

Pogue went on without a pause, "Which raises some complications, Sergeant Major. When you and the proctors responsible for protecting the heirs and administering the test failed with the others, some of us hoped a succession fight would start, allowing an outsider or some unauthorized heir to take the throne." Pogue kicked back for a minute before sitting forward to continue, "Of course, this boy represents a minor problem that can be remedied easily enough."

"He is the *heir apparent*, Admiral, not a problem to be remedied," Ward stated firmly.

"Now, now, Sergeant Major. Does he know what happened to the others who tried to pass the test?"

Ward stood taller and answered straightforwardly, "No, sir. He has not been informed of who the others were or what exactly happened to them. It is contrary to the parameters of the test for me to give him that information."

Pogue smiled broadly, as did his exec. "Well, let me inform him, since I am not a proctor and not bound by the *parameters of the test.*" Turning, his eyes focused on Hugh directly. "Your Highness," he began, his voice dripping venomous honey, "only the most worthy may be emperor, which is why there is a Test of Heirs." Pogue stopped to exam Hugh, head-to-foot before smiling condescendingly.

"Although I can't see what you bring to the table. For some reason you have a personal proctor who will walk you through every step of the way as you take the test." Pogue sniffed and shook his head. "It is a test, Your Highness, impossible to pass except for exceptional persons like Charles Roland. Many have died trying. In my opinion, you would be better off killing yourself now and avoiding the pain. Regardless, Ward will be there right to the end of the ordeal, your end."

Pogue's eyes bored deeper into Hugh. "The reason you will fail is that the test evaluates character more than anything else. That same nonsense about the emperor being only the most worthy is what you obviously lack. After your insufferable behavior at the air lock, I'm surprised you got this far. You really are an irritating young boor. When Cyrus, a good man for all his flaws, took the common test, one of his cousins, his sister, and a brother failed. Even that usual route to getting the Galactic Starburst has a low pass rate. The heirs I know of who survived the coup have all failed the full test." Pogue's smile turned shark-like as he gazed hungrily at Hugh. "They all died trying. And for what, an empty oath? Only a fool would do something like that." Giving him a dismissive look, Pogue said, "Of course, you'll be dead soon, so it doesn't matter."

Turning to address Ward, Pogue continued, "He could be useful as a figurehead and I know someone who might make that work. The empire needs something to draw it back together, and he could be just the ticket. You will need to go along, of course, as will he, but I am sure he'd rather be a live figurehead than another failed, dead test taker. We both know he has no chance. If Phil Ambruster couldn't pass, how could he?"

"Deftly put," Ward answered. Hugh hoped his eyelid hadn't fluttered at the code word. "Since we're getting all the cards on the table, what about these TechMech guys? Where are they from and how many are there?"

Hugh felt a double buzz on his shoulder. Remembering Ward slapping him as he strode into the entry port, he understood. They had just received the *go* from the teams outside.

Pogue shrugged his shoulders, eyes returning to Hugh as he answered Ward, "They are moving in a swarm through this arm of the galaxy, swallowing up systems as they go, and leaving devastation behind them. They're pretty low-tech, actually, relying on graviton drive, so they are slow and vulnerable. Unfortunately, there are lots of them. They seem to think they are on the side that won the Battle of Lost Earth. Other than that, who knows?"

Ward shook his head and spoke suddenly, "I am choosing door number three, and so is His Highness." He cocked an eye at Hugh.

Hugh's tone returned to normal, feeling great relief at not having to playact with this pompous buffoon any longer. "Of course, Sergeant Major. Let's get the show on the road. May I ask how we're getting out of here?" Hugh's gun slid almost subconsciously from his holster into his hand and steadied on Bhat, not Pogue.

Ward chuckled as Pogue's expression reflected his astonishment at Hugh's change in demeanor. "Excellent imitation of Doña Carlota, by the way. You always did have a way with that as a boy. Why are you covering the exec, sire?"

"He's got a shoulder holster with a pulsar under the dress blouse, I think. All he has to do is tip it, and we're in a world of hurt."

Pogue began to turn an alarming shade of puce as Hugh and Ward's chatting totally ignored him. Bhat intelligently remained completely still.

Pogue blew up, "You're in the middle of my ship! Your crew is captured or dead by now. Give up while you can." He snarled to the exec, "Paul, take their arms and get security in here. We'll get those King's codes from the sergeant major."

Kevin Dunn took a two-handed stance, pointing straight at Bhat's head. "Not recommended, sir." Out of the corner of his eye, Hugh saw Kennion move up beside Kevin and Gail move closer to Ward.

"So, how are you going to get past my entire crew, Sergeant Major? You're dead; you just haven't laid down in your grave, yet. This boy is not worth dying for. Join us and we can reestablish the empire."

Gail, whom Pogue seemed to have forgotten in all the turmoil gave a silvery laugh. "Same old Ham, always underestimating other people. We will be leaving, however. I think you might be surprised what a little Amazon power, with a Fleet Elite team, can do."

Pogue's face went blank. "Amazons? Fleet Elite Marines? I thought you only flew the ship. When did you go Amazon?"

"After my husband and children died in the coup," Gail answered, voice as cold as liquid helium. "I still don't know if you were part of it or I'd kill you right now. However, we need to get the heir through the rest of the test, so I'll put off finding out the truth until later. I suggest you be gone when I return if you were with the rebels."

Hugh turned his head enough to see that Kennion had his sidearm trained on Pogue's head, Dunn having readjusted his stance to cover him, too. Carefully avoiding coming between Kennion and Bhat, Ward stepped up to Bhat, relieving him of his pulsar and communicator. Hugh turned to watch as Ward tapped his own communicator with a staccato pattern. A reply came, three pulses, a short and two long. Ward nodded and smiled.

Appendix M: Miscellaneous Imperial Documents

Commissioning Form: CNS BRING IT
Accepted from trials: February 29, 3211
Shipyard: Periastron 3, Planet Periastron, Glove System, Prime Sector
Type: Cruiser
1000ft by 100ft by 75ft—7 decks
3 hydroponics/environmental spaces; 3 power rooms; preon drive primary with gravitonic backup
Main bridge: standard configuration; 1/3 back from nose, auxiliary bridge 1/3 forward from rear
Weapons: 10 missile bays, 40 anti-missile pods, 12 2-man gun pods, 12 3-man laser pods, 2 armories, 6 missile magazines, fifty missiles each at full load, 1 kinetic weapon bay with max of 5 weapons
Full complement: 34 officers, 146 Noncommissioned officers, 318 enlisted and technicians; 498 total crew

25

When Needs Must

Cruiser *Bring It*

2225 BBMT 24 October 3473

TO HUGH CASCADE, WHAT HAPPENED next seemed to occur in slow motion. From the corner of his eye, he realized that a pistol seemed to materialize in Hamilton Pogue's hand and began blazing away. The first round spun Sean Ward to the ground. From behind him, where Tim Kennion had been standing, he heard something heavy hit the ground as the sound of a third round went off. Where that last round went, he hadn't a clue. The next moment, his pistol bucked twice in his hand, returning to level with smoke curling from the barrel, his two shots sounding like one, followed a split second later by one additional report.

Hugh's vision now narrowly focused on only two things: Bhat and Pogue. His finger remained taut against the trigger, watching for movement, any motion at all, from the exec or Pogue. Commander Bhat lay sprawled as a rag doll, lifeless, but Hamilton Pogue grasped his stomach, trying desperately to stanch the blood pulsing through his fingers. Hugh, with a monumental exercise of will, eased his finger away from the trigger, eyes still targeted on Pogue, watching as he slowly slumped to the floor from the chair, his life coursing away.

Hugh took a moment to survey the situation, while keeping Pogue under his gun, noting in passing the hole where Bhat's heart had been. Glancing quickly behind, he saw a bloody red third eye in the middle of Kennion's forehead, while Ward bled from a gash on his head. Neither Kevin Dunn nor Gail Felt appeared seriously injured.

Hugh refocused on Pogue, ignoring everything and everyone else in the scene, zeroing in on the man who had wanted to control or dispose of him with as little emotion as he might have ordered a dinner wine. As far as Hugh could tell, Hamilton Pogue didn't much care what happened to Hugh or anybody else, as long as he, Pogue, ended up on top. Hugh pretty much now felt the same way about him. As he thought about this, Hugh discovered, to his surprise, his finger beginning again to tighten on the trigger pointed now at Pogue's head. He found it harder this time to ease off.

Hugh heard Gail's voice, as from a great distance, "Dunn, see what you can do for Captain Pogue."

Kevin Dunn's normally cheerful voice growled back, "Sergeant Major first. Then, if that scum is still alive, we can fix him up so the hangman can finish the job."

"Sergeant!" Gail's command voice took over, "Take care of the captain. Now!"

Dunn stepped into Hugh's vision, careful not to interrupt his line of sight to Pogue. He handed Hugh his gun before coming within reach of the captain. Putting pressure on the wound, he slowed the flow, then demanded, "How do we call your medics? You're dead in sixty seconds unless they get here, ASAP." Pogue, already losing consciousness from blood loss, could only nod at a button on the bottom of the chair arm above him.

Dunn stabbed the button with a bloody hand, leaving a smear on the expensive upholstery. "Med teams to Captain Pogue's quarters, stat. He is bleeding out from a stomach wound. Need another team for lesser injuries." He put both hands back into the bloody gore in Pogue's middle.

Hugh heard Gail hiss, "Did you have to tell them who got shot?"

"Guess not, ma'am. But ships' crews seem to respond best when their captain needs them."

"Which means security is on the way with them."

"You said take care of the situation, and I did, ma'am," Dunn responded, without contrition. "We better make sure Peterson and Jebet are ready for visitors."

Grabbing Dunn's gun from Hugh, Gail stepped forward, and his tunnel vision abruptly expanded. Suddenly, he noticed the bloody gash on her arm, but she seemed to be holding the pistol steadily enough. Her hands were bloody, too, evidently from someone else's blood, because he could see very little blood flowing from her wound. Turning his head, he saw Ward down on his back, his face a bloody mask, barely moving, a strip of cloth wrapped around the temple and forehead.

Gail caught his look. "He should be okay. Head wounds are especially bloody because brains need so much blood, which is why I have no idea why his head is bleeding so much." Her attempt at humor helped calm him. Continuing, she said, "He'll be okay, Hugh. Make sure Peterson and Jebet are ready for company." Hugh nodded, appreciating how the use of his first name had relaxed him.

Opening the entry hatch, he came eye to eye with Pete Peterson while Abdul Jebet watched the corridor. "We've just completed a little disagreement over imperial policy. Captain Pogue decided he wanted to appeal to a higher court, which means he needs medical assistance, as does the sergeant major. Let medics in, no guards. You may want to step in here, keeping the hatch open, because they may decide to shoot first. Pogue is definitely critical and has to get help fast. We have to avoid a shooting contest if we want to help him." At that moment, they could hear feet pounding down the corridor toward them. An alarm klaxon sounded at almost the same time.

Peterson shook his head. "These people can't be trusted. We found six heavily armed men in the yeoman's office across the hall when we arrived, so we jammed the lock electronically."

Hugh became aware of someone in the office across the corridor beating furiously on the hatch. Apparently, they couldn't get out, so he ignored them. Peterson went on talking, "I don't think it's a good idea to have all of us in Pogue's cabin. We'd be trapped if we do that, sir. More flexibility if we control the corridor between the hatches." The habit of calling an officer *sir* in an emergency apparently overwhelmed the newfangled *sire*. "We'll close off the corridor. I'll take the next bulkhead up and let the medics in from there. You can escort them in. Jebet will take the bulkhead toward the entry port in case they try to flank us. Fleisch and Klostermann can pull us out that way, if necessary." After a second, he added, "Or Gail's girls can, wherever they are."

Hugh nodded in agreement. Not strictly chain of command, but it worked for now.

Peterson hadn't seemed to notice Hugh agree with him. "You okay, Your Highness?" he asked after a moment. "You look a little pale."

Feeling increasingly lightheaded over the last minute, his knees started to buckle. His stomach began to lightly heave like a touch of the flu. "I'm not feeling very well all of a sudden."

"Shock," Peterson stated authoritatively. "First time you shot someone?" He hurried forward to the hatch as he spoke and dogged it shut.

"Yeah," Hugh answered, his stomach becoming more rebellious by the second. He almost staggered, his head reeling badly now.

Peterson gave him a compassionate look. "Yeah. First time in combat, I shot someone up close and personal, I puked my guts out afterward, too. Killing people really isn't a normal thing for folks to do. Throw up and get it over with. We still have lots to do today."

Someone began banging on the other side of the hatch. Peterson's suggestion almost did bring his breakfast up to land all over the corridor, but he fought it down. His head cleared a little as he did, enough for him to focus on the hatch as Pete keyed the com unit. Hugh noticed a jammer attached to that hatch. Peterson must have completely burned out the door latch mechanism on the office since, apparently, they had only brought two jammers and Jebet must have attached one at the other end of the corridor.

"Open up!" demanded a voice through the bulkhead communicator.

"I will, as soon as you do two things: security team backs off and medics come through unarmed. No negotiation," Peterson answered.

The voice on the other side came back hard, *"No way. Put your arms down and we come in. Surrender and it will go easier on you."*

Hugh stepped up, now in icy control as adrenaline chased away the nausea. "Pogue is bleeding out thanks to his own stupidity, but he's not dead yet. Don't you make it fatal. Security team stays back; medics come in unarmed. Five seconds is about all the time Pogue has left."

A different voice answered almost immediately, "Got it. We're ready to go. Security team is back."

Peterson cracked the hatch to check the corridor. He seemed satisfied, so he opened it wider to let in the medical team. As they stepped through the hatch, Hugh saw they were both well over six feet tall and looked more like wrestlers than medics. Pete nodded at Hugh, giving him a warning hand signal. Hugh backed toward the hatch to Pogue's quarters, five meters away, pistol ready. Peterson kept the hatch between him and the medics, gun up, until he could close it.

The medics stepped past Peterson carrying their bags. As the first one reached Hugh's hatch, they popped guns out of the bags. Not swiftly enough, however. Peterson, having already dogged and locked the hatch one-handed as they went past, screwed a gun into the eye socket of the rear medic even as he made his move. Hugh, however, dropped his pistol instead, attacking barehanded. He flipped his medic to the ground, a move much easier in normal gravity than the two G's he had been training in. His right knee landed between the medic's shoulder blades. He let out a "woof," as all the air left his lungs. Hugh gripped the man's wrist. A little more pressure and he could easily break it.

Hugh growled roughly, "Either of you really a medic or just security goons?"

"Yeah," grunted back Peterson's man with the same voice he recognized from the hatch, "we do both on this ship."

Hugh stood, dragging his man upright, before roughly shoving him through the hatch. Dunn looked up, blood to his elbows as he did. "About time," he complained harshly. "Pogue almost died while you two were dancing out there."

His medic dropped to his knees and quickly dug out a pouch of sera to replace the lost fluids. Whatever else he might be, from Hugh's experience the man certainly acted like a medic. Having regained his breath, the medic slid a needle expertly into Pogue's arm, the fluids quickly entering the almost bloodless body. He now added shock drugs and then started to probe, trying to tie off the severed artery. Partially successful, he quickly attached a second bag and then tapped his communicator, "Doc, admiral's in bad shape. Need your help, stat." He continued to work without waiting for a reply.

"I'm on my way," came the reply.

Hugh jabbed his medic. "What's your name?"

"Zane," came the testy response.

"Listen, Zane. Be sure the doctor knows not to bring weapons other than his knives. If he does, you'll be needing a new doctor because I'm losing my patience."

"I'll tell 'im," he sneered. "Who do you think you are, anyway?"

"The heir apparent," Hugh answered matter-of-factly. Even though occupied in trying to save Pogue, Zane's head snapped around, giving Hugh a hard stare. Hugh just stared back, his face showing nothing.

Dunn nodded and vouched, "Better believe it." Dunn had returned from the washroom while Zane worked, able to get most of the blood off. He took over watching the medic work, gun rock steady and focused on a point midway up Zane's back. A shot there might not kill him but would almost certainly paralyze him. From the look on his face, Zane understood it, too.

As Hugh turned to go back into the corridor, the place they would need the most manpower, something strange about the chair lying on its side drew his attention. Examining it more closely, he found two open compartments, one in the right arm and another high on the backside. It suddenly dawned on Hugh that the guns Pogue and Bhat had used to wound Ward and Gail and kill Kennion came from these hideouts. In shock, he realized they had assumed that Pogue and Bhat were unarmed after they had taken the guns they knew about. Hugh promised himself silently to never let that happen again. Turning, he saw Gail kneeling beside Ward, trying to make him more comfortable by putting a cushion under his head. His eyes were barely open.

Bitterly, she commented, "I knew that weasel better than anyone here. I'm the one who told you how bad he could be, and yet I let him sucker me into thinking he had surrendered. He always kept an ace up his sleeve."

Hugh nodded. "Like a medical team made up of security goons," he murmured. "I wonder what he has these bully boys do in their spare time?" He actually didn't want to know the answer: he felt certain he probably wouldn't like it. Shaking himself, he straightened up, before heading into the corridor in time to hear someone new banging for admittance. Hugh saw Peterson's medic on the deck trussed up with tape and supplies from his own bag in the corridor. *Fleet Elite can be very resourceful.* Hugh dragged him a little farther down the corridor, then stood, picking up his pistol from where he had dropped it when subduing Zane. Steadying the pistol against the cabin hatch. "If that's the doc, let him in. I'll take him to Pogue."

Peterson just nodded and then spoke through the hatch communicator. "Doctor only, no weapons. Bring your bag with all your knives and toys, but if you try to use them any other way than medically, we'll record your bad judgment on your tombstone."

"Fine," came the single, rock-sure reply. He certainly sounded like a doctor to Hugh, supremely confident in his control of himself and his ability to command the situation.

The doctor stopped in the hatchway, examining Hugh narrowly, every inch of him proclaiming that as a doctor he should be in charge. Peterson simply motioned him forward with his pistol. "You're not searching me?" he asked in surprise.

Peterson shook his head. "I'm a dead shot and snake quick, so you can take your chance if you want. Besides, your captain really does need your help. One word of caution, His Highness here," said Peterson, motioning toward Hugh, "is at least as fast as I am and he doesn't distract easily at all, so don't try anything."

The words *His Highness* seemed to stop the doctor in shock. "You don't mean this boy is the emperor?" He stood frozen in the corridor.

"Nope, just heir apparent. For now, anyway. You have a traitor to save, though, so you better be quick about it. Last I heard, he could use a priest more than a doctor."

The doctor deflated a bit as Peterson spoke. Hugging the bag to his chest, he hustled in. Taking in the situation at a glance, he brusquely began giving orders, "You there," indicating Dunn. "Clear that table. Zane, help me get the admiral on the table so I can operate." Dunn just stood watch. "I said *move*, Marine," ordered the doctor

Hugh interrupted, "Dunn, get the other medic in here to help. Zane, you clear the table. Captain," he said to Gail, "please help keep an eye on things. Sergeant Major looks like he is almost back to being ready for duty."

Gail, who had been stroking Ward's head, looked distinctly embarrassed for a moment before standing. Ward, for his part, appeared somewhat cross-eyed and possibly suffering from a concussion. *Definitely not ready to report for duty, much less action of any kind.* Regardless, Gail quickly brought up her pistol as Zane pushed everything from the wet bar onto the floor, all but the glassware that he carried to a sofa. Dunn came back in after a moment with the other medic. Nantz, according to his name tag. The doctor then began working on his patient while keeping up a steady stream of invective toward Pogue's assailants. Hugh just ignored his verbal abuse, as did Dunn.

Dunn watched from a position in a corner where he could observe the doctor while keeping an eye on part of the corridor. Hugh, standing against the same bulkhead, took the corner where he could not be seen from the corridor. As the operation progressed, Gail moved Ward and herself into an inside corner that could not be seen from the passageway.

Finally, the doctor, Davison, from his name tag, ran out of outrage about the time he finished sewing up Pogue. "That should hold him for a minute or two. Touch and go, but he may pull through. He'll need to be moved to sick bay immediately," he demanded.

Gail, on her communicator almost the entire time Davison had been operating, looked up. "He'll stay here," she stated in a steely voice.

Davison puffed himself up, turning a bright red before he began to bluster, "He must be immediately moved to an intensive care unit. He may die or develop a serious infection if he isn't. I need to hit him with a full gamut of antibiotics. Operating in here may have killed him just as surely as that bullet, but I didn't have any choice! He would already be dead if I hadn't." He obviously expected his every word to be accepted as law, and a mere commander ignoring him, especially with the health of an admiral on the line, stunned him.

Gail Felt looked remarkably unmoved by his imperious demand. Pointing toward the bedroom, she simply stated in an almost dismissive tone, "There. Now."

Davison's face turned from red to an alarming purple. Opening his mouth, he almost choked on the words struggling to be unleashed, plugged by the instantaneous appearance of Gail's pistol. Davison, suddenly cross-eyed, tried to focus on what appeared to be an enormous tunnel lined up unwaveringly just two inches from the bridge of his nose. Hugh watched as the doctor's eyes widened, color draining from his face.

Gail asked conversationally, "Doctor?"

Davison turned on the medics and began screaming to cover his fear, "Get him into his bed! Now!"

Gail grabbed Hugh's arm firmly. "Keep focused. His anger is nothing compared to us being dead, sire," she hissed quietly.

Hugh nodded, steadying his pistol on the medics. After the doctor settled Pogue on his bed, Hugh caught his eye. "Now the sergeant major, Doctor." The doctor sidled past Hugh as if terrified of him. Only Hugh and his people knew this impression of him, as a stone-cold killer, didn't exactly match reality. Before entering this cabin, he had never shot anything except game before in his life. His face gave away nothing now, but his gut had discovered a huge difference between shooting people and animals. Sims weren't really the same, either. *Not at all the same.*

Dunn and Gail kept the medics under their gun sites as the doctor proceeded to treat Ward in stony silence with a surly frown. He settled Ward onto the couch after finishing.

Ward struggled to sit up, but the doctor pushed him back, his returning professional manner not encouraging disagreement. Ward not being up to his usual ability to go fifteen rounds with a grizzly bear, the doctor easily won the contest.

An interesting thought occurred to Hugh while Davison treated the sergeant major, but he waited until the doctor straightened up to pursue it. As Davison stretched his back, Hugh commented, "Good work, Doctor."

Davison turned and glared at Hugh. "What else would you expect with a gun pointed at my spine. I need to report to Commander Jay, the second officer, since Bhat is dead." He gave a brusque nod of his head to the corpse still lying behind the chair against the wall.

He keyed the com unit.

After a moment of reflection, Hugh nodded, "Go ahead and call but please be very careful as to what you say. Tell Commander Jay that the admiral is resting, though he really should be in the ICU. Bhat is dead and the medics are alive but trussed up like Christmas turkeys."

The screen remained blank while a man's disembodied voice answered, *"Tell them to surrender. If the admiral dies, they do, too."*

Hugh spoke from out of visual range of the com, "If you try anything, he certainly will die. The doctor'll let you know every hour what the admiral's status is. Out."

He cut the com. "Sit, Doctor." Davison looked around and decided that Pogue's overturned chair would be the most convenient spot. Setting it back on its feet, he settled into it. "How long have you been practicing? Do you have a family?" Hugh asked.

Davison glared before answering, "Twenty-five years. Fifteen years on Beacon in private practice and then ten years after the coup in the navy. I had a family before those crazies destroyed the empire. Lost my wife, a son, and his family in the coup; heaven knows where the others are."

Hugh felt sympathetic. He definitely empathized with the man. "So how did you end up out here?"

Davison gave him a hard look. "The admiral needed a doctor before deploying to Sector Thirteen to check out rumors of rebellion, so he drafted me. We got out there and went nosing around."

As he talked, the doctor began to warm up. With the air of a natural gossip, he leaned forward. "We may have set off the rebellion in Thirteen. We had just arrived at Admiral Traynor's supernova when everything blew up. We laid low, not really participating, just flying back and forth between the various factions, trying to get a handle on things, I guess. In fact, we barely escaped from Task Group 13-2 when the rebels concentrated on them in their hiding place. I never could figure how they knew those ships were in that nebula, but they killed a lot of them. It looked like the rebels were going to take over the whole sector when a loyal task group ambushed Traynor. I heard he blamed Pogue personally for the losses. What did he expect? Pogue supported the loyalists." Davison added expression by shrugging his shoulders for emphasis. "Well, by that time, we had gathered this little squadron together from odds and ends, so we took off with Traynor hot on our heels. Since then, we have been trying to stay together and stay alive."

Davison took a breath and glared at Hugh once more. "And then, here you come, upsetting everything, claiming to be emperor, and causing all kinds of problems."

Ward's voice rasped a little drily from the couch, "He is the heir apparent, Doctor. So, if you don't mind, more respect is in order."

Davison spun with surprise to see Ward sitting up in a shaky sideways slant on the couch but managing to hold his gun rock steady. The doctor blanched a bit, his earlier fear returning. "Put that down; you need rest," he ordered.

Ward sagged back a little more before nodding. "You may be right about my need for rest," he allowed, "but you will show respect to His Highness."

Davison gave Hugh a speculative look. "Before you got here, we heard a report of another fake emperor coming through, looking to raise a fleet."

Ward couldn't muster enough energy to sit up straight. "I told that self-centered oaf not to tell anyone. We're trying to get this done quietly."

Davison became intrigued, leaning toward the sergeant major. "Do what quietly?"

Ward just clammed up, taking on a poker face. "Nothing at all, just a private matter."

The doctor sat up, excitedly. "You're looking for a new Galactic Starburst? You're on the quest?"

Hugh, momentarily stunned that the doctor seemed to know about the test, blurted out, "What do you know about it?"

Ward gave him a quelling look, but too late. The doctor's face beamed with a beatific smile as he settled back. That changed quickly to one of calculation as he gave Hugh a most unnerving head-to-toe examination. Hugh felt as if he were a prize animal on the auction block in one of the market towns near the estate.

Clearing his throat, the doctor ventured, "The admiral told the command group you were claiming to be a Cascade. You wouldn't be related to Trevor Cascade, would you?" Then, seeming to grasp for the proper social convention, choked out, "Your Highness?"

Hugh relaxed a little, this conversation could be going much worse. "Yes, I am. Did you know my father, Imperial Warlord Trevor Cascade?" Hugh felt that the greater the distance and grandeur he could impart to his father, the more leverage he would have with the doctor.

"Yes," squeaked Davison, before swallowing and starting again. "Yes, I knew him slightly. My son held a minor civil position at court and ran into him from time to time." The doctor even puffed a little at this reminder of past pride and reflected glory from his important son. "He and his wife were both there that day," his voice now betraying the deep grief he still felt at the real loss of family and friends.

"Everyone died, all but," he continued, "Admiral Pogue."

"*Captain* Pogue," Hugh corrected in an absent tone. The pistol still rested dead center on the doctor, although Hugh sounded relaxed.

"Captain Pogue," amended the doctor hastily. "Anyway, he told the crew your ship carried another fake heir, claiming to be the son of Trevor Cascade. He told everyone that years ago he had personally reviewed the footage and reports and knew that all of Trevor Cascade's children were dead. You won't have any sympathizers among the crew."

During the discussion, Ward had inched around on the couch so he could watch Davison's face. Ward asked, "Doctor, are the ships of this squadron commanded by rebels or loyalists?"

Davison shook his head as if to clear it after being hit. He struggled to form an answer to such a simple question. He obviously knew all the officers in the fleet and which side they stood on as Pogue had gathered up ships. Ward's question obviously brought all of what he knew into conflict with what Pogue and Bhat had said over the years. Without even mentioning it, Ward planted the big question: Which side had Pogue really been on? Hugh easily read that in his reactions. Poker playing had taught him how to be a skilled reader of people.

After another moment, the doctor answered in a whisper, "All but the *Elmira Hayes* are commanded by officers from former rebel ships we picked up. All of them have personally given their oath to Pogue." Pausing for a moment, he added, "There is an exception. The corvette *Hayes* has managed to keep its crew and officers together. Captain Pogue tried several times to transfer officers onto her, but her captain, Lieutenant Brennan, absolutely refused. Claimed it would cause morale problems." Davison paused for a moment. "A close friend of his commanded the destroyer *Lemanton*. The destroyer's captain died while being arrested for mutiny, by the exec Pogue had assigned to her ship."

Hugh waited, letting the doctor come to his own conclusion. His gut told him that arguing with him now to prove the point would be exactly the wrong move.

The doctor pondered another minute, then sadly regarded Hugh. "That just makes things worse. You know you're not getting out of here alive, don't you?"

Hugh startled him by smiling, a broad, carefree grin. "We'll see." Stepping to the door of the bedroom, he checked to see how things were with Dunn and the medics. Tied up, nice and tight. Pausing for an instant, he ordered decisively, "Bring in Zane. I have a few questions he and his friend can help with."

Shutting the door, he gave Ward a wry smile. "Best way out? Trade the traitor or break the command group?"

Ward shrugged. "Good question. The women have the entry port air lock under control at the nose. Fleisch has set up a heavy weapon covering the hatches inside the entry port on the *Bring It* side, so anyone trying to force entry onto *Ambrose B* will have a tough time even getting to the air lock. If necessary, Sheila can blow the attachment passageway and standoff, but then she'd be blown away by this ship. Hard to break into a ship like the *Ambrose B* since the skin can be polarized, which makes wearing a suit on it, to cut a hole, a losing proposition. So, our ship is secure for now, as long as we stay attached."

Hugh thought as Dunn appeared, half dragging Zane. Ignoring Zane, he spoke to Dunn, his face hardening, "Drop our friend on the deck, Dunn. Right next to the exec. Then get back in with Pogue and the other one."

Zane landed hard on his side almost nose to nose with Bhat's wide-eyed dead face. He couldn't move away, unfortunately, tied so tightly he could barely squirm. He just lay still, glaring.

Ward appeared supremely indifferent. "Doctor," he asked, "did these boys ever torture anyone for Pogue, to keep them in line?"

Zane swore at Davison. "Keep your mouth shut or it will go harder with you later."

Ward just smiled. "That answers that," he said with satisfaction. "Now for some information." Looking straight at Zane, he continued, "Who is really next in command here after Bhat and Pogue?" Zane gave him a hard look in return and just kept his mouth shut.

Ward glanced at Hugh. "I'll need your help on this, Your Highness. I'm a little under the weather still. Please grab a sharp knife from the doctor's kit." Hugh stood a minute as he weighed his options. He then went to the doctor's bag and grabbed several scalpels.

"Wait," wailed the doctor. "You can't do this, it's not legal!" Hugh ignored Davison, just knelt by Zane, face blank.

Ward gave Zane a calculating stare. Matter-of-factly, he began, "The heir apparent is very skilled in skinning and dressing animals. He is about to use those skills on you." Turning back to the doctor, he shook his head. "It is very legal, Doctor. If we were going to have a trial for Zane, we would be concerned about where the evidence came from." Ward shrugged. "However, Zane will never have to worry about standing trial; too many obstacles, legal and otherwise, in the way. Plus, since we do need to get His Highness out of here safely, we need information. His Highness, of course, can't be tried except by a full court of sector lords, which no longer exists. He can pardon the rest of us, so there is no problem with the courts." Appraising Zane once more, Ward nodded as if he had made a momentous decision. "Let's start by stripping the tendons in his hands and then we'll move on to the feet and legs."

Zane's expression became more and more alarmed as Hugh calmly examined the selection of scalpels available to him before picking a couple and laying the others down. Flipping Zane on his back, Hugh slammed his knee into his solar plexus. Zane's "ooph" as his breath exploded out of him, combined with his clear terror, normally would have brought pity. Hugh felt none at all. There were too many ghosts hovering around this man—men and women he'd destroyed without pity.

Zane bucked and rolled, desperately throwing himself about in panic, trying to get away even as he struggled to regain his breath.

"You haven't even asked a question. Why aren't you going to ask a question?" Zane finally wheezed out, desperately.

Hugh just shook his head, tapping the scalpel in his hand. "I figure to speed the process up, we carve you up quickly, and your partner will be much more helpful. Easier on us, easier on him. Plus, it is easier on you, you don't have to suffer hours of pain just to keep your honor intact. Everybody wins."

Zane stared in horror. His reaction told Hugh what he needed to know about him. If this man hadn't tortured people to death, he had at least stood by watching and knew how long it could take. The very idea scared him to death. Gasping, he begged, "Why don't you just ask a question? I still can say no, but it might be something I can talk about."

Hugh glanced at Ward for a moment, who shook his head. Hugh just looked down with a sad expression. "Sorry, we're in kind of a hurry."

"Please," begged Zane. As a crazed look came into his eyes, he added, "Your Highness!"

Hugh contemplated Zane for a minute. A full minute, during which hope flickered in Zane's eyes, keeping him just this side of sane. Hugh shrugged. "As long as you're being polite, we'll give it a try."

Sitting back on his heels, Hugh examined Zane dispassionately again before nodding at Ward. "I would rather not even have to talk to this thing, but he did properly address me as *Your Highness*, so you ask him. Otherwise, I'll just get the job done. *Quickly*," he added with feeling. It made him feel dirty to even play this role. He would never have tortured Zane to death. He hated seeing even injured animals suffer.

Ward nodded gravely. "Yes, Your Highness." Turning on his best sergeant drill instructor demeanor, he looked down at Zane. "Your name?"

"Weston Zane."

"How many people have you tortured for Pogue?"

NAVWAR OFFICER BASIC COURSE

Appendix L: Imperial Military Training
Standards Introduction to Astroplotting

Naval Officers Basic Course
issued 3411 with revisions

Precise location of ships and systems is essential to successful military operations and for the civil administration of the empire. Emperor Dave in 2491 created this area of specialization in conjunction with a standard objective coordinate system not based upon the erratic motion of Earth, a minor planet in the Orion-Cygnus Arm of the galaxy.

To successfully pass this section, a midshipman must be able to plot on the galactic X, Y, and Z axes the location of a series of star systems in both imperial and Terran coordinates.

26

The Narrow Ledge

Cruiser *Bring It*

0105 BBMT 25 October 3473

AN HOUR LATER THEY FINISHED. During that time, Dr. Davison had checked several times on Hamilton Pogue's condition before reporting in a few minutes earlier. Sweat dripped from medic/security goon Weston Zane but, more pronounced still, he reeked of fear and shame. The doctor had ceased commenting long since, his face ashen with shock as Zane confirmed Pogue being a traitor and a prime mover of the coup. Pogue's specific responsibility had focused on identifying the locations of all the heirs at the time of the initial strike that had resulted in the deaths of so many innocents, including the strike that had killed Davison's family. Pogue hadn't actually called in the kinetic strike, but he could have stopped it, or at least warned people to flee. The doctor stood quietly, as if in a trance, before turning back toward the bedroom, firm determination etched on his face. As Hugh watched him, he felt certain the doctor heard his long-dead son, daughter-in-law, and wife crying to him for justice from the grave. Hugh caught his arm and firmly pulled the doctor back into the chair.

Davison pleaded with him, "Your Highness, if there is any justice in this galaxy, let me kill him!"

Hugh's eyes filled with pain and compassion. "You have good reason to kill him, as do I. We're not the only ones. Sergeant Major Ward, Captain Felt, and billions, maybe trillions of others, are in line ahead of us. However, I don't think you would be able to live with yourself if you killed him. You're too good a man, Doctor. Plus, we need him if we're to get out of here."

Standing, Hugh gave Ward a thoughtful look. "If we take him to the *Ambrose B* as a hostage, we can take off, but his co-conspirators are just as likely to blast us so they can be number one."

Ward nodded. "The problem with any mutiny is that, once legal authority is destroyed, it can't be reestablished without buckets of blood. Maybe not even then. We are in a bind I can't see a high probability of getting out of." He stopped, frowning. "Sire?"

A flashing emerald-green cursor on what should have been a dead screen at Pogue's workstation had distracted Hugh. *How long has that been on? What? Now it's blinking deep, bright blue.* Had he seen it on earlier? He remembered carefully giving the room a thorough once-over while the doctor treated Pogue and Ward. He would have noticed it, even if just as a mental note. The cursor now turned golden. *What does that mean?*

"Your Highness?" prompted Ward a second time. Hugh recognized the exaggerated patience in his voice, 99 percent certain that Ward now felt more than mildly irritated by Hugh ignoring him. But, in this situation, something as out of place as that suddenly flashing cursor might be the difference between making a bad plan without knowing it and stumbling onto a good one.

"Sergeant Major," responded Hugh, still not giving him his full attention, "do you remember Pogue's computer screen being open when we came in?"

The complete non-sequitur seemed to throw Ward out of his stride. "Your Highness?" came the puzzled reply. "I can't remember."

Hugh mused on, half aloud as the cursor now flashed red. "I don't remember for sure. It's on now, however, and there is a small camera icon showing that we are being watched. They've likely seen much of what has gone on the last hour."

Hugh caught a motion from Ward. Watching him closely now, he saw a series of thoughts cross Ward's mind. Impatiently, he waited for Ward to speak to him. Facing the monitor across the room and to the side of the couch, but talking to Hugh, Ward commented as if at a tactical briefing, "Whoever it is wanted us to notice them by enabling a camera icon and then blinking that cursor at us. They could have continued to monitor in secret, so what do they want?" The cursor now turned amethyst purple.

Hugh agreed with the analysis. Fleet Elite relied on stealth and secrecy to accomplish its missions. Ward had drummed into him: *Be seen, you die.* Violating that rule, someone had just stepped into the open in a free-fire zone and sent up a flare to get their attention. It raised interesting, and dangerous, possibilities.

"Sergeant Major?" Hugh began, "if someone can monitor the captain's day cabin secretly, I would guess they have set up a monitor in the bedroom also." The cursor simply continued to blink, neither confirming nor denying Ward's theory. It now having cycled to white against the black, he continued, "Also, they haven't transmitted any threats or demands, which indicates what to your mind?"

Ward thought for a moment and then stood shakily. "We need to get Captain Felt in here." But before he could even go a step, he slumped back, dizzily.

Hugh bit his lip as he looked at the situation. He didn't want to leave Zane and the doctor alone with Ward this weak. He pointed at Davison. "Please get Dunn to drag this *person* into the bedroom and then send Captain Felt out. After you do that, please stay there until we call you."

"I could help," Davison suggested.

Hugh shook his head. "You already know too much for the good of our long-term health. Or yours, for that matter. Let's take it slow and see what happens."

The doctor nodded and stepped quickly into the bedroom. Dunn came in and, without a word, dragged Zane, none too gently, back with him. He didn't ask for an update, either. Hugh expected that Dunn didn't need to ask. He'd seen Dunn skillfully worm information out of people before, and he'd have both Zane and the doctor in there to work on.

Gail closed the door as she returned. Seeing Ward slumped back against the couch, she walked over and sat beside him, propping him up. "What's up, sire?" she asked.

Hugh indicated a chair. "Grab that and sit so you can see the monitor better. Someone has been watching us secretly and just let us know. Let's see what they have to say for themselves." Gail got up to pull the chair next to Hugh, then sat. Hugh asked conversationally, "Can you hear and see us okay?"

Yes, blinked into life on the monitor in white type. Not showing any surprise, all wore poker faces, perhaps the strongest tell they knew the stakes in this game: their lives and the empire.

"I take it you are in a private area but still need to be careful?"

Yes!

"You are not the acting commander or a member of the command group?"

No.

Hugh became thoughtful. "We'll let that go for later. You've been listening in. Do you have a suggestion for our little predicament?"

Surrender?

Hugh just shook his head with disgust.

The computer reply read, *Can't take a joke? I will have the sensors in the Oort cloud simulate a full-on TechMech assault. The other ships will head to the cloud to pick up leakers that get through.*

"Then what?" asked Hugh.

Elmira Hayes *stays here under* Bring It*'s guns, which is standard procedure. Admiral Pogue doesn't trust LT Brennan.*

"And?" prompted Ward.

You tell Commander Jay you are taking Pogue to your ship. He will follow the security cameras showing you moving the admiral to your ship, so everyone will back off. Jay won't do anything to harm Pogue. As soon as you're aboard and away, I will take a shuttle to the Hayes *and follow you out of here.*

Hugh asked a question that he burned to know the answer to: "How do we keep *Bring It* from following us or just blowing *Ambrose B* up as soon as we're off?"

They won't be able to. Trust me.

Hugh turned his back on the camera, giving Gail and Ward a quizzical look. He waited for options. Gail and Ward's incredulous expressions told him all he needed to know about their feelings. Gail spoke for both of them, "It's crazy. Trust someone we don't know to do things we can't monitor and hope to get away?"

Behind Hugh, the computer displayed a simple line. *Do you have a better plan?*

Hugh turned back as he saw his counselors' eyes swivel back to the screen. "Captain Felt," Hugh asked formally, "what do you have from your team?"

Gail's face became mulish and she refused to open her mouth. Hugh glanced at Ward for support; he shrugged. Hugh added, "If this person has eyes in the captain's quarters, there are probably eyes and ears everywhere. I would say it is even possible our com channel has been identified, even if the signal hasn't been decrypted. All they need is a fix on the transmission site to find the team. So, where are we?"

Gail's expression remained mutinous, but she answered. "We have the supplies and fuel on board, but *Bring It*'s guns and missiles are live. We have no way of turning them off at this point as we are stuck far from all the control lines and nodes, which means we can't get away without being blown up."

Hugh leaned toward her, intently. "Without help, you mean."

"Yes, Your Highness," she answered formally, "without help."

Hugh turned back to the screen, although he supposed the person monitoring them could see him whichever way he faced. He wanted to see the response from the screen, however. "Why should I believe you and rely upon you?"

Why not? came the response.

"Because we may create so much havoc for *Bring It* that they're glad to see us go."

And blow you up as you sail away, anyway. The string of letters, looking like an explosion, trailed the cursor as it crossed the screen.

"Maybe yes, maybe no. But again, why should I trust you?"

The cursor blinked for seconds in purple again before starting to write again. *My team and I were accidentally assigned to Pogue's ship. We decided, while we were here, to monitor the situation and keep our heads down. By the time we figured out which side Pogue supported, our only option would have been an IED within the ship. It would have been suicide. We watched as Pogue carefully transferred out or killed every loyalist he and his men could find. I've lost my entire team because of that.*

After a pause, it continued, *He filled their slots with mutineers, which makes this ship completely loyal to him. Almost. I don't know of anyone else besides myself for sure. I have almost blown up the ship several times, just to have it over with. This is the first time I have been able to see a way off while still carrying out my plan.*

Hugh nodded and then asked Ward, "Suggested actions?"

Ward's lips tightened before answering, "Stupid tactically, but apparently the likeliest way out. I'd flunk a cadet who chose this course. Too many guns, too many ships, too many people who think we're the bad guys." Gail just nodded.

Hugh turned back toward the screen. "Start the ball rolling," he ordered formally. "How long?"

It will take several hours for the signal faking an attack to get to the cloud without being detected, and then back. Can't send out an archeonB signal without Commander Jay knowing.

Nodding once more at the screen, he politely thanked him before looking at Gail. "Get the doctor," he requested. "We need to take care of our prisoners."

Hugh pulled Kennion's body behind the bar and then Bhat's, straightening them out.

Davison stepped timidly back into the main cabin, then waited quietly while Hugh finished laying out the bodies. Ghastly puddles of human fluids remained, but at least the bodies lay out of sight. The intervening period of enforced meditation with Dunn seemed to have sobered him considerably.

"I need you to knock out the medics, Doctor. Then we can talk." Hugh's face remained neutral, neither severe nor encouraging.

Hugh observed Davison's increasing agitation while he considered the ramifications of helping Hugh and others to this extent. "Well—," he began to stutter.

Ward cut him off. He obviously felt better. "Either you do it or I do it and, quite frankly, I don't care if they survive an injection they get from me. Your choice."

Davison hesitated another moment before getting his bag. He quickly set up two shots of a strong tranquilizer. He then looked up, pleadingly. "This will knock them out, but I have to live on the ship after you leave, so could you do it?"

Gail smiled understandingly. "I'll do it. Back in a minute."

Hugh sat again and motioned Davison to a chair. "You're not obligated to stay here, Doctor. We have a good chance of getting away, and I'd say Pogue has a very slim chance of survival."

Davison gave them a searching look. "You really mean that, don't you?"

"I really do mean it. I am offering you a chance to choose a probable death here with Pogue, either by him or some other way, or possible escape and a return to the empire."

Davison thought a moment and then looked up, pained. "What about my family?"

"Didn't they die in the coup?"

"I mean my family here. I have a wife and child on Nighthawk; a lot of us do." Hugh appeared stunned for a moment before Davison went on, "We never thought we'd ever get back, so we started over out here. We've been here years, and this system is our home now. I can't leave them. Who would take care of them?"

Hugh looked over at Ward, feeling completely out of his depth. They couldn't take the time to get people off the planet, much less find a civilian transport. What could he do? He'd been alone the last ten years, so he could understand what it meant to Davison.

Glancing around, he saw the cursor blinking innocently white again on the blank screen. Quickly seizing his only thought, he asked, "Which shuttle are you taking?"

Davison's confusion at the non-sequitur only heightened when Hugh followed up the comment with, "If Davison has a family he won't leave behind, at least some of the people on the corvette will feel the same way. You could have a mutiny if you don't get a civilian transport and take them with you. Which shuttle?" Hugh insisted.

Davison craned his neck around to see who they were talking to when one word popped onto the screen, *port, a cargo shuttle,* in green. After a second, a string of words followed in black. *I will take him if you rendezvous with the corvette and take me with you.*

Hugh queried Ward silently, who shrugged. His nonverbal response loudly said, *Your decision. You're the boss.*

Hugh shook his head and grimaced. "Thanks for the help, Sergeant Major."

Ward actually grinned back at him. "Comes with the territory, Your Highness, comes with the territory. If you can't make simple life-and-death decisions for a few hundred people, how will you be able to do it for billions?" Although said lightly, the truth in his answer bit deeply.

After the last hour, Hugh felt much older than eighteen. "Ward, get on the com and make arrangements for safe passage to the *Ambrose B.* Doctor Davison, you accompany the medics to sick bay, after which, you are on your own to get to the shuttle. The corvette will be on its own to get the crew's families and then go home, and I mean to Seventh Fleet, not Thirteenth Sector, the best way they can." Taking a breath, he faced the screen, although he had no idea exactly where in the room all the cameras watching him were. He formally declared, "On my honor, we will rendezvous with the *Elmira Hayes* before we leave the system and pick up our unknown benefactor before continuing on our way to Earth."

Ward nodded and called the bridge over the desk com. As he went through the chain of command to Commander Jay, Hugh gave the doctor an intent stare. Finally, he spoke, sounding quite young again, asking a question that had just occurred to him. "Doctor, if we hadn't been able to get your family away, what would you have done?"

Davison shrugged. "Well, Your Highness, I can tell you that you wouldn't have left the ship alive. Losing one family is all the pain any man should have to endure in a lifetime."

Hugh gave him a sympathetic smile. "I'm glad you didn't have to try and stop me; I would have hated to kill such a fine family man and doctor." Davison started to smile back before Hugh's deadly seriousness hit him. Hugh continued, "You're a bad liar, so it's better that you've been able to report him being alive."

Hugh spoke seriously as he continued, "I have a mission to save hundreds of billions, maybe trillions, of people and I will shoot anyone who comes between me and that job, regardless of how worthy his motives." Hugh's face hardened again. "It would probably have given me sleepless nights thinking about your widow and child, but I would have done it and lived with the consequences later. I'm glad it worked out this way."

Davison gave a heartfelt nod and agreed, "So am I, Your Highness, so am I."

Ward seemed to be arguing with someone over the com screen as Hugh turned away from the doctor. "I don't care if you are the next most senior commander of this flotilla. Get off the line so I can speak with Commander Jay."

"Sergeant Major," drawled an over-bred voice, a tone favored by some of the cluster capitals as well as people from Beacon. To a real extent, he sounded quite a bit like Doña Carlota with her aristocratic drawl but much more condescending than she ever acted, even to the most obnoxious people she dealt with. "You don't understand. You have no choice but to surrender. You are in the middle of that ship, in the middle of this fleet, in the middle of this solar system. So, if you would be so kind?"

Hugh stepped into range of the com screen and saw a trim little man, one might even say dapper, with the rank pips of a lieutenant commander. "Lieutenant," Hugh spoke using his best Doña Carlota Gonzalvez y Rodriguez del Castillo air of superiority, ramming the smug superiority squarely back in the cretin's face while deliberately downgrading his rank, "why are you giving my man here trouble? We are leaving, of course. I am the heir apparent, and I will be obeyed! Now put Commander Jay on."

Shock crossed the lieutenant commander's face at his first glance at Hugh followed by fear. "Warlord?" he whispered. Hugh, at the moment, must have looked remarkably like his father, Trevor.

"Your name, Lieutenant," Hugh demanded imperiously.

The face on the other side of the com contorted with a variety of emotions before he got control of himself. Sneeringly, he spoke again, "I am Wilby Dent."

Ward sat up. William Dent had been a part of the coup attempt stopped by Trevor Cascade and Doña Carlota. He'd been present at the man's execution for treason.

Wilby Dent continued to speak. "My father was wrongly convicted of treason, when it was that usurper, Emperor Cyrus, who was the traitor. He killed my father. And so I helped start the Restitution Movement to remove the usurpers and return my family, as descendants of Emperor Benjamin, to their rightful place as rulers of the em—."

Another call broke in, splitting the screen as Dent remained online but muted. An icon in the corner indicated that this had been relayed by the planetary archeonA facility. Hugh recognized the face on the screen: Morgain uch Roberts. She smiled broadly. "What a pleasant surprise, all of us on this call together. By the way, good to see you, Sergeant Major." She flashed him her blinding smile, and Hugh felt the tug of her charisma. "I understand you have made a bit of a mess there, but are stuck." Her face hardened into a mask of fury as she turned her attention to Dent. "As for you, your usefulness to me is at an end. I am on my way to claim my prizes even as we speak." Dent's transmission abruptly ended. She refocused her attention on Ward. She gave that blinding smile again, but this time it repelled Hugh. "Here is my offer: surrender. I might even let

Cascade's boy live if you do it quickly. But decide now. I want you and the bag, and yes, I know about it because when I was an heir, one of my proctors talked before you pulled her. You have ten seconds." She looked like a cat that got the cream.

Hugh gave Gail the cut sign. The abrupt end of the transmission most certainly would irritate Morgain, and he would have enjoyed seeing her expression, but he didn't have the time.

He disabled the com from taking inbound calls. "I think that was just about enough from her," he said. "I may actually feel a little bit of sympathy for Mr. Dent; she's clearly planning on killing him."

Ward grimaced. "She's come far in her plans. Back toward the end on Deft, she contacted us claiming to be empress and offering to let us go free if we gave her Doña Carlota." A shadow crossed his face as the memory came back. "Obviously, we laughed her off. We didn't have a full understanding of how many she had pulled into her orbit and how far she'd come in convincing others."

Hugh nodded. Looking at the screen, Ward asked, "Can you get your diversion going now?"

The screen blinked blue again, *It'll be a while. The Oort cloud sensors are a long way out there. Before I can tie into the archeonB sensor net, I have to use old-fashioned light speed radio. It takes hours for radio to hit the first relay, so it won't be detected.*

Dent's a pompous, arrogant, little prick. He commands one of the cruisers and it's heading toward solar north on my screen. My guess is that he decided he should make himself scarce before Morgain shows up. As for Morgain, though, she is a totally different story. Don't underestimate her power. I can personally attest that she is pure evil.

Hugh turned to the doctor and saw the raw hate on his face. Whether it was for Pogue, Dent or Morgain, he didn't know. Gently, he told him, "There is nothing you can accomplish by staying here. Your family needs you, and so does the empire, so make it to the shuttle. Are there oxygen masks in that bag?"

"Three." Davison said.

Ward nodded. "Good thought. Dunn and the others have rebreathers as part of their kit, so we have just enough with Kennion's."

"What?" asked Davison.

Ward sank back before he answered, "The next attempt to kill us by Commander Jay may very well be with gas. Could be toxic, might be sleeping gas or an incapacitant. We need the masks to get out of here if he uses something like that, whether here or in the corridor."

"Probably the corridor, Sergeant Major," Dunn suggested from the other room. Hugh agreed. Only someone incredibly stupid, which didn't describe Pogue, would allow any kind of access to the air ducts of his own quarters. Pogue seems to have had a healthy survival instinct."

Ward concurred. "So, now we wait."

After Davidson made his regular health report on Pogue, another hour started. Standing slowly and gingerly, Ward walked carefully to Kennion to strip the extra equipment off of him, including his com, before handing it to Hugh. Hugh didn't need two coms, but you never left one for the opposition.

"Need to see if Pogue has another arms cache," Ward suggested a bit breathlessly.

Hugh nodded. "I'll do it; sit down before you fall down. Where should I look?"

Ward directed the thorough examination of the cabin, inch by inch. Finally, Hugh found a hidden panel. Inside were more arms and a few grenades. Grunting with satisfaction as Hugh handed out the goodies, Ward commented, "Experience searching for contraband hidden by Marines and spacers over the last thirty years certainly comes in handy from time to time. Now that we have more firepower, we have surprise on our side. They know what we came in with from the security monitors. How do you think we should leave, Your Highness?"

"A standard level two clearing operation, no shooting unless they open the ball." Ward nodded as he tried to stand again, then slumped back. Hugh shook his head, a tight fist forming in his gut. "I'll brief the troops," he grunted. This would be his first live-fire operation. His shoot-out with Bhat and Pogue had been too brief to be called anything other than an old-fashioned gunfight. Definitely not the same thing.

Dunn opened the hatch. "Pogue and the medics are wrapped up and sleeping." He left it open.

After a while, Ward broke the silence. "We'll be moving fast when we go. Make a blanket stretcher for Pogue. We're leaving the medics here. When Pogue's people get here, they'll probably take them right to sick bay. If not, it doesn't matter. Just be ready. We have to hope they release the doctor in time."

"Aye," Dunn answered sardonically. "When we tie up the doctor, we could slide a knife under him so he can cut himself free if they don't do it."

"Good thinking, Kevin," Hugh agreed. He felt relieved for getting Kevin's help in worrying about the details. He really couldn't do it all himself. Dunn ducked back into the bedroom, hatch still open.

THE MANUAL FOR COURTS-MARTIAL (MCM)

Revised 3277 AD by Order of the Emperor, Charles Roland

No changes are made in the definitions of infractions and crimes against good military order and discipline. A single change is made in punishment as follows:

"In times of insurrection or disorder as defined by the Imperial Fleet or Imperial High Command, any individual, whether acting passively or actively, supporting any mutiny or mutineer, will be guilty of mutiny. The penalty is death. The mandated form of punishment is spacing without a suit in the presence of fleet personnel when possible. Summary execution is permitted by any commander into whose hands a mutineer may fall. Formal trial of any person involved is not required. Reestablishment of good military discipline is of primary concern."

27

Time to Go

Cruiser *Bring It*

0255 BBMT 25 October 3473

HUGH CASCADE FELT KEYED UP after prepping for the run to the ship, but now they could only wait. Time dragged to a stop, their watches not seeming to move at all. Even Hugh, used to waiting while stalking game or on maneuvers, began to feel the strain. He finally ground his teeth, a sure sign of frustration. He knew it but couldn't help himself. *Had Commander Jay somehow stopped everything? Could he be playing mind games by stretching things out before hitting us? Does Jay think I will call and beg to surrender? Fat chance*, he snorted.

What now?

He desperately wanted to *do* something, not just wait. He must be patient, a virtue he definitely didn't love at the moment. One more time he ran down his equipment list, making sure the mini gas mask, now hanging around his neck, could be quickly pulled on if Jay decided to flood the passageway with incapacitants.

Time continued to churn his insides. After a second hour finally dragged past, *Ambrose B*'s coms silently vibrated. A string of letters ran across the coms on their wrists.

Gail Felt smiled in relief. "An alarm message just came in from the Oort cloud of a big attack. Everyone but the *Elmira Hayes* and *Bring It* have been ordered out to fight." She tapped a message and got the response. "Sheila says the order came from a Commander Jay."

"Time to go." *And it might be a sneaky trap.*

He caught a change on the monitor in red. *That's for real! My message didn't have time to get out there and back.* His startled expression stopped Sean Ward in the bedroom door as he moved to help Dunn.

"Sire?"

"This attack is apparently the real thing, Ward. They may need every ship."

"They may also have enough or too few. Your decision, sire. However, what is the mission?"

Hugh struggled for a moment. The people in this system were not under his command nor were they his responsibility to protect. His duty lay to billions upon billions back home, people he had sworn to serve, many of whom would die if he didn't pass the test and acquire a new Galactic Starburst.

Steeling himself to the grief it would cause if this system went down due to his decision, he faced the monitor. "Get to the shuttle. Wait for the doctor as long as you can. We're on our way now."

Ward stepped to the corridor hatch. "Peterson, help Dunn with the stretcher. We're moving out."

Hugh tied the doctor up loosely as they walked out, sliding one of the scalpels from the med bag under him. "This should help you when they come in behind us. Good luck." Davison nodded, looking suddenly frightened by the thought of what might happen after Hugh and the others left.

Hugh opened up the ship's com again. "Commander Jay, we are headed to our ship with Pogue. Back your people out of our way. Out." Before Jay could answer, he shut off the com and stepped out into the corridor.

Abdul Jebet burned out the electronic latch on the hatch on the down-ship side of the passageway, then carefully aimed his laser rifle at the manual wheel that opened the blast hatches if the power failed. At more than one hundred fifty pounds, only a really big man could lug around the monster load of a laser rifle with its power pack and spare barrels, which quickly burned out in a fight. Hugh knew he couldn't have carried it and done anything else, maybe not even toted it by itself for any length of time. Fortunately, Jebet fit the bill. Easily holding the rifle steady, he fired a measured shot into the wheel, turning it to slag. Jay would have to blow the door in or use a torch to cut it out in order to follow them. Hugh smiled grimly. Since no ship commander wanted to blow out blast doors that might be needed unexpectedly, it would take the better part of half an hour to open it the old-fashioned way with a cutting torch.

As Jebet fired, Commander Jay demanded from a com screen in what Hugh noted to be an excellent command voice, "What are you doing? You are destroying my ship! Stop that!"

Hugh figured his last call had removed the *Do Not Disturb* block, which let Jay's call through. He answered Jay, "We don't want surprise visitors sneaking up behind us. Just play nice and you'll get your ship back in one piece when we leave."

"You have no idea how much trouble you're in!" Jay threatened harshly. Hugh decided that continuing to argue with someone this fundamentally out of his depth would just be a waste of time. That said, Hugh had neither the inclination nor time to explain it to him. He disabled the com.

While Hugh was speaking to Jay, Jebet crowded past Kevin Dunn and Pete Peterson to get to the forward hatch. Hugh followed them, with Gail and Ward coming last. After Ward gave Jebet a sign, he cracked the hatch, flash grenade at the ready. A four-man team, their automatic weapons trained on the hatch, covered the corridor ahead of them. Jebet called out to them, "We have Pogue on a stretcher and we're coming through. He is next in line, so move back! You fire and he's likely to get hit." Stepping forward, grenade ready, pin pulled, laser rifle pointed at the team still blocking the corridor, he bellowed, "Move!"

Weapon barrels rising, they slowly backed off. Jebet led, followed by Pogue on the blanket stretcher carried by Dunn and Peterson. Jebet's laser rifle pointed unwaveringly at the rebels while Dunn and Peterson's weapons hung around their necks and shoulders. Hugh knew they could fire one-handed if things got dicey. Unfortunately, if that happened in the narrow confines of the corridor, no one would likely survive the firefight. From his place behind the stretcher, Hugh could barely see anything up ahead. Worse, the gas mask hanging from his neck chafed and made it hard to turn his neck from side to side. His trigger finger lay tensely along the trigger guard so he wouldn't accidentally fire off rounds and get people killed. It already ached with the tension. Moving quickly forward, he stopped just behind the hatch combing where, if shooting started, he would have a tiny bit of cover from which to fire back. Gail tugged on his shirt to get him to back up even more. He ignored her, staying as close to the hatch as he could, just behind Peterson. *I wish I had taken point!*

He saw Jebet replace the pin in his grenade before leading off again. He hadn't known Jebet had been carrying an armed grenade. The thought of what would have happened if he had accidentally dropped it caused sweat to break out all over him. Glancing left and right, he saw that only two doors opened onto this section of corridor between the hatches. He jammed them quickly shut before slagging them, just in case. He moved on past the next hatch. Hugh watched intently as Jebet slid up carefully to the first of the four cross-corridors between them and *Ambrose B*. His stomach knotted as Jebet peeked around each corner with his skinny eye. *Jebet looks tense,* he decided, his own body subconsciously mimicking what he read from Jebet.

Behind him, he heard a scraping noise. Hugh whipped his head around, slipping his finger into the trigger guard. He froze, shocked by what he saw. Gail stood on Ward's bent knee looking into an air vent. "Clear," she whispered. "It's only six inches high." Ward looked even paler than before. He just nodded as Gail hopped down.

Hugh chewed himself out. *I should have thought of that. There might have been a sniper or gas canister.* Turning back forward, he saw Jebet passing through the next hatch with Peterson and Dunn close behind. Hurrying to catch up, he gave the cross-corridors a once-over. From the hatches at their ends, metal dripped from their locks. Jebet must have shot them, too, but being so focused on Gail and Ward had caused him to miss it. Stepping into the next section, he saw Jebet checking out the only two doors in this section.

"Missile Bay," Jebet identified to the right. He slagged the lock. "Missile Bay," he called for the left one and repeated the procedure. Standard layout for a cruiser like this one. Carefully, he moved up to the second cross-corridor, repeating the procedure.

Hugh's nerves were tight as a guitar string, an instrument he had tried but failed to master. That irrelevant thought irritated him as he forced his concentration back toward the front. He heard Ward breathing hard but didn't turn around. He'd have to leave getting Ward to the ship up to Gail. If things went bad, Hugh was the only reserve available to pull things out, which meant he needed to keep his mind on business.

Jebet slid through the next hatch. They were halfway there. Four doors on both sides of the corridor now. Jebet fused each door lock before creeping up to the last cross-corridor. Hugh verified that the cabin hatch locks were thoroughly slagged as he passed each one, making sure they didn't get a nasty surprise that could kill all of them. Sweat began to drip down to his chin from his hairline. At any moment, poison gas could come out from vents or a gun barrel could pop into view and open up. A spray of bullets in this corridor would leave no one standing.

Their progress forward seemed to crawl. It had taken just a few minutes, on arrival, to reach Pogue's cabin from the entry port, but the return journey seemed to stretch out endlessly. Then Jebet stepped into the entry port, only twenty-five minutes by Hugh's watch from starting this journey up-ship. Sweat drenched Hugh as if he had run several kilometers in full gear.

He relaxed as he approached the connection to the *Ambrose B*, watching as Gail securely dogged the three entry port hatches before jamming their locks. Reaching the entry port access, Ward, pale as a sheet, sagged against the hatch frame of the final lock. Hugh walked over to give him a hand. Standing, Ward shrugged off the help before shuffling off. *Stubborn as a mule.* He took out a jammer retrieved from Kennion's pouch before they had left, turning it on. It blacked out all cameras and scrambled vocal pickups in the area. Up until that point, they had wanted to be seen with Pogue. Now, Jay being able to watch them turned into a liability.

Without ceremony, Dunn and Jebet dumped Pogue on the steel deck, just excess baggage now that they didn't need him anymore. Regardless, they had no room for him on *Ambrose B*, so he would be staying here. As he hit the deck, Pogue grunted in pain, even through the heavy-duty pain killers given him by Davison. Dunn and Jebet quickly returned to protection detail mode, heading into the air lock to *Ambrose B* ahead of Hugh. Verifying everything secure, they waved Hugh in.

It had likely taken *Bring It*'s crew at least five minutes to get through the jammed hatches back by Pogue's cabin. That should have given the doctor twenty minutes plus to get to the shuttle while *Ambrose B* finished getting out of range—of the guns but not the missiles. If the unseen person didn't stop *Bring It* from firing missiles at them, Hugh would have only a minute or so to regret his decision to trust him.

Dunn and Klostermann half carried Ward down the connector between them. Gail ran ahead to the bridge as Jebet secured the air lock and blew the entry port connector. The *Bring It* entry port air lock automatically sealed when the connector suddenly lost pressure. Hugh followed Gail to the bridge while Dunn helped Ward the rest of the way to his cabin.

Gail had her headset on by the time Hugh reached his station, everything ready to go. It normally took at least an hour from a cold start to get the engines going, so Sally and Sheila must have kept them warm while Hugh visited Pogue's quarters. *Good idea.*

Gail spoke into the headset, "*Ambrose B* requesting permission to undock and leave station, over." The standard formula startled Hugh, but he smiled and then began to laugh. Sally joined him and Gail looked at them coolly, simply saying, "A taut ship always follows correct communications procedures," at which point, she joined in laughing.

The incoming com signal sputtered at them while they laughed, *"Hold position,* Ambrose B. *Where is Admiral Pogue? What is your course? Respond, over."*

Gail ignored the increasingly angry com officer trying to get her attention. "Sal, lay a tight beam on *Elmira Hayes.* Advise her that we will rendezvous near Nighthawk once they pick up *Bring It*'s port shuttle. Make sure the shuttle identity is clear, and they confirm. That will be *Bring It* 2-Bravo headed for them."

"Wilco," answered Sally Carr, as she proceeded to connect.

Hugh busied himself with the sensor screens. At this distance from the Oort cloud, he could only read drive signatures. He watched the rest of Pogue's squadron approaching the Oort cloud on preon drive when a gravitonic drive signature burst out of the rocks and ice ahead of them. At almost a light-year from the sun, signals took a long time to be relayed, arrive, and then be deciphered. However, within a light-year, preon and graviton drives could be identified essentially immediately from the disturbance they made in the underlying fields. A quartet of gravitonic drive emissions quickly followed the first one, erupting from the Oort cloud headed for Nighthawk. Drives on two of the four suddenly fluttered and died while a third ship simply disappeared. Pogue's squadron hadn't reached the cloud yet, so the destruction of those ships must have been due to mechanical failure, probably from ramming headlong into objects in the Oort cloud. Pogue's squadron reached the Oort cloud just as a larger group busted out. Many of them also flickered out, having brushed too close to objects on the way through. The rest required personal attention. The squadron obligingly gave it to them.

Hugh leaned into the screen, totally engaged in the fight, wondering how many ships must have run into the ice and rock of the lacunae just to get these few ships through. *How many ran into atomic mines? The pilots flying those ships must have known most would die trying. Why would they do it?* He decided he really didn't need to know the answer to that question. Thinking about those who would do something like that and the suicidal drive that animated them, could give anybody nightmares.

As *Ambrose B* headed toward Nighthawk, a cargo shuttle shot away from *Bring It* on a course for *Elmira Hayes*. Moments after breaking cleanly away, *Bring It* exploded in a sunlike blaze of glory.

"I guess that answers the question as to whether we can trust whoever is on shuttle 2-Bravo," commented Gail dryly. "Thank goodness Dent's cruiser left hours ago. That could have really been messy."

Sally looked up. "*Hayes* wants us to meet up out here. They are comming ahead for their families to get to a merchant ship at the capital space field. By the time *Hayes* arrives near Nighthawk, the merchant ship should be up to join them and head for deep space together. We are fifteen minutes from docking."

Hugh nodded but didn't say anything, his attention focused on the battle at the edge of the Oort cloud. He knew he didn't belong in that fight and, more importantly, his responsibility did not include this system. Those people flying the fleet ships had long ago foresworn themselves, thereby losing all right to call on him for help. Yet, he wanted to be out there with Pogue's squadron, fighting the barbarian horde, protecting the innocents in this system who believed that the fleet of the Core Empire had sworn to protect them. The choice to not stand with them against the evil sweeping in from the stars racked his soul. His mind knew what choice he should make, must make, but his heart screamed at him to stand up to the barbarians he could see, not those a thousand parsecs away. So, he stood cheering on Pogue's ships, the least he could do.

One of Pogue's ships blew up and then another. His knuckles gripped the edge of the console so hard they were white. The TechMech ships died even more quickly as they fought the fleet ships facing them. None were getting through. Still, Hugh watched in suspense to see if the battle would ever end. A tap on his shoulder startled him, making him jump, so intense had been his concentration.

"We're nearing *Hayes*, sire," Gail said in a normal voice. Hugh's emotions were now raw, an open wound. A third member of the squadron died and a core of TechMech ships began forming up on this side of the Oort cloud. Why didn't everyone feel what he did? He couldn't run from this fight! Hugh's face became a mask of rage and grief. "Our passenger, Your Highness?" Gail reminded him formally.

That helped refocus Hugh on what needed to happen here. His duty now lay in judging if this person, who claimed to have helped them and who appeared to have been responsible for *Bring It* blowing up, should be allowed aboard. Alive. The potential threat to the empire if this person were to kill Hugh suddenly hit him. Now he understood Doña Carlota's concern about him running around without protection. His decisions were no longer just about him, if they ever had been. Back on *Bring It*, he had promised to take this unknown aboard, but also knew that if this person gave any indication he would compromise the mission, then he couldn't be allowed to live. Hugh, alone, would have to make that decision, having taken part in too many simulations, participated in too many scenarios, not to know the rules of the game. *Game*, he snorted derisively. Something else to dream about endlessly if he were required to give the order to space him.

Standing, he strode purposefully forward without another glance at the board. At least he could appear confident. Besides, nothing he said or did could possibly affect the outcome of the battle at the Oort cloud. He had to now focus on the life coming before him, in the here and now, that he must judge. By the time Hugh reached the air lock, the monitor showed a single figure had already jetted over from the shuttle and started the entry procedure. Dunn and Peterson stood patiently waiting for their passenger, sidearms out and up. As soon as their passenger entered the air lock, *Ambrose B* shot away toward deep space above the ecliptic. *Elmira Hayes*, presumably, had sped away as well, racing to its rendezvous with the merchant ship bringing their families, before heading back toward the empire.

Hugh cleared his mind as the lock cycled open, preparing himself. Stunned by what he saw, his jaw dropped. Short, raven hair surrounding an oval face. The golden hard suit of a naval flyer. Striking green eyes. *It's a girl?*

She came to attention under the guns of Hugh's bodyguards and saluted. After a second, Hugh returned the salute, still in something of a daze, before he shook himself, snapping his jaw back into position. "You are?" he asked, sounding to himself as if he were still a little befuddled. This beautiful girl, probably his age, had made their escape possible? He had expected a man. An older woman like Gail, with plenty of experience, wouldn't have been a surprise because blowing up *Bring It* must have taken amazing guts and a coolheaded intellect.

Hugh felt supremely grateful at the moment that the girl didn't laugh at him. In a pleasant voice, she simply said, "Maeve Ellyllyon, Ensign, reporting as ordered, Your Highness."

Acknowledgments

I would like to thank my wife, Sandy, for the many hours of diligent work and advice in creating this book and for her patience in allowing me to spend so much time in my own world. Many thanks go to those who have read it and provided feedback especially my brother, David, whose help has been especially insightful. My family deserves special appreciation for patiently enduring endless conversations about characters and plots and for offering suggestions. Thanks to Craig and Leighn for their invaluable technical help with computer theory.

I would also like to thank Nicholas Armbruster, PhD, for his invaluable reference work, *The Core Empire*, published 4 April 3555 on Beacon by Wilhelm House. Without the insights and carefully researched background materials, I could never have finished this book.

My editor, Andy Zack, needs special thanks for his invaluable help and patience in bringing this work to completion, as well as the rest of the fine people at Endpapers Press.

Finally, I would like to recognize the dedicated members of the United States armed services who are the inspiration for many of the scenes in this story. However, no person, living or dead, has been the basis for any character.

www.ingramcontent.com/pod-product-compliance
Lightning Source LLC
LaVergne TN
LVHW050928080826
845145LV00001B/243

* 9 7 8 1 9 3 7 8 6 8 8 8 8 *